VANISHED

VANISHED

KAREN ROBARDS

DOUBLEDAY LARGE PRINT HOME LIBRARY EDITION
G. P. PUTNAM'S SONS
NEW YORK

This Large Print Edition, prepared especially for Doubleday Large Print Home Library, contains the complete, unabridged text of the original Publisher's Edition.

G. P. PUTNAM'S SONS
Publishers Since 1838
Published by the Penguin Group
Penguin Group (USA) Inc., 375 Hudson Street, New York, New York 10014, USA • Penguin Group (Canada), 90 Eglinton Avenue East, Suite 700, Toronto, Ontario M4P 2Y3, Canada (a division of Pearson Penguin Canada Inc.) • Penguin Books Ltd, 80 Strand, London WC2R 0RL, England • Penguin Ireland, 25 St Stephen's Green, Dublin 2, Ireland (a division of Penguin Books Ltd) • Penguin Group (Australia), 250 Camberwell Road, Camberwell, Victoria 3124, Australia (a division of Pearson Australia Group Pty Ltd) • Penguin Books India Pvt Ltd, 11 Community Centre, Panchsheel Park, New Delhi–110 017, India • Penguin Group (NZ), Cnr Airborne and Rosedale Roads, Albany, Auckland 1310, New Zealand (a division of Pearson New Zealand Ltd) • Penguin Books (South Africa) (Pty) Ltd, 24 Sturdee Avenue, Rosebank, Johannesburg 2196, South Africa

Penguin Books Ltd, Registered Offices: 80 Strand, London WC2R 0RL, England

ISBN-13: 978-0-7394-6798-5
ISBN-10: 0-7394-6798-0
Printed in the United States of America

This is a work of fiction. Names, characters, places, and incidents either are the product of the author's imagination or are used fictitiously, and any resemblance to actual persons, living or dead, businesses, companies, events, or locales is entirely coincidental.

To Christopher, in honor of your sixteenth birthday this month. This beats a car, yes? No? Love always, Mom

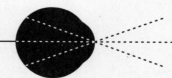

This Large Print Book carries the
Seal of Approval of N.A.V.H.

To Peter, my technical support even while he's away at college.

To Chris, whose tales from the teenage trenches never fail to make me laugh.

To Jack, who shared *Inkheart,* as well as many other wonderful books, with me.

To Doug, who puts up with us all and loves us anyway.

To my parents, Pete and Sally Johnson, with love.

To my three brothers, Tod, Bruce, and Brad Johnson, who are still making my life interesting.

To my sister Lee, otherwise known as mini-me, who takes all my teasing with good grace.

To Peggy, lifelong friend.

To my wonderful editor, Christine Pepe, whose kindness and patience know no bounds and whose deft editorial touch is much appreciated.

To my agent, Robert Gottlieb, who does such a fantastic job for me.

To Leslie Gelbman and Kara Welsh and the entire Berkley group, with a whole boatload of thanks for your friendship and support.

To Stephanie Sorensen, publicist extraordinaire.

And finally, to Ivan Held and the rest of the Putnam family. If it takes a village to raise a child, it takes a family to publish a book. Thank you.

VANISHED

1

Sarah Mason had always thought that when Death finally came calling for her, he would be better-looking. You know, sort of like Brad Pitt in *Meet Joe Black.* The kind of guy you actually wouldn't mind taking off with. The jerk wearing the cheap plastic skeleton-face Halloween mask was maybe twenty, around five eight and scrawny, a dark-complected Caucasian with long, greasy black hair, a single fat silver hoop earring, and a fuzzy goatee poking out from under the mask. His high-tops were white, his oversized Hornets T-shirt was red, and his denim shorts were long and so baggy that they threatened to go indecent with any too-sudden move. In other words, tonight Death was definitely not heartthrob material. He wasn't even borderline impressive.

Then again, the gun he was pointing at her was big and bad. So big and bad that, Sarah realized as her shocked brain resumed minimal functioning, she'd quit breathing the moment she'd set eyes on it.

"You! Lady! Get over by the cash register!"

No doubt about it. The mask might hide his mouth, but he was yelling at *her*, aiming that big black gun at *her*, his movements agitated, jerky. She could see his eyes through the egg-shaped holes in the plastic. They were shiny black, the kind of shiny black that usually indicated pupils dilated from drug use, and they darted nervously around the convenience store aisle where he had her trapped.

She stood stock-still, unable to move. Caught in that state of suspended animation in which the horrible event that was occurring seemed, for the first few seconds, no more real than a bad dream, Sarah continued to stare numbly at him.

I don't believe this. I just came out for dog food. . . .

"Move!" he screamed when she didn't.

Her heart leaped. Her mind raced. She swallowed convulsively.

"Yes. Yes, okay."

Jolted back into horrible reality by the sheer volume of his shout, Sarah hugged the big blue bag of Kibbles 'n Bits—the urgent lack of which had brought her to this, her neighborhood Quik-Pik, at shortly after eleven p.m.—close to her chest, and moved.

"Hurry up! Hurry up!" He was practically waving the gun at her in his agitation, shifting from foot to foot, his too-shiny eyes roaming all over the place.

"It's okay." She drew on every day of her four years of experience in dealing with criminal types as an Assistant District Attorney for Beaufort County, South Carolina, to keep her voice even. As acting head of the Major Crimes unit, she ordinarily ate penny-ante thugs like this for breakfast. But this wasn't a courtroom, and his future wasn't at stake here: Hers was. What she wanted to do, *needed* to do, was forge a human connection between the two of them. It was a basic tenet of the Women Against Rape class she helped teach: Make the perpetrator see you as a person and you're less likely to be harmed. "Just stay cool."

"I *am* cool. Don't you be tellin' me to stay cool. Who you to be like, *stay cool?*" His voice went shrill with indignation.

Okay, wrong thing to say.

"Get yo' ass over to that cash register." He bounced up and down on the balls of his feet, thrusting the gun toward her like a foil, and Sarah instinctively braced in anticipation of it going off. *"Now."*

Sarah gave up on the whole *try to make a connection with the criminal* concept, quickened her pace, and lowered her eyes while she thought desperately, trying to come up with an angle, some way to get out of this mess. She'd managed to call 911 on her cell phone as soon as she'd realized that a robbery was going down at the front of the store. That was the good news. At the time, dog food in hand, she'd been fleeing toward what she presumed was the back exit, heading toward the hall that led to the restrooms and beyond. Before she'd had a chance to say a word in response to the operator's brisk 911 this guy had come charging out of the ladies' restroom and down the hall and she had been forced to change her path and thrust the still-connected—she hoped—cell phone into her purse. Where it remained.

Since it was her cell, though, even if the operator didn't just automatically disconnect the silent call, even if the operator followed through, the address that would come up was her home. There was no way to connect the call to this location at all.

That was the bad news.

Even worse news was that even if the cops realized what was going down, if they knew it was her, they probably wouldn't come anyway. Just at that moment, she was pretty sure she was riding the number-one spot on their least-favorite-persons list.

"Dumb bitch," the robber said, the words just barely muffled by the mask.

Sarah's hackles rose instinctively. *Bitch* was one of those words that pushed her buttons, even thought she'd been called one often enough that she should by all rights have gotten over it by now. *Don't answer,* she cautioned herself. She was almost even with him by this time, close enough to smell his acrid scent. Apparently, either he didn't believe in showers or nerves were causing him to experience a serious case of deodorant failure. Whatever, he reeked. The aisle was only about three feet wide. She was going to have to put herself within a few inches of him to get past. Goose bumps raced over her skin at the prospect. Of course, they could have been caused by the frigid breath of the cold cases to her left hitting her arms and legs, which were bare because she was wearing shorts and a tank top in deference to the ninety-degree heat outside, but she didn't think so. She was pretty sure that prickly feeling she was experiencing was pure, galloping fear.

Which, in a weird kind of way, was actually a positive. She'd thought she'd lost her fear of death sometime during the past seven hellish years. In fact, deep in the dark of night when things got really bad, she could have sworn she was looking forward to it. It was probably the whole getting shot bit that was freaking her out now, which was perfectly understandable. Nobody in their right mind wanted to take a bullet. Especially over a quick run to the store for dog food.

"What, you got shit for brains or something? I said *move.*" Skeleton Boy glared at her. He was bobbing impatiently, making coins or keys or something metallic in his pocket jingle.

"Yes, okay." Sarah kept her voice soothing as she ostentatiously picked up the pace. Her flip-flops made quick little slapping sounds against the hard, smooth floor. It was interesting to realize that the closer she got to him, to that unsteady gun, the harder her heart pounded. However her mind felt about it, her body clearly wasn't okay with the prospect of imminent death. She was breathing fast, she could feel herself breaking out in a cold sweat, and her stomach was tying itself in knots. Even her knees felt weak.

What did it say about her life that being scared to death almost qualified as a good thing?

"You okay back there, man?" the second robber, the one at the front of the store, called.

"Yeah," Skeleton Boy answered. "Everything's under control." His gaze swung back to Sarah. His voice dropped. "I'm warning you: Don't fuck with me. *Run.*"

The look in his eyes turned deadly as he pointed the gun at her. Sarah got the impression that now his machismo was at stake, and obediently broke into a ragged little trot. *Street Survival 101: Never mess with a punk's self-image.* Averting her gaze, she hunched her shoulders, making herself as small as possible. She deliberately didn't look at him, didn't make eye contact. And because she didn't, because she kept her eyes lowered as she slogged past him, she spotted the little girl hiding beneath the round table piled high with packaged doughnuts at the end of the aisle.

There was a white plastic skirt covering the table, but the skirt was on crooked. On this side it lacked a good eight inches of reaching the floor. The child was lying on her side and had curled up into as small a ball as possible, but Sarah could plainly see two tan, thin, and dirty legs pulled up tight against her chest; a pair of equally tan, thin, and dirty arms wrapped around the legs; a bright yellow T-shirt and blue shorts; bare feet; and a small face half-hidden by a tangled fall of long, coffee-colored hair. The little girl was looking right at her, her eyes huge and dark and afraid.

Sarah blinked. Her breathing faltered. Her eyes connected with the girl's terrified gaze for a pregnant instant that seemed to stretch into a pulse-pounding eternity. Her heart started banging in her chest—and then she recovered her wits enough to jerk her eyes up and away. He might follow her gaze. . . .

Please, God, don't let him see the child.

"Get the damned drawer *open,*" the other robber—she thought there were only two—shouted at the woman behind the counter.

"Yes, sir."

The cash drawer popped open with a rattle and a *ping* just as Sarah emerged from the end of the aisle. She could see the pair of them now, the woman behind the counter looking down at the still-quivering cash drawer, the robber on the other side of it with his gun trained on her. The cashier was about sixty, short, plump, and grandmotherly, her salt-and-pepper hair curling around her face, her red uniform top hugging matronly breasts. Her mouth was trembling as she looked fearfully at the robber.

"Put it in here." He thrust a flimsy white plastic grocery bag at her. She shook visibly as she complied, scooping money from the cash register into the bag with quick, clumsy movements. This guy was taller and chunkier than Skeleton Boy, and seemed calmer, too. At least his gun wasn't bobbing and weaving all over the place and he wasn't jingling like a set of wind chimes in a gale. He had the same dark complexion and greasy-looking black hair, and she wondered briefly if maybe the pair were brothers. This guy's hair was tied back in a ponytail to reveal a raised white scar on the side of his neck. Diamond studs, six or more in decreasing size, marched single file up the whole outside of his ear. No goatee, or at least none that she could see beneath his gray plastic wolfman mask. His black T-shirt had the sleeves torn off, revealing a tattoo on his left biceps. Sarah squinted. It looked like some kind of bird—an eagle maybe? Whatever it was, she would definitely recognize it if she saw it again.

Tonight's goal number one: survive to identify that tattoo for a jury.

"Did you look everywhere? Is she it?" Wolfman demanded urgently as he glanced their way. Sarah took care not to meet cold, dark eyes that revealed none of the nerves Skeleton Boy was obviously feeling. This guy was the bad guy, the one who called the shots, she realized. *He* was the leader. And if push came to shove, probably the killer. The thought made her shiver.

"Yeah," Skeleton Boy answered.

"You sure?"

"Hell, yeah, I'm sure. Why do you always got to treat me like I'm some kind of god-damned retard?"

"I was just askin'."

"Well, stop asking and let's get this over with."

Through the big glass windows that fronted the store, Sarah could see that the gas pumps were deserted. Except for her blue Sentra, the parking lot was deserted. The intersection in front of the Quik-Pik was deserted. Beyond the halogen glow of the parking lot, the night was black and still. She and the cashier—and the little girl un-der the table—were on their own. Through the big, round security mirrors that flanked the checkout station, she watched Skeleton Boy coming up close behind her. He shot nervous glances out at the parking lot, jin-gled the change in his pocket, and shuffled his feet. His gun shook slightly as he pointed it at her back.

At the idea that a bullet could smash into her flesh at any moment, Sarah's heart stuttered. However she might feel about Death in the abstract, tonight, here in this over-air-conditioned Quik-Pik, she realized that she definitely did not want to die.

"That all you got?" Wolfman practically went over the counter as the cashier, tears running down her cheeks now, tried to hand him the partly filled grocery bag, which he thrust roughly back at her in a gesture of fierce rejection. "Lift that drawer up. That's where you keep the big bills. Think I don't know that? Don't you be trying to pull something on me." His gaze shifted from the cashier to a spot over Sarah's left shoulder: Skeleton Boy. "You look in the restrooms?"

"I told you. *Yeah.*"

"Okay, okay, just making sure."

Sarah felt something prod her in the small of her back just as the cashier lifted the now-empty black plastic cash drawer out of the register. A glance up at the mirror confirmed her worst fear. Skeleton Boy was right behind her—and the mouth of his big, black gun was now pressed firmly against her spine. It was all she could do not to flinch and pull away, but she was afraid that any unexpected movement on her part might make his unsteady trigger finger contract. With a tremendous effort of will she stayed perfectly still, gritting her teeth while cold sweat washed over her in waves. The mirror told her that she looked parchment-pale, big-eyed, haggard, and basically scared to death. Her tightly compressed lips were thin and bloodless; her short, layered black hair, still damp from the shower she'd taken at the gym just before heading home, was slicked close to her head so that her eyes and strong cheekbones seemed to dominate her face; and her back was hunched like an old woman's as she clutched the ten-pound bag of dog food to her too-thin frame with both arms. She was only thirty-one but she looked older, years older, she realized with a sense of shock. Put the blame on color-leaching fear or the complete absence of makeup or the ghastly lighting all she wanted, but the truth was that she barely recognized the gaunt-cheeked, hollow-eyed, haunted-looking woman staring desperately back at her through the mirror.

Once, a long time ago, so long ago she

could hardly remember, she'd been pretty. . . .

"Where's the fucking money?"

Wolfman's sudden roar made Sarah jump and brought her attention crashing back down to the scene in front of her. As her gaze refocused, Wolfman surged over the counter and grabbed the cashier, who was clutching a single fifty in her hand, by the hair. The fifty fluttered to the floor near Sarah's feet. The money bag dropped onto the counter with a *plop.* The cashier gave a little high-pitched squeal that was immediately silenced as Wolfman slammed her head down hard against the top of the cash register with a metallic *clang.*

Sarah's stomach twisted. Her mouth went dry. Her eyes, huge with pity and fright, stayed riveted on the cashier.

"You gonna tell me? Huh? Huh?"

As Skeleton Boy scooped up the fallen fifty and stuffed it in his pocket, Wolfman slammed the woman's forehead into the cash register twice more in quick succession.

"Huh? Huh?" *Clang. Clang.*

Inside, Sarah screamed. Outwardly, she gritted her teeth and clenched her fists in impotent rage but made no other move. She had to do *something*—but there was nothing she could do except watch in silent horror. Anything else, she knew, would simply refocus the violence on herself.

At the thought, she went clammy with fear.

The cashier's shrill cries deteriorated into sobbing moans as Wolfman ground her forehead against the cash register's unforgiving metal with deliberate brutality. An answering sound, a barely audible whimper, came from the little girl hidden under the table. Sarah's eyes widened as it registered. She caught her breath, but dared not look around.

She was sweating bullets now. Her heart thudded.

Stay quiet. She sent the fierce mind-message to the child. Then, in case the kid wasn't receiving, she appealed once again to a higher power: *Please God, keep her quiet. Don't let them find her.*

The thought that they might sent icy terror shooting through Sarah's veins. However ambivalent she might feel about the value of her own life, she found that she could not bear the idea of a child, a little girl, being hurt. And that she and the cashier were both going to end up hurt, or worse, Sarah now had little doubt. With a sinking feeling, she accepted the reality that the situation was rapidly deteriorating. From experience, she knew that violence, once initiated, tended to escalate.

Even as the realization caused little curls of panic to twist through her stomach, Wolfman yanked the cashier's head all the way up. The woman sobbed and gasped noisily, her eyes wide, her mouth open. Behind Sarah, Skeleton Boy jingled louder than ever. The air conditioner blew. The refrigerator units hummed. There were so many different sounds that apparently Sarah was the only one who heard the child give a little cry—or at least the only one who recognized the sound for what it was.

Don't come out, she willed the kid urgently. She could feel trickles of sweat rolling down between her shoulder blades. Her heart pounded like a long-distance runner's. Her mouth was so dry that her tongue felt like leather.

"Where's the fucking money?" Wolfman roared again, letting go of the cashier's hair at last.

Dazed and crying, the woman slumped against the counter without answering, supporting herself on her elbows. Her sobs were painful to hear. A two-inch gash had opened in her forehead just above her left eyebrow, deep enough so that a white line of fat showed in places around the edges. Rooted to the spot with horror and at the same time still hideously attuned to the child hidden beneath the table, Sarah could only watch as blood began to fill the cut and spill down the woman's face. The cashier—her name was Mary; Sarah could read it on her nametag—glanced up and locked eyes with Sarah for a timeless moment. Her eyes were puffy and swollen, welling over with tears and dark with pain and fear. The irises were a soft blue faded by age. *Help me,* they seemed to beg, and Sarah's heart turned over. But there was nothing she could do that wouldn't make things worse for all of them.

Thwack. Wolfman delivered an openhanded slap to the side of Mary's head, which caused it to snap to one side.

"Oh!" Her hand flew to the spot. She slumped lower, trembling violently, her eyes huge pools of fear.

"Where's the fucking money?"

"That's all. I swear, that's all." Mary's voice was so thick with tears that the words were hard to understand. She sobbed louder as the robber thrust his face toward her menacingly, and dropped her gaze to the counter as if she were afraid to look at him. "Oh, Jesus, have mercy on me. Oh, Jesus, please have mercy."

Out of the corner of her eye, Sarah caught a flutter of white. The table skirt had moved, she realized. The little girl must have changed positions to get a better view.

Sarah's heart skipped a beat. Her breathing suspended. The robbers had to have seen—but after a few tense seconds in which she quivered with horrified anticipation, she realized that they hadn't.

Stay under there, she urged the girl silently, even as she kept her gaze glued to the sobbing Mary. *For God's sake, please, please stay quiet and don't come out.*

Wolfman rounded on Skeleton Boy. "Didn't you tell me this time of night they usually have a couple thousand in here?"

"Yeah, Duke, they do. They always do."

Wolfman went very still. His gaze stayed fixed on Skeleton Boy. The air between them suddenly crackled with tension. Fresh terror stabbed through Sarah as she realized what she had just heard: Wolfman's name was Duke. *She—and Mary, and the child—now knew his name.*

Worse had just taken a toboggan ride straight downhill.

"Did you just say my name? Are you fucking *stupid?*" Duke's voice seethed with repressed rage before his gaze snapped back to the cashier. "I'm gonna ask you one more time: *Where's the money?*"

Mary, looking even more terrified than Sarah felt, sucked in air.

"They—they came to get it early tonight. Just after—after ten. This is all I've taken in since. I wouldn't lie to you. As Jesus is my witness, I wouldn't lie to you." Blood and tears comingled on her cheeks. Beneath the gore, her skin had gone gray.

"God*damn* it." Duke turned to glare at Skeleton Boy. Sarah caught another flutter of white out of the corner of her eye. She could almost feel the weight of the child's watching eyes. Her throat tightened. Her stomach turned inside out.

Don't move. Don't make a sound. . . .

"You can't blame this on me," Skeleton Boy protested.

"Shit I can't." Duke's gaze shifted to Sarah. "Get her purse." Then he addressed her directly as Skeleton Boy yanked the purse from her shoulder. "Anything in there?"

"About forty dollars. And credit cards." Sarah was surprised at how steady her voice sounded. Inwardly, she was pretty much a quivering blob of jelly. Her legs felt as limp as overcooked spaghetti, and her heart was beating like the wings of a trapped wild bird. She no longer harbored any doubt at all: Sometime in the next several minutes, she and Mary were going to die. And if she didn't stay quiet and hidden, the kid was going to die as well.

Whatever happens, please don't let them find the child.

"Where's your purse?" Duke demanded of Mary. Urgency came off him in waves now. Skeleton Boy had stopped jingling. Sarah could hear small sounds that told her he was rifling through her purse.

Mary still slumped over the counter. She was breathing hard, bleeding, shaking, crying. A steady stream of her blood dripped onto the black countertop, spotting it red.

"In . . . in the back." Her voice was faint, quavery.

In the back. Great. Fantastic. Just where they didn't want to go. It didn't take psychic ability to realize that "in the back" was a bad thing. At least while they were up front there was a chance somebody might pull into the parking lot and see what was going down and call the police.

"How much you got in it?" Duke grabbed Mary by the arm and shook it when she didn't answer immediately. "How much?"

"A couple dollars."

"Shit." He shot another venomous glance at Skeleton Boy. "This whole thing's a piece of shit."

He took a step back, snapped his gun up, and shot Mary in the face. Just like that. Without any warning at all. Sarah's jaw dropped as, before she had a chance to even begin to grasp that it was happening *now,* the sound of an explosion practically blew out her eardrums and the left side of Mary's face went missing. Blood and gore blew backward in a cloud of red mist, splattering the cigarette cases and the shoplifting monitor and the second of the two big, round mirrors and everything else on the far side of the counter with crimson. Mary didn't scream, didn't cry out, didn't make a sound. She just dropped like a stone, disappearing behind the counter, gone. There must have been a thud as her body hit the floor, but Sarah couldn't hear it over the sudden terrible ringing in her ears. A new smell—the sickening mix of blood and body effluvia that she had learned meant fresh death—assaulted her nostrils.

Her stomach turned inside out. Her heart stuttered. The Kibbles 'n Bits bag slid from her suddenly nerveless arms. She didn't hear that hit, either. All she could hear—and the sounds were partly masked by the relentless ringing in her ears—were Skeleton Boy's curses and a high-pitched, terrified keening that for a moment she thought must be tearing its way out of her own tight throat.

Then she realized that it wasn't, and realized, too, with a fresh little thrill of horror, where the sound was coming from. Her gaze slid sideways. The child . . .

"Mary! Mar-eee!"

Sarah's heart leaped into her throat as

the little girl, tangled dark hair flying like a banner behind her, burst from beneath the table and dove toward the cashier's station. The table, upended by the force of her exit, hit the floor with a crash. Boxes of dough-nuts flew up in the air, landed, and skid-ded everywhere.

"What the hell . . . ?" Duke whirled around. Skeleton Boy, swallowing the last of a string of curses, followed suit. For the briefest of milliseconds, they were appar-ently too astonished to do anything but gape as the little girl, shrieking like a siren, hurtled toward them.

"Fuck." Duke's momentary paralysis van-ished. His gun snapped up and he took quick aim at the screaming child.

2

"*No,*" Sarah cried. Powered by a sudden burst of terror-fueled adrenaline, she turned and shoved Duke as hard as she could. Caught off guard, his attention focused on the onrushing girl, he stumbled sideways against the counter—*and dropped his gun.* The weapon clattered to the floor and skidded away toward the display of assorted chips in the middle of the nearest aisle.

Sarah's eyes widened.

A chance. They had a chance. . . .

Heart leaping like a jackrabbit, blood

pumping a mile a minute, Sarah seized it, springing past Skeleton Boy in less than the time it takes to blink. She grabbed the little girl, who had nearly reached them by that time, by the arm. Even as the still-shrieking child glanced up at her with big, brown, terror-filled eyes, Sarah reversed course in a flash, taking advantage of the child's forward momentum to pull her behind her in a mad dash for the door.

"Come on."

If the child even tried to resist, Sarah never noticed. The girl was tiny, bird-boned, no more, Sarah guessed, than six or seven years old, and light as a feather. Everything was in motion. There was noise, confusion, and upheaval everywhere. The child screamed in continuous shrill blasts of sound as Sarah towed her willy-nilly behind her. Skeleton Boy cursed, pivoting, already raising his gun, already trying to get a bead on them as they raced for the door. Having dived after his gun, Duke, cursing a blue streak, too, came up off the floor like a rebounding gymnast with it in hand.

"Shoot 'em! Shoot 'em!" he shouted to Skeleton Boy.

"I am! I am!" Terror heightened Sarah's

senses so that everything seemed magnified. The cold stream of the air-conditioning suddenly felt like icy Death breathing down her neck. Beneath the screams and shouting and the drumlike pounding of her own heart, she thought she could hear every shuffle of the robbers' feet, every inhalation of their breath, every metallic *snick* of their weapons. The sickeningly-sweet smell of death intensified, mushrooming so that it filled her nostrils. Her surroundings blurred into a streaming kaleidoscope of color as she fled for what she knew was her life— and the child's. The warmth of the little girl's frail wrist became the only point of reality in what suddenly felt like a waking nightmare. Her own movements seemed to happen in slow motion, as if she were struggling to run through deep water. Her arm felt heavy as lead as she stretched for the door handle, which was just inches away from her fingertips now. The robbers were behind her, but she could see their reflections in the shiny-black plate-glass windows.

Skeleton Boy leveled his gun. Watching his only slightly blurred image, Sarah screamed to wake the dead. Her heart gave a sickening lurch. Her pulse raced. Duke, on his feet now, bounded toward them. The hand holding the gun jerked up, leveling off just past his waist.

Sarah's skin crawled. Any second now, she was going to feel a bullet slamming into her back. . . .

Then she made contact with the door handle and felt cool metal beneath her flattening palm as she shoved the heavy door wide and raced through it and across the sidewalk. A blanket of steamy-thick August air enfolded her in a welcoming embrace. Stars twinkled overhead. A pale crescent moon sailed high. Behind her, the screaming child felt as weightless and insubstantial as a kite.

Go, go, go. . . .

A quartet of patrol cars, sirens blaring, red lights flashing like beacons in the inky night, rocketed toward the parking lot from different directions.

Thank you, G—

Even as she sent the prayer winging skyward, Sarah felt a tremendous blow, like she'd been smacked in the side of the head with a baseball bat. Pain exploded inside her skull. The force of the impact knocked her off her feet, sent her flying. Wide-eyed, stunned, she watched what looked like the whole department's worth of cruisers converging on the scene as pellets of glass rained down around her like hail.

The store windows had shattered behind her.

A rat-a-tat exchange of gunfire going off like a string of firecrackers just above her falling body made her instinctively duck her head. Then she smacked down on the pavement, cracking her skull against the ground so hard that she saw stars. She tumbled across unforgiving asphalt. Her arms, knees, and chin shredded and stung. Coming to a stop at last, she moaned, then curled instinctively into a ball. Something warm and wet gushed over her right cheek.

Blood, she realized as her fingers brushed it and came away crimson. Then came the sickening realization: It was *her* blood.

Panic welled inside her. *Oh my God, I've been shot. . . .*

"Two guys! Over there on the left!" A man's voice. A cop's. Not close.

"They're making a break for it!"

"Halt! Halt! *Halt!*"

"Look out! He's got a gun! *Shit!*"

A single shot. A burst of gunfire. A cry.

"Maurice!" Duke's shout was a wail of anguish.

"Drop your weapon! *Drop your weapon!*"

"Okay, okay! Just don't shoot! Don't shoot me!" The voice was Duke's, and it was ragged with fear. There was a distant *clank,* as if he had dropped his gun. No sound at all from Skeleton Boy.

"Get your hands in the air *now!*"

All Sarah could see of this as it went down was a stampede of shiny black feet rushing past her. She lay where she had fallen, paralyzed with shock, barely able to breathe.

It hurts. It hurts. . . .

Seconds later, a pair of those shiny black shoes stopped inches from her nose, then a second.

"It's Sarah Mason, all right." A uniform crouched beside her. The world was coming in and out of focus so that she couldn't be completely sure, but Sarah thought it was Art Ficus, a patrol officer she knew fairly well if casually. Their brief interactions had always been cordial. "Looks like she's been shot."

"Well, ain't too many people gonna cry

about that," the other uniform grunted, moving on. The voice was familiar: Brian McIntyre. Of course. She'd last heard that voice just after lunch, when she'd listened to his recorded deposition in her office. She hadn't liked it any better then.

Art touched her shoulder, then picked up her wrist, feeling for her pulse. Her arm was limp. Scarily so. But she could feel his touch.

"Sarah. Can you hear me?"

Yes. Sarah tried to respond. To her surprise, she discovered that her mouth wasn't functioning. At least, it opened, but no sound came out. She worked her lips, moved her tongue, tried to ignore the horrible raw-meat taste of her own warm blood trickling into her mouth.

Am I dying? Is this what dying feels like?

All fear, all urgency, seemed to have left her now. In its place were curiosity, disbelief, maybe a touch of sorrow. The whole situation seemed unreal.

I don't want to die.

The thought was strong, forceful, conclusive. No ambiguity there at all. Despite everything, now that push had come to shove she was definitely going to go with remaining among the living. But then, she wondered suddenly, did she really get to choose? Does anyone ever get a choice?

It occurred to Sarah that there was something urgent she needed to remember, needed to communicate to Art before it was maybe lost forever to the encroaching darkness that was creeping in to claim her, although try as she might, she couldn't quite think what it was.

"We need an EMT over here!" Art shouted urgently. His fingers left her wrist. She felt them next pressing against her neck just below her ear. With the tiny part of her mind that was still attuned to such things, she knew that he must be having trouble finding a pulse because he was continuing to search for one. Then she realized that he was waving an arm in the air to attract attention, and got the impression that he wasn't happy with whatever his fingers pressed to her neck were telling him. "EMT! Over here!"

She could hear him, hear the shouts in the background, hear the sirens and the commotion going on all around, but it all seemed to be receding, as if she were being drawn ever further away.

Was this how dying happened? Did you just kind of float off into the atmosphere? Not so bad after all . . .

Then Sarah remembered what it was that had been tugging at the trailing strings of her consciousness, and sucked in air. She immediately grew more alert as a new kind of dread coursed through her veins.

"That's right," Art was muttering. "Breathe, damn you, breathe."

"The girl," Sarah enunciated with herculean effort. The child had been screaming when Sarah had been shot. She could remember the shrill sounds, remember the feel of the little girl's wrist in her hand. Then had come the blow to her head. She'd lost her grip as she had been hurtled to the ground, and after that the child had been silent. No more screams. No more contact. No more anything.

Where is she?

Tarry fumes radiating up from the still-warm-from-the-sun pavement, coupled with fainter smells of car exhaust and gas and gunpowder and her own blood, curled up her nose and down her throat, threaten-

ing to choke her. Staying conscious required every ounce of willpower she possessed. She was woozy, running on a whole
lot less than all cylinders, but she was almost certain that the little girl had stopped
screaming at almost the exact moment she
herself had been shot. Since then, nothing.
Not a peep. A chill raced like an icy finger
down her spine as she considered the ramifications. What had happened to the
little girl?

Find her. Sarah felt her mouth moving, but
no sound came out.

"Don't try to talk." Art's hand left her
neck. He stood up, waved urgently. "Damn
it to hell! *Over here!*"

Had the child been shot, too? Was she lying somewhere nearby, hurt and bleeding?
It was dark, the parking lot was full of shadows, the whole area was a sea of noise and
confusion—it would be easy to overlook
one small, crumpled child.

"Where's . . . the girl?" In her mind, at
least, the question was loud and sharp.

No response. Had Art heard? Had she
even spoken? Her lips had moved, but
maybe once again there had been no
sound.

Sarah's gaze swept desperately over the area she could see, which didn't encompass a whole hell of a lot. The convenience store was behind her. In front of her were Art's legs, an expanse of black asphalt, gas pumps in their halogen-lit islands, and the intersection with its red light, which was presently just changing to green. Across the street a Chinese restaurant and a used-car lot were dark, already closed for the night. A dozen or more cop cars and a pair of ambulances, all with sirens wailing and roof lights popping, jammed the convenience store's parking lot and the streets on either side of it. More black-and-whites raced through the intersection even as she watched. A police van screeched to a halt just inside the parking lot, disgorging uniformed personnel who hit the ground running. Helmets, body armor, rifles—was it the SWAT team? Jesus, the PD was going all out. Further out, past the stroboscopic lights of the emergency vehicles, it was impossible to see anything, but Sarah got the impression that onlookers were gathering on the other side of the street in front of the People's bank that anchored that corner. Everywhere she looked there was chaos—but no sign of the child.

Sarah tried to lift her head. A terrible shooting pain ricocheting like a pinball through her skull made her abandon the attempt. Dizziness swept over her in a cresting wave. Panting and nauseated in its wake, she lay still again. Her left ear was squashed flat against the pavement. She was picking up the sirens, the shouts, the thunder of onrushing feet, as vibrations now more than sounds, she realized, and realized too that with every second that passed she was getting more and more out of it again. As long as she didn't move, she figured, she had a fighting chance of remaining conscious, aware. Now that she was motionless once more, her head didn't even hurt. It just felt kind of tingly and weird. Like the rest of her.

Probably not a good sign.

Before she could let go, before she could surrender to the blackness that lapped around the edges of her mind like an incoming tide, she had to know that the child had been accounted for. Until she knew that the little girl had been found, she had to do her best to hang on.

"We got a victim down inside the store," someone yelled behind her.

"Holy mother of God . . ."

Clearly they'd found Mary.

A gurney rattled past, then another. More people—EMTs—arrived, crouching beside her. One grabbed her wrist. Fingers moved through her hair. . . .

Sarah tried again, putting everything she had into it.

"The girl . . ."

"What girl?" The EMT—it was a woman, whom she didn't even try to identify— pressed a gauze pad hard against Sarah's head just behind her right ear. It should have hurt, but it didn't. *Funny that she should worry about not feeling pain. . . .*

The woman spoke over her shoulder. "Get a mask on her."

"She was with me." Forcing the words out took all Sarah's strength. "A little girl. In the store with me . . ."

An oxygen mask clamped over her mouth and nose, cutting off her voice. The welcome flow of fresh, sweet air distracted her. She inhaled deeply, once, twice. The threatening blackness receded slightly. Conversely, the pain increased.

"Anybody see a little girl?" the woman yelled as a cervical collar was clamped around Sarah's neck. "She says there was a little girl in the store with her."

The responses Sarah could hear were all negative. Panic tightened her throat, caused her heart to race. Where was the child? She had to be nearby. If they just looked, they would certainly find her. . . .

She made urgent noises beneath the mask.

"Ready to roll?" a man's voice asked as a stretcher slapped down onto the pavement beside her.

"Yeah," the EMT answered, while, inwardly, Sarah screamed *no.* She wasn't going anywhere until she knew about the girl.

She tried to reach for the mask, tried to lift her head, tried to tell them they had to wait, had to find the child. Her movements were quick, instinctive—and a huge mistake. The resultant shaft of pain was so intense—so *excruciating*—that she had no more than a split second to register her error before the blackness finally succeeded in whirling her away.

To her surprise, the next little girl Sarah saw was her own daughter, Alexandra.

Alexandra Rose Mason. "Lexie" for short. Her snub-nosed, freckle-faced, plump-cheeked child was looking directly at her, her denim-blue eyes wide and solemn, her strawberry-pink mouth unsmiling. Sarah felt an aching, longing flood of pure love as her gaze rested on that sweet little face. Hungrily, she drank in every tiny detail of Lexie's appearance. Her face was just-washed clean, and her long, coppery curls were brushed into two neat ponytails tied up with narrow satin ribbons that almost exactly matched her eyes. She was standing perfectly still, which was unusual for a five-year-old who was practically a study in perpetual motion, who ran or danced or bounced (never walked) everywhere, who loved T-ball and soccer and swimming and camping and horseback riding and just about anything else active and outdoors. Lexie generally had smudges on her face and scabs on her knees and tangles in her hair, but just now, in her favorite baby-blue T-shirt and denim skirt, she looked just-escaped-from-the-bathroom fresh.

Sarah knew from experience that such perfection wouldn't last long.

"Hello, Mommy," Lexie said, smiling at her. Lexie smiled like she did everything else, with her whole heart. Her eyes sparkled, her cheeks glowed pink, and her lips stretched into a grin so wide that Sarah could see almost every tooth in her head—including the loose front one that should be falling out any day now.

Sarah smiled back, although she didn't dare say a word.

"Emma's brought cake," Lexie continued excitedly, and the warm rush of pleasure Sarah had felt at seeing her began to fade. "It's her birthday. She's six. When will it be my birthday?"

October twenty-seventh.

"Will I be six?"

Yes.

"Emma and I will be the same age again then," Lexie said. "But now she's older. She told me so." She frowned as if the newly advanced age of her friend was a worry, but then her expression cleared and she was once again her usual blithe self. "Do you think I'll get a trophy today?"

Today being the occasion of the end of T-ball season cookout. The celebration was being held at Waterfront Park, and it was marked by a picnic and the giving out of awards. Although the children didn't know it yet, the parents had gotten together with the volunteer coaches to make sure that this year everyone would be recognized with a small blue-and-gold trophy. Recalling that, Sarah felt a bittersweet pang. Lexie loved trophies. So far in her life she had collected two, one for successfully completing her swimming lessons and one for the previous spring's soccer season. They were accorded a place of honor on her bedside table, which really didn't have room for the addition of a third, even if it was the small one she would get today. Maybe Lexie could be talked into moving them to the bookcase in the living room, although Sarah doubted it. Her only child had decided views on the way things should be done, and a very definite mind of her own. And she had decreed that her bedside table was the place for her prized trophies.

But that was a problem for later. Sarah's concern at that moment was not to spoil her daughter's pleasure in the coming surprise.

I don't know, sweetie. We'll have to wait and see.

"Can I go get some cake now?"

Cold panic rushed through Sarah's veins. *No. Wait for me.*

"It's my favorite. Chocolate with chocolate frosting. And there are pink roses on it. Please, Mommy, please?"

No, no, no, Sarah screamed in her head, but Lexie clearly heard something different, because she gave Sarah a beaming grin, then whirled and went dancing away.

Unable to stop her, Sarah's breathing grew ragged as she watched the bouncing little figure growing smaller. After a moment, Lexie switched from dancing to skipping, a new skill she had proudly mastered just days before. *All the other kids can skip,* Lexie had told her sadly at the end of her kindergarten year. So Sarah had spent the best part of the summer, in what little free time she had after work, taking her daughter out on the sidewalk in front of their apartment building and doggedly demonstrating the fine art of skipping. Weeks of effort had paid off just in time for the start of the new school year and the huge big deal that was first grade.

"I'll save you a piece, Mommy," Lexie

called back over her shoulder and sent her a last beaming grin.

Sarah could feel her heart cracking in two.

Come back, baby. Please, please come back.

But Lexie kept going, blissfully un-aware.

As she watched her daughter moving far-ther and farther away, Sarah was in such pain that it hurt to draw breath. Long pony-tails bobbing, plump little legs pumping in the awkward bunny-hop gait that she was so proud of, Lexie looked so happy, so sweet, so carefree. . . .

No, no, no, no, no.

Tears leaked from Sarah's eyes. Terrible wailing sounds tore at her suddenly raw throat. Her body twisted and turned in a fu-tile effort to escape the anguish that she knew was coming.

Lexie. Lexie.

But Lexie didn't turn again, as Sarah had known she wouldn't. There was no redoing the past. It was irrevocable, carved in stone, over and done.

Her own harsh sob woke her. She gave a

shuddering gasp, her eyes blinked open, and Lexie was gone. Again.

A terrible desolation filled her, leaving her colder and darker and bleaker than the Arctic at midnight.

A dream. It had been nothing more than a dream. Of course.

You'd think you'd be used to this by now, she told herself grimly as she struggled to breathe through the crushing weight that seemed to have descended on her chest. But she wasn't, and once again the pain was almost unendurable. It gripped her heart with hawklike talons and held on tight. Her body trembled, her breathing came in harsh, ragged gasps, and her cheeks were wet with tears.

Lexie.

She moaned, heard herself, and stopped.

Okay, get a grip. Let it go. You can do this.

But despite her fierce resolve, the pain refused to release her. In those first few waking seconds, Sarah couldn't seem to marshal up the steely determination necessary to force it from her consciousness. The only good thing about it was that it made the physical pain she was suffering seem insignificant in comparison. Her heart was a quivering mass of raw nerve endings screaming in hellish torment. Compared to that, what did it matter that just about every part of her body ached, or that the right side of her head felt fat and swollen, or that she had the mother of all headaches? None of that even began to register when measured alongside the monstrous agony that seemed to have taken up permanent residence somewhere deep inside her soul.

Will there ever come a time when it doesn't hurt like this?

Sarah was pretty sure that she already knew the answer to that: No, not in a million lifetimes.

The only thing to do was grit her teeth and move on.

It required real effort to turn away from the lingering images of the dream, but she did it by concentrating fiercely on the present. It was, she had learned, the only way to cope, to survive.

Okay, first things first. Why did she feel like she'd been run over by a truck? That was the burning question of the moment, and she forced herself to grope around inside the groggy recesses of her memory for an answer. She was lying down, on her back, with her head slightly elevated, on a soft, resilient surface that she assumed was her bed. For a moment she lay blinking up into the darkness surrounding her, trying to fathom why the room was so cold, trying to identify the source of the faintly vinegary smell, trying to ferret out the reason for the rhythmic beeping that seemed to originate from somewhere just behind her head. Then she realized with a jolt that it was unfamiliar darkness. This was not her bedroom, not her bed. And as her eyes adjusted she realized, too, that the darkness was not absolute. It was tinged with a weird greenish glow that just barely allowed her to see shapes and shadows and movements.

Even as she registered that, Sarah's eyes widened and her heart skipped a beat. She tensed, then winced at the pain of it without ever shifting her gaze. Because the reason she knew she could discern shapes and shadows and movements was that in the dark, shadowy corner of the room, something was moving, rising, solidifying. Eyes riveted on the form that was suddenly taking on substance before her eyes, Sarah could do nothing but watch with a racing heart as the tall, broad figure of a man loomed suddenly out of the darkness, closing with swift purpose on where she lay.

3

"You awake?"

The growling voice was familiar: Jake. Sarah's tense muscles relaxed, and her breath escaped in a soft sigh. Over the past seven years, by infinitesimal degrees, Jake Hogan had become the closest thing to family she had left. He had seen her through the worst time of her life, providing advice and moral support and practical help when she had most needed it. Since then he had been a strong shoulder to lean on as she had worked first on surviving, and then on putting herself back together again. In turn, she had nursed him through a divorce and various other assorted crises, the majority of which were of his own too-stubborn-for-his-own-good making. They knew most of each other's secrets, shared a taste for fishing, the University of South Carolina Gamecocks, and the occasional stupid horror movie, and in general had a good time together on the increasingly rare occasions when they hung out. Since his private investigative firm did much of its work under contract for the DA's office, which meant that he pretty much moved in the same career circles as she did, they had each other's backs professionally, too. A nice bonus to the relationship was that on the few occasions when she needed a male escort to an event, she could usually count on being able to press Jake into service. A downside was that he was congenitally allergic to phone chat and shopping malls, so the whole girlfriend niche in her life was basically left unfilled.

"Hey." Her greeting sounded weak to her own ears. Her tongue felt thick, and she had to swallow twice before she could get even that single syllable out. Also, either she was moving or the room was. Or something inside her head was really, really out of whack.

She was going with the latter.

"You were doing some pretty good moaning there. You in pain?" The light over the bed clicked on. Sarah blinked, wincing at the sudden brightness. For a moment all she could see was the slightly unfocused outline of Jake. At six feet one inch and right about two hundred twenty pounds, he pretty much filled her field of vision. He was thick-chested and broad-shouldered, built like the high-school football star he had once been, now gone slightly to seed. If, at age thirty-nine, he was just a little soft around the middle, it was about the only thing about him that was soft. His features were bluntly masculine, his jaw was broad and bulldog aggressive, and both his cocoa-brown eyes and thin-lipped mouth were hard, even in repose. He had Cherokee blood in him somewhere, and it showed in the harsh blade of his nose, the crow blackness of his short-cropped hair, and the swarthiness of his skin.

"Some." The word, emerging as it did from her sandpaper-dry throat, was scarcely more than a croak. She felt disoriented, nauseated, and just plain bad all over, and her thought processes were moving so slowly that she could almost feel the gears clanking in her brain. One reason she wasn't thinking all that clearly, she realized, was that her mind was still ensnared by the last lingering cobwebs of the dream. *Lexie . . . No.* She wasn't going there. Not consciously. Not if she could help it. Not again. "Nothing I can't deal with."

"Tough girl, hmm?" His voice was dry. His hand, big and warm, wrapped around hers. She hadn't even realized how cold her hand was until she registered the comforting heat of his.

"Don't start, okay?" She wiggled her fingers experimentally, then, just as a precaution, tried moving her toes. At least everything seemed to work.

"If something hurts, you should say so. That's why they invented doctors. And pain medication."

Sarah didn't reply. What he saw as her refusal to ask for help even when in his opinion she desperately needed it had long been a source of irritation to him. At the moment, though, she just wasn't up to rehashing old beefs with Jake. She felt too awful.

Her vision was fuzzy, she realized, as Jake's face blurred. In an effort to focus properly, she tried frowning at her surroundings, but frowning hurt so she gave that up in favor of a cautious squint, which proved slightly more successful. She was in a hospital room, she saw with a little spurt of mingled alarm and surprise, on a narrow hospital bed with what felt like a football helmet strapped to her head. The greenish glow she'd noticed before he had turned on the light emanated from a monitor near the head of the bed. She had to turn her head slightly to see it. The steady beep came from another monitor. An IV pole holding a half-empty bag of fluid stood to her left. Its long, clear tube snaked down to her arm. To her right, in the far corner of the small room, was a black vinyl recliner. From its position, she realized that Jake must have been sitting in it until her distress had drawn him to her side. Other than that, there was a beige-curtained window; a small bedside table with a phone, a pitcher, glasses, and a remote-control unit on it; and a darkened TV attached by a metal arm to the wall, and that was about it. Typical hospital, but at least she'd somehow managed to score a private room.

She still wasn't quite clear on how or why. "What . . . happened?"

"You don't remember?" Jake's thick black eyebrows twitched together as he studied her face.

"N-not really." What she remembered most vividly was Lexie standing by her bed, Lexie turning away . . .

Sarah's heart gave a piteous hiccup before she frog-marched her thoughts back to the present, in which she realized to her chagrin that her eyelids felt hot and heavy and her nose felt stuffy and her cheeks were still damp. Probably he could tell she'd been crying. Not long ago, she'd promised him that she didn't wake up crying anymore, and it had been almost true. Maybe, if she was lucky, he would think these tears stemmed from the pain in her head.

He let go of her hand, then touched her damp cheek with a blunt forefinger.

"Bad dream, honey?" His voice was infinitely tender.

Okay, so she was never that lucky and he had the occasional perceptive moment. Plus, he knew her pretty well.

"Yeah." The single syllable was grudging. "Lexie?"

"Yeah." Sarah took a deep breath as she admitted it, and then, in an effort to dismiss the subject, lifted a cautious hand toward her right temple, where the worst of the pain seemed to be centered. That was a mistake. Her head gave a huge throb, the room revolved, and if she hadn't dropped her hand and closed her eyes right then, she was pretty sure she would have passed out. "I feel . . . really weird."

"I'm not surprised."

She thought he might have said something else, but if he did, she missed whatever it was as despite her best efforts she faded right out of the picture again.

The next time she cracked open her eyes, faint fingers of sunlight probed around the edges of the still-drawn curtains. No lights were on, and the room was full of shadows, but she could still see well enough to make out her surroundings: Yep, that part was real enough; she was definitely in the hospital. For a moment she lay perfectly still, almost afraid to move, breathing in the antiseptic smell that had puzzled her before, listening to various faint hums and beeps as the equipment around her did its job. This time the hit-by-an-eighteen-wheeler feeling wasn't a surprise, and neither was the pair of size-twelve Nike sneakers resting soles-up on the pale blue blanket that covered her bed. She looked past the shoes to discover Jake sprawled in the recliner. He was wearing the same rumpled khaki shorts and dark blue T-shirt he'd been wearing when she'd seen him last. His long legs were crossed at the ankle with his feet propped on the edge of her bed, his brawny arms were folded over his chest, and his head was tilted back, pillowed by the top of the chair so that the dark-stubbled underside of his chin was exposed. At first she thought he was dead to the world, but then she saw that his eyes were half-open and looking at her.

"So," he said. "Back among the living?"

She cautiously opened her eyes all the way and was pleased when nothing bad happened. "Seems like it."

His feet hit the floor and he sat up, yawning and stretching hugely. "How you feeling?"

"Like crap." Actually, that was an under-

statement. Her head pounded like somebody was going to town in there with a jackhammer. Her knees, elbows, chin, and left
hip all hurt in varying ways and in varying
degrees. Her throat was parched. Her
mouth felt like it was stuffed full of cotton
balls. "Is there water?"

"Sure." He stood up, poured water into a
glass, added a straw, and held it for her.

"Thanks." She drank, and the cold water
helped. The condition of her head and most
other body parts remained unchanged, but
her throat was no longer dry and the cotton
had left her mouth, which were pluses. She
still felt a little groggy as her mind battled to
emerge from the layers of fog clouding her
thought processes, but it occurred to her
suddenly that Jake's presence in her hospital room was surprising. Last she'd heard
from him, he'd been snorkeling in the
Florida Keys with his latest bimbo—uh, girlfriend.

"Aren't you supposed to be on vacation?"
she asked as he returned the glass to the
table and dropped back into the chair with
another wide yawn. "What are you doing
here?"

"Morrison called me."

Morrison was Larry Morrison, Beaufort County District Attorney and Sarah's boss. He was also a fishing buddy of Jake's, which had its good points and its bad ones. It sometimes enabled her to get a feel for Morrison's position on various topics without asking him directly, which was a plus in the career department, but she also occasionally got the feeling that he and Jake were ganging up on her, which she didn't like.

"What time is it?" A galvanizing thought had just hit her out of the blue, and she struggled to rise on her elbows. Her conclusion as her head spun and the room seemed to turn a slow cartwheel around her: not happening. Abandoning the effort, she closed her eyes and sank back with a groan. "I've got to get up. I have to be in court at nine. The Parker case."

"Not today you don't. I wouldn't worry about it; I'm sure Morrison's made arrangements for somebody to cover for you." He glanced at his watch. "Anyway, it's eight forty-two."

Translation: She had about as much chance of making it to court on time as she did of flying to the moon. Sarah's hand moved to her head, which felt as mobile as if it were encased in about half a ton of concrete. Her fingers encountered layers of rough-textured cloth, explored further, and finally she determined that her head was swathed in a surprisingly heavy gauze turban.

Her eyes popped open as memory resurfaced in a flash.

"I got shot," she said in surprise.

"You did indeed." There was an edge of grimness to Jake's tone. "Turns out it wasn't much more than a flesh wound, fortunately, plus a pretty good concussion when you hit the pavement. You lost some blood, though. And some hair."

Her eyes rounded. "Oh my God, they must have thought I was going to die for sure if Morrison called you in Florida."

"I was home. I got home yesterday afternoon, as a matter of fact."

"But . . ." It might be happening in fits and starts, but her mind was gradually ratcheting up to full wattage despite the pounding in her head. "This is Thursday. You weren't supposed to get back until Sunday."

He shrugged. "Something came up at work, so I had to cut the trip short."

"Bet   Donna"—the   twentysomething
blonde's name popped into her head right on
cue—"loved that."

"Danielle. And she was very understanding."

But suddenly Sarah was no longer concerned with Jake's girlfriends. As her memory returned in full, her eyes fixed on his
with an almost painful intensity.

"Mary—the   cashier—didn't   make   it,
right?"

"Nope." Jake picked up the curtain cord
that dangled next to him and started idly
playing with it. Sarah had observed before
that when he wanted to mask the depth of
his response to something, he had a tendency to fidget with his hands. Well, hardened prosecutor that she was, she was
bothered by Mary's death, too. The woman
had been an innocent victim, the killing absolutely senseless. If the case was given to
her to try—which it wouldn't be, because
she was a fact witness, and because of the
whole range of conflict-of-interest concerns
that such an assignment would stir up—
she'd go for the maximum sentence. And
get it, too. Mary deserved no less.

"The little girl who was with me in the

store. What happened to her?" The sense of urgency she had felt the previous night was back, blunted slightly by, she presumed, the passage of time and/or the drugs dripping into her veins.

Jake's brows knit. "What little girl?"

"She was hiding under a table. When Mary got shot, she came screaming out, and I grabbed her and ran. I still had hold of her when I got shot."

Jake stopped playing with the cord and gave her a long, assessing look.

Sarah had no trouble interpreting that look. She glared at him. "What, do you think I'm nuts now? She was *there.*"

"I never said she wasn't." His tone was placating. "This just happens to be the first I've heard about it."

Still, Sarah bristled. "Could you check?"

Jake inclined his head in a slow nod. "Easy enough."

He stood up, stretched, and walked toward the door, flexing his apparently cramped shoulder muscles and rolling his head around on his neck as he went. While Sarah watched in growing surprise, he pulled open the door, stuck his head out, then had a low-voiced conversation with someone in the hall outside, whom she couldn't see. By the time he closed the door and came back toward the bed, she would have been frowning if she hadn't already discovered that as far as her head was concerned, frowning was a bad thing.

"Who were you talking to?" She could already tell by his carefully blank expression that whomever it was knew nothing of the little girl.

"Morrison put a uniform on the door. Until we get this sorted out."

Sarah forgot and frowned, then grimaced—which hurt, too—and finally managed to relax her face in the teeth of her natural reactions. "What sorted out?"

"Figuring out who shot you."

By this time Jake was standing beside the bed, drumming the fingers of his left hand on the mattress as he looked down at her. His eyes were bloodshot, his hair was rumpled, and he badly needed a shave. She realized that, any snatched catnaps in the chair notwithstanding, he hadn't had any sleep. At the moment he looked tired and irritable and unwilling to face the day. Actually, sort of like she felt, minus the big, white turban and the pain.

"It was either Duke or Skeleton Boy," she said impatiently, "and if I had to hazard a guess I'd say Duke. He was the one who shot Mary. Legally, though, it doesn't matter. They're both facing felony murder charges regardless of who pulled the trigger. Forget them. What I want to know is, where's the little girl?"

The tightening of his jaw and the narrowing of his eyes told its own tale. He didn't have to say a word: She knew just from looking at him. He had his doubts that the little girl had even existed.

Her lips compressed. "Look, there was a girl. My best guess is that she's six, seven years old. Not quite four feet tall, thin, with dark hair and eyes and skin. Maybe Latina." At the telling flicker in his eyes she added forcefully, *"Nothing* like Lexie."

"Hmm." As a response, that was not exactly a ringing endorsement of her sanity. Sarah was trying to summon the energy to get mad when he added, "The way it was told to me is that you were outside while the two perps were still in the store behind you when you got shot. That sound right?"

Sarah thought about it for a second. The

moments before the bullet hit her were becoming increasingly clear in her mind. Like a snippet from a horror movie, she could see Mary's head exploding, hear the child's terrified screams. She could almost taste her own fear as she grabbed the little girl and ran.

She nodded, the movement cautious because of the precarious state of her head. "I'd just made it out the door. I was holding the little girl's wrist."

"Then unless you turned around to face the store at the last moment, neither one of the punks inside could have pulled the trigger. The doctors here, with the concurrence of the ME, who stopped by the hospital last night to examine you just to make sure after the question was raised, determined that the shot that hit you was fired from somewhere in front of you."

"What?" Sarah frowned in astonishment, then just as quickly stopped. *Ouch.* "I never turned around. I ran out of the store with the little girl and never even looked back." As she mentally replayed the sequence of events, she narrowed her eyes in concentration. *Crap, that hurt, too. Okay, for the next few hours at least, the byword was Ex-*

pressionless-R-Us. "The store windows shattered *after* I got hit, I'm almost sure. I remember hearing them go."

Jake nodded as if that confirmed what he already believed.

"The working theory is that three people were involved in robbing the store. One's in jail right now, one got shot and is in critical condition in the ICU here under twenty-four-hour police guard, and the third, the one who shot you, is still at large. I'm guessing he was acting as a lookout and panicked when the robbery started to go south. If he exists, they'll get him."

This time, Sarah knew better than to frown, or to widen her eyes, or to do anything that involved moving a muscle group higher than the tip of her nose. One thing she'd always prided herself on was being a quick learner.

"What do you mean, *if* he exists? If I was shot from the front, he has to exist." At Jake's expression, the tiniest degree of doubt crept into her voice. "Doesn't he?"

"It's always possible that the shot was fired by someone else."

No frown. Is this hard or what? "Like who?"

Jake shrugged. "Don't know, yet. Maybe somebody with a grudge."

"Against me?" The notion was slightly shocking. "You've got to be kidding. Me? Little Miss Sweetness and Light?"

That won her the slightest of wry smiles. "Every prosecutor makes enemies. Including you, Maximum Mason."

The nickname, courtesy of some of the defense attorneys she'd come up against during the course of her career, failed to rankle.

"So I do my best to keep criminals off the streets. So sue me."

"I'm just saying, not everybody loves you like I do."

"Victims love me. Bad guys fear me." It was a takeoff on a baseball cap he had that read *Women love me, fish fear me,* and it earned her another of those slight smiles.

"Funny."

Sarah would have frowned thoughtfully if frowning had been an option. Jeez, being shot in the head was better than Botox for keeping wrinkles at bay. Maybe she could bottle it and make a fortune.

"If it was somebody with a grudge, then he would almost have had to be following me and waiting for an opportunity to take a shot. Or . . ." Her voice trailed off as a thought occurred. Jake lifted his eyebrows at her inquiringly. Their gazes met. "Brian McIntyre was one of the first cops on the scene."

The words were heavy with significance.

Jake grimaced. "You know, not to belabor a point, but taking on the PD like that might not have been the smartest decision you ever made."

Indignation stiffened Sarah's spine, which made her head lift, which in turn made it pound punishingly while the room tilted around her. She slumped back against the pillow, defeated. "I didn't take on the PD. I took on two cops. Who were accused of rape."

"By a hooker hired for a bachelor party that got out of hand. I'm telling you right now, that's a case you're never going to win."

"You know, the thing about being a pros- ecutor is we don't get to choose our clients. We just have to take what we get. So maybe Crystal Stumbo isn't a vestal virgin. So what? She was hurt. She was bleeding. They roughed her up. What was I supposed to do when she came to me, tell her that the law doesn't apply to her? As far as I'm concerned, it applies to everybody." Sarah took a breath, realized that she was doing what he called "getting up on her soapbox" again, and continued in a milder tone. "Anyway, she was hired to *dance* at the party."

"Strip. She was hired to strip. And she has a prior conviction for prostitution."

"In Atlanta. She came to Beaufort to make a fresh start."

"Sarah." Jake met her gaze, came to a full stop, shook his head, and bit back whatever else he had been going to say. Clearly he wasn't up to continuing the argument at the moment. It was one they'd had before and would have again. He had his position; she had hers: otherwise known as the wrong and the right. "In any case, I don't think Brian McIntyre is the shooter, simply because he must know that you have no chance of getting an indictment against either his partner or the other guy." Sarah's mouth opened, and he held up a hand to quell her protest before she made it. "The PD might not like you right now, but I don't think any of them are stupid enough to take a shot at you. Probably there was a lookout man. Probably that's the answer. If so, then he gets caught and the problem goes away."

So file that away under something to worry about if and when she needed to. In the meantime, she had other priorities. A clawing sense of urgency sharpened her voice.

"Jake. I want that little girl found."

Jake's eyes were unreadable as they met hers. "You putting me on the clock on this?"

"Yes." Since he did a lot of work for the DA's office—which included a fair amount of work for her—technically, she could assign the job to him officially, for pay. But because of budget constraints, and because it was possible that having Jake search for the little girl might, in Morrison's eyes, fall under the heading of using department resources to resolve a personal issue and thus be an ethical no-no, and also because there was just the teeniest, tiniest part of her mind that was beginning to fear that just maybe she *had* imagined the child, she hated to tie this to the DA's office in any formal way. "Uh, no. Please find the little girl for me, Jake?"

"You want a freebie," he interpreted correctly and sighed. It was acquiescence, and she knew it. "The store had security cameras. There should be a tape. In a perfect world, the PD would already have it secured. I'll track it down and have a look."

Smiling hurt, too, Sarah discovered. "Jake, ol' buddy, ol' pal, you're the best."

"Yeah," Jake said, his tone dry. "Look, if you want, I . . ."

A brisk knock on the door interrupted. Before either of them could say a word, Morrison stuck his head in.

"Hey, there. You awake? You decent?" He pushed on through the door as he saw that she was, indeed, awake, and that both she and Jake were looking at him. Decent was a whole different matter. Sarah was suddenly conscious of being dressed in a barely-there green hospital gown with nothing underneath. Moving cautiously out of deference to her head, she slid a quick glance down her body to make sure she was covered and tugged the blanket up close around her neck. In her opinion, giving the boss an eyeful wasn't a rung on the ladder to success. "So how's our heroine?"

Jake frowned, and Sarah started to follow suit before she remembered: bad move. *Ouch again.*

"Heroine?" they echoed in almost perfect unison.

"That's what they're saying." A tall, thin man in his early fifties, Morrison grinned at Sarah cheerfully. His bony, intelligent face creased into deep folds beside his mouth, and lines radiated out like spokes around his eyes. They were hazel, magnified slightly by rimless glasses that had a tendency to slide down his aquiline nose. He was balding, elegant, politically connected, and— Sarah's personal favorite of his traits—ran a loose ship. His primary focus at the moment was getting elected governor of the state in two years, which in practice meant that his assistant DAs were responsible for the day-to-day grind of handling the nearly overwhelming workload of the prosecutor's office. Hard work was rewarded with more hard work, which led to a lot of turnover. In fact, Sarah had scored her promotion to acting head of Major Crimes when her boss, John Carver, had suffered a stroke on the job in mid-May. They were still hoping Carver would be able to come back at some point; if not, Sarah had been assured by Morrison that the job was permanently hers. Morrison had learned he could depend on her to get the job done, and Sarah had learned that she could depend on him to stay the hell out of her way, which worked out for both of them. He was a shark, ruthless and aggressive in pursuit of his goals, but since he mostly focused that side of his personality beyond the walls of his office, Sarah liked him immensely. Just now, in a well-tailored navy blue suit, crisp white shirt, and red power tie, he looked like one of his own campaign posters as he strode across the room to the TV. "I saw it on at the nurses' station as I was coming in. Look at this."

He punched a button and the TV came on. A cartoon filled the screen. For a moment, Sarah stared at it in bewilderment. What was he trying to say with that? That she was a Powerpuff Girl? Not exactly the image she was shooting for.

"Grab the remote," Morrison said impatiently. Jake picked it up. "Scoot on over to Channel Five."

The television blinked, and then Sarah found herself watching Duke, in handcuffs, being hustled toward a police cruiser. It was night, the Quik-Pik was in the background, and lots of flashing red lights on the periphery of the shot signaled the presence of many more emergency vehicles in the near vicinity. Clearly, a TV film crew had arrived on the scene in time to capture at least some of the previous night's events.

". . . has been identified as twenty-two-year-old Donald 'Duke' Coomer," Channel 5's bubbly blonde Hayley Winston said from the TV, as Duke was unceremoniously loaded into the back of the patrol car, "whom you see here being taken into custody. Now, in other news . . ."

"Shoot, we missed it." Morrison sounded disappointed. "Go to Channel Three. Quick."

Jake complied—and Sarah sucked in air as all of a sudden she was confronted with a grainy image of herself shoving Duke, then turning to grab the little girl, who was as real and solid as Sarah had been 99.9 percent sure she was.

Thank God, she *wasn't* crazy. Hah! She'd known it all along.

The tape—clearly it was the store's security tape, which just as clearly the PD had *not* secured—was silent and not all that clear, but Sarah's mind instantly supplied the missing details. Mary had just been shot; the little girl was screaming. . . .

". . . bold action by Beaufort County Assistant District Attorney Sarah Mason saved her own life and that of an unidentified young girl during the armed robbery last night of the Quik-Pik convenience store at the corner of Lafayette Street and Highway Twenty-one . . ."

On the screen, Duke was running forward and Skeleton Boy was doing his ants-in-his-pants dance on the balls of his feet. Both of them were taking aim with businesslike handguns. Sarah and the little girl were no longer in the frame; they must have just made it out the door. The tape only clearly covered the inside of the store. . . .

"Sources tell us that police were alerted by a nine-one-one call from Ms. Mason's cell phone, and tracked it first to her residence and then to her vehicle, which was parked outside the convenience store only a few blocks from her home. They arrived to discover the robbery in progress. . . ."

On the screen, the store window shattered and a flash of light blasted from the

muzzle of Duke's pistol—*almost* simultaneously.

"We need to get that tape." Jake glanced
at Sarah. "See what I mean?"

She saw what he meant, all right: The
elapsed time between the muzzle flash
they'd just witnessed and the explosion of
window glass was nonexistent, or even in-
verse: They were talking nanoseconds here,
but it had certainly looked as if the window
had blown out first. Of course, it was possible that muzzle flash routinely occurred after the bullet had left the gun. Who knew?
She certainly didn't. In any case, the
elapsed time seemed much too brief for
Duke's bullet to have been the cause of the
shattered window—she thought. But then,
she wasn't a forensics expert. They would
need one. . . .

Suddenly, Mary's face appeared on the
screen. The picture looked like it had been
taken from a driver's license or something
similar. Looking at it, Sarah felt her stomach
cramp into a tight little knot.

"Killed in the crime was fifty-seven-year-
old Mary Jo White. Mrs. White had been
working at the Quik-Pik for almost two
years. She leaves behind . . ."

"Turn it off," Sarah said, closing her eyes. She didn't want to know any more about Mary, about the life she'd been snatched away from, about the family she'd left behind. Later, maybe, but not right now. Right now she just couldn't take it.

". . . three children and four grandchildren. She . . ."

Morrison's cell phone began to ring.

". . . was a widow who worked nights in the store so that she could be home during the day to care for her grandchildren. She . . ."

"Turn it off."

Saying it with enough force to make sure she was heard hurt her head, but not as much as listening to the news report. She represented victims of violent crime on a daily basis, and thus should by all rights have been immune to the horror of Mary's fate, but she wasn't. In those few minutes of shared terror before the other woman had been killed, she and Mary had connected. Mary's death felt like a personal loss. For today, for this morning at least, while she was hurting and vulnerable and struggling to make sense of what had happened, she just couldn't take any more of those.

The TV clicked off, courtesy of Jake, who still held the remote. In the sudden near silence, Sarah listened to Morrison say into his phone, ". . . running a damned zoo over there. One fuckup after another. Well, be glad it's not us. Yeah, keep me posted."

He disconnected just as Sarah opened her eyes to discover that he was frowning heavily.

Nice that somebody could.

"What?" Jake asked.

But Morrison was looking at Sarah. "The guy they took to the jail—the one involved in the Quik-Pik robbery—hanged himself in a holding cell about an hour ago. Donald Coomer. They just found the body."

It took Sarah a second to realize that he was talking about Duke.

4

"Shit," Jake said.

Morrison shrugged and tucked his phone back into his jacket pocket. "We know he's guilty. The crime's on tape. He would've got the death penalty, no doubt about it. All this does is speed up what would have been the eventual outcome anyway, and save the county the cost of a useless trial to boot."

"The whole thing stinks like a pissed-off polecat." Jake shook his head. *"Jailhouse suicide* my ass. When an inmate dies in custody, you can usually thank either another inmate or a cop, and you know that as well as I do."

"The other guy—his partner—was high," Sarah said. "Totally strung out. Maybe Duke—Coomer—was, too. Maybe he crashed. Maybe he crashed and realized what he was facing, and did it."

Jake looked unconvinced. "Maybe. Maybe not."

"So you think this was murder?" Morrison sounded skeptical. "That this guy was killed, what, by a cop in retaliation for shooting Sarah here?"

Jake and Sarah looked at each other. Given the ongoing rape investigation, their silent mutual consensus was *not.* Although that still left a host of other possibilities open.

"Whatever happened, it's one more black eye for the King administration." Despite Morrison's frown, Sarah could detect a note of glee lurking beneath his words. He and Franklin King, Beaufort's mayor, were locked in a no-holds-barred battle to be the Democrats' nominee for governor. And, since South Carolina was a die-hard Democratic state, the Democrats' nominee almost always won. Maybe one in every five elections would put a Republican in the statehouse. Sarah had no illusions that that was why Morrison hadn't objected when she had pressed to file charges in the Crystal Stumbo case: The police department was heavily allied with the mayor. Burn one, and you could see scorch marks on the other before the match was out. And Morrison really, really, *really* wanted to burn the mayor.

"Maybe the lookout got picked up last night on some other charge." Jake sounded like he was thinking aloud. "He'd know he was facing a death-penalty rap if he got fingered. That's a pretty good motive to murder your buddy, wouldn't you say? The other perp's still under twenty-four-hour police guard, right?"

"Yeah, just like Sarah here." Morrison looked at Jake. "I still think suicide's the most likely scenario under the circumstances, but you never know. Run a check on who else was in the vicinity when Coomer checked out, would you?"

Jake nodded. "Will do."

"Do you really think I need police protection?" Sarah barely remembered not to frown as she put the question to Morrison. She still felt a little woozy, a little out of it,

but not enough to keep her from experiencing a momentary *frisson* of fear at the
thought. In a weird kind of way, she almost
welcomed the feeling. Like the first green
buds of spring, this newfound concern for
her continuing existence could be a sign
that she was starting to come alive again
at last.

"Probably not, especially now that
Coomer's out of the picture. He and the
other guy, Maurice Johnson, who it turns
out is Coomer's cousin, by the way, would
be the threat to this third guy, not you. You
never saw who shot you, right?"

"No."

"Then you're probably in the clear." Morrison shrugged and grimaced. "There was
so much confusion when you were brought
in last night that we all thought better safe
than sorry."

"Good thought." Jake's voice was dry.

Sarah ignored that, as did Morrison. She
kept her focus on her boss. "The little girl in
the store—the one you just saw on the
tape—is she under police protection?"

He shook his head. "Not as far as I know.
No one said anything to me about a little
girl. That tape you just saw was the first I

ever heard of her." His cell phone began to ring again. He answered; listened; said, "Yeah, I'm coming" into it; then disconnected and glanced at Sarah and Jake. "Well, gotta run." Already on the move, he lifted a hand in farewell. "Places to be, things to do. You know how it is, always busy. Glad you didn't bite the big one last night, Sarah."

"Aren't we all." Jake's voice was even drier than before.

"Wait." Panicking a little, Sarah shifted to watch him go, and for her efforts was stabbed by various assorted pains. Morrison paused with one hand on the doorknob to glance back at her inquiringly.

"I'm supposed to be in court at nine," she said. *"Parker versus South Carolina.* Liz Wessell is the judge, and you know how she gets when people don't show up. Tell me you've got somebody covering for me."

Morrison waved a dismissive hand. "I sent Duncan. She loves him. He's asking for a postponement. Should be no problem; everyone knows what happened with you." He grinned at her. "Way to burnish the image of the office. The TV stations will be replaying that tape for days. Assistant District

Attorney saves little girl: We're talking PR out the ass."

With that, he was out the door. Sarah watched it close behind him, then shot a triumphant glance at Jake, who was still standing beside the bed. "Told you there was a little girl."

His lips curved up at the corners. "Hey, I never doubted it for a moment."

"Yeah, right." She eyed him with some severity, then sighed as she shifted again in search of a more comfortable position. "Never mind. Just find out what happened to her for me, would you? I'm assuming she wasn't shot."

"If she was I'd know about it. And it'd be all over the news."

"That's what I thought, too."

"Maybe she just ran on home. A little girl like that, she was probably scared out of her mind."

Terrified. The child had been terrified. If she tried, Sarah could still see the look on her face—and hear her screams.

It was an effort to shake the images away.

Sarah focused on the few bits of information she had. "She knew Mary—the cashier.

When Mary got shot, she burst out from under the table, screaming her name."

"Tough thing for a kid to see."

"Yeah." Sarah took a deep breath and did her best to block the memory out. *Tough thing for anybody to see.*

A quick rap on the door presaged the arrival of a nurse, who entered before either Sarah or Jake could respond.

"And how are you feeling this morning?" The woman sent Sarah a bright smile. A tall, plump fortysomething with spiky brown hair and tortoiseshell glasses, she was wearing blue scrubs and pushing a well-loaded metal cart with squeaky wheels. "Here's breakfast, and then I just need to do a little check . . ."

"I'm okay. And, uh, okay." Sarah, distracted, watched as Jake did a quick little two-step to get out of the way.

"I'm out of here," Jake said as the nurse popped a thermometer under Sarah's tongue, then picked up her wrist to check her pulse. "I'll be back later. Abbott's just outside the door if anything comes up."

Abbott being the cop. Knowing Jake's loathing of needles and most other doctor-related things, Sarah was only surprised he'd stayed by her side so long. He must have been really worried about her.

"You doing okay with the IV?" The nurse pressed the flesh around the needle to be sure it was still securely in place beneath the tape. Jake blanched and headed for the door.

"Yes, fine. Jake . . ." There was a note of urgency in her voice.

He was already halfway out the door.

"I know." He glanced back over his shoulder at her. "Find the girl."

"Yeah. Thanks." He had his hand on the knob when she bethought herself of something else. "Oh my God. Jake." Brows lifting, he glanced over his shoulder at her again. "Sweetie-pie. Would you stop by my house and let him out? And feed him?"

Jake groaned. "Why me?"

"Because you're here. Because you're my best friend. Because you have a key to my house," she said in as beguiling a tone as she could muster. She would have fluttered her eyelashes at him, but she was getting good now at remembering about the no-movement-above-the-tip-of-the-nose rule. Also, the nurse was doing something to the bandage around her head, and it was probably best if she didn't make any sudden movements just then. "Because I haven't been home since I left for the store last night, and by now Sweetie-pie really, really needs to go out. Because he loves you."

Jake snorted.

"Please?"

His mouth tightened. Sarah almost smiled: Good lawyer that she was, she recognized capitulation when she saw it.

"You owe me," he said.

"I know. Lots. Thank you."

"Are you *laughing?*"

"No. Of course not. Besides, laughing would hurt my head." She bethought herself of something else, and her momentary amusement drained away. "Oh, and, um, would you mind stopping somewhere on the way to my house to pick up some dog food? I'm out, which was why I was at the Quik-Pik last night in the first place."

"Did I ever mention that you are a giant pain in my ass?"

"Frequently."

He almost smiled himself at that, she could tell. Then, before he could succumb, he let himself out the door.

"He likes Kibbles 'n Bits," Sarah called after him. Then, with a sigh, she surrendered to the ministrations of the nurse.

The thing about Sweetie-pie was, he wasn't. He was eighty-plus pounds of inertia mixed with a liberal sprinkling of bad attitude for seasoning. Not that Jake could particularly blame him for the bad attitude part. The dog was ugly with a capital U, the kind of badass dog that you expect to see in fight rings or guarding some pothead's primo fields, and he'd been forced to go through his nine years of life answering to the name of Sweetie-pie in public. The humiliation of it had to be huge. Every time he thought about it, Jake could almost forgive Sweetie-pie for the loathing with which the dog routinely regarded the world around him. *Almost.*

That second qualifying *almost* came as Jake cautiously let himself into Sarah's modest brick house—the house that she'd had to buy because no apartment or condo or rental property would let her move in complete with Sweetie-pie—to be greeted by a hair-raising snarl.

"Hey, Sweetie-pie. Hello to you, too."

Closing the door behind him with some reluctance—call him chickenhearted (Sarah would), but feral growls just seemed to automatically imbue him with the urge to retreat—Jake looked cautiously around for Sarah's cherished pet as he headed down the small entry hall to the kitchen, which, like the rest of Sarah's ranch-style house, was Spartan in the extreme. Plain white walls without pictures or plates or other decoration. Mini-blinds rather than curtains. Dark hardwood floors. The minimum of furniture.

The necessities of life, but not its comforts.

That was Sarah to a T.

Jake swallowed the last of the Snickers bar he'd picked up at the Thornton's Mini-Mart on the way over, drained the foam cup of coffee he'd snagged from the same source, and called it a breakfast. As he put down the bag of Kibbles 'n Bits he'd obediently purchased on the solid-surface counter—it was white, like the appliances, while the cabinets and small rectangular table and four chairs in the center of the room were some kind of dark wood—he glanced up at the clock over the refrigerator.

It read nine twenty-five. Christ, he had things to do. The good thing about running his own business was, yes, his hours were flexible. The bad thing was, if he didn't work, he didn't eat. Or pay the light bill. Or the mortgage. Or make payroll. Or . . . the list was endless.

He'd promised Morrison the results of the Perry investigation, which involved re-enacting the timeline that was the chief element in a murder suspect's alibi, by five p.m. today. He'd promised Fortis Insurance Company a dossier on a gang who routinely crammed older cars full of people, drove the freeways, then slammed on their brakes in the middle of traffic so that they would be rear-ended and could subsequently claim injuries for everybody in the car, by five p.m. today. He'd promised Eli Schneider, a prominent local attorney in private practice, a report on the amorous activities of one of his client's soon-to-be-ex-wives by five p.m. today. And those were just the major things his poor sleep-starved brain could recall at the moment. When he got into the office, he was sure a thousand and one other things that required his attention would be waiting.

And then there was Sarah. Always Sarah.

The hell he'd gone through last night when he'd heard she'd been shot didn't bear thinking about. By the time he'd arrived at the hospital, he'd been in a cold sweat. Even after the doctors had told him that as far as bullet wounds went, hers was relatively minor, he hadn't been able to relax. Then he'd been faced with the question of who had shot her and why. In his judgment, the chance that somebody had used that robbery as a cover for attempted murder was remote, but it existed. The chance that a third participant in the robbery, always supposing there was a third participant, would be looking to silence a witness who had never so much as set eyes on him was equally remote but could not be entirely dismissed. Now that he had given the matter more thought and incorporated the death of Donald Coomer into the mix, though, another possibility had occurred to him. A third robber posted outside the store, watching the job go south and wanting to eliminate the only people who could identify him before he ran, might well have been firing at either Coomer or the other guy, Coomer's cousin, and hit Sarah by mistake.

Or . . . well, he was still thinking through alternate or's. The only surviving witness besides Sarah was the little girl pictured with her in the video, who, thankfully, had turned out to be one hundred percent flesh and blood. He needed to track her down ASAP, both for Sarah's peace of mind and his own. It was unlikely that whoever had shot Sarah might be eliminating witnesses who hadn't even seen him and, thus, hunting for the child, too, but not impossible. Before he could breathe easily again, before he could shrug the weight of this from his shoulders and the worry of it from his mind, he'd have to find answers to every one of those questions. And in the meantime, just to be on the safe side, he needed to take what steps he could to ensure that Sarah stayed safe.

But instead of getting a running start on any of that, here he was attending to the number-one item on his morning's agenda: arranging breakfast and a potty break for Sarah's hound from hell.

Time to face facts: Could anybody say "whipped"?

Oh, yeah. He could.

"Sweetie-pie! Come on, boy."

The dog was nowhere in sight. A growl,

low and menacing, reaffirmed that Sweetie-pie was alive, somewhere within earshot, and aware of his presence. The sound came from the far end of the hall where the two bedrooms were located: Sarah's, where the dog probably was holed up, and the spare room. Jake knew that spare bedroom well, having spent more than a few nights in it himself over the years. Nights when he'd been too drunk to drive home, other nights when she'd needed him to stay. Nights when one of them had worked overtime to keep the other sane.

But he had always slept in the spare bedroom, never in her bed.

For a long time now, he'd forbidden himself to think of sex and Sarah with the same brain wave. Over the years, because he'd immediately purged his thoughts when he'd messed up and done it, the two had become something like mutually exclusive in his mind. Luckily, he didn't need to have sex with Sarah. There were lots of women he could, and did, have sex with. And she—as far as he knew, she hadn't had sex with anyone at all in the seven years that he'd known her.

He didn't know how he would react if she ever did.

Something to work through when and if it happens, Jake thought wryly as he opened the back door. For now, and the foreseeable future, they were Best Friends Forever, as the card she'd gotten him for his thirty-ninth birthday last month had humorously put it. At the time, he'd read it, grimaced, and nearly asked her: *So what happens if I'm tired of being best friends?*

But he hadn't, and the moment had passed. Then he'd been busy and she'd been busy and—last night she'd been shot.

The ramifications of his reaction to that were something he was going to have to sort through later, when he had time—and a clearer head.

For the moment, though, here he was, stuck babysitting Cujo. The only thing to do was get it over with.

"Sweetie-pie," he crooned, feeling idiotic. This was what being BFF with a woman got you: all the headaches of an affair with none of the privileges. Hell, if Sweetie-pie was in as bad a mood as it sounded like he was, Jake might be the one making a quick dash out the exit in the next couple of minutes.

"Here, Sweetie-pie."

An ominous clicking of toenails on the hardwood floor warned him: Sweetie-pie was on the move.

Jake pushed the screen door and held it open so that the dog, when he appeared, could go right on out. The backyard beyond was small, neat, and fenced in. Actually, double-fenced in. An industrial-strength chain-link number was backed by a recently added six-foot-tall privacy fence that ringed the place on three sides. The new neighbors on the left had a cat. A pampered and beloved cat. Also known as Sweetie-pie's Holy Grail. Thus, the need for fencing that kept Sweetie-pie from even so much as glimpsing temptation.

In Jake's opinion, it wasn't so much *if* as *when* Sweetie-pie would be having cat for lunch. But Sarah, of course, didn't see it that way.

A quick glance at his watch told him that it was now nine thirty-five. He could feel impatience building, but he did his best to keep it from showing up in his voice. Besides being ugly and bad-tempered, Sweetie-pie was also highly attuned to the emotions of the humans around him. "Sensitive," Sarah called him, although the description made Jake roll his eyes. The thing was, though, if Sweetie-pie wasn't feeling the love, he was perfectly capable of turning around, hightailing it back to wherever he was emerging from, and staying there until he was forced out. Jake pictured himself having to roust the dog out from under Sarah's bed with, for example, the aid of a broom, and almost shuddered. That was a place he wasn't going to unless he absolutely had to.

"Come *on,* Sweetie-pie!"

He'd thought his voice was still in saccharin mode, but clearly there was a false note in there somewhere because Sweetie-pie, who rounded the corner just then, responded with a lip-curling snarl, in the process showing off a set of gleaming white choppers that would have done the great white in the *Jaws* movies proud.

"Good dog," Jake said, lying through his teeth. He flapped the screen door invitingly. "Want to go out?"

Still snarling, Sweetie-pie hesitated, fixing his beady black eyes on Jake like Tony Soprano eyeing a possible FBI plant. Jake grimaced, reminded himself that he had too much manly pride to abandon his post, and did his hundred-thousandth mental head shake at Sarah's choice of a pet. The dog was a mixed breed with the head of a pit bull and the muscular body of a rottweiler. His coat was short and rough, mostly black with a few tan markings. Each of his paws was the size of one of Sarah's hands. His tail was long and thick and carried low; none of this stupid tail-wagging stuff for Sweetie-pie. He was not—repeat, *not*—a tail-wagging kind of dog.

The thing was, Sarah loved him. And Jake could even kind of understand why. She and Lexie had rescued him from the pound when he was a six-month-old, badly abused puppy. Little Lexie had named him Sweetie-pie (and was that the mother of all misnomers, or what?). Despite their subsequent tender care of him, he had never lost his distrust of the human race. Particularly, the male half of the human race.

The thing was, though, he loved Sarah. And, Jake presumed, he had loved Lexie, too.

Which was reason enough for Jake to be standing there in Sarah's colorless kitchen, trying to coax the stupid mutt to go outside and make use of his favorite tree.

"Out, Sweetie-pie."

Jake flapped the screen door again, a little more forcefully this time. Sweetie-pie, who knew him perfectly well, even though, as he continually made clear, he wasn't particularly thrilled about the acquaintance, quit snarling and started walking, stiff-legged, toward the door. He still eyed Jake evilly, his lip still curled to show a warning glimpse of teeth, but he wasn't growling. Jake counted that as a plus. As he passed Jake, the dog's shoulders tightened as if he were expecting a kick or a blow; Jake, for his part, tensed, too, with a quick prayer for the continued well-being of his bare calves. But détente held, and Sweetie-pie slunk on out the door, across the porch, and down the steps without incident. Jake, for his part, blew out a sigh of relief and closed the screen. Sweetie-pie glanced back over his shoulder at the sound, then hiked his leg with gusto on the honeysuckle at the bottom of the steps.

Jake couldn't help but suspect that he was being dissed.

The next hurdle would be coaxing the animal back inside, but that was a problem for later. For now, Jake poured the Kibbles 'n Bits he'd brought into the dog's dish, filled his water bowl, cast a quick glance out through the screen to make sure that Sweetie-pie was doing what he was supposed to be doing and not chomping cat, then headed toward the single bathroom at the end of the hall to answer nature's call himself.

He was halfway there when he heard it: faint, tinkling music, the likes of which he'd never heard in Sarah's house before.

What the hell?

His steps slowed, his brows twitched together, and he listened hard.

When you wish upon a star . . .

It took him a minute, but then he recognized the tune despite the tinny, offbeat rendition. In the next breath, he realized that it was coming from Sarah's bedroom. From behind her closed bedroom door, to be precise.

Her closed bedroom door that she always, always left open because Sweetie-pie liked to snooze under her bed.

The weird little vibe that had kept him alive during his nine years as an FBI agent shivered through his gut. The music was harmless, a plaintive child's tune, but its presence there, at that moment, in Sarah's supposedly empty house, creeped him out. He knew, without knowing exactly how or why, that something ominous lay beyond that door.

Instinctively, Jake reached for the Glock that had once been as much a part of him as his arm or leg, only to remember that, in his new, calmer existence as a private investigator, he'd left it locked in the desk in his office.

Shit.

He could drive to the office, retrieve it, and return.

He could call the cops and let them search the house.

Or he could arm himself with the ridiculously small knife in his pocket, take three strides, and throw open Sarah's bedroom door.

Okay, so he was too impatient for the first and too macho for the second. Or too stupid. Whatever.

Holding his breath, listening to the music that now struck him as downright eerie, he pulled the knife out of his pocket and opened it. It wasn't big, but it was his and he knew what to do with it if he had to. Gripping it, he walked quietly to the end of the hall, turned the knob, and threw open the door.

And then went motionless with shock.

5

Toys were strewn all over the room. A Barbie doll. A two-foot-long pink plastic Corvette. A magic wand. A small purple hand mirror with flowers twining around the glass. A prancing black horse. A stuffed unicorn.

When you wish upon a star . . .

The creepy little tune filled his ears even as he realized what he was seeing: Lexie's toys. Untouched for years, they'd been stored in Sarah's closet. Now the left side of the sliding, mirrored closet door was ajar. The large blue box where the toys had been kept was tilted on its side, with tissue paper spilling out across the dark floor like drifts of snow. He spied its lid halfway under the dresser, lying on its back.

A breath of frigid air touched his cheek, and it occurred to him that the room was unnaturally cold. *Ghostly* cold.

Christ, man, get a grip. Blame the air-conditioning system and the closed door.

There was nothing—no one—there.

A quick glance around confirmed it: unless someone was hiding under the bed or in the other side of the closet, the room was empty. Like the rest of the house, Sarah's bedroom was small and simply furnished. The queen-size bed was placed against the wall opposite the door between a pair of fifties-era double-hung windows. It had a plain oak headboard and a white spread that reached the floor. It was, as he would have expected, knowing Sarah, neatly made. The mini-blinds were closed so that despite the bright sunshine outside, the room was dim. The nightstand on the right side of the bed held a lamp, an alarm clock, a telephone, and a book. Opposite the bed was an oak dresser with no clutter at all on its surface and a rectangular mirror above it. Those were the room's only furnishings.

They looked exactly as he would have expected them to look if Sarah had been the last person in the room. If he'd interrupted a burglary, the burglars had disturbed nothing but the closet.

No. Correction: the toy box in the closet. *Okay, so that was weird.*

The thing was, he was virtually certain: No burglar could have gotten past that dog.

Unless, maybe, someone had crept in through the window and shut the door on Sweetie-pie while he was out of the room.

And played with Lexie's toys?

Jake's mind reeled. *How unlikely was that?*

But still.

Moving warily, Jake crossed to the windows and checked: They were closed and locked. Then he walked to the closet and, being careful not to disturb the upended toy box or the clouds of tissue spilling out, opened the right side just enough so that he could get a good look at the closet's interior. It wasn't deep, not a walk-in, and a glance was enough to assure him that no one was hiding inside. As far as he could tell, everything was in place. Her clothes hung from the rod in a progression of typical Sarah neutrals. Her shoes—maybe six or so pairs ranging from sneakers to medium-high heels, nothing fancy—rested on a small rack at the back of the closet. The overhead shelf was neatly organized with a row of clear plastic bins.

The toy box had been on the floor at the back left side of the closet. He knew, because he'd watched her place it there. As far as he was aware, it hadn't been touched in the four years since.

Now someone had opened the closet, tipped the box on its side, and scattered the majority of the contents around the room.

The question was, who?

Jake was still pondering the answer to that as he dropped to his knees to take a quick peek under the bed. Nothing, not even a dust bunny, except the old plush dog bed Sweetie-pie liked to sleep on.

When you wish upon a star . . .

The tune was getting to him. Jake set his teeth, got to his feet, and followed his ears to the source of the sound: the stuffed unicorn.

The toy was lying on its side. When he picked it up, the music stopped.

He frowned as he looked down at it. It

was clearly the toy of a very young child, maybe a foot long from its velvety nose to its tail of iridescent yarn and fifteen or so inches tall if measured from its satin hooves to the tip of its glittery, gold horn. Except for the horn, a silky blue ribbon tied around its neck, and a pair of blue glass eyes with im-possibly long silver lashes, it was all white velvet and satin. Beneath the plush, he could feel something hard in its middle, something that he guessed was the mecha-nism that caused it to play music. He saw no button or on-and-off switch or any other obvious means of starting and stopping the music, but when he turned the unicorn over to check out its underside, the tune started again of its own accord.

When you wish upon a star . . .

Somehow, in this context, the high-pitched tinkling was managing to give him the willies. Shaking the feeling off as best he could, Jake quickly turned the unicorn right side up. The eerie little melody stopped. He tried it again, experimentally: On its side, the music played; upright, it was silent.

A hell of a toy to get a kid. Jake was will-ing to bet that Sarah had been heartily sick of it long before she'd had reason to pack it away.

The pertinent part of the whole thing, though, was that somehow the unicorn, and the other toys, were now strewn over the dark wood floor of Sarah's bedroom instead of stored safely away in the closet.

Could Sweetie-pie have somehow gotten into the box of toys? It didn't seem likely. Just like with the tail-wagging, Sweetie-pie wasn't that kind of dog. As far as Jake knew, Sweetie-pie ate, slept, growled menacingly, and went out. He was about as playful as a tree.

Jake looked down at the toy in his hand, thinking hard.

It could not have happened since he himself had been in the house. No way had a burglar gotten past him this morning, either to get in or out. The house was too small. If a human being had done this, it had to have happened sometime before he had arrived on the scene, probably last night while Sarah was in the hospital.

Unless Sarah had done it herself.

Jake's eyes swept the room again. The toys were strewn haphazardly over the floor, as if a careless child had opened the toy box and flung the contents out one at a time. He couldn't imagine Sarah, highly organized Sarah, for whom these items were precious relics, doing such a thing.

On the other hand, he had an equally hard time imagining a burglar doing such a thing. There was, as far as he could tell, no point in it. Anyway, the house showed no signs of having been broken into, and, once again, there was Sweetie-pie. He, personally, had faced countless gun-toting thugs ranging from petty thieves to arms and drug traffickers to white-collar criminals with more to lose than he'd ever make in ten lifetimes, but nothing had ever given him pause quicker than a close encounter with Sweetie-pie.

And he'd been acquainted with Sweetie-pie for years. He prided himself that he was on the dog's short list of people he didn't hate.

Any stranger breaking into Sarah's house and encountering Sweetie-pie would have been out of there before his eyeballs had snapped back into his head.

Which kind of deflated the whole toy-obsessed-burglar scenario.

But if a burglar wasn't responsible, and

Sarah wasn't responsible, that pretty much left the dog. It was straight out of Detection 101: Eliminate all the things that couldn't have happened, and, ergo, what was left was what *had* happened, however unlikely it might seem.

What he was left with here was the dog.

The bedroom door had been closed.

That was a problem. If Sweetie-pie was the culprit, how had he gotten into the bedroom with the door closed?

Okay, say the door had been open to begin with. Sarah always left the bedroom door open, so that was likely. If the dog had begun tearing things out of Sarah's closet, maybe he'd gotten rambunctious enough to have somehow bounced the door shut behind him. Maybe he'd galloped out of the room with, say, one of the toys in his mouth. Or something.

Imagining Sweetie-pie with a complete personality transplant might be a stretch, but it was the best explanation Jake could come up with for what he was seeing.

Unless Sarah had done it herself.

Jake didn't even like to think about that. That scenario opened up all kinds of possibilities that he really didn't want to have to contemplate.

One way to find out was, simply, to ask her.

Jake grimaced at the thought. If she hadn't pulled the toys out, and he didn't think there was any way in hell she had, telling her what he had found in her bedroom would, at the very least, upset her. It would rip the scab off her just-barely-crusted-over despair.

He couldn't do it. No way was he causing her that kind of pain. Not unless he absolutely had to.

Whatever had happened here, she didn't have to know about it. He could fix it, make it go away.

With that in mind, Jake righted the toy box, picked up some tissue, and wrapped up the unicorn. Then he carefully stood it upright in the box and wedged it in place with some plastic trophies that hadn't spilled out, so that it wouldn't tip over and the damned song couldn't play. He picked up the Barbie, the car, the wand, the mirror, and the horse, wrapped them in tissue, and stored them away, too. Finally, he put the lid on the box, set the box back where it had rested undisturbed for years, and slid the closet door closed.

Mission accomplished.

He glanced around. Now everything in Sarah's bedroom looked just as neat and orderly as it always did. No harm, no foul.

Just in case the culprit *was* the dog, Jake closed the bedroom door behind him and tested it to make sure it was securely fastened. It was. *Unless Sweetie-pie chews a hole through the wood, he ain't getting in,* he thought with satisfaction. Then he did a quick search of the rest of the house, checking windows, looking around. Everything was locked up tight. Nothing was out of place.

The bottom line was, nobody was in the house. And as far as he could tell, nobody had been in the house.

"You pull those toys out of the closet?" he asked Sweetie-pie once, with the aid of a trail of strategically placed dog treats, he'd managed to lure the animal back inside. The dog was busy scarfing up his food by then and didn't even bother to snarl. He ate as fast as he could, with his tail tucked between his legs and a wary eye on his surroundings as if scared that somebody—

namely Jake, who had never even so much as called him a bad dog to his face in all the years of their acquaintance—was going to do something mean to him while he ate.

Jake sighed. In Sweetie-pie's case at least, you could take the dog out of the junkyard, but you were never going to be able to take the junkyard out of the dog.

The mind boggled at the idea of him romping around with Lexie's toys.

But if Sweetie-pie wasn't guilty, then who was? And was there any way the ransacked toy box could be connected to Sarah's getting shot? They seemed like two totally unrelated events, but . . .

Jake was still pondering the possibilities as he locked the back door and then left by the front, after making doubly sure that both were secure.

As he drove away he was no closer to an answer than he had been when he'd first opened Sarah's bedroom door, but he felt more uneasy than he had in a long time.

Sarah was released from the hospital at a few minutes after five thirty p.m. Hospital rules required that she be brought down to the pickup area in a wheelchair, which had struck her as ridiculous when the nurse had shown up in her room with one. But now, as she stood up on the pavement and attempted to negotiate the curb and then manage the few steps from the wheelchair to Jake's car in the suffocating heat, she found that she was unexpectedly lightheaded and actually grateful for Jake's hard hand beneath her elbow. Not that she ever meant to let him know it. If he somehow guessed how bad she suddenly felt, he'd hustle her back inside so fast their feet would kick up a dust trail.

"You take care, now," the nurse said as she turned the chair around and headed back into the bustling lobby. Sarah waved in response, caught a glimpse of herself in the tinted window of Jake's car, and grimaced. She looked kind of like the dead heroine in Tim Burton's movie *Corpse Bride,* only with short hair and pale rather than blue skin. In other words, not so good. It didn't help that a big, flesh-colored Band-Aid was stuck on top of the two-and-a-half-inch-long wound just above her right ear and that the hair around it had been clipped close to her scalp. The effect was something less than stylish, and since she had way too much scheduled not to show up for work the next morning, she spent a frantic few seconds mentally trying out various hairstyles that might cover up the damage. Coming to the conclusion that nothing was going to work and that, in any case, while she might go the blazer-and-slacks route to cover up her skinned elbows and knees, her skinned chin was going to be impossible to hide, she sank glumly into the passenger seat of Jake's Acura RL.

"Seat belt," he reminded her, and closed the door. The vehicle, which was running, was black with a black interior. The seat was hot against the backs of her bare legs despite the blasting air conditioner, and she shifted them restlessly without managing to escape the broiling leather. He'd driven straight from his office to pick her up, a ten-minute ride. With the outside temperature at ninety-seven steamy degrees, the car was taking a while to cool down. She was wearing her "office emergency outfit," brought to her by her administrative assistant Lynnie Sun, which she kept at work in case she ever needed a quick change of clothes. It consisted of a slim khaki skirt, a sleeveless

white blouse, a navy blazer, fresh underwear, pantyhose, and heels. At the moment,
the blazer and pantyhose, along with the
pain pills the doctor had given her and instructions for caring for her wound, were
stuffed into a plastic bag that Jake had
just tossed in the back. It was too stickily
humid for more than the bare minimum of
clothing.

Moodily, she watched through the windshield as Jake walked around the hood to
the driver's side, popping something—
probably candy—into his mouth as he went.
He had the worst diet of any adult she'd
ever met, subsisting mainly on coffee and
candy during the day, with a rotating selec-
tion of fast food—McDonald's, Pizza Hut,
KFC, Long John Silver's, you name it, if it
was greasy and fattening he ate it—for dinner. Unless, of course, he was in a hot-and-
heavy phase with one of the Blondies (her
own private nickname for his succession of
twentysomething girlfriends, every single
one of which had been a va-va-va-voom
blonde), in which case either the girl cooked
him a meal or they ate out somewhere
slightly more upscale—and, hopefully, nutritious.

The thing about the Blondies was, they were all so similar it was hard to keep them straight. You had to hand it to him, though: Clearly he knew what he liked, and he stuck to it.

Jake slid in beside her, slamming the door, and she turned her poor aching head, which felt heavy as a boulder as it rested against the top of the seat, sideways so that she could look at him.

"Thanks for coming to get me."

He grunted by way of a reply as he put the car in gear and they pulled away from the curb. Since she'd seen him that morning he'd shaved, and changed clothes, too, trading in shorts and T-shirt for dark gray slacks and a pale blue dress shirt, now almost as rumpled as the clothes he'd slept in had been. At the moment, the collar of his shirt was open and the sleeves were rolled up past his elbows. She presumed he'd discarded a jacket and tie somewhere during the course of the day. Just like hers, a lot of his work required court appearances, which in turn required business dress.

"So tell me again why they're letting you go today?" He sounded testy. He *looked* testy. And tired. The skin around his eyes was puffy, and the eyes themselves were bloodshot. His brows didn't quite meet over his nose, but they came close, which was never a good sign. He was a big guy, broad-shouldered and muscular, taking up more than his fair share of space in the front of the car. If she hadn't known him so well, she probably would have found him intimidating.

But he was Jake, and she did know him that well, and it had been many years since he'd been able to intimidate her. Although, occasionally, he still gave it the old college try.

Sarah shrugged. "No reason to keep me, I guess."

The truth was, they'd wanted her to stay for at least one more night. *As a precautionary measure,* Dr. Solomon had said. But she was sick of the hospital, sick of people popping in every five minutes, sick of being poked and prodded and feeling like she was on display. The local news programs ran replay after replay of the store's security video, not that she watched: After Morrison had left, the TV in her room remained firmly off. But she knew what was on the air anyway, because innumerable people told her about it as they stopped by to check on her, commiserate, or just get a firsthand look at what one of the nurses on her floor kept telling visitors was the "heroine of the hour." Everyone from the hospital staff to her own administrative assistant *(Et tu, Lynnie?)* to the woman who lived across the street from her had dropped in and talked the subject to death. Two detectives from the Beaufort County PD had come by to take her statement. Mark Kaminski, a fellow assistant DA who Morrison had already assigned to prosecute the still-at-death's-door Skeleton Boy, aka Maurice Johnson, should he recover, had showed up to quiz her about details of the crime. She had tried quizzing him back in turn, just to see what he knew, but since she was a victim and would be a witness at any subsequent trial, he wasn't allowed to tell her anything even if he knew anything to tell, which, as Johnson had not regained consciousness since the shooting, he assured her he didn't. Later, when the cop outside her door had decamped for a long lunch, Channel 5's Hayley Winston had managed to sneak in, complete with a cameraman, requesting an interview. Sarah had been surprised into stammering out answers to a few questions before the hospital staff, which she'd urgently summoned with her call button, had shown up and shooed them out. Everybody wanted to know what it had been like inside that store, and the truth was that she could hardly stand to think about it, much less talk about it. An innocent woman had been violently murdered right in front of her eyes, and the image now haunted her every time she closed them. To make things worse, her own brush with death had left her not traumatized exactly, but certainly badly shaken in a way she couldn't share with anyone. For so long now she'd thought she wanted to die, but when Death had finally stared her in the face, she had discovered that she wanted to live after all.

The knowledge continued to unnerve her. She felt almost like a stranger in her own skin. To *not* want to die—what was that? When had it happened? It was a seismic shift in the way she interacted with the world, and she hadn't even seen it coming. It was just suddenly there.

Not that she meant to tell Jake any of that. Mother hen that he was, he'd worry if he had the slightest clue about what was going on inside her head. Then, being Jake, he'd do something about it. Like march her right back inside the hospital, tie her to a bed if need be to keep her there, and summon a crack team of psychiatrists to probe her psyche.

Okay, so probably she could use some help with her mental health. Today was definitely not the day.

"You're taking tomorrow off, right?" Jake accelerated, and the Acura pulled smoothly out onto Highway 21. Heat vapor shimmered off the pavement, rising lazily toward the baby-blue sky. The four-lane road was packed with traffic, most of which was heading out of town at a slow crawl. Since they were coming from the hospital, though, today they were actually traveling toward town, which was a good thing. Beaufort was just at that moment experiencing its small-town version of evening rush hour, which generally lasted for about thirty minutes, tops. The problem was, Beaufort was hemmed in by water on all four sides, which made it to all intents and purposes an island. There was one major road heading west, where most of the population lived: Highway 21. If you pictured Highway 21 as a python with its head at the Atlantic Ocean, then rush-hour traffic was a rabbit the python had swallowed for dinner: It moved slowly along toward the tail in one solid clump. Not that Sarah had much firsthand experience with rush-hour traffic. She rarely left the office before seven thirty or eight. But still, she knew that by six p.m. on weekdays, everyone who *didn't* lack a life was usually home and traffic was back to its usual state, which was the next thing to nonexistent. The city was laid-back like that, particularly in the summer, when after work the majority of the townsfolk were engaged in boating or golfing or gardening or throwing impromptu barbecues in their backyards. Beaufort was a socializing kind of town, an aristocratic kind of town, a lazy, set-in-its-ways, you're-a-stranger-if-you-haven't-lived-here-all-your-life kind of town. She, personally, had lived full-time in Beaufort for a little more than four years, and yet she was still an outsider. And that was something that was never going to change.

"Well," Sarah said guiltily. On the right, a strip mall complete with a fast-food trifecta of McDonald's, Taco Bell, and Pizza Hut was siphoning cars from the road, and Jake gave it a wistful glance. Before he regained his focus, she made a stab at redirecting his thoughts.

"So what did you find out about Duke? Donald Coomer?"

Jake shrugged and changed lanes to avoid the line of traffic pulling into the mall.

"He's definitely dead."

"Care to elaborate on that a little?"

"He was alone in one of those holding cells in the basement of the jail because they were getting ready to take him over to the courthouse for arraignment. Apparently, he got hold of an extension cord and used it to hang himself from the grille in the door."

"How long was he alone?"

"Bill Canon was the supervisor on duty. He swears not more than ten minutes."

"Who had access?"

Another shrug. "To those cells? Who didn't? Cops, sheriff's deputies, officers of the court, lawyers—hell, the cells lock from the outside. Anybody with access to the jail could have just turned the knob and walked in."

Sarah knew those cells. Like the jailhouse itself, they were older than dirt. Each was about six feet square, solid concrete except for the acoustic-tile ceiling, with a metal door complete with a small, open, steel-barred window and a metal bench built into one wall. There were no security cameras in the cells themselves, but the hall outside was covered.

"Did you check the security camera in the hall?"

"Wasn't working at the time."

"Oh." They were on the bridge that spanned the Coosaw River now, and steel struts flashed by outside Sarah's window. Below, a tugboat pushed a barge loaded with coal toward Port Royal Sound. She registered this only peripherally. Her mind was busy turning over the possibilities. "That's not good."

"No."

"Any clue how he got hold of the extension cord?"

"Nobody knows. The popular theory is that it was somehow left in the cell. They're checking it for fingerprints, but I don't expect much."

"So was it a suicide or not?"

"For my money? Not. But at this point, that's just a gut feeling." Now that they were off the bridge, traffic was speeding up again. Jake braked for a red light and glanced at her. "Speaking of gut feelings, what do you feel like for supper?"

They had just passed a Long John Silver's on the left and an Arby's on the right. Sarah figured the fast-food restaurants must be giving off subliminal messages now.

She shrugged. *She* wasn't hungry. "Your call."

The light turned green and they drove on.

"I already checked and you got nothing worth talking about in your refrigerator. You want to pick up something on the way to your house or you want me to order in pizza?"

Sarah made a face at him. "For your information, in the *freezer* I have lasagna and chicken cordon bleu and New England pot roast."

He snorted. "Frozen diet dinners. I saw 'em. Yum."

"They're *good*. And healthy." She sighed. There was no winning this battle, she knew, so she might as well surrender now and save herself the effort. "I'm not even hungry, but if you have to, pizza. Veggie."

"Good choice." His tone was slightly satiric. That he would order a meat-lovers pie for himself went without saying.

"You don't have to babysit me, you know. I have a headache, and my hairstyle's on life support, but other than that I'm fine. If I had my car"—which was at the police impound lot, she'd discovered courtesy of Lynnie—"I'd have driven myself home."

"Good thing you don't, then."

"I need to pick it up."

"Already done. I had Pops"—his grandfather, who worked for him—"do it. It's in your driveway."

"Wow. Thanks. You're amazing."

"So I keep telling you."

She smiled. "I—"

His cell phone rang, interrupting. Fishing it out of his pocket, he glanced down at the number, muttered something indecipherable, and answered.

"Yo."

"Hi, Sugar Buns. I've got pork chops ready to throw on the grill. How soon can you get here?"

Sarah was able to hear every word clearly, and she recognized Donna's—*oops, Danielle's*—breathy tones.

"Sounds good, babe," he said into the phone, shooting Sarah, whose smile had morphed into a smirk, a hard glance. "I can't make it, though."

"You can't make it!" Sarah could almost see Blondie pouting. "But I bought *pork chops.* I told you yesterday I was going to, and you said *great.*"

"Something came up."

"Something always comes up with you. All you do is work. Work, work, work. We even had to cut our vacation short so you could come back to work."

"I know. I'm sorry. Put the pork chops in the refrigerator and we'll do it tomorrow."

There was the tiniest of pauses. To Sarah's discerning ears, it was clear that Blondie was vacillating between throwing the mother of all hissy fits and making nice. If she'd been sure about her man, Sarah's bet was that she would have gone with the hissy fit, but that was the thing about Jake: The girls he dated were *never* sure about him. They were probably all masochists, and keeping them guessing was part of his appeal.

"Promise?" Danielle went with making nice.

Jake's mouth quirked up at the corners. "Unless something comes up."

Well, at least he was honest.

Danielle inhaled sharply. Then, after a couple of seconds in which the issue hung in the balance, she chuckled, the sound throaty and intimate. "You are the biggest tease!" Her voice turned seductive. "Just so you know, I bought a new nightie just for *you-ou . . .*"

Jake's eyes cut to Sarah. If he'd been five years old, he would have been squirming uncomfortably in his seat about now. She puckered her lips and blew a silent kiss his way.

He looked back at the road, cleared his throat, and spoke into the phone. "Look, I've got to go. I . . ."

"It's black. And lacy. And you can see right—"

"Hold that thought, okay?" Jake interrupted hastily. "I'll talk to you tomorrow."

"I just want you so m—"

But if that was going to be a confession of undying lust, it was lost forever because

Jake muttered a hasty "bye" and disconnected.

"How old is she?" Sarah couldn't resist
asking as Jake put the phone down on the
console between the seats.

He shot her a look. "Twenty-five."

"If she's the one I'm thinking of, she's hot.
You should definitely go check out her pork
chops."

"Didn't anyone ever tell you it's rude to
listen to a private conversation?"

"What, I was supposed to stick my fingers in my ears?"

"Something like that."

"Well, golly gee, next time I just might do
that—Sugar Buns."

His lips tightened, and she was ready to
swear that a hint of red crept up over
his cheekbones.

"So she's into pet names. So what?"

"Come to think of it, that one's actually
kind of appropriate. You really do have a
nice ass."

This time, the look he shot her came
complete with narrowed eyes. "You want to
drop it, please?"

"But that Sugar Buns thing was so cute."

"Sarah."

"Okay. I get it. I'm embarrassing you. I'm sorry."

"The hell you are." The red was fading, but it had definitely existed, Sarah noted with interest. Jake continued, "Danielle's a nice girl. If you got to know her, you'd probably like her."

"Keep her around long enough and I'll probably get to know her." As far as Sarah was concerned—and, she suspected, as far as Jake was concerned, too—the Blondies were practically interchangeable. None had ever lasted longer than six months, and most of them far less. Jake had been seeing Danielle for something on the order of five months. In other words, she was almost past her use-by date.

Jake grunted. Sarah translated that to mean "end of conversation." They were nearing the downtown area now. The historic district with its rows of beautiful white mansions was perhaps a mile ahead. Jake slowed down to keep from crowding a horse-drawn carriage loaded with tourists that rolled out of a side street and proceeded to bowl along directly in front of them. The horse was gray and resigned-looking, the open-topped carriage was black and bedecked with flowers, and its occupants were laughing and chatting with the top-hatted driver, who was half-turned in the seat as he regaled them with Beaufort's history. Sarah knew the spiel: The town was one of the few that had survived General Sherman's Civil War–era march to Georgia intact, largely because the Union troops had found the place so uniquely charming (all right, strategically located) that they had commandeered it for a headquarters. The antebellum mansions that crowded the old downtown streets and waterfront had emerged from the war unscathed, and now the most magnificent of them provided Beaufort County with its claim to fame as thousands of tourists flocked to visit them each year.

"You know," she said as Jake passed the carriage and sped up again, "I can eat pizza perfectly well on my own. Or better yet, New England pot roast. You really don't have to miss Danielle's pork chops on my account."

Jake slowed, then turned left onto Bay Street. The houses in this area dated from the Victorian era, which made them relatively new in Beaufort terms. They were not quite mansions, but they were large and old and ornate, set back from the street on beautifully manicured fescue lawns surrounded by wrought-iron fencing. Giant, glossy-leaved magnolias shaded overflowing gardens. Tall cypress and Spanish moss–laden live oaks lined the streets. Flowering azaleas in shades of pink and coral crowded close to large gingerbread-trimmed porches where the residents sat in swings and rockers gossiping as they watched the world go by.

"Just so you know, I'm not just eating pizza with you, I'm staying the night. Unless you'd rather stay at my place?"

Sarah eyed him. The truth was, she realized as she considered the matter, she was *glad* that he wouldn't be leaving her alone tonight. The knowledge that last night someone had tried to kill her gave her the jitters when she allowed herself to think about it. Not that she was about to admit to that. It might give him way too much insight into exactly how fragile she was feeling. Usually, she was Miss Independence personified.

"There's Sweetie-pie," she reminded him. He grimaced, signifying that the thought of hosting her dog for the night did not appeal, just as she'd known it wouldn't. He and Sweetie-pie were something less than bosom buddies. For the sake of putting on a good show, she dredged up a challenging tone. "Anyway, what would happen if I told you that I just really need to be alone tonight?"

"I'd tell you to lock yourself in the bathroom when we get to your house, because that's about as alone as you're going to get." There he went, being all unsympathetic to her needs again, just as she had expected. Thank goodness. "I don't know whether you realize it or not, but you lost your police coverage about three hours back. Frist"—Lowell Frist was the Chief of Police—"says they can't afford to provide you with round-the-clock protection. Anyway, the official line is they don't think you're in danger."

"And you do?"

Jake's jaw tightened, just fractionally but enough so that Sarah knew that he was truly worried about her. The knowledge sent a chill down her spine.

He shook his head. "I don't know."

They had nearly reached her neighborhood by this time. Sandwiched between the old rich in their historic mansions and the new rich in their glitzy bedroom communities were her people—the "no rich," as she called them, who made their homes in the small houses and apartment buildings that had built up around the historic district in the years after World Wars I and II, before the suburban building boom began. The residents were a hodgepodge of everything from large families of recent immigrants to retirees on a fixed income to working singles like herself. Small businesses dotted the area, which boasted significantly more concrete than grass. As Jake slowed for a red light, Sarah saw her not-so-friendly neighborhood Quik-Pik at the other end of the block. Even from that distance, she could tell that it was closed. The parking lot was roped off with yellow crime-scene tape and a pair of squad cars were stopped at the curb. One of the uniforms was just exiting his cruiser. As Sarah watched, he climbed nimbly over the yellow tape and headed toward the building where, presumably, the investigation was still under way inside. Ordinarily, it would have been a closed case by now and the store would have been back in business, but the fact that an officer had shot and killed a suspect would delay the natural order of things. The PD would be extra-careful about covering its ass.

"Shit," Jake said. "I wasn't thinking. I should have come another way."

"What other way?" There really wasn't another way to get to her house from the hospital that didn't involve at least passing within sight of the Quik-Pik. She lived only four blocks away. "Anyway, don't worry about it. I'm fine."

And she was, until she saw the message board out front that usually advertised gas prices. In the wake of the tragedy, its big, black magnetic letters had been changed to read:

Mary Jo White 1939–2006
Rest in Peace

And then, at the very bottom, somebody had added *Pray 4 Us.*

Her throat was suddenly tight. Her vision blurred. A knot formed in her chest. The horrible memories ran through her mind like a movie on fast-forward: the terror on Mary's face, the gunshot, the screams . . .

Much as she might want to, she realized, there was no escaping the terrible reality of what had happened. The random evil that lurked in the world had once again forced itself into her life, into her tiny allotment of breathing room, without warning. One moment everything was all fine and dandy and hunky-dory and the next—not. The safe, sane fabric of everyday existence was ripped violently apart, and afterward nothing could ever be the same.

That was why she had become a prosecutor: to do battle with that random evil. Maybe that was even the reason she was still alive.

She had to believe that there was a reason.

If she could find the strength to fight for people who couldn't fight for themselves, then good would come out of evil, and evil would ultimately lose.

Or so she'd been telling herself for the past seven years. Maybe she was even starting to believe it.

They had just passed the Quik-Pik and were accelerating through the intersection in what Sarah guessed was an effort on Jake's part to beat the light and get the unwelcome view behind them when her eye was caught by a gaggle of children. They were coming out of the ramshackle house on the other side of the intersection that had recently been converted into the Wang's Oriental Palace Chinese restaurant. There were four—no, five—of them, all with hair of so dark brown it was almost black, all with deeply tanned skin, all thin, all dressed in well-worn, almost ragged clothes. The tallest was a boy of, Sarah guessed, around ten. The youngest was a girl barely past the toddler stage. The rest were a boy and two girls in stair-step sizes. They were walking away from the car, so Sarah couldn't see their faces, but she was sure—almost sure—that the second-tallest child, the girl with the long, dark hair holding the littlest one's hand, was the little girl she had last seen screaming as they fled from the Quik-Pik.

"Jake," she said urgently. "Pull in here."

6

"What?" Jake glanced at her, frowning.

"It's the little girl, I'm almost sure. From the store. There." Fingers already fumbling to unbuckle her seat belt, Sarah pointed toward the children.

Looking where she indicated, Jake pulled the Acura into Wang's lot and drove to the far end of the parking area where the pavement ended in a jumble of broken asphalt and scruffy grass. The children were already walking away along the narrow gravel alley between the restaurant and a tall privacy fence on the left that separated the commercial area from the house next door. A mix of yellow sunflowers and thorny purple thistle and leggy ragweed grew tall against the unpainted fence. A battered Dumpster surrounded by untidy piles of discarded boxes and crates made the alley impassable for anything as large as Jake's car.

"Stop," Sarah said, and Jake did. Even as she opened the door and tumbled out (anything more graceful was beyond her at present) the children crowded around a black plastic trash bag that had been left beside the Dumpster. They opened it, peering down inside it at the contents, talking quietly among themselves.

"Hey. Hi." Sarah was a little woozy, a little wobbly in her beige pumps with the sensible two-inch heels as she headed down the alley toward the children, but determination, as she had observed before, made up for a lot. Her knees might feel about as solid as mashed potatoes, and her head might feel like it was going to explode any minute, and the spicy scent of Chinese food drifting on the sultry air might be giving her stomach fits, but at least she was moving in the direction she wanted to go, and that was what counted.

"Hi," she called again, waving. A broken piece of pavement caught her toe and she stumbled but managed to regain her balance after a few staggering steps.

The whole gang looked at her, their eyes wide. It took no more than a glance for Sarah to be sure: The tallest girl—and she was talking several inches under four feet here—was the little girl from the store. Her hair was a jumble of tangles that badly needed brushing, her yellow T-shirt—*was it the same one from the night before?*—was stained and ripped at the shoulder, her once-red shorts had faded to a well-worn pink, and her thin legs and bare feet were grimy. Like her build, her features were small and delicate. The warm gold of the early-evening sunlight confirmed Sarah's earlier impression, registered under the previous night's far harsher fluorescent glow: The child was pretty. And obviously neglected.

"Remember me?" Sarah asked, trying for a reassuring smile. It didn't work. Or rather, it did, only not quite in the way she intended. Her target, still clutching the hand of the youngest of the group, let out a muffled scream and backed away from the trash bag, her mouth hanging open, her eyes round as doughnuts. The little one, either sensing the older girl's fear or feeling like her fingers were being crushed in a death grip, started to bawl. Noisily.

"No, wait, it's okay." Anxious that they not be frightened, Sarah stretched her smile into a friendly grin (and never mind the pain in her head) as she lengthened her stride to close in on them. Bad move. Her head throbbed, her vision blurred, and she lost her balance and tottered sideways before catching herself with a hand against the side of the building.

"Run," the girl cried, and to Sarah's astonishment they did, just like that, snatching up the garbage bag and pelting down the alley like deer catching wind of a hunter. The girl grabbed the toddler by both arms, swung her off her feet, balanced her on her hip, and ran away like that, in a way that told Sarah she'd had a great deal of practice at it. She was fast, too.

"Wait."

Sarah tried running after them, only to be brought up short by Jake's hand grabbing her arm and her own realization that for her, today, running just wasn't in the cards. Anyway, there was no way she was catching up with them: They were already scampering around the far edge of the privacy fence and out of sight. Sarah stared after them, surprised and disappointed and even a little hurt. From her point of view, she and the child had bonded through their shared horrific experience. From the child's point of view, obviously not.

"That went well," Jake said.

She glanced over at him. He was a pace or so behind her, with his hand wrapped around her upper arm as if he feared she would take off in hot pursuit despite her battered state if he let go. The setting sun was behind him, making him look tall and broad and casting his face in deep shadow. But she had no trouble at all discerning that his lips were twitching.

"Do you think she didn't recognize me?"

The lip twitching evolved into a full-fledged grin.

"The thing is, you're staggering around like Frankenstein, you're skinned up and bruised and have a bandage on your head, and the last time she saw you, you were lying shot and bleeding on the pavement. So maybe it wasn't so much that she didn't recognize you as that recognizing you wasn't a real positive experience for her."

Sarah's lips compressed. "Are you saying that I look bad enough to scare small children now?"

He laughed. "I'm just saying I can understand why she ran." He was drawing her back toward the car as he spoke.

"But I saved her life! She must know I mean her no harm."

"She probably thinks you're a haunt. Or a zombie. Or some other boogie come out of the grave to get her."

She had left the car door open in her excitement, Sarah realized as they reached it. Jake bundled her back down into the seat with swift efficiency. She didn't resist. Galling as it was to admit it, that brief chase had left her utterly exhausted. There was no way she was going after them under her own steam, determination or not.

"That's ridiculous," Sarah said crossly as he closed the door on her. By the time he slid in beside her, she had her seat belt on. "I just wanted to make sure that she's okay."

After putting the car in gear, he circled it back around the parking lot toward the street. "She's okay. I told you earlier she was okay. You don't have to worry about her."

He had called her during the course of the afternoon to report that he had located the child for her. Not that she had doubted that he would. Jake was a crack investigator, which was why the DA's office used his (expensive) freelance services so extensively. And he was utterly reliable, at least as far as she was concerned. Whatever she asked of him, she could pretty much count on him to do if it was humanly possible.

Despite his reassurance, Sarah still felt anxious. Craning her neck, she tried to see through the backyards to the next street over, which was where that particular turn at the end of the alley logically led. It was impossible. Chain-link fences, honeysuckle hedges, staggered rows of houses—there was too much in the way.

"You don't think she's in danger from whoever shot me? The third robber, if there is one?"

Jake shook his head. "I don't think so. She's a little kid, to start with, which means that even if he exists and she did see him, which I don't think she could have, given the logistics of the whole thing, she was so

scared and upset at the time that she probably wouldn't be able to identify him anyway. And if she did, her identification
wouldn't be worth much for just those reasons."

"You're presuming that a third robber
would be intelligent enough to realize that.
From what I saw, the two in the store were
dumb as rocks."

The Acura was back on the street now,
heading toward Sarah's house. For a moment Sarah toyed with the thought of asking Jake to drive around and see if they
could find the children, but then she dismissed the idea. For now, it was enough to
know that the little girl was alive and well
and relatively safe. If she wasn't in danger—
and for the moment Sarah was willing to accept Jake's judgment about that—there
was certainly no point in scaring her senseless. Besides, she'd already given herself
the mother of all headaches chasing after
the child, to say nothing of spaghetti knees
and an allover glaze of sweat. And for what?
In a word, rejection.

The kid clearly wanted nothing to do with
her.

She settled back into the seat with a sigh.

"So tell me about her."

Jake dug an open package of peanut M&M's from his pocket, dropped it in the cup holder nearest him, and proceeded to fish a couple out and pop them in his mouth. Sarah watched him with narrow-eyed disapproval.

"Hey, I didn't have time for lunch, okay?" He knew her well enough to correctly inter-pret her expression, and also not to bother offering her an M&M. "You want to know about the kid or not?"

"Yes." Chiding him about his eating habits was a waste of breath. Not that that usually stopped her from doing it, but the thing was, she just wasn't in the mood to at-tempt Jake improvement right then.

"Okay." He braked, turned left onto Jack-son Street, fished out more M&M's, and crunched them down, too. "Her name's Angela Barillas. She, her single mother, and four siblings—I think it's a pretty safe guess that those were her siblings we just saw—live in the Beaufort Landing complex, at forty-two Yamassee Court, apartment two-C."

Sarah knew that apartment complex: It consisted of some twenty run-down brick buildings with six apartments in each. The residents tended to be either recent immigrants or the working poor. It was maybe a mile and a half as the crow flies from her house—and she had once lived in a complex just like it. The memory was unwelcome. Even as she pushed it from her mind, it made her feel cold all over.

Jake continued: "She's nine years old, in fourth grade at Riverside Elementary, and except for being upset about what happened to the cashier, who was a neighbor, she's doing just fine. Apparently, she ran on home after you got her out of the store. None of her family even knew that anything out of the ordinary had happened to her until they saw her on TV this morning. The police tracked her down around noon today, got no answer at the apartment, then tracked the mother down to Walgreens where she works one of her two jobs. When the mother took them to the little girl, the kid said she didn't say anything about the robbery because she'd snuck out and was afraid of getting in trouble."

Jake had told her all this over the phone earlier.

"She's small for nine," Sarah said. "And

what kind of nine-year-old is sneaking out at night anyway?"

Jake shrugged. "What I know about nine-year-olds you could write on the back of a bottle cap. If you want, I can contact Child Protective Services, and they can check the family out."

Sarah shook her head. "I'd rather look into the situation myself first. You start getting government agencies involved, and anything can happen." She hesitated, then added in a softer tone, "That garbage bag—what do you think was in it?"

It bothered her to think it might be food. That they might be hungry . . .

"No idea." Jake looked at her. "Sarah. There's only so much one person can do. You're working twelve-hour days as it is, and carrying God only knows how many pro bono cases besides. You're teaching that rape class at the community college. When they're short drivers, you deliver food for Meals on Wheels. You—"

"So I like to stay busy," Sarah interrupted, her tone defensive.

"I know you do." His voice softened. "All I'm saying is, you don't have to take on this family and its problems."

"I'm not planning to 'take them on.' All I want to do is just make sure that little girl is all right."

"You saved her life and now you're responsible for her forever?" Jake's voice was dry.

"Something like that." Sarah refused to be drawn. It was an ongoing thing—she fussed at Jake about his eating habits, his constant parade of ever-younger girlfriends, his laissez-faire approach to life. He fussed at her about overworking, getting too involved with people and things he termed lost causes, and being too uptight in general. They'd argued over variations of those topics so often in the past that now only a lift of an eyebrow, a curl of the lip, or a sidelong glance was necessary to get their point across.

"Fine. Do what you want." It was clear that he knew he wasn't going to be able to talk her out of checking up on the child.

"I will."

Sarah's brick ranch was located on Davis Street in a block of small, single-story and split-level homes. It was a quiet, middle-class area with sidewalks, fenced backyards, and cars parked along the street.

Jake pulled over in front of her house—as he had promised, her Sentra was in the driveway—and they got out. She retrieved her mail from the box, waved to old Mr. Lunsford across the street, who was out mowing his grass, and with Jake beside her, headed inside. After the plush green lawns of the wealthier parts of town they had just passed through, her postage-stamp-sized yard was almost embarrassing: It was sun-crisped in spots, and the only plants offering up serious competition to the crabgrass were the dandelions. A pair of scrawny yuccas sported wilting blooms on either side of her front stoop; small, round shrubs marched in a bedraggled line against the brick; and a single hardy palmetto provided the only spot of shade in the angle where the front walk met the driveway. The wrought-iron window boxes that hung beneath all three front windows, courtesy of a previous owner, provided the only note of distinction. Unfortunately, they were empty. In the four years that she had lived in the house, she'd never gotten around to planting anything in them. Next spring, she vowed to herself, she would. And never mind that she'd made that vow before and, anyway, whatever the opposite of a green thumb was, she apparently had it.

"Woof." Sweetie-pie greeted her at the door, smiling his wide doggy smile at her. She bent clumsily—like everything else she had done today, bending hurt—to give him a hug. He responded with an enthusiastic full-body wriggle.

"Hey, puppy. You glad to see me?" she asked him, and took the lick he bestowed on her cheek for a *yes.* When she straightened and headed for the kitchen, he followed close on her heels, pausing only to throw a low, all-purpose growl over his shoulder at Jake, who had just stepped inside the door.

"He's glad to see you, too," she translated for Jake, who rolled his eyes. In the kitchen, she opened the door and let Sweetie-pie out. Then she kicked off her shoes and sat down barefoot at the table to go through her mail, which, as usual, consisted of bills, bills, bills, and advertisements. Jake followed her into the kitchen, glanced around, then headed toward the back of the house. Without really paying much attention to what he was doing—Jake had had the run of her house for many years now—she registered his quiet footsteps, listened to him opening doors and moving from room to room, and got the distinct impression that he was searching the house. Her lips quirked a little—Jake tended to err on the side of caution—and she meant to ask him if he expected to find the bogeyman hiding under her bed, but when he reached the kitchen he was on his cell phone, ordering pizza. By the time he finished she'd forgotten all about it because her cell phone rang and she was busy talking, too.

It was Ken Duncan, one of the three assistant DAs who reported to her, wanting to know if she would be in court the next morning. There had been no problem getting a postponement of the Parker case, he told her, but *Helitzer vs. South Carolina,* which was on the docket at 9 a.m., was stickier. Helitzer's lawyers were objecting to any postponement. They wanted their motion to dismiss heard.

"I'll be there," Sarah assured him, glad Jake had wandered out of the kitchen again while she talked.

"You gonna be home for a while? They sent over some documents today you probably ought to be aware of. I can drop them off if you want."

"That'd be good, thanks," she said, just as Jake came back into the kitchen. She and Duncan discussed other upcoming cases for a few minutes, and then she disconnected. She was exhausted, aching all over, and her headache was ratcheting up like it was swinging for the fences again, but as she met Jake's gaze, she stiffened her spine and tried to look like she felt just fine. He'd clearly heard every word she'd said, and allowing herself to look even one-tenth as wiped out as she felt would give him too much ammunition for what she knew was coming.

"I thought you were taking tomorrow off," he said.

Was he predictable or what?

Jake leaned against the counter, frowning at her and swirling the contents of his glass so that the ice cubes in the golden-brown liquid clinked against the sides. He had helped himself to some perfectly healthy, unsweetened sun tea from her refrigerator, to which he had added five—count 'em, five—packets of Sweet'N Low from the sugar canister where she kept them. She knew because she could see the empty little pink paper packets right there on the counter beside him. Good thing she didn't keep sugar in the house. If she did, he would need insulin about now.

"You know what? You have a real problem with your sweet tooth." It had the double virtue of being true and at the same time serving as a possible distraction. As she spoke, she started looking through the advertisements as though she actually found them of interest. "You ever thought about going into sugar rehab?"

"You have a real problem with overworking," he retorted, undistracted. "Would it kill you to take another day off?"

Sarah sighed.

"Tomorrow's Friday. I'll get finished early. But I have to be there for a little while at least.

"What's so important that you can't postpone it while you recover from getting *shot in the head?*"

"For one thing, Mitchell Helitzer's lawyers have moved for a dismissal. The hearing's at nine."

Jake frowned. "There you go, that's another one of your lost causes. You actually think you're going to get a conviction against *Mitchell Helitzer?*"

Okay, so Mitchell Helitzer was a former Gamecocks quarterback *and* a scion of one of Beaufort's oldest, wealthiest families.

"He killed his wife, Jake."

He took a sip of tea and lifted his eyebrows at her. "He claims she fell down the stairs. You got any witnesses to say she didn't?"

The answer was no, and he knew it. This was another of their running discussions.

"There was way more blood in that stairwell than there should have been if Susan Helitzer had just fallen and hit her head. Plus, she landed on her face, and there was damage to the back of her head as well. I think he came up behind her and hit her with something. Like a hammer."

"Head wounds bleed a lot, and she could have hit the back of her head in the fall. Those stairs are steep, and they're concrete." He shook his head at her. "You're going to need more than that if you're bound and determined to go for capital murder."

He was right, and she knew it. Playing devil's advocate was one of the things Jake did really well. With what she considered truly commendable maturity, she stuck her tongue out at him.

"Hey, there's enough there that I was able to convince Morrison that I could make a capital murder charge stick."

Jake grimaced. "The reason he's letting you go for it is because the media's in love with this one. If the DA's office seems to be playing softball with Mitchell Helitzer, then it's all over TV that the rich and famous get special treatment in Beaufort County. He wants to be governor. He can't afford to hand the Republicans a stick like that to beat him with."

So he was right again. It didn't make her any less certain that Mitchell Helitzer had cold-bloodedly murdered his wife.

"Oh, go investigate a divorce case."

His lips quirked mockingly at her. "You know I'm . . ."

Right, he was going to say, she knew, but before he could finish, there was a knock at the front door. Sweetie-pie, who was still outside, bounded onto the back porch and started barking frenziedly in warning.

"Pizza," Jake said over the din, and went to answer the door.

Sarah took advantage of his absence to grab the pain pills the doctor had prescribed for her from the bag Jake had left on the counter. She swallowed a couple with a quick drink of water. If Jake knew how badly her head hurt, she'd be lucky not to find herself marched right back to the hospital.

They ate in the living room with the TV on and Sweetie-pie at Sarah's feet, sitting side by side on the brown leather couch that stood beneath the big fifties-era picture window that looked out on the front yard when the mini-blinds were open, which, just at present, they were not. The couch matched the love seat on the left and the chair and ottoman combination on the right. Upon buying the house, she had made a single quick trip to Evans, the local discount furniture store, where she'd purchased the set, along with just about everything else she'd needed for the house. The couch-loveseat-chair combo served the dual purpose of being functional and at the same time, with the addition of a matching set of three oak tables and a pair of brass lamps, filling the room. There might not be a lot of color or pizzazz, but the room was presentable and reasonably comfortable, and that was all Sarah cared about.

The pizzas were on the coffee table in front of them. Jake tucked in hungrily while Sarah, who didn't have a big appetite at the best of times and had practically none right then, nibbled at hers. Like Jake, Sweetie-pie was a confirmed carnivore, so she fed the dog bits of sausage and ham cribbed from Jake's pizza—which, as she pointed out, was actually doing Jake a favor as it saved him from just that much more artery-clogging grease—and grinned when Jake gave her—and Sweetie-pie—the evil eye. Fortunately, the pain pills did their job: instead of feeling like an evil elf was sitting on her head, pounding it with a hammer, she just felt faintly, almost pleasantly, woozy.

Duncan, still wearing his suit and tie from work, arrived just as they were finishing. He was a nice enough looking guy, about five ten and lean, with wavy light brown hair that was starting to thin a little on top and bright blue eyes. At thirty-five, he was newly divorced from a cheating wife—the office gossip network was nothing if not efficient—and an object of interest to Lynnie and most of the other single women in the office. He'd been with the DA's office for almost two years, having previously worked for a while in the private sector, and was a good lawyer if a little overconcerned with his won-lost record, which made him very careful about the cases he took on. In other words, like a lot of lawyers she knew, if he didn't think he could win, he wasn't going to play. Which, actually, made him a good person to have on her team.

"Oh, hi," Duncan said to Jake in mild surprise as he stepped inside the house and spotted him over the half-wall that separated the entry hall from the living room. Sarah, meanwhile, dragged Sweetie-pie, who was expressing extreme dislike of Duncan in his usual inimitable way, toward the back door. Jake, who was still parked in front of the TV, merely waved in reply, and Duncan followed Sarah at a cautious distance on into the kitchen. Once Sweetie-pie was safely outside, Sarah sat down at the table and took the file that Duncan, who was sitting now, too, pulled out of his briefcase and handed across the table to her.

"I didn't know you had a thing going on with Hogan," Duncan said, low-voiced, as

Sarah opened the file and started reading the newest sheaf of papers.

"He's a friend." Sarah glanced up as she replied, and was surprised at something that flickered briefly in Duncan's eyes. Something she couldn't quite put her finger on but that took her slightly aback nonetheless. Was it interest in her as a woman? Pure prurient speculation? Or something else entirely? Whatever, time to shut him down. "And this is your business because . . . ?"

His gaze as it met hers was calm and steady. Whatever she'd thought she'd seen in his eyes was gone now. Had she just imagined it? Probably. Between the pills and the gradually rebuilding headache and the trauma of the past twenty-four hours, she knew she wasn't quite as needle-witted as she liked to think she normally was. In fact, she was starting to feel more than a little spaced-out.

"Just curious is all." Duncan shrugged and smiled at her ruefully. "Word around the office is you don't date."

"I don't," Sarah said with a hint of bite, hoping to put the final nail in the coffin of whatever he was thinking, and looked pointedly back down at the papers. He was silent as she finished reading them, then glanced up at him again, all business. "This is the basis of their motion to dismiss?"

He nodded. "That's it."

"What is?" Jake asked from the doorway. He had discarded his shoes, Sarah saw, and looked very much at home as he padded across her kitchen toward the sink in his socks. Duncan shot him a covertly assessing glance, and it struck Sarah that as aggressively masculine as Jake was, people might have a hard time believing that the two of them were just very close friends. Sarah thought of her own bare feet and the pizzas on the coffee table and realized that, to somebody like Duncan who didn't know the true situation, she and Jake must indeed look pretty intimate. Which they were, of course, but not in that way.

"They've got an affidavit from an expert witness swearing that the blood spatter in the stairwell where Susan Helitzer died is consistent with a fall down the stairs," she told him as he opened the cabinet beneath the sink and extracted a black plastic garbage bag from the box she kept there. Of course, she could see Duncan registering that Jake knew exactly where her trash bags were kept. This was going to be all over the office tomorrow, and she accepted the truth of that with an inward sigh and filed it away under the heading of just one more thing to deal with when she had to.

"Oh, yeah?" Jake asked as he straightened, trash bag in hand. He didn't say I told you so, but then, he didn't have to. His expression said it for him. Sarah gave him a narrow-eyed look as he headed back toward the living room. His answering smile was more on the order of a self-satisfied smirk.

"Want to save the rest of your pizza for breakfast?" he called back to her as he disappeared around the corner.

Oh, so tactful. She could see by Duncan's expression that despite her earlier disclaimer, he was speculating wildly about whether or not she and Jake would be sharing a mutual breakfast. Which they would be, of course, but, once again, not in that way.

"No." Her tone was blighting in the extreme. The thing was, ordinarily she would have saved the pizza, for breakfast or otherwise. It wasn't in her nature to waste things, and Jake knew it. But with Duncan's curious gaze on her, saying yes would have been like pouring fuel on the gossip fire.

"Suit yourself." Jake's response was way too cheerful. He knew what he was doing, the turkey, and was enjoying himself at her expense, she could tell.

A few minutes later, Duncan got up to leave and Sarah walked him to the door. It was full dark outside by this time, and porch lights were on up and down the street. A slight breeze rustled the palmetto's leaves. It was still hot, as it always was in Beaufort in August, but the humidity had lessened slightly and the air smelled of honeysuckle and freshly mowed grass. Down the street, a group of children whooped as they chased lightning bugs in a neighbor's yard. Music spilled from the open window of a car driving past.

"You sure you don't want me to fill in for you tomorrow? You're not looking so good," Duncan said as he stepped out onto the front stoop.

"Thanks a bunch," Sarah said dryly.

"Oh. I didn't mean it that way." The only light on the stoop was what spilled out through the open front door so it was difficult to tell, but Sarah could have sworn he was blushing. "You do look *good,* I mean, you always look good, except . . . um . . . I only meant, um . . . what with what happened and all, maybe you would rather not . . ."

"I'll be in court at nine." Sarah put him out of his misery. "Thanks for dropping the file off."

"Oh, um, yeah, glad to. Anytime."

With a shrug and a wave, he walked down the steps like he was happy to escape and cut across the lawn toward his car. Sarah closed the door and turned around to see Jake emerging from the living room with the now-bulging trash bag in his hand.

"Well, he wasted his night." Jake headed for the kitchen.

"What do you mean?" Sarah followed him.

"It's pretty obvious he was hoping you'd be alone. My guess is he's trying to work up the nerve to ask you out."

"He brought me the Helitzer file!"

"Yeah. Uh-huh. Makes a good excuse, doesn't it?" Jake grinned at her over his shoulder as he opened the back door, clearly intent on taking out the trash. Sweetie-pie, who must have been napping on the back porch, leaped to his feet and let loose with an explosion of barking. Jake dropped the bag and jumped back. Dog and man locked gazes, with Jake all wide-eyed and Sweetie-pie glowering at him through the screen. Sarah laughed.

"Damn mutt," Jake muttered under his breath, and, recovering, retrieved the bag.

"He loves you. He just has trouble show-ing it." Still grinning, Sarah walked past Jake, who snorted and pushed open the screen. As Jake eyed him warily, Sweetie-pie slunk into the kitchen, casting an evil glance at Jake as he passed. "I'm sorry he scared you."

And that was payback for his teasing.

Jake didn't take the bait, however. He just grimaced and went on out the back door as Sweetie-pie headed in the opposite direc-tion, presumably making for his preferred sleeping spot under her bed.

"I'm going to take a shower," Sarah called after Jake.

Without waiting for a reply, she headed toward the bathroom. She was dead tired, aching all over, and despite the pills, her head was starting to really hurt again. She was going to take a shower and go to bed. As Scarlett O'Hara so famously put it, tomorrow was another day.

She only hoped it would be better than the last two.

In the end, concerned about protecting her wound from the drenching effects of the shower, she opted for a bath instead. While the tub filled she brushed her teeth, then stood, eyeing her reflection in the mirror above the sink. By the familiar light of her own friendly bathroom fixture, she still looked awful, she decided glumly after a critical examination of as much of herself as she could see. At five foot four, she weighed one hundred and three pounds, which was twenty less than she'd weighed seven years ago. She'd known she was getting too thin, of course, and her reflection confirmed it. Her eyes—they were the same denim blue as Lexie's, and thus she could hardly bear to hold her own gaze—were deep-set and shadowed. Her face, with its delicate features, had once been strikingly attractive, but now it was not; it was too thin, with her bones seemingly trying to push through her skin. Add to that her pale complexion;

straight, black-as-night eyebrows; and the reddened scrape on her chin where it had hit the pavement, and she was, indeed, just about enough to scare small children. A nurse had helped her shower before she left the hospital, so at least her short, black hair was good for one more day. Or maybe *good* was the wrong word. Say, rather, it was clean. Her nape-length hairstyle with its graduating layers in front was great for work, strictly wash, add a little mousse, and wear. It was not so great, however, when it wasn't moussed, or for hiding a flesh-colored Band-Aid nearly the size of a dollar bill.

On the other hand, the good news was, she was alive.

Mary wasn't . . .

Forcing that thought from her mind, Sarah stepped into the tub and sank into the blissfully hot water. To most of her poor, abused body, it felt wonderful; to her scraped elbows and knees, it stung like nobody's business. As it was almost impossible to keep all four joints out of the water at once, she bathed fast and got out, dripping, then staggered a little as her head swam unexpectedly. Luckily, she caught herself on the sink before she went to her knees. Hanging on to the rim of the sink for dear life, taking a series of deep breaths, she stayed that way until she got her balance back. Then she dried quickly, pulled on the blue knee-length T-shirt she wore to sleep, tied her white terry-cloth robe over that, and went out to say good night to Jake.

He was in the living room again, sprawled on the couch with his feet in their black socks propped on the coffee table. The remote was in his hand, and, typical man, he was flipping channels. He looked up as she appeared in the doorway and lowered the remote. A glance at the TV told her that he was watching the *News at Ten.* Hayley Winston was on the screen, a vision of blond perkiness as she talked about a pileup on Highway 17.

"You look dead beat," Jake said. "Head hurt?"

Oh, yeah. "A little. I'm going to bed."

"Yell if you need me."

"Count on it," Sarah said and started to turn away. Then she glanced back over her shoulder at him. "Jake?"

"Hmm?" His attention was on the TV again. He looked so right slouched on her couch, so big and dark and rumpled and dear, that she smiled a little.

"Thanks," she said softly.

His eyes shifted to her face.

"For . . . ?"

"Being here. Staying the night. Coming to the hospital. Everything."

"No problem."

His eyes moved back to the TV and suddenly widened. Sarah followed his gaze, compelled by the surprise in his expression.

Lexie's face was on the screen, chubby and smiling, her coppery hair brushed into fat ringlets that framed her face. Sarah recognized that picture instantly: It was her daughter's school picture, taken the third week of kindergarten.

The shaft of pain was so unexpected that she couldn't breathe.

". . . a particularly poignant side story," Hayley Winston was saying. "Assistant District Attorney Sarah Mason, who pulled nine-year-old Angela Barillas to safety in last night's tragic convenience-store robbery, is herself the victim of a tragedy. Viewers may remember that her five-year-old daughter, Alexandra, was . . ."

The TV clicked off just like that, Jake having made good use of the remote.

He was on his feet then, moving toward her, his eyes dark with concern.

"Sarah . . ."

The pain vibrated inside her like a tuning fork. It twisted through her stomach, shivered along her nerve endings, oozed out of her pores. The intensity of it never faded, and yet there was a horrible familiarity to it. Once again she had to wonder, *How could anyone hurt like this and live?*

"Sarah." Jake's hands were on her shoulders, big hands, warm hands that pulled her close to his chest. For a moment, just a moment, she allowed herself to rest against him, allowed herself to be weak, to lean against his solid strength, to draw comfort from his presence, his concern.

But then she forced herself to breathe, in and out, slow and steady, forced herself to push the pain away, forced herself to grit her teeth and stiffen her spine and dismiss what she had just seen from her thoughts. If she had learned nothing else in this hard school, she had learned that the only way to survive was to be strong. To be strong, and refuse to dwell on what she had lost.

She lifted her head from his chest and took a step back. Still, he didn't let her go. His hands were strong and steady on her shoulders. His eyes searched hers.

"I'm okay." Her voice was surprisingly clear. She saw in his eyes that because she was hurting, he was hurting, too, and that comforted her a little. For his sake, she managed a small, hopefully reassuring smile. "It's okay. Really. Seeing . . . *that* . . . was unexpected, is all."

He looked unconvinced, but she couldn't help it. She'd done all the pretending she could do.

"Sarah . . ."

"I'm going to bed," she said, not letting him finish because she just couldn't take any more, couldn't take any more pain, couldn't take any more shocks, couldn't take any more sympathy. "Don't worry about me. I promise, I'm fine."

"Yeah." He sounded faintly skeptical, but his hands dropped away from her shoulders.

"Good night." She turned away from him, heading back toward her bedroom with her back straight and her head held high.

"'Night." His voice, low and deep, followed her down the hall.

Except for the faint glow from the living room, it was dark in her bedroom. Leaving the door open as she always did so that Sweetie-pie could get up and get a drink of water if he needed to during the night, Sarah took off her robe, pulled back the covers, then got into bed without bothering to turn on the light. She needed sleep, craved sleep, welcomed sleep as the only refuge from pain she knew.

She had a formula, a tried-and-true formula that had gotten her through 2,587 of the darkest of dark nights. Listening to the rhythmic sounds of Sweetie-pie breathing under the bed, she curled into a ball under the covers and repeated every prayer she had ever heard, saying them over and over silently until they ran together in her mind, until she was lost in the promise of peace they offered, until she was, finally, swallowed up by the mindless oblivion of sleep.

Tonight, she didn't even dream. She slept deeply, heavily, for how long she didn't know. She knew only that when she was jolted awake at last, the house was dark as a cave and still. For a moment, she couldn't think what woke her.

Then the phone on her night table rang, its peal shrill and insistent.

That's what had awakened her, she realized, and she groaned as she groped for the phone. Her head throbbed, her mouth was dry as toast, and throwing off the clutching fingers of sleep was surprisingly hard. The pain pills had made her woozy before. Maybe sleep intensified their effect. The luminous numbers on her bedside clock read one thirty-two a.m., she saw as the phone shrilled again just as her hand closed around the receiver.

The only news that it was possible to get at that time of night was bad news, and the most likely source of bad news was work. They needed her at the jail, they needed her at a crime scene, they needed . . .

"Hello." Her voice was thick with sleep as she spoke into the receiver.

"Mommy. Mommy, come get me. I'm scared." The voice broke on the smallest of sobs. "Mommy, where are you?"

Sarah gasped and sat bolt upright as the little girl's tremulous voice went through her like an electric shock.

It was Lexie. Lexie, who seven years before had walked away from her to go get birthday cake and vanished without a trace.

7

"Lexie!" Sarah cried into the receiver, but it was too late. Lexie was already gone, and the only sound that reached her ear was the dull hum of a dial tone.

Lexie had hung up.

No, no, no.

"Lexie!" she screamed into the phone, scrambling out of bed, clutching the receiver in such a tight grip that her fingers hurt. Her heart pounded so hard she thought it might burst. "Lexie, Lexie, Lexie, Lexie, Lexie!"

The dial tone was her only answer.

"Lexie!" Sobbing, Sarah sank to her knees on the hard wood floor, holding onto the receiver like a lifeline. Her pulse thundered against her eardrums. Her gut twisted into a thousand hard knots. "Oh, God, *please.*" Then she spoke into the receiver again, frantically: "Lexie! Lexie!"

"What the hell?" The bedroom light snapped on, and quick footsteps came toward her. From under the bed, Sweetie-pie exploded into a volley of warning barks. "Shut up, Sweetie-pie," Jake said fiercely, and the dog did. Then, on an entirely different note, Jake said, "Sarah?"

"Jake!" She was on her knees, clutching the receiver, cradling it to her ear. She looked up at him, wild-eyed. "Jake, it was Lexie. She called me. Just now. It was *Lexie* on the phone."

"What?"

"It was. It was her voice. It was Lexie. Oh my God, Jake, it was Lexie." Sarah caught her breath, then screamed into the mouthpiece again. "Lexie! Lexie, where are you? Lexie! Please talk to me. *Please.*"

No answer but the dial tone. She started to sob in harsh, ragged gasps.

"Sarah." Jake crouched down beside her,

wrapped a hard arm around her heaving shoulders, and tried gently to remove the receiver from her grasp. She resisted, hanging on for dear life. It was a link to her daughter—her only link to her daughter. . . .

She sucked in air, regained control of her voice again.

"Jake. It was *Lexie.*"

"Honey. Let me listen."

His fingers closed over hers, and he gently lifted the receiver toward his ear. This time she didn't resist. But she didn't let go, either. She couldn't. Lexie was on the other end of that line. She could never, ever let it go. Her daughter was there—somewhere. Somewhere, *somewhere.*

Where? Oh, God, where?

"Lexie," she whimpered, her voice tremulous as the pain, sharp as a knife, sliced into her anew.

"Hello?" Jake said into the phone. "Hello?"

After a moment, he shook his head at her and lowered the receiver. Sarah still clung to it, looking at him with a mixture of fear and dread and hope that made her shake all over even though she knew it was too late, even though she could plainly hear the monotonous drone of the dial tone for herself.

Lexie . . . It was a primal scream inside her head.

"All I'm hearing's a dial tone. There's no one there, Sarah." Jake's tone was heavy with sorrow for her.

"It was Lexie. I swear to you, it was Lexie." She was panting, sweating, trembling. Her fingers still clutched the receiver so tightly that her knuckles were white. Panic clawed at her insides. She had to find Lexie. She couldn't, *could not,* lose her again. "Oh my God, check the caller ID."

Even as she had the thought, Sarah rose up on her knees so that she could see the phone itself. Her fingers scrabbled frantically over the dial pad. Urgently, she punched the button to call up the number of the last incoming phone call.

The display read *unknown caller.*

Sarah felt like a giant hand was squeezing her heart.

Think. You have to think.

"Star sixty-nine," she gasped aloud. She was once again talking to herself more than him, although she could feel him behind her, hear his breathing, sense his growing concern.

Dial star sixty-nine, and it automatically told you the number of your last incoming call. Once she knew the number, she could find Lexie. Fingers trembling, she punched the buttons.

Please, God. Please, please.

Then she put the phone to her ear and listened with stuttering heart and bated breath.

"This is your call return service. TouchStar service cannot be used to call this number, trace this number, or enter this number on your list."

"No," Sarah moaned, folding like an accordion so that her back was parallel to the floor. With her legs bent beneath her, she clutched the receiver to her chest with both hands. "No. *No.* Oh my God, *Lexie.*"

"Sarah, don't." Jake leaned over her, wrapping both arms around her rocking body, holding her tight. She could feel the solid weight of him, feel the smooth warmth of his skin, feel the slight abrasion of his chest hair against her arm. With the tiny part of her mind that could still register such things, she realized that he was naked except for his boxers. She barely noticed, and didn't care. There was only one thing on her mind: Lexie.

"Okay, I need you to tell me exactly what happened here." He sounded so calm, too calm. Her back stiffened and she straightened, pulling free of his embrace and looking at him with raging disbelief. Under the circumstances, how could he sound like that?

"I already told you: Lexie called me. On the phone. Didn't you hear it ringing just now?"

She tried for calm, too, tried to slow her racing thoughts so that she could make sense of what was happening. But with her heart thudding and her stomach churning and her mind darting from possibility to possibility like a crazed bee, it was almost impossible to think even halfway clearly. All she knew for sure was that her whole body cried out for her daughter, *who just minutes ago had been on the other end of that phone.*

"I didn't hear anything except you screaming for Lexie." Jake's voice was flat, emotionless. He was watching her carefully,

Sarah realized as she met his gaze. As if he thought . . .

"Of course you didn't hear the phone ring. There's no extension in your bedroom." Then, as what he was really saying percolated through her agitation, she gasped, "You're not thinking I imagined it, are you?"

Hanging unsaid in the air between them were the countless times, in the first days and months and years after Lexie's disappearance, when she had thought she'd seen her daughter in passing cars, only to follow them and find out it was some other little girl with red hair. When she'd thought she'd heard her daughter's voice, only to rush toward the sound and discover another laughing child. When she'd thought she'd felt her daughter's presence behind her, only to whirl around and discover Lexie wasn't there.

The psychiatrist she'd seen in the second year following her loss, when she'd been struggling to take up her law studies again, had told her that what she was experiencing was so common that there was even a name for it: *searching behavior.*

It didn't happen nearly as often now, but still, sometimes . . .

"I didn't imagine it," she cried when Jake didn't say anything, which in a way was more telling than words. "I didn't dream it, I didn't make it up. It's real, it happened. Lexie was on that phone. Jesus, I can prove there was a call. It's there on the caller ID."

The caller ID might read *unknown caller,* but it at least showed a record that a call was received at one thirty-two a.m. If there hadn't been such a record, she realized, she might have begun to doubt what had just happened herself.

But there was a record. Thank God for the record. Thank God for small mercies: She had that one tiny shred of proof that Lexie had called.

Lips compressing, Jake got to his feet and leaned over the phone, reaching for the number pad, clearly intent on confirming that the call had indeed come in.

"I told you she called," Sarah said as the display lit up. Still clutching the receiver tight, she stumbled to her feet. Adrenaline pumped through her veins. Her heart pounded. Her mind whirled round and round like it was trapped on one of those dizzying amusement-park rides. Her fight-or-flight response was working at capacity,

but she couldn't focus, couldn't figure out
what to do next. The only thought that was
coming through loud and clear was: *We're
wasting time.*

"We've got to find a way to trace that call.
I'm telling you, it was *Lexie.*"

Jake straightened to face her, his eyes
dark, his face a study in concern as he absorbed her desperation.

"Okay," Jake said. She knew that tone,
knew she was being humored. Even barefoot and nearly naked, he exuded solid
strength. The thing was, though, just at this
moment she didn't need solid strength. She
needed *belief.* And help.

"Walk me through this," he continued.
"The phone rang, right? You answered it.
Then . . ." His voice trailed off as if to en-
courage her to continue.

"It was *Lexie.*" Sarah sucked in air, fought
to remain rational, fought not to lose it altogether. Desperately, she tried to force her
sleep- and medication- and injury-impaired
brain to rev up to maximum firepower. She
wanted to run outside screaming Lexie's
name, wanted to dart through the sleeping
city in a frenzied search for her daughter,
wanted to pound on every door and beat on

the window of every passing car and root through every dark basement and alley and wooded area until there was literally no stone left unturned.

"It was Lexie on the phone. She remembered the number. Thank God I kept it the same. She said . . . she said . . ." Sarah fought to remember. " 'Mommy, help me.' And she said she was scared. And then she started to cry and said, 'Mommy, where are you?' "

Tears welled into Sarah's eyes. Anguish threatened to overwhelm her as she looked down at the receiver in her hand, then back up at Jake. He was just looking at her, pity in his eyes, doing nothing at all, and she was doing nothing at all, too, except clutching the buzzing receiver and staring back at him. Meanwhile, Lexie was out there somewhere, needing her, wondering where she was. Sarah looked frantically at the windows, the doors. Her hand clenched tightly around the receiver.

"Why are we standing here? We have to trace the call! We have to call the police!"

She realized that she was almost screaming the words at him only when he grimaced.

"Sarah," he said, his voice deep and low. She saw that he was hurting for her, and saw, too, from the hard, dark compassion in his eyes that he still didn't believe the truth. "Honey . . ."

"It was *Lexie!*" she shouted, maddened at the idea that he didn't seem to understand. She gripped the receiver in both hands, almost beside herself at the thought that they were losing valuable time. Her palms were sweaty on the hard plastic. Her heart galloped like a runaway horse. More than she had ever wanted anything in her life, she wanted to be able to pour herself down that receiver and along that phone line to reach her daughter. Lexie was there, on the other end of that line, just out of reach.

What to do? What can I do? I have to find Lexie . . .

"Okay, just calm down." Jake reached for her, sliding his hands around her upper arms and pulling her close against him and wrapping his arms around her so that she was enveloped by his heat, by his strength, by the warm, familiar smell of him. He was offering comfort the best way he knew how, the only way he knew how, and she rejected it fiercely.

"*Calm down?* You've got to be kidding." Sarah wrenched herself out of his arms, glared at him, looked down at the receiver in her hand, and then placed it carefully on the night table beside the phone. "Don't you dare hang that up," she warned him. Then, "I need your cell phone. Where's your cell phone?"

Hers was with her purse, which had been impounded as evidence by the police. Someday, maybe, she'd get all that stuff back. But for now, when she needed it most, it was lost to her. *Was that the way things always worked or what?*

"On the night table by the bed."

In the spare bedroom, she knew he meant. Darting around him, she ran for the spare bedroom, flipping on the light switch as she passed it so that the lamp beside the bed came on, taking in the rumpled bed and his discarded clothes puddled on the floor with a single, searching glance before spotting her quarry, his slim, black cell phone, and snatching it up.

The police. They had to trace the call. They had to mount a search before the trail grew cold again.

With shaking hands, she flipped open the

phone and started punching in 911. The mini-blinds weren't closed all the way, and in the places where the narrow slats didn't quite meet, she could see the blackness of the night outside. Lexie was out there in that blackness. Lexie, who had always been afraid of the dark.

At the thought, Sarah's heart lurched and she gasped for air.

Hurry, hurry, hurry . . .

"Sarah. Wait a minute." Jake's hands closed over hers, preventing her from hitting that final 1. He was right behind her, reaching around her, far bigger and stronger than she was and with the advantage of surprise, too, so that when he took the phone out of her hands and closed it, there was no way she could have prevented it. "Just hold on."

"What do you think you're doing?" She rounded on him in a fury, grabbing for the phone, trying to wrest it from him.

He hung on to it, warding her off as best he could. "Listen to me. . . ."

"What's wrong with you? Give me that phone."

"Damn it to hell, Sarah." He tossed the phone into the middle of the bed and, when she would have dived for it, caught her, wrapping his arms around her, holding her fast, her back to his front. She struggled wildly, straining to reach the phone, beating his imprisoning arms with her fists, kicking her heels into his bare shins.

"Ouch! Shit!"

"Let me go! Are you *nuts?* I have to call the police."

"Would you just *listen?* What makes you so sure it was Lexie?"

"You think I don't know my own daughter's voice? I'd recognize it anywhere, in the furthest reaches of the universe, in the deepest, darkest hole on earth, *anywhere,* do you hear? She sounds exactly the same. My sweet baby . . ." Sarah's voice broke as she strained to get away from him.

"That's just it, don't you see? Sarah, honey, it's been seven years. Lexie wouldn't sound exactly the same. She was five years old *then.* She'd be—what?—twelve now? I doubt you'd even recognize her voice."

"It was Lexie. It was Lexie . . ." Even as Sarah continued to struggle, the truth of what he was saying hit her with the impact of a bucket of cold water to the face. Lexie's voice on the phone had sounded *exactly the same.* As if she were still five years old.

It couldn't be.

"Oh no. No, no, no. " The inescapable logic of that ground into her solar plexus like a punishing fist. All the air rushed out of her lungs, her knees gave way, and she sagged toward the floor. If Jake's arms hadn't been around her, she would have fallen.

"Sarah . . ."

"It was her," she said. She realized that she was desperately clutching at straws even as she uttered the words. "It was *her.* I recognized her voice. We've got to call the police."

"Sarah." Jake managed to get an arm beneath her limp knees and swung her up into his arms. She clutched at his broad shoulders, breathing hard, shell-shocked as the horrible truth became ever more inescapably apparent.

"You were asleep," he continued inexorably. "You're recovering from a concussion. You're on pain pills, for God's sake. The point I'm trying to make here is that you may be coming at this with impaired perception."

The point he was trying to make, ever so delicately, was that it couldn't have been Lexie. As much as she hated to face it, she had to look at the facts. The voice had been that of a very young girl. A twelve-year-old would sound different. . . .

"I'll get the call traced," Jake promised, sitting down on the edge of the queen-size guest bed with her on his lap. His thighs were warm and firm beneath her legs. His chest was wide, well-muscled, and covered with a wedge of fine, black hair. His arms kept her imprisoned there when, if she could have, she would have run screaming from the room. "We'll get to the bottom of this. But you need to get hold of yourself first."

"It was Lexie." But her protest was weak now, because she knew, *knew,* that for five-year-old Lexie to be calling her seven years after she had disappeared was impossible. *Knew* it. But still . . .

Remembering that high-pitched little voice, her heart clutched.

"It couldn't have been Lexie, Sarah." His arms were comfortingly tight around her as he read what she was feeling in her eyes, then said aloud the words she couldn't bear to accept.

"Who was it, then?" she cried as the awful pain ripped at her, rearing up in his hold and glaring at him like it was all his fault, like he was the one who was making the whole thing so impossible. "If it wasn't Lexie, *who was it?* Can you tell me that?"

The skin around his eyes tightened, his jaw hardened, and she knew that he hated saying what he was getting ready to say to her.

"Most likely it was a crank call."

A crank call. The thought was hideous— monstrous, even.

"No," she said. Then, as the probable truth of it began to seep inexorably across the sea of pain and denial and hope she was adrift on, she added piteously, "Who would do such a thing?"

"I don't know." He shook his head. By the bright light of the overhead fixture, he looked about as pale and haggard as it was possible for a swarthy-skinned man to look. His black hair was mussed from sleep. Stubble darkened his jaw. His eyes were almost black with a reflection of her own pain; his mouth was tight with it. "You've been all over TV in the last twenty-four hours. You saw part of that piece about what happened to Lexie yourself. So did just about every household in the area. And that's only the coverage we know about."

"Somebody would have to be sick to do something like that." *Sick* was how she herself was feeling, sick to her very soul, sick to death with the same kind of raw pain she had felt in the days and weeks and months immediately after Lexie's disappearance. The pain had never gone away, but it had been lessening, turning into a dull ache that she had learned to live with, to deal with, to accept, much like an amputee experiencing twinges in a missing limb. But now the sharp, tearing agony of it was back in full force, and she quivered at the impact.

She couldn't bear it—but she had no choice *but* to bear it. That was another of the lessons she had learned in that very hard school.

His arms tightened around her as if to still her trembling.

"There are a lot of sick people out there."

"Are you sure . . .?" She answered her own question before she even finished it, finally accepting the hard, cold truth. "It couldn't have been Lexie, could it? Oh, God, it couldn't have been."

"No. It couldn't have been." His voice

was very quiet as he delivered the death blow to her last remaining sliver of hope.

Sarah had seen the abyss before, so she recognized it as it yawned before her now. As she once again found herself trembling on the brink of the bottomless pit of grief and despair that awaited the unwary, she knew enough to pull back from the edge. Sucking in air, she fought for control. Tears leaked out of her eyes, ran hot and wet down her cheeks. Clamping her lips together to prevent herself from bawling like a baby, she buried her face in the hollow between his shoulder and neck, burrowing against him, concentrating on his enveloping warmth, on the comfort of his familiar smell, on the muscular strength of his body against hers. Jake had walked through the darkness with her before; she clung to him like a rock in a raging sea now, as she fought to keep from falling prey to it again.

"Sarah." His hands stroked comfortingly down her back, and she realized that she was shuddering as if in the grip of a high fever. She felt something brush her hair—his lips, she thought, and clung tighter still. Thank God for Jake, thank God for him, he could help her get through this if anyone could. . . .

"I'm okay," she said, as much to reassure herself as him. But she wasn't okay, she could hear the not-okayness in the ragged timbre of her voice, feel it in the tremors that continued to rack her. Her throat was raw and her eyes burned and she hurt, physically hurt, in a way that was far different and far more painful than any physical trauma she had ever endured.

"You were right about calling the police. I think that's the thing to do here. We're going to tell them you had a crank call." Jake's mouth was right next to her ear. He spoke very deliberately, as if he wanted to make sure his words sank in.

"Yes. Okay." Sarah was working hard to get herself back on an even keel, gritting her teeth in an effort to control her trembling, trying to regulate her breathing, trying to slow her racing heart. Inside, she felt shattered. *A crank call—of course that's what it was. A cruel, terrible joke.* Exhaling slowly, she forced the words out. "We need to trace it."

"If it's humanly possible, it'll get traced, don't worry. I'll make sure of it." He seemed to hesitate. She could feel a new tension in his body, hear a reluctance in his tone that told her that something else was up. Something more. It took an effort, but she managed it: Taking a deep breath, stiffening her spine, she lifted her head from its sanctuary on his shoulder to look at him inquiringly. He met her gaze, searched her face, and she knew for sure: More bad news was coming her way, and he hated like hell being the messenger boy.

"What?"

"There's something else you need to know," he said, as Sarah sniffed and snuffled and dashed the last lingering tears from her eyes. His mouth tightened as he watched. She didn't cry often, and, since the early days, rarely in front of him, but it got to him when she did, she knew. Jake was a softie like that.

"So spit it out." The tears were all but vanquished, and her voice was stronger now.

He grimaced. "When I stopped by to feed Sweetie-pie this morning, those toys in your closet were scattered all over your bedroom floor."

It took Sarah a second to realize that he

was talking about Lexie's toys. Her heart started tripping all over itself again. She tried to breathe slowly and carefully in an effort to settle it down.

"What do you mean?"

"The box was tipped on its side, and the toys were thrown around the room. I thought the dog might have done it."

"Sweetie-pie?" Sarah thought about that for a second, then shook her head. "I don't think so."

"The house was locked up tight. Your bedroom door was closed. I don't know how else it could have happened."

She hadn't kept all Lexie's toys, just the ones her daughter had loved the most. When she had moved from the duplex where she and Lexie had lived into this house, she had stored the toys in her closet. To her knowledge, the box hadn't been touched since.

"That's . . . *strange.*"

Jake was watching her closely. "Yeah."

Lexie's toys scattered. Lexie's voice on the phone—Sarah's eyes widened. A tremor raced over her skin. Despite her best efforts, her heart began to race. Could Lexie possibly be there, in the house? Could she be trying to get in touch with her mother? Sarah had heard tales in which spirits tried to contact loved ones via moving real-world objects, via otherworldly phone calls, and she and Lexie had been close, so close, that if such a thing were possible, Lexie would be trying her hardest to reach her, to get back to her in any way or form she could. But to believe such a thing was to believe, first, that ghosts existed; second, that they could contact the living; and, third and hardest, that Lexie was dead.

It was reality, Sarah knew, that her daughter was probably no longer among the living, but even after all these years she still couldn't face it.

As far as she was concerned, Lexie was out there somewhere. Her reason might tell her otherwise, but her heart, her poor broken heart, would never abandon hope. Not as long as she herself lived.

"What?" Jake had been watching her face.

"Call the police," Sarah said, and he nodded.

Jake reached for his cell, picked it up, and dialed. Sarah heard the words coming out of his mouth but registered none of them. Concentrating with every fiber of her being, she replayed the voice she'd heard on the phone in her head.

"Mommy. Mommy, come get me. I'm scared. Mommy, where are you?"

Every syllable, every intonation, had sounded like Lexie. Even "scehwed" for scared—Lexie hadn't been able to say her r's. But no matter how much Sarah wanted to believe, it couldn't have been.

Could not have been.

By the time officers Mike Steed and Tyson Dryer showed up, Sarah was calm. She'd had enough time to internalize the fact that she was most likely the victim of a vicious prank. That didn't keep her from feeling like her heart had been ripped to shreds. But at least she was able to talk to the cops without breaking down.

They took a report and left, polite enough but behaving as if what had happened to her was slightly less serious than a fender bender. The chances of them following up in any but the most perfunctory of ways Sarah rated as practically nil. She had the feeling that if Jake hadn't been pals with the dispatcher, no one would have bothered to come out at all. As a prosecutor, she should have rated better treatment. If she hadn't been so destroyed inside, she would have been angry.

All of a sudden, it was hell being a pariah with the police department.

"I called a friend at the telephone company who promised to do what he could to have that call traced," Jake said when the cops were gone. "And I've got your answering machine in the kitchen set up to record all incoming calls just in case whoever it was calls back. If the phone rings again, let the machine answer it."

At the very idea, Sarah felt herself start to tense up. But she nodded agreement.

They were still in the kitchen, where the interview with the cops had taken place. Sarah sat at the table; Jake leaned against the counter. Sweetie-pie, who had made his dislike of uniformed police officers unmistakable, was in the backyard. Despite the fact that she was wrapped up tightly in her thick, white bathrobe and had pulled white athletic half-socks on her feet, Sarah was freezing with a cold that she suspected was too bone-deep to blame on the air-conditioning. Besides, Jake, in the slacks and shirt he had worn earlier, seemed perfectly comfortable with the temperature. Before the cops had arrived, Jake had poured her a glass of milk—skim, the only kind she kept in the house—and had ordered her to drink it, on the theory, she knew, that whatever it was in milk that made people sleepy might have a calming effect. It still sat in front of her, barely touched.

"Tired?" Jake asked.

Only then did Sarah realize that she had both elbows on the table and was resting her pounding head in her clenched hands.

"Yes." She glanced up at him. She *was* tired, in spirit as well as body. The shattering phone call seemed to have drained every last reserve of strength she had left.

"You gonna finish that milk?"

Sarah looked at the almost-full glass in revulsion. "No."

He moved then, picking up her glass and pouring the contents down the sink. Sarah knew this because she could hear the liquid gurgle as it went down the drain, and then the clink of glass against metal as he set the glass down in the stainless-steel sink. Her eyes were closed, though, and her head once again rested on her hands, so she didn't see a thing. She longed to surrender to the physical exhaustion that demanded she rest, but her mind wouldn't cooperate. Even as her body surrendered, her mind continued to race.

"Come on, bedtime." He spoke from behind her, and she could feel his hands close around the back of her chair. Sarah blinked, lifted her head, and looked up at him, then glanced at the clock over the refrigerator: three twenty-three a.m. Not quite two hours since she'd heard Lexie's—no, *not* Lexie's—voice on the phone. It didn't seem possible that so little time had passed. It felt like an eternity.

The pertinent fact, though, was that it was still night. If they went to bed now, they could still get another three or three and a half hours of sleep.

Weary as she was, Sarah didn't think she would ever be able to sleep again.

But there was no point in depriving Jake of his rest.

"Right." Summoning every last ounce of determination she had left, she stood up. Her head swam, and the pounding on her skull increased tenfold. The pain pills either weren't doing their job or were wearing off.

"Okay?" He gave her a narrow-eyed look.

Sarah nodded, straightened her shoulders, and went to let Sweetie-pie in. The dog bounded inside when she opened the door, shaking himself all over. It was only then, as droplets of water from his coat hit her, that she realized it was raining. Not heavily, but in a gentle downpour that would most likely be gone by morning.

Tears in heaven. The title of the Eric Clapton song sprang into her head, eerily appropriate.

"You go on. I'll turn off the lights," Jake said.

Sarah nodded again, and followed Sweetie-pie down the hall. She could feel Jake's worried gaze on her until she was out of his sight, but trying to reassure him was beyond her at present. It was all she could do to put one foot in front of the other, to stay upright until she reached her bed, where it would be okay to collapse. Then, in the darkness, she could grieve and mull over what had happened until she had sucked all the juice from it, and at the same time fight to put this behind her. The hours remaining until dawn would be spent in a private battle to regain her emotional footing, she knew. It was scary to realize how precarious was her grip on the normal, everyday life she had painstakingly rebuilt for herself.

She would be damned before she would let it all collapse over a few scattered toys and a crank phone call.

The light was still on in her bedroom, Sarah saw as she neared it, and she could hear the scooting noise Sweetie-pie made as he scrambled under the bed. Thank God she had Sweetie-pie, she thought. At least she would have another living, breathing creature there in the dark with her to keep her from feeling so alone.

Lexie was alone. Alone in the dark and the rain.

The thought stopped Sarah dead in the bedroom doorway. Closing her eyes and sagging against the door jamb, she gritted her teeth against the pain it caused and did her best to will it from her consciousness. She could not entertain such images and function, as she knew from bitter experience.

Taking a deep breath, she forced her eyes open again—and found herself looking at the phone.

The receiver no longer rested on its side

on the night table. Someone had hung up the phone.

Sarah's stomach knotted.

Steed and Dryer had been in the bedroom. Jake might well have been, too; he'd been out of her sight during some of the time she'd been talking to the cops. Any of them could have done it. After all, there was no reason not to. It had been a crank call, nothing more, and the caller was long gone the moment the call ended. Keeping the phone off the hook would do no good at all.

Sarah knew that. She even knew that now that Jake had the answering machine rigged to record incoming calls, it was probably better that the phone was hung up, in case whoever it was called again. Then, at least she would be able to replay the call and listen to the voice over and over again until she knew, in her own mind and heart, that it wasn't Lexie. Memory was unreliable. As a prosecutor, she knew that. Eyewitness testimony, which, ironically, was the most persuasive to jurors, was in actual fact the least reliable testimony of all. The way she remembered it, the voice had been Lexie's. But like everyone else's, her memory was almost certainly unreliable, too.

That was a fact, plain and simple, and she accepted it as such. But looking at that phone in its cradle, Sarah felt like her last link to Lexie had been severed.

The pain was sharp and intense, like an ice pick to the heart.

But she didn't make a sound. She just stood there and endured as she had learned to do, breathing slowly, in and out, knowing that there was nothing to do but weather the pain until, as she knew would eventually happen, it gave up and went away. Or at least lessened enough so that she could function again.

"What now?" Jake said behind her. Startled, Sarah opened her eyes and glanced over her shoulder at him. She hadn't even heard him approach.

Speaking was beyond her for the moment, she discovered when she tried. Instead, she shook her head and gestured toward the phone.

Frowning, he looked past her, then clearly saw the restored receiver and realized what it meant to her. His jaw hardened and his gaze swung back to her. She must have looked as stricken as she felt, because what he saw in her face made his eyes darken and his lips thin.

"It was a *crank call,* Sarah. You know that."

It took everything she had, but she managed to nod acknowledgment.

His mouth twisted, and from his expression it was obvious that her nod had done nothing to ease his concern.

"Okay, you can't stay in here." His voice was rough. "Come on, you're sleeping with me."

Sarah took a deep breath.

If I sleep with Jake, then I won't be alone in the dark after all.

At the thought, some of the tightness in her chest eased. She nodded jerkily, then turned and walked toward the spare bedroom.

8

Sleeping with Sarah was, in so many ways that he couldn't even begin to enumerate them all, a mistake, Jake admitted wryly to himself some fifteen minutes later. That was the main problem with being BFF with a woman: He was a guy, with all the normal guy instincts, while grief and guilt and God knows what else had turned Sarah into a virtual nun. He knew as well as he knew his own name that she had no awareness of him sexually at all.

So far at least, he wasn't quite enough of a jerk to do anything to try to change that.

The house was dark and quiet except for the gentle patter of rain on the roof and the faint hum of the air-conditioning. A little bit of gray from the night outside filtered in through the blinds, so despite the fact that every light in the house was off, he could see the outlines of things, like the tall chest against the pale wall opposite the bed and the curves of Sarah's body snuggled against him. They were wrapped up all warm (too warm for him, but at first she had been shivering) and cozy in the bed in the spare bedroom. Rendered sleepless as a rock by the circumstances despite being absolutely bone-tired, he was lying on his back with his head on a pillow and one arm tucked beneath his head, shirtless and barefoot but at least having had the good sense to keep on his pants. She was nestled against his side, wearing nothing but that loose T-shirt thing she slept in, her head on his bare shoulder, his arm around her, holding her comfortingly close. Even while his heart was breaking for her, even while he was furious as hell at whoever had made that call and done this to her again, even while she was being so brave and lying so still and trying to pretend that she was asleep, which he knew good and well she wasn't, the sweet femininity of her body pressed to his was slowly driving him around the bend.

In all their years of best friendship, he had never actually found himself sharing a bed with her before. Right there and then he vowed, as God was his witness, that he was never going to sleep with Sarah again.

Unless, of course, there was down-and-dirty sex involved.

Which he refused to allow himself to even think about.

Get thee behind me, Satan.

The problem was, though, that with every breath he drew, he could smell the faint floral scent of her shampoo. He could hear the quiet rhythm of her breathing. He could feel the warmth of her breath stirring the hairs on his chest. He could feel the silkiness of her skin against his, and the heat of her hand resting on his left pec, and the whole soft weight of her pressing into his side. More specifically, he could feel the small, firm roundness of her breasts. They were the size of not oranges but maybe tangerines, with soft puckered nipples that clearly proclaimed her lack of awareness of him as a man, and one was jutting into his rib cage just below his armpit and the other rested on his chest. Another name for them, he reflected, was torture in the flesh. To add insult to injury, he could feel the indentation of her slender waist, and the firmness of her stomach, and the curve of her thighs. One of her legs lay across his, and he could feel the shape and heat of it through the thin cloth of his pants. Knowing that said leg was bare, just like the rest of her underneath that T-shirt, was the final straw. The awful truth was that he was in the process of getting the mother of all hard-ons, and the fact that he was having difficulties of that kind was making him feel guilty as hell.

She needed him tonight, not as a lover but as her best friend.

Which, if you wanted to call a spade a spade, sucked eggs.

"Jake."

He'd known she wasn't asleep.

"Hmm?"

"Has anything—anything at all—come in on Lexie lately?"

So much for pillow talk. He felt a fresh welling of anger at the bastard who'd made that call, who was putting her through this just when he'd thought, hoped, she was starting to finally heal.

"Nothing of any substance. Not since that TV show got a tip about a little red-haired girl having breakfast with an old man at a Denny's. It turned out to be his grand-daughter, remember?"

He could feel her slight nod. She was lying still, too still, and by her very stillness he was able to gauge the depth of her pain. His arm tightened around her, hugging her closer. There was nothing else he could do.

Goddamn that son of a bitch to hell.

"You know I would have told you if there'd been anything new." He was careful to keep his voice gentle and his personal concerns out of the arena. She was upset, hurting. One thing she didn't need at the moment was any additional complications from him. "It was a crank call, Sarah. You need to let it go."

He took her indrawn breath for instinctive resistance. When she exhaled, slower and deeper, he knew she was accepting the truth of his words.

"Not knowing is the worst," she murmured, her voice thick. He guessed that her throat was tight. "I just keep imagining that she's out there. That she needs me." She paused, took another breath. "It's hell."

"Sarah . . ." His gut tightened at the pain in her voice. The pain that, no matter how much he might want to, he couldn't ease for her. "It's been seven years. You've got to go on with your life."

"I know." She was breathing harder, working at breathing, and he knew that she was trying not to feel, trying to push the pain away. "It's just—*hard.* Especially when things like this happen. Do you think that it could have been more than just a crank call? That somebody might be trying to get back at me or something?"

"Like the Beaufort PD?" His voice was intentionally dry. Since he couldn't help her in any other way, he tried to turn her question into a distraction. "It's possible. But it's also kind of subtle for them, and anyway, you've been ticking them off pretty regularly for the last seven years and they've never tried anything like this before. Remember how mad they were when you came to me initially?"

"Yeah." Her voice softened, and he guessed that she was picturing, as he was, their first meeting. Six weeks after Lexie's disappearance, she'd burst into his office, breathing hard, determination oozing from her every pore. Fresh out of the FBI, he had just bought out his grandfather's ailing private investigative firm, and was standing on a chair as he did his best to nail a sagging curtain rod back into the crumbling plaster of the reception room. The force of Sarah's entrance had sent the front door slamming back into the wall, and startled him so much that he'd taken an instinctive step back and fallen off the chair. Dorothy McAllister, the sixtysomething secretary-cum-receptionist-cum-assistant he'd inherited from Pops, was in the back somewhere sorting through files, so he'd been left to face his first walk-in client alone, while lying flat on his back with an overturned chair at his feet and a grimy gold polyester curtain, which he'd grabbed in the fall, draped around his head.

"I need to speak to whoever's in charge here." Her manner had been abrupt, authoritative, like someone accustomed to running the show. He had known immediately that she had some serious issues, because she spoke to him as he lay sprawled at her feet without so much as cracking a smile at the ridiculousness of the situation. In fact, she didn't even seem to notice it.

"That would be me." Brushing the curtain from his head, he scrambled to his feet and held out his hand. "Jake Hogan."

"Sarah Mason." He remembered thinking how pretty she was, with the black hair she'd worn long then cascading around her shoulders, and eyes as big and blue as Port Royal Sound fixed on him with almost frightening intensity. She'd been heavier then, too, in a good way, slender rather than skinny and with curves in all the right places that filled out her jeans and yellow T-shirt in a way designed to make a man sit up and take notice. A fox, he remembered thinking, and then she'd said the words that had brought them to this place, her spare bedroom, tonight.

"I need you to help me find my daughter."

A finder of missing persons was not what he wanted to be. Those kinds of cases, as he knew from high-school summers spent helping his grandfather, were uniformly small potatoes. The money and stability were in things like long-term security work, government contracts, and large-scale insurance investigations. Not the penny-ante stuff like missing persons, petty theft, and divorces that had been his grandfather's bread and butter—and ultimate financial downfall. To save the firm, Jake planned to take it in a whole new direction.

"The police . . ." he began, shaking his head, truly regretful that he couldn't help her. But he had issues of his own, like a high-maintenance, Northern-bred wife who hated Beaufort and hated the fact that her hotshot FBI agent husband was in the process of morphing into a small-town private dick and, he sometimes thought, *hated him;* a nearly defunct family business that it had cost him almost all his hard-earned savings to buy; a newly widowed father who was having a midlife crisis about ten years too late and had ditched said business to run off to Acapulco with a rich multiple divorcée; and a grandfather who was having real trouble letting go and just retiring already. And those, plus a seriously depleted bank account, were just his major problems. The minor ones were too numerous to mention.

In other words, this was not the moment to succumb to the desperation in a pair of big blue eyes.

". . . they're probably your best bet when it comes to a missing person."

She shook her head. He couldn't help but note, with what he hoped was covert admiration, the flush that added roses to a complexion that was already a glowing golden tan—and the way her breasts jiggled ever so slightly with the vigor of her movement.

Okay, so he was human. *Shoot me.*

"The police seem to think her father took her. He didn't. I know he didn't."

Jake folded his arms over his chest—and never mind that his elbow still tingled from where he'd banged it on the floor—and lifted his eyebrows at her inquiringly.

"He didn't want to be a father. That's one of the reasons why we got divorced." It was also, Jake discovered later, why they had gotten married: Sarah had gotten pregnant at nineteen, and, determined to give her child the kind of stability that she herself had never known, basically bulldozed her boyfriend into marrying her. With predictably disastrous results. From what Sarah had told him, the short-lived marriage—the guy had split the scene when Lexie was a little over a year old—had been a pitched battle from the start. Her husband was a handsome loser, a pothead who'd dropped out of college to try his luck on the drag-racing circuit, and Sarah the Determined had made up her mind to whip him into the kind of father she thought her child deserved.

Jake's loyalties were all with Sarah, but he couldn't help feeling a certain sneaking sympathy for the guy. He'd experienced Sarah in makeover mode himself.

"The police think because I was going after him for all the child support he never paid me, that he had a reason to take her." The words had come spilling out of Sarah's mouth. She'd started wringing her hands, and her tone had grown increasingly tense. "And they're telling me that he doesn't seem all that concerned about her disappearance, which they seem to think just about clinches it. Oh, they say they're following other leads, but it's been *six weeks.* My baby's been missing for six weeks. I have to try something else."

Jake had no trouble in interpreting that "something else" to mean him.

"Why'd you pick me?" He had some trouble keeping the exasperation out of his voice. The case was six weeks old; missing-persons cases were notoriously difficult at best, and this one involved a child. Unless the noncustodial father really did have the kid, the prospect of a happy ending wavered somewhere between slim and none. And he didn't want to be the one to have to tell this pretty lady that her baby wasn't coming back.

"They said you were an FBI agent. Some of the girls where I work. I'm an intern at the DA's office."

He had found out later that she'd just completed her first year of law school at USC in Columbia, and was only in Beaufort for the summer because of the internship. As it had turned out, she had stayed a year looking for her daughter, and then, after she'd completed her law degree, had taken a permanent job at the DA's office and returned to Beaufort to live. Always hoping something, some new information, would turn up. Always looking for Lexie.

She must have read his intention to turn her down in his face, because she reached out and laid a hand on his forearm. Soft, pretty, feminine hands—with the nails bitten to the quick. He'd felt the impact of her touch clear down to his toes.

"Please. I need help."

He'd always been a sucker for a damsel in distress. He knew this about himself, and thanked God that he had learned to fight the tendency.

"I'm expensive," he warned, just as a way to get her off his back without having to say no outright. "Something like this'll probably run you, oh, say ten thousand dollars plus expenses, with no guarantees. And I'll need half of it up front."

She caught her breath. Her face fell. Her hand dropped away from his arm.

"I . . . don't have that kind of money," she said, and he watched the beautiful rosy color drain from her face, watched her mouth go all pinched and tight, watched her eyes take on kind of a bruised look that gave him his first inkling of what the last six weeks must have been like for her. "The most I can pay right now is five hundred dollars."

Looking at her, he could tell that even the five hundred dollars was a stretch, that it would take every last cent she could earn, beg, or borrow to give him that. All he had to do was tell her the truth, that five hundred dollars would pay for just about a day of his time, which, unless the kid popped up out of the woodwork somewhere, wasn't going to get the job done. Then she would be gone and he would be free to get on with getting his new business up and running.

What he said, really slowly and calling himself an idiot every breath of the way, was, "Well, you know, that might work. See, the thing is, we do have kind of a payment plan."

In the end, he hadn't even taken her five hundred dollars. Of course, he hadn't found Lexie, either. The trail was too cold by then, and despite all the help he'd managed to pull in from his friends at the FBI, the investigation was too bungled. The Beaufort PD, miffed that she'd turned to a private investigator for help, had proceeded to turn on her, investigating her up one side and down the other for the possible murder of her daughter. That had come to nothing in the end—they hadn't been able to find so much as a single shred of evidence that Sarah had been anything but an exemplary mother—but it had further muddied the waters of what had really happened to Lexie. His own private opinion was that Sarah's daughter had been taken by a sexual predator and killed within a few hours of her disappearance. After seventy-two hours, the chances of recovering a missing child alive hovered around zero. Best-case scenario: maybe, one day, somebody might stumble over some remains. Then, at least, Sarah would have closure.

But for Sarah's sake, he'd never stopped looking.

"It just seems like a lot's happened," Sarah-in-the-present said into the dark, and moved, as if she was trying to find a more comfortable position. Just like that, Jake was whisked out of the past and dropped back into her way-too-hot bed with a jolt that caused him to grit his teeth. Her tone, and her movements, told him that she was now focused on something besides Lexie. Unfortunately, that helped his own predicament not one jot. The warm, soft hand on his pec slid back across his chest until it pillowed her cheek, trailing fire every inch of the way. Her legs shifted, too, reminding him forcibly that he had a shapely female thigh basically riding his leg.

"A lot?" Jake echoed intelligently as he tried to ignore the thigh—the naked, burning-hot thigh—that was creeping innocently up his obscenely receptive leg as they talked.

"The robbery. Mary being killed. Me getting shot. Duke—Donald Coomer—dying. You finding Lexie's toys spread around my bedroom. The . . . thing tonight." Her tone was thoughtful, and it was clear that she didn't have the least inkling of the discomfort she was causing him.

The slight hesitation with which she referred to the "thing," which he had no trouble interpreting as the phone call, told him that it still preyed on her mind. More guilt was heaped like coals inside his brain. Despite the assault her emotions had suffered, she was adult enough to struggle past her pain and try to find a reason for what had happened. He, with all the maturity of a horny seventeen-year-old, just wanted to get laid.

"You think they're all connected?" Thinking clearly was difficult when your mind was struggling to stay out of the gutter, Jake concluded grimly. He only hoped he didn't sound as slow-witted to her as he did to himself. The good news was, he was no longer in danger of being busted because her leg was no longer sliding up toward the

Danger Zone. The bad news was, now it was sliding down.

Somebody call the fire department.

"I don't know," she said. "What do you think?"

That if he didn't get her off him soon he was going to be Exhibit A for proof of the existence of spontaneous combustion.

"Could be coincidence."

"Wait a minute, aren't you the guy who's always saying that there's no such thing as coincidence?"

Maybe when he was in his right mind. Her thigh was sliding up again, and her hand was on the move, too, smoothing the hair in the center of his chest as if he were a cat she was unconsciously petting.

Christ almighty.

He exhaled, slowly and carefully. "Seems like a stretch to connect what happened with the robbery to the rest."

"You think?"

Not at the moment. In pure self-defense, he made his own moves, shifting his legs subtly sideways, flattening his hand over hers so that her fingers were stilled. It was a measure of how sexually unaware she had become that she didn't even seem to notice what she was doing, or his reaction.

Concentrate, slimeball.

"If you're looking for a connection, the strongest possibility is that the thing with the toys might be connected to the phone call. Although I still can't see how anybody got past that dog." At least he was able to string two coherent sentences together again.

"You said yourself somebody shot me. On purpose."

"Maybe on purpose." *Okay, it was a little easier to think now. Not a lot, but a little.* Her thigh was lying against his, not on top of it. "Whoever did it could have been aiming at the perps in the store, remember."

"Or they could have been aiming at me."

"Even if they were, that doesn't mean there's a connection with the phone call."

"No. But it doesn't mean there's not, either." Her tone was thoughtful. "That phone call—it was cruel. Whoever did it wanted to hurt me."

Her fist slowly clenched beneath his flattening hand. Her nails lightly scored his skin as they moved, and her fingers raked through his chest hair. She shifted positions again, sliding that thrice-damned thigh back up over his leg, and he had to grit his teeth to keep from groaning aloud. He only hoped that she would ascribe his silence for the minute or so it took him to unclench his teeth and reply to his careful consideration of her statement.

"That doesn't necessarily mean it had to be someone who knows you. It could have been anybody who saw that story about Lexie on TV." Despite his best efforts, his voice sounded strained to his own ears. He realized suddenly that *all* his muscles were tensed. Realized, in fact, that he was lying there in that nice, soft bed of hers, stiff as a board from head to toe. "Or even somebody who heard your name mentioned and re-membered what happened. There was a lot of publicity at the time."

And if there was any justice in the universe, he was earning major brownie points here for his iron self-control.

"So you're saying that everything that's happened over the last two days is just a random series of unconnected events?"

Even though he was maintaining tight visual contact with the ceiling in an effort to keep his focus somewhere besides his physical reactions to the woman beside him, he could feel her looking at him. His mistake lay in looking back.

Her head had shifted on his shoulder so that her face was tilted up toward his. Her eyes were dark pools in the pale oval of her face. He could see the smooth slope of her cheek, and the gentle curve of her lips.

Which were just inches from his. God help him, he could feel the warmth of her breath feathering over his mouth.

He wanted to kiss her. More than he had wanted almost anything else in his life. The fierceness of it stunned him. His heart was pounding, he realized. His hand that was curled around her shoulder had tightened. And that wasn't all that had tightened, either. Almost painfully.

All he had to do was dip his head . . .

"Jake?" Her eyes were narrowing at him. *Shit.*

Not dipping his head required every bit of self-control he could summon. He lay still as a log, gritting his teeth, closing his eyes in an effort to shut temptation out, concentrating on getting his breathing under control, his impulses under control.

You can't do this. Not now. You're family to her. She doesn't have anybody else.

"Are you okay?" Her hand flattened against his chest so that the imprint of it burned into his skin like a brand, and then she once again slid that tormenting leg up his thigh.

"Mmm." Somehow, from somewhere, he found the strength to keep his mouth to himself, his hands to himself, his self to himself, and roll away.

"Where are you going?" she asked as his feet hit the floor and he all but sprang up off the mattress.

"Bathroom," he managed in a strangled tone, and with what he considered true nobility, he kept his back turned to her and walked steadily away.

He stayed in the bathroom a long time. When he finally walked back into the spare bedroom, he was braced for questions, at the very least. But to his relief, she was all bundled up in the covers, breathing quietly with her back to the door, and to all appearances sound asleep.

Moving carefully so as not to wake her, he lay down on top of the covers, on his back, with one wary eye on the curvy bundle next to him. With her under the covers and him on top of them, even if she turned over and snuggled close, they should be all right.

But she didn't move, and eventually he, too, fell asleep.

What woke him was the pressure. Warm and intimate, it brushed against his ass then snuggled close, reminding him that he wasn't alone in bed.

His first groggy thought was that Danielle was feeling him up.

His second was that it wasn't Danielle.

Then he remembered just who it was he had slept with, and his eyes opened wide. It took no more than an instant to register that he was facing the window, that daylight was pouring in through the cracks in the blinds, and that he was lying on his side almost at the edge of the bed, looking at a wide expanse of empty mattress and rumpled bedding where Sarah should have been.

Somebody was behind him, though, caressing his backside through his pants. Somebody who clearly wanted him bad.

Sarah?

She'd said he had a nice ass . . .

Even as he had the mind-blowing thought, Jake cast a hopeful glance over his shoulder. What he saw was a sleek black head resting on the mattress behind him. It came complete with a squared-off muzzle and an inquisitive nose that was busy sniffing at his crack.

Ewww!

"Goddamn dog!" he yelped, jumping a foot in the air and landing flat on his back in the middle of the bed.

Sweetie-pie, startled too, also jumped back. Then he snarled, showing every one of those *Jaws*-worthy teeth.

Jake glared at the dog, who glared back. The dog did him one better, however: While Jake's glare was silent, Sweetie-pie's was augmented by a blood-chilling growl. The growl deepened menacingly, the dog's hackles rose, and it suddenly occurred to Jake that exchanging dirty looks with Sweetie-pie might not be the smartest thing he'd ever done. Backing down from a fight wasn't in Jake's character: He was a former football player, Marine, and FBI agent, for God's sake. A warrior by nature and training. Saying "die" just wasn't something he did.

On the other hand, Sweetie-pie was a big dog with a bad attitude and a whole lot of teeth—and he stood between Jake and the door.

Faced with a mohawk-sporting, teeth-baring hellhound, Jake did the only thing he could.

He bellowed "Sarah!" at the top of his lungs.

9

"Your Honor, I'm sorry to have to say it, but what we have here is an overzealous prosecutor. You know Ms. Mason's record as well as I do: She's extremely, perhaps even *overly,* aggressive when it comes to any case that she perceives to be about violence against women. We submit that in this case she is simply wrong: The evidence doesn't support the charge. And we have the expert testimony to prove it."

Pat Letts, Mitchell Helitzer's high-priced defense attorney, slid the blood-spatter evidence across the polished walnut dais to

Judge Amos Schwartzman, who was sitting behind the bench in Courtroom D of the Beaufort County Courthouse, otherwise known by lawyers, cops, and other insiders as Thunderdome. A managing partner in Crum, Howard, and Gustafson, Letts was a blonde in her late thirties, nearly six feet tall in her four-inch Manolos, with a killer figure that was set off by a short, tight, lime-green knit suit that clung to her curves like a slightly elongated tube top. His Honor, a plump, grandfatherly type with a shiny dome and bifocals, was known to have an eye for the ladies. That eye, and its fellow, were practically popping out of his head now as he drooled over the counsel for the defense, who was standing beside Sarah in front of him.

"This is the basis of your motion to dismiss?" Judge Schwartzman asked.

Letts nodded. "Yes, Your Honor."

Judge Schwartzman slid the bifocals up his nose and dropped his eyes to skim the paperwork. Letts cut her eyes at Sarah and smirked. Sarah, who sometimes worked out with her at the gym they both belonged to, knew that Letts was as aware of Judge Schwartzman's appreciation of eye candy as she was, and had dressed to take full advantage.

Crap. Wish I'd thought of that. But she hadn't. She'd been in such a rush this morning that she was lucky to be dressed at all, and anyway, she possessed neither a bright knit suit nor a killer figure to flaunt.

"You're asking for this to be dismissed without prejudice?" That meant that the case could not be reinstated at a later time. Judge Schwartzman looked at Letts over the top of his bifocals as he asked the question.

"Yes, Your Honor." Letts smiled at him. She was wearing more makeup than usual, too, Sarah noted, including bright red lipstick, and was working her sex appeal for all it was worth.

Ah, well. All's fair in love and court proceedings.

"Your Honor, we have our own expert witness who will dispute their witness's conclusion as to the import of the blood-spatter evidence." Sarah slid her own hastily composed rebuttal across the dais. If she couldn't compete in the glamour Olympics, she would use what she had and go with pathetic. Her suit was black polyester

(ADAs couldn't afford the pricey stuff, like Letts's thousand-dollar St. John), knee-length, worn with plain hose and two-inch black pumps. Whatever the opposite of exciting was, that's what she had going on. On the other hand, she knew from her mirror that she looked thin, pale, tired, and—thanks to her scraped chin and the impossible-to-miss Band-Aid behind her ear—like a crime victim who was lucky to be alive to make it into court today. *Work it, Sarah, work it.* She fleetingly touched her Band-Aid and made big, sad eyes at the judge, and never mind that the healing wound under the Band-Aid tugged unpleasantly. "As we are all sadly aware, violent crime is on the rise here in Beaufort County, and violence against women accounts for a large percentage of the increase. The prosecutor's office is swamped with the sheer volume of such cases. Whatever opposing counsel says, we do not choose to prosecute lightly, believe me, especially in a case such as this. The death of Susan Helitzer is, as you know, receiving a lot of media attention. In light of the violent manner in which she died, the lack of witnesses and the questions surrounding the case, the DA's office would quite simply be negligent if we did not closely examine the circumstances surrounding her death. We have in fact done so, and we firmly believe we have the evidence necessary to prove that her husband, did commit felony murder. For that reason, we ask that you not grant opposing counsel's motion to dismiss."

Sarah had Judge Schwartzman's attention now, and took advantage of the opportunity to lift a not-quite-steady hand to her oversized Band-Aid again and wince as if she were the victim of a painful twinge. The judge looked sympathetic, Letts shot her a withering look, and Sarah felt a flicker of triumph.

Take that, Jessica Rabbit.

Letts promptly counterattacked. "The *death* of Susan Helitzer was a great tragedy, as everyone agrees. Her family, including her bereaved husband, Mitchell"—who, control freak that he was, was sitting right there at the counsel table, listening to the proceedings, although he wasn't legally required to be in court that morning at all— "are rightfully devastated. But it was an *accident.* If you read the report of my expert witness, Dr. Norman Seaver, who as even opposing counsel knows is a renowned expert in the field, you will find that the blood-spatter pattern clearly proves that the cause of death was an accidental fall down the stairs." Letts took advantage of Judge Schwartzman's frowning focus to fan her face as if she was suddenly hot, then unfasten the top button on her jacket so that the lacy white camisole she was wearing beneath peeked out. Then, sotto voce, she added: "Whew, it's warm in here."

The judge smiled at her. "It is indeed."

Yikes.

"Your Honor, our expert is Dr. Edward Kane from USC, who has testified before this court many times. I don't think that even Ms. Letts would care to call his credentials into question," Sarah said. Actually, the report in front of the judge had been written by her, over the feverish hour and a half before court convened, from information obtained over the phone from Dr. Kane's assistant, because, wouldn't you know it, Dr. Kane was currently on a Caribbean cruise and couldn't be reached just when she most needed him. But Dr. Kane *was* their expert, and she knew how he was prepared to testify, and, anyway, judges didn't need to know everything. "All we are asking is for the opportunity to bring this case before a jury. Let the good citizens of Beaufort County decide whether or not Mrs. Helitzer's death was an accident."

With the judge's eyes now on her, Sarah took a little tottering sidestep as if her poor, wounded head was so messed up she was having trouble keeping her balance, then clutched the edge of the dais for support. Brushing her Band-Aid with her fingers again, she tried to look wan, which wasn't a stretch. Despite being juiced on oceans of caffeine and adrenaline, and strengthened by a good dose of righteous determination to see justice done, she felt wan. Plus, she was ignoring the mother of all headaches.

"Are you all right, Ms. Mason?" Judge Schwartzman asked, low-voiced, his brow knit with obvious concern. Sarah nodded bravely. Besides doing her best to garner a sympathy vote, she was gambling on the fact that Judge Schwartzman was smart enough to glean the other thrust of her message: The electorate is watching. You don't want to screw this one up.

She gave him a weak smile.

"The fact that I'm standing in front of you

this morning should tell you how strongly I feel that this case needs to go to trial, Your Honor," Sarah said, just to drive the message home. "The doctors at the hospital wanted to keep me another day. But I wanted to be here to make sure you understood that *this was a cold-blooded murder.*"

"Your Honor . . ." Letts began indignantly.

Judge Schwartzman waved her into silence.

"I'm ready to rule," he said. "Motion to dismiss is denied. The trial will proceed as scheduled."

With that he banged down his gavel. It was over.

Yes. Sarah did a mental fist pump.

The court reporter stretched her cramped fingers, the bailiffs hustled in a defendant from the holding room, the deputy exchanged low-voiced conversation with the judge, and the spectators in the gallery emptied and refilled the pews. *They're changing the guard at Buckingham Palace,* Sarah thought as she headed back to retrieve her things from counsel table. Letts, flinty-eyed now, shot Sarah a disgusted look and hurried over to talk to his client, whose naturally florid face had flushed bright scarlet in honor of the ruling. On his feet now, Mitchell Helitzer was maybe an inch shorter than his defense attorney, but he was probably three times as wide so, in Sarah's opinion, it all evened out. At forty-seven, he was a bulldog of a man with curly, ginger hair and the air of a bully, who looked ill-dressed even in his obviously expensive pale gray suit. His wife, Susan, whom Sarah had never met, had been slender and petite, which Sarah knew from reading her autopsy report. She wouldn't have been able to put up much of a defense when her burly husband attacked her.

"I gotta know, what's in this witch hunt for you?" Helitzer demanded of Sarah as they all met up at the swinging gate that hung at the bar of the court. Anger radiated off him in waves. His piggy blue eyes hated her. Sarah had a momentary flash of Susan Helitzer's autopsy photos and briefly considered beaning him with her briefcase, but professionalism stopped her. Besides, she would get him in the end. The death penalty or life in prison without parole would hurt a whole lot longer than a clout upside the head.

"Justice for Susan," Sarah told him at the

exact same time as Letts, looking scandal-
ized, said, "Mitch! Hush your mouth!"

Grabbing his arm, she shoved him
through the gate and practically strong-
armed him up the aisle.

Sarah followed.

"Just so you know, we're going to ask for
a postponement of the trial," Letts said over
her shoulder as they neared the end of
the gallery.

"We'll fight it. We're ready to go to trial
now," Sarah replied. Which wasn't quite a
lie. She'd had her work cut out for her to get
this case, which she had inherited along
with John Carver's job, in order to make the
previously scheduled trial date in time. Her
erstwhile predecessor had been something
less than a master of organization, and
she'd had to go back over everything from
forensics to witness interviews to the timeline, correcting countless errors along the
way. Coming on top of everything else that
went with settling into her new position,
preparing for this trial had required a herculean amount of labor. But then, as Jake
frequently pointed out to her, she had no
personal life, so she'd been glad to put in
the time. The trial was scheduled to start

two weeks from Monday, and by then every last piece of the puzzle should be in place. If not, she was definitely ready to wing it until it was.

"Well, we're not," Letts snapped, and used Helitzer, who was glaring at Sarah over his shoulder, as her own personal battering ram to push through the swinging mahogany doors into the busy hallway beyond.

"Nice to be loved by all," a voice drawled in her ear just as she was getting ready to follow suit.

Sarah jumped. She didn't have to glance back, though, to know who it was: Jake. He must have been in the gallery, watching.

Feeling absurdly like a kid who'd been caught playing hooky, only in reverse, she pushed on through the double doors with him behind her. The muted noise of the courtroom changed into the free-for-all bustle of the hallway. Aged dark pine paneling lined the walls, and the light streaming through the tall windows at either end was diffused by the waviness of the hundred-year-old glass. There was a modern annex, but this part of the classically designed courthouse dated from before the Civil War. Its age added gravitas to the hundreds of proceedings that were carried out within its walls each day, but the lighting was poor, and the air-conditioning was sporadic at best. Sarah spent so much time in the building that the faint, musty smell that no amount of Lemon Pledge could erase was as familiar to her as the scent of coffee, and she knew its every nook and cranny. Four wide halls connected to form a square around each of four floors, and Courtroom D was on the second. The worn marble floors were slick from decades of being walked on, so instead of striding, the crowd sort of shuffled from room to room. Sarah often thought that someone should come take one of those opinion polls the politicians were always carrying on about here: a more diverse cross section of South Carolinians was impossible to imagine. All sexes, all races, all ages, all income levels came together to battle it out in Thunderdome.

"Why aren't you at work?" she asked him, on the theory that the best defense was a good offense. When she'd left the house at shortly after six thirty a.m., he'd been snoring like a chain saw, hugging the far edge of the bed and lying on top of the covers. He'd been flat on his stomach, his hands under his pillow and his broad, bare shoulders hunched as if he were feeling the cold, so she'd been nice enough to drape a quilt over him before she'd left him lying there and headed for her office, to which she had known he would strenuously object. Since then, he had shaved, presumably show-ered, and changed into a tan jacket with a pale blue shirt, navy tie, and pants, which told her that he'd gone home before coming to the courthouse.

"I am at work. I have to testify for Morri-son in the Price case this morning. The question is, why aren't you at home?" He fell into step beside her.

For one of the few times that she could remember, she didn't welcome his pres-ence. The thing was, she had somewhere she needed to be, somewhere that she pre-ferred he know nothing about. And she had to be there in—she took a surreptitious peek at her watch—a little more than four minutes.

Of course.

She shrugged. "Last night, after you ran off to the bathroom, I decided that phone call came from someone who was trying to get under my skin. And if I let them get under my skin, they win. I don't like that idea, so here I am not letting it get to me."

They got caught up in the sea of harried people hurrying toward the ornate double staircase that wound four floors up and down, and automatically picked up their pace to match.

"What about your head?" There was a tightness about Jake's lips and eyes that told her that he disapproved of her being out and about under the circumstances. Unfortunately for him, though, his approval wasn't required. "Or does ignoring a bullet wound and a concussion fall under the whole not-letting-it-get-to-you thing?"

Gripping the iron banister with one hand, Sarah segued into the line of people moving down the stairs. With a deft maneuver, Jake managed to stay beside her.

"I've got a headache," she admitted. "But I'd have the exact same headache even if I stayed home, and I really needed to be here to make sure that motion to dismiss wasn't granted."

Among other things, but she wasn't going to get into that.

"Good job on that, by the way," he said.

They reached the bottom of the stairs and she got out of the slipstream of people headed for the metal detectors. He moved with her, and she glanced up at him. His eyes glinted down at her. "You had me worried, I have to admit. For a minute there, when you were standing in front of Schwartzman, I actually thought you might be going to faint."

"Thank you," she said, and permitted herself the briefest of grins. Of course, he knew what she had done and she knew what she had done, but talking about it here in the middle of the courthouse where anyone could overhear was a bad idea. Gossip was the lifeblood of the Beaufort legal community, and with the Helitzer trial coming up, she didn't want to find herself on Judge Schwartzman's bad side.

"Hey, Sarah, I saw you on TV yesterday! Great thing you did!" a voice called out behind her. Sarah glanced around to see Ray Welch, a junior lawyer who worked for the midlevel firm Bailey and Hudson, waving at her as he got on the elevator at the other side of the lobby. There were only four servicing the whole building, and they were old and cranky and always full, so she and most of the other people who spent a lot of time in the courthouse had given up on them long since and just used the stairs.

"Thanks," she called, and stopped walking, pressing her back against the wall to keep out of the way of the herds of people walking past. Jake stopped in front of her, and she glanced up at him again to discover that he was frowning at her.

"You know, it's just barely possible that there's somebody out there who wants to kill you," he said, planting a hand beside her head and leaning toward her so that his words went no further than her ear. "Which is why I spent last night at your house, remember? And what thanks do I get? First you leave me at the mercy of that monster of a dog, and then you show up right in the middle of the damned courthouse, which is just about the first place that any halfway intelligent person who wanted to shoot you would look."

Sarah cast a covert glance toward the door at the far end of the hall that opened onto the small back staircase leading to the basement. She needed to be down there in a little less than—her gaze fell on the big clock on the wall opposite—three minutes. Preferably without Jake.

"If someone wants to shoot me, the courthouse is probably the safest place I could be," she retorted under her breath. "They've got metal detectors, remember?" She cast a significant look at the well-manned entrances. "No guns allowed."

Jake's brows twitched together, which Sarah knew meant she'd scored a hit.

"So was Sweetie-pie a problem?" she continued hurriedly, before he could re-group and continue the argument.

"Not at all," he said, his tone way too affable for his narrowed eyes. "Unless you consider it a problem that he held me at bay on the bed for something like twenty minutes after he woke me up by sniffing my ass. I had to throw the quilt over him and run like hell to get out of the house."

Sarah's eyes widened at the picture this conjured up, and then she giggled. A real, girlish giggle, the likes of which rarely emerged from her throat anymore. Jake's harsh face softened as he watched her, and a reluctant smile touched the corners of his mouth.

"You should laugh more," he said. Then,

the smile vanishing, he added in a quieter voice, "Sarah. You're killing yourself here. You need to stop running as fast as you can."

Their eyes locked, and Sarah saw in his that he knew the real reason she was going about business as usual today: Work was the only way she knew to keep her mind off Lexie. If she didn't have work to occupy her, if she didn't keep going and going and going until her mind was numb and her body limp from exhaustion, then grief would fill her heart until it exploded into a thousand little pieces.

But this was not a conversation she wanted to have, not even with Jake. Maybe in some distant future, when her pain had dulled to the point where it no longer had the power to lacerate, but not today.

"I have a job," she said with a defiant tilt of her chin. "That's why they pay me."

His lips compressed. He started to say something more, but before he could get the words out, his cell phone rang. He fished it from his pocket, looked at the read-out, frowned, and answered.

"Hogan."

"We got trouble here, Hoss," said the

voice on the other end. Thanks to all the commotion around them, Sarah could barely hear the words coming through the phone, but she had no trouble identifying the speaker as Pops, otherwise known as Phil Hogan, Jake's grandfather. Nobody else called Jake "Hoss."

Jake sighed and met Sarah's gaze. His grandfather was eighty-six, and so far the word "retirement" didn't seem to be part of his vocabulary. Despite a touch of arthritis and the occasional senior moment, he was as spry as a man half his age, and still routinely put in forty to fifty hours a week as an employee of the agency he'd founded.

"What?" Jake asked in a resigned tone.

"Begley is threatening to pull the DVS security contract," Pops said. "Unless . . ."

Sarah missed the rest, because she took advantage of this fortuitous interruption to edge away from Jake.

"Gotta go." She mouthed the words, added a jaunty little wave, and merged into the eddy and flow in the hallway with the alacrity of a fish that had just managed to wriggle off a hook. Jake turned, straightening away from the wall to frown after her, but she ducked into the crowd and was able to scoot safely away. The thing was, she knew he would strongly object to what she was about to do, and would have no hesitation in trying to argue her out of it until she went deaf from listening.

She was still recovering from a gunshot wound, a concussion, and a pair of extremely traumatic nights, for God's sake. There was no earthly reason that she could see to add the stress of a lecture from Jake if she could avoid it.

The back staircase was little used, and Sarah was alone as she walked down it and pushed through the heavy metal door that opened onto Thunderdome's lowest level. There were more people hurrying along the hallway she stepped into—people always seemed to be in a hurry in the courthouse— and she exchanged greetings in passing with a lawyer she knew. The basement was huge, with limestone walls and a damp smell that no efforts at dehumidifying had ever managed to get rid of, and had once been used exclusively for storage. As the population of Beaufort had increased and space in its courthouse had grown tighter, it had been converted into offices on an as-needed basis. In the eighties, the city had hired a contractor to do an official remodeling, with an eye to standardizing the whole thing. The result was a warren of identical rooms, most of them windowless, with narrow, halogen-lit hallways running in a criscross pattern that was enough to confuse the hell out of anyone who didn't know exactly where they were going. Fortunately, Sarah did, but that was why she wasn't exactly surprised to see a bone-thin woman with a mane of improbable red hair teetering along in front of her. She was wearing a hot-pink tank top, a black micromini, sheer black stockings, and impossibly high heels, and the metal-beaded fringe on her black suede shoulder bag jingled with every step. She also looked lost.

"Hey, Crystal," Sarah said with resignation as she came up behind her.

"Sarah." Crystal turned with surprising grace considering the shoes, and Sarah got an eyeful of abundant cleavage swelling above the tank's scoop neck. Crystal's double-Ds were her ticket, and she was clearly a firm believer in *if you got it, flaunt it,* which would have worked for Judge Schwartzman, but unfortunately, the judge they were scheduled to see was Liz Wessel.

"I been looking for Suite thirty-nine like you said, but I guess somebody forgot to put the numbers on the doors."

"They're over the doorbells." Sarah pointed to small brass plaques over the doorbells that had been installed beside each door when they had been ordered locked for security purposes. The numbers etched into them *were* small, and hard to see in the iffy light. Sarah had never noticed before, probably because she knew where everything down here was.

"Can't believe I missed *that.*" Sarcasm etched Crystal's voice.

Looking at her over-endowed client critically, Sarah had a small epiphany and slid out of her jacket. That left her in a short-sleeved white blouse, which wasn't the way she usually liked to appear before Liz Wessel, who was a stickler for dressing to show respect for the bench. In this case, however, Crystal's need was clearly greater than her own, so Sarah was prepared to make sacrifices.

"You look cold," she lied, holding out her jacket to Crystal. "Why don't you put this on?"

Crystal looked at her like she'd lost her

mind. "What, are you kidding? It's, like, ninety degrees in here."

Sarah sighed. So much for trying to be tactful. "Look, the judge we're going to talk to is a *woman,* all right? Things would probably go better if you would cover up."

Crystal looked down at herself and frowned, then looked back at Sarah. "Oh, is she one of them jealous types?" Sarah nodded, praying that the action wouldn't be caught on a security camera or something and come back to bite her at a later trial. "No need for that. She wants 'em, she can get 'em. They only cost five thousand dollars for the pair. Judges make plenty of money to afford . . ." She caught Sarah's eyes and broke off. "Fine."

She took the jacket and shrugged into it. It fit reasonably well, and Sarah realized that, except for the notable exception of the double-Ds, she and Crystal were pretty much the same size. With that distraction out of the way, Sarah was able to focus on the rest of her client. Crystal was maybe thirty-five, with a Malibu-caliber tan that went oddly with her flaming hair and hazel eyes. Her brows were plucked into an improbable arch, she had a little pug nose, and her lips, beneath their coating of shiny, hot-pink gloss, were thin. She was attractive in a hard-eyed, take-no-crap kind of way. She looked like a woman who had seen a lot and done a lot, and would ultimately live to regret most of it.

"Wait," Crystal said as Sarah started to ring the bell for Suite 39.

"What?" Sarah paused with her finger on the bell.

"I got a call at work last night. Some man. He told me to get out of town or I'd be sorry."

Sarah frowned. The memory those words conjured up caused her throat to tighten, and she thrust it from her mind. The moon must have been right last night for harassing phone calls.

"You recognize the voice?"

Crystal shook her head. "No."

"You think it was about this case?"

Crystal nodded. "I think it was one of them cops."

"You have any proof?"

Crystal shook her head again. "No."

There was tension in her face now, and her right hand was opening and closing nervously over the clasp of her purse. Clearly, the call worried her.

Sarah's gaze was direct. "You thinking about getting out of town?" If her complaining witness was preparing to fly the coop, she needed to know.

"I don't want to. I just got this new job at Godfather's"—which billed itself as a "gentleman's lounge," but was, in reality, the city's premier strip joint—"and the money's real good." A smile widened her thin face. "Plus, I got a new boyfriend."

"That's nice." Sarah let a beat pass. "You're waiting tables, right?"

"Uh-huh."

A couple of secretaries walked by, chatting animatedly about the upcoming TV season. They were, Sarah gathered, looking forward to the resumption of *Desperate Housewives.*

"I watch that," Crystal said as they disappeared down the hall. "It's real good."

"Is it?" Sunday nights for her were spent preparing for Mondays. "Look, you know you can still drop this if you want to. Nothing's set in stone yet."

Crystal's jaw tightened stubbornly. "And let them get away with what they done to me? They *raped* me. I may not be a member of the Junior League like some of these women around here, but I got rights. I'm a person, too."

So Sarah had assured her when Crystal had approached her at the Women Against Rape class three Wednesdays before and told her what had happened to her the previous night. It was still true, and Sarah was willing to do everything in her power to help Crystal exercise those rights. The only thing was, Crystal lived in a far different world than she did, a world where cops wielded a lot of power and women like Crystal were considered disposable. Sarah had explained before she had agreed to file charges what Crystal would likely face in the aftermath, and every word of it was coming true. But as long as Crystal wanted to prosecute, Sarah was going to do what she could to help her. Even if she took some heat, too.

"You sure?" Sarah asked one last time, her finger hovering above the bell.

"Yeah, I'm sure."

So be it. Sarah rang the bell, and they were admitted into Judge Wessel's chambers.

"So you want a TRO, is that right?" Judge Wessell, a slim, fiftyish woman with short, brown hair and blue eyes, looked at Sarah with a slight frown. She was on her way to court and was dressed in her black jurist's robes. At the moment, however, she was seated behind the massive walnut desk that dominated her office. Her young male assistant was hovering impatiently in the doorway. Sarah and Crystal stood in front of the desk, Crystal fidgeting nervously and Sarah trying to ignore the sound of clicking fringe. Sarah had just finished explaining the merits of her request, not forgetting to throw in the phone call Crystal had received, and from Judge Wessel's grim expression was cautiously hopeful of success.

"Yes, Your Honor." Asking for and being granted a temporary restraining order in cases such as Crystal's was fairly routine. What wasn't routine here was the identity of the subject being ordered to stay at least one hundred yards from the complaining witness.

"You have proof that Officer McIntyre has been harassing Ms. Stumbo?"

"We have a picture, Your Honor. It was taken by Ms. Stumbo three days ago from the front window of her home." Sarah handed over the letter-sized computer print-out that Crystal had given her.

"I took it on my digital camera," Crystal said proudly.

Although the photo had been taken at night, there was enough illumination from a nearby street light to clearly show a black Mustang parked alongside a Dumpster in what appeared to be a trailer park. A mail-box was in the shot, and the numbers on it provided proof of location. Unfortunately, the person in the driver's seat was not read-ily identifiable. He appeared to be a male with dark, slicked-back hair, but his features were blurred because the car windows were tinted.

"I can't identify this as Officer McIntyre. I doubt if you can, either." Judge Wessel's tone was astringent as she looked up at Sarah.

"See the license plate?" Sarah pointed to the picture. "I had it blown up." She put another computer printout in front of the judge. A license plate filled the page. The image was something less than sharp, but the numbers were decipherable. "That's Officer McIntyre's personal vehicle. See, here's the registration from the Department of Motor Vehicles verifying it."

Judge Wessell looked and nodded. "I see." She pursed her lips, frowning as she stared down at the papers in front of her. Then she gave a brisk nod, reached for a pen, signed the papers Sarah had put in front of her with a flourish, and pushed them back toward Sarah, who picked them up. "Very well, I'm granting the order. This isn't clear-cut, you realize, Officer McIntyre may have had a perfectly legitimate reason for being in that location, but I won't tolerate even the appearance of witness intimidation."

"Thank you, Your Honor," Sarah said as Judge Wessell rose. As Her Honor conferred with her harried-looking assistant, Sarah stowed the papers in her briefcase and hustled Crystal out of there before her client could say or do or reveal anything (okay, any two things) that might prejudice the judge who might well preside over the trial in which she was the complaining witness.

Sarah had learned long since that it was always best to keep in mind that whoever had said that the courtroom was a slice of life had got it only partly right: What it was really was a slice of staged life. The judge and jury saw only what was put in front of them. One of the tricks to conducting a successful prosecution lay in presenting the best possible version of the victim. To that end, she and Crystal were going to have to have a wardrobe consultation before the trial's start date.

"I'll see if I can't get those papers served on Officer McIntyre today," Sarah promised Crystal as they walked back toward the stairs. She was once again wearing her jacket, and Crystal was once again jiggling all over the place.

"That'll keep him away from me, right?" Crystal asked as Sarah pulled the stairwell door open for her. A man coming through gave Crystal's assets an admiring glance. Crystal smiled flirtatiously at him, and he almost walked into Sarah in his bedazzlement.

"Oh, excuse me," he said, noticing her only when she stepped out of his path. Sarah sighed as he walked away still blinking, and pushed her bodacious client on through the doorway.

"Yes, it will," she said, picking up the conversation again.

Should was more like the truth. In Sarah's experience, TROs had never kept anyone who was really serious about getting close to a victim from doing so, but they were useful as a tool. Lawyers were usually able to secure stronger sanctions—like jail time—when the TRO was violated. Of course, sometimes that wasn't much help to the victim. In Crystal's case, however, the fact that McIntyre was a cop and presumably valued his job should work in her favor. If he violated it, he would be looking at suspension from the force as well as jail time.

"You think I could get one against my landlord?"

"What? Why?"

"My rent's late. Look, this whole thing has really affected my earning power. I tried to explain to him I got *raped,* but every time I come home, fifteen minutes later he's there banging on my door. He was there this morning. I had to wait till he was gone to leave. Maybe I could get one of these TR-whatever things on him to keep him away until I get the money together."

Sarah sighed again. They were trudging

up the steps by this time. Or at least Sarah was trudging. She wasn't quite her usual Energizer Bunny self, she was discovering as the day wore on. Besides her headache, her knees hurt and her leg muscles felt weak. In fact, she felt kind of weak all over. If it hadn't been for the metal banister, which she was using to pull herself up, she wasn't sure she would have made it to the first floor.

"A TRO doesn't work on landlords," she said. What she needed, she decided, was more caffeine. *Way* more.

"But it works on cops, right? All cops? Or just him?" Crystal reached the top of the stairs and pushed through the door. Sarah followed, heaving an inner sigh of relief. The climb, and the conversation, were taking their toll.

"Just him." Casting a quick look around the crowded hall, she was relieved to see that Jake was nowhere in sight. "Why, have other cops been bothering you?"

"There's been other cars, some of 'em parked in front of work." Crystal shrugged. "This was the only one I got a picture of. I just got my camera."

"Next time you see one, take another picture. And call me."

Sarah's cell phone, which had been returned by the police that morning in a large Ziploc bag along with the contents of her purse—the purse itself was still being held as evidence—went to town just then. At something of a loss without her purse, she'd dropped her phone in her blazer pocket and stored her wallet, cosmetics, etc., in her briefcase until she could replace her purse. She had set the phone on vibrate before she'd entered the courtroom earlier, and now it was having spasms in an effort to call attention to itself. Fishing it out, she frowned down at the number on the readout.

"I need to take this," she said to Crystal, who kept on walking with a wave and an airy "Later."

"Hey," Sarah said into the phone.

10

"Thought you ought to know," Jake said on the other end of the line. "We got a good lead on the third robber."

"Oh yeah?" Sarah stopped walking and leaned against the wall with one hand pressed over her open ear, the better to hear him with.

"Childhood friend of the other two, name of Floyd Parker. Donald Coomer and Maurice Johnson hung with him all the time. Johnson's sister places him with them up to half an hour before the robbery."

"Where'd you find her?"

"Hospital. Johnson's still critical, and his clan has gathered."

"So was this friend there, too? Did somebody pull him in for questioning?"

"He's at work. Big D's Tire Service. They're sending a squad car to pick him up right now."

"Thank God." Sarah felt a stirring of relief. Despite her stalwart efforts not to dwell on the possibility that there might be someone out there who actually wanted to kill her, it would ease her mind to know that the guy who'd put a bullet in her head was off the streets. Just in case he decided to try it again. "Where are you, anyway?"

"Heading toward work. Where are you?"

"Still at the courthouse."

"Planning to stay there?"

"For a while. I'll be here until at least two, and then I need to stop by the office. When I get done there, I'll probably call it a day."

Jake snorted. "What, are we talking seven, eight p.m. here? On a Friday night? How about this: In honor of your war wound, I'll swing by and pick you up at five thirty and we'll do dinner. Somewhere nutritious. With vegetables. You pick the place."

"Be still my heart." Sarah couldn't help

smiling. Then a thought occurred. "Wait a minute. You're forgetting the pork chops."

"Oh." The way he said it told Sarah he really had forgotten. "I'll tell Danielle something came up."

"Again? She's gonna love that." Even as she shook her head, she felt a little twinge of regret at the idea of forgoing an evening out with Jake. Since the robbery, she'd been taking stock, a little, and something she'd realized was that Jake was right up there with work and Sweetie-pie as one of the three things that made her life worth living. On certain occasions, in his company, she'd even been almost happy. As happy as it was possible for her to be, anyway, with Lexie gone. If it hadn't been for Jake, she didn't think she would have made it through last night. In the aftermath of that phone call, she had craved warmth, and support, and human contact. She had clung to Jake out of raw need, holding tight to what felt like the only anchor in her disintegrating world, and finally, when the worst of the pain had ebbed, had found her usual safe harbor in his arms. When he had left her to go to the bathroom, the sense of loss and, yes, abandonment that had flooded her had been as powerful as a rogue wave. It had also been a wake-up call. Depending on Jake for emotional stability was an error of potentially devastating proportions. In the end, every single person in the world was alone, as she knew from bitter experience. Jake was a crutch, and instead of letting herself lean so hard on him, she needed to concentrate on building up the strength to get through this on her own.

Which was why she had pretended to be asleep when he'd returned to bed. She had felt comforted and cared for in his arms, and just knowing that he was there, that he shared her pain and heartbreak as much as anyone could, had helped her push the worst of the agony away. But that was the thing: This was *her* pain, *her* heartbreak. He couldn't shoulder even part of her burden for her. No one could. She had to bear the heavy weight of it herself.

"She'll understand," Jake said. "She's an understanding kind of girl."

"You're fooling yourself, pal." She had things she needed to do after work anyway, Sarah remembered. Important things. Like, um, more work. And laundry. "You go on and eat your pork chops and don't worry about me. I have things to do myself."

"Like what?"

"Wouldn't you like to know?" She felt the weight of a gaze on her, glanced up, and saw Larry Morrison heading her way, with Ken Duncan trailing in his wake like the tail on a kite. "Look, I've got to go."

"Sarah." Jake's tone was suddenly serious. "Until Floyd Parker is actually in custody, and until we know for sure that he's the guy who shot you, keep in mind that you could still be in danger. Be careful, okay?"

"Yeah, I will." Sarah didn't much like the way Morrison was looking at her. "Talk to you later."

Closing the phone, she dropped it back in her pocket and straightened away from the wall to meet Morrison head-on.

"Sarah."

"Hey, Boss." Behind Morrison, Duncan was looking worriedly at her.

Uh-oh. Something was in the wind.

Morrison's gaze shifted beyond her, then returned to her face.

"Walk with me, would you?"

He curled a hand around her arm, and Sarah found herself walking beside him back the way she had come, toward the far end of the hall where the basement stairs were located. The reason, she deduced, was because it was out of the steady stream of traffic proceeding from the entrance and the metal detectors to the stairs, and thus they had at least a slight chance of talking without being overheard.

"So, what's up?" Being cornered like this by Morrison was never a good thing, and tension tightened her stomach.

"First the good news. The unsub who shot you? We think we may know who he is."

"I heard."

Morrison shot her a quick, frowning look. "You've got good information, then. I just found out myself. Care to tell me who you heard it from?"

"Nope."

"Never mind." Morrison's voice was dry. "I can guess." He cleared his throat. "Anyway, I just got off the phone with Amperman at the PD, and he told me that they were putting the guy in the car as we spoke. He's in custody, and he's looking good to be our unsub. Of course, nothing's set in stone yet, but you can probably breathe a little easier."

"That *is* good news," Sarah said, and cast a wary glance at him. "So what's the bad news?"

"I got a call a little earlier from Pat Letts. She wants you pulled from the Helitzer case. She says you're unfairly prejudiced against her client and she's threatening to go to the judge with a petition to have you removed."

Sarah snorted, and her stomach relaxed. This was fairly routine stuff, part of the chess game regularly played between defense attorneys and prosecutors.

"She's just bent out of shape because her motion to dismiss was denied."

"I heard." Morrison's eyes twinkled at her suddenly. "Actually, I talked to Amos Schwartzman, who filled me in. He says you're looking pretty wobbly, and I agree. So Duncan here is going to take over the rest of your cases for today, and you're going home. Understand?"

"What?" Caught by surprise, Sarah stopped walking and stared at him in momentary incomprehension. Fridays were always busy, and she had a truckload of things she needed to do. Besides . . . "No!"

Morrison stopped, too. The twinkle had

disappeared in favor of an authoritative stare. Duncan, who was looking at her over Morrison's shoulder, gave her a sympathetic grimace out of their mutual boss's view.

"I *said,* you're taking the rest of the day off. And the weekend. I don't want to see you anywhere near the office until Monday morning at the earliest. If I do, you're fired."

"What?" Sarah was pretty sure that last part was a bluff.

"You heard me. Monday morning at the earliest."

"But I've got a hundred and one things . . ."

Morrison interrupted, shaking an admonishing finger at her nose. "Face it, Sarah. You need the time off. Take it. That's an order."

She was still spluttering protests when he gave her a stern look, said "I mean it," and walked away to talk to Judge Jefferson Prince, who had just emerged from the basement and greeted him with a hearty clap on the back. Sarah's mouth closed with an angry snap. Duncan, who had stayed beside her, came in for a furnace-caliber blast from her eyes.

"Hey, it wasn't *me,"* he protested, taking

a hasty step back and flinging up the hand that wasn't holding his briefcase. "All I do is take orders around here, too."

Jake's business, and also his residence, was located in one of the less impressive of the colorful, three-story Victorian houses that formed a loose semicircle around the acres of huge white mansions anchoring the historic district. It was pale yellow with white shutters and a great deal of gingerbread trim. The front door was painted *haint* blue to ward off the evil eye, and a discreet pewter plate of the size approved by the town council had been affixed to the door. It read *Hogan & Sons Investigations.* Never mind that Jake, the current owner, had no sons, or indeed any children at all, and only one sister who was married, lived in Atlanta, and had a six-year-old daughter. Never mind that his father, to whom the "& Sons" had originally referred, was an only child. The business had been founded fifty-two years previously by his grandfather, who, when he had given it its name, had been hoping for a basketball team's worth of boys from his late, long-suffering wife. And he was not a man who easily relinquished his dreams. As he had said when Jake had suggested changing the name to simply Hogan Investigations: "Nothin' doin'. You're the one what's gonna make that name fit."

Jake's reply had been, "Yeah, Pops, don't hold your breath."

But he had the feeling his grandfather was. Figuratively speaking, of course.

Now, as he pulled his Acura into the paved area that he shared with the dentist's office next door, which was another converted Victorian house, this one painted periwinkle blue, he saw the red Harley at the end of the lot and shook his head. Pops, who racked up speeding tickets by the dozen, whose car Jake had threatened to take away a multitude of times, who couldn't work a cell phone, refused to touch a computer and was mystified by the ancient VCR he'd owned for ten years and had never yet figured out how to program, had bought himself a brand-new, state-of-the-art motorcycle in honor of his eighty-sixth birthday two months ago.

"Just like the one I rode in the war," he'd said happily when he'd first dumbfounded Jake with it. "Well, except for being red. And new. And having all that electronic stuff on it. And being so danged expensive."

Jake had been saying almost-hourly prayers ever since.

"So what's this about DVS?" he asked Dorothy as he walked through the small, thoroughly modern reception room—formerly the house's entry hall and front parlor, which a decorator had updated for him with pale gray walls and chrome-and-black-leather furniture—toward the more spacious office area in the back. Like the business itself, Dorothy was a Beaufort institution that he had acquired from his grandfather. She admitted to being seventy, he suspected she was at least five years older, and she had worked for Hogan & Sons for the last thirty-two years. Her snow-white hair was pulled back into a no-nonsense bun at her nape, silver-rimmed spectacles framed her gray eyes, and her plump face had its fair share of fine wrinkles. Round as a teakettle, homey as Aunt Bee, she favored what local denizens called "housedresses," short-sleeved, mid-calf length rayon dresses in bright flower prints, which she wore with sensible lace-up shoes. Widowed twenty years ago, she had two children, both of whom were in their forties now, and had not missed a day of work since Jake had taken over the agency.

"You'll have to ask *him.*" Jerking her thumb toward the sliding glass doors that opened onto the deck (two of Pop's im-provements to the building, which included the conversion of the top floor into the apartment in which Jake now lived, all car-ried out in the days before the city had got-ten picky about such things), she barely glanced up from the up-to-the-minute Mac she had learned to operate with the ruthless efficiency with which she did everything else. Her tone was grim, and Jake gathered from it that she didn't approve of something his grandfather had done. Suppressing a sigh—with four senior-something and two twentysomething employees, he sometimes felt as if he were running a kindergarten rather than a business—he headed toward the deck.

And stopped short with his hand curling around the handle and his nose just inches from the sliding glass door.

Danielle perched on the deck railing, her long, blond hair done up in a cute ponytail, her tanned and toned body clad in the Lycra shorts and exercise bra that she routinely wore to work. Which, since Danielle was an aerobics instructor at the local Y, wasn't as odd as it sounded.

Pops sat in one of the cushioned metal deck chairs that had come in a set of four along with the glass-topped table, complete with a bright blue sun umbrella. He was leaning back in it so that its two front legs were inches off the deck, with his booted feet (since he'd bought the Harley, he'd taken to wearing boots on even the hottest days) propped on a lower rail. He was wearing a black T-shirt and jeans. A big, open bag of marshmallows rested on the table within easy reach. Even as Jake watched, he snagged a marshmallow from the bag and casually pitched it over the rail.

Jake practically ground his teeth.

"Old fool," Dorothy not quite muttered.

Family loyalty prevented Jake from agreeing—out loud.

He slid open the door and stepped out into the steamy heat of a low country morning. A pair of giant live oaks that predated the building by a good fifty years twined branches in the marshy backyard, gray Spanish moss dripping from their limbs, providing ample shade for the section of deck where Pops sat under the umbrella while Danielle, a foot or so to Pops's right, toasted happily in the sun. A heron took flight at the rattling sound the door made, soaring up into a cloudless azure sky. Beyond the deck, the intercostal waterway rolled by, its soft turquoise waters reminding him of the boyhood hours he had spent fishing its depths with the wiry old man who was even now, as he pitched another marshmallow over the rail, grinning unrepentantly at him.

"Hey, Hoss."

"Jake!" Danielle slid off the rail with a blithe disregard for the possibility of splinters in interesting places and greeted him with an enthusiastic hug and kiss. Jake hugged and kissed her back, somewhat less enthusiastically. For the last couple of weeks now, he'd been getting that restless feeling that he'd learned from experience usually meant it was time to move on. Danielle was pretty and sweet and energetic and . . . maybe that was it. Maybe she was too damned energetic. She always had something going on, a plan, some fun event scheduled for them to share, when sometimes all he wanted to do was just stretch out on the couch and watch sports on TV.

"I thought I told you not to feed the gators," Jake said, directing his irritation at his own lack of fun-ness at his grandfather. Danielle's arms were looped around his neck now. By default, his arm loosely circled her waist.

"I'm not feeding the gators," Pops protested, flicking another marshmallow over the side. "I'm feeding Molly."

Despite having Danielle clinging to his side like a barnacle, Jake made it to the rail in time to see the falling marshmallow snapped out of the air by a ten-foot-long gator sunning itself on the concrete walk that led across to the small dock where his fishing boat was tied up. It was so close that if it had stretched out its neck another couple of inches, it could have rested its head on the lowest step of the three that led up to the deck.

"That is just so cool," Danielle said.

Jake cast a dark glance over his shoulder. "Damn it, Pops . . ."

"Molly's not a gator." Pops pitched another marshmallow. "She's family."

The quick snapping together of a pair of

three-foot-long jaws ratcheted Jake's irritation level up a notch. "If that gator eats another dog . . ."

It wasn't an idle worry. Last summer, one of Big Jim the dentist's patients had brought her poodle to the office and, mindful of the dangers of leaving pets in cars in such heat, left it tied to a tree instead while she ran in to pick up some X-rays. When she came out, the leash was there, a few tufts of apricot fur were there, but the dog wasn't. Instead, as she had hysterically told the police, she'd seen the tail of a big ole gator sliding away into the water.

Then Big Jim's ditzy new assistant had volunteered helpfully that the old man who worked at the detective agency next door kept gators as pets. The police had come calling, Pops had allowed as how he didn't keep 'em as pets but did feed 'em sometimes, and the upshot of the matter had been a summons to go to court for maintaining a public hazard. Plus a threatened lawsuit by the bereaved pet owner, which had required Sarah's services, along with the cost of a new poodle, to squash.

Since then, Jake had been firmly opposed to the feeding of gators, any gators up to and including Molly, on agency property. The business didn't need the ill will, or the potential liability. He, personally, didn't need the aggravation.

But did Pops listen? About as well as gators flew. Which was to say, not at all.

"I never did believe Molly got that dog." Pops took his feet off the rail so that his front chair legs hit the ground with a dull *thunk.* "For all anybody knows, a human coulda took it. Or it could have just plumb run off. If that prissy woman was *my* owner, I woulda hightailed it first chance I got, for sure."

Having heard Pops's theories about the fate of the missing poodle more times than he cared to remember, Jake just curled his lip at his grandfather and swiped the bag of marshmallows off the table by way of a reply. Danielle, who'd listened to this exchange with widening eyes, clung even tighter while casting the gator a newly nervous look. Jake looked, too, and was ready to swear the thing was smiling at him now. Its jagged yellow teeth were more visible than before, and its bulbous golden eyes, which were fixed on him, were open wide and had taken on a devilish kind of sparkle.

Jake would have said *shoo* to it, but he was pretty sure the gator wouldn't, and when a gator had a mind to stay, there wasn't, he had discovered, much a person could do to change it. Short of dynamite, which he unfortunately didn't have.

"She sees them marshmallows." Pops stood up and stretched, catching his hands behind his back and flexing his arms. He was a fit five nine, though he claimed that he'd once been as tall and wide as Jake and had shrunk with the years, and was as energetic as a forty-year-old. Actually, Jake reflected, the old coot was probably more energetic than he was himself. He was also bald as an egg, tan as cowhide, and wrinkled as crepe paper. The gleaming silver motorcycle that was airbrushed on the front of his T-shirt caught the sun as he moved. Underneath were the words *Road Hog*. His jeans were bootcut Levi's. With built-in holes in the knees. That he'd paid good money for. You could say lots of things about Pops, but you sure couldn't say he wasn't stylin'.

"You keep swinging that bag around, you're gonna have her right up here with us in a minute," Pops warned.

"Oh, gosh, now you're scaring me." Danielle shuddered theatrically. Her arms tightened around Jake's neck and she snuggled closer into his side. Jake gave his grandfather a skeptical look but stuffed the marshmallow bag down deep in his jacket pocket just in case.

"So, what brings you here this morning?" he asked Danielle, maybe a little less graciously than he could have. Two killer animals in one morning were probably two more than any sane man should have to deal with. To say nothing of the kind of people who actually got attached to said animals. No wonder he was feeling slightly out of sorts. Probably this edgy feeling he was experiencing had nothing to do with Danielle at all. Probably it was all about marshmallow-scarfing gators and saber-toothed dogs—and Sarah. Definitely there was some worry about Sarah in the mix.

"I made a pineapple upside-down cake last night. I was going to take it to work with me for everybody to share, but then I remembered how much you liked the last one I made, so I thought I'd drop it off for you instead."

"Why, thank you," he said, and felt her

arms tighten like a noose around his neck as she beamed at him.

The thing about Danielle was, not only was she hot, and good in bed, but she could cook up a storm. With that combination, any man with a lick of sense ought by rights to be thinking about gold rings and mortgages about now.

Jake barely repressed a shudder at the thought. Keeping it casual, he let his arm drop away from her waist and kind of took a step back, which caused her stranglehold on his neck to loosen and brought his hip up against the rail at one and the same time. To complete his escape, he would have hiked himself up to sit on the rail if the whole turn-your-back-on-the-gator-while-you've-got-marshmallows-in-your-pocket scenario hadn't just then played itself out in his mind.

The resulting debacle just might give the nickname Sugar Buns a whole new meaning.

Nope, he wasn't going there. He kept both feet on the ground and cast a wary glance at the gator, which hadn't moved.

"Cake was good." Pops smacked his lips reminiscently. "I had a nice big piece."

"Thank you." Danielle's reply was accompanied by a modest smile. She had only one hand on his shoulder now, so Jake counted that as a step forward.

"She's a great cook," Jake said, digging deep for the enthusiasm that seemed to be eluding him for the moment. The thing was, he knew she was thinking about gold rings and mortgages even if he wasn't. And the other thing was, he already knew it just wasn't going to happen. Not with Danielle. Not then, not in six months, not ever.

"Speaking of cooking," Danielle said. "I also made corn pudding and baked apples to go with the pork chops. And I've got some green beans, and I can do macaroni and cheese if you want."

"Now that sounds like some meal," Pops said, while Jake's mouth, which was clearly experiencing disconnect with his brain, watered reflexively.

Danielle turned her Bambi-brown eyes on Pops. "You're welcome to join us."

Pops grinned. "I'd sure like that." He glanced at Jake mischievously. "Don't worry, I'll leave early."

It required an effort, but Jake managed to push the tantalizing image of macaroni and cheese out of his head long enough to take stock. Danielle had switched gears from her previous emphasis on sex, sex, and more sex, and was now obviously operating under the maxim that the way to a man's heart—and that gold ring—was through his stomach. All right, it probably was, but as long as there was a McDonald's left in the world, Jake figured he could hold out.

"The thing is," he began, and Danielle's brows twitched together and her hand fell away from his shoulder even before he could finish.

"Something came up?" Her tone was sweet as honey. Too sweet. Didn't match the snap in her eyes at all. Damn, maybe he was using that phrase too much if the women in his life were starting to anticipate it before it even left his mouth.

"Yeah." Jake strove for apologetic, but to his own ears it sounded vaguely sheepish instead. "What can I say? There's a lot going on right now."

"That's it." Her back went ramrod straight. Her cheeks flushed. Her ponytail quivered. *"That's it.* I'm tired of always being put off for your *job.* Either you put me first for once or we're *over."*

Pops opened his mouth to butt in, and Jake shot him a stay-out-of-this-or-die look.

"I can't put this thing tonight off." Again he tried for apologetic, and again he missed the mark. He could tell by the quick clenching of Danielle's fists at her sides. "I would if I could."

"Fine." She stormed past him toward the door, throwing the words at him over her shoulder. "Fine. That's it for me, then. I am so out of here."

The sliding glass door rattled back to crash against its frame with enough force to make Dorothy, who was still working at her desk, jump in her chair and look up with a startled expression. Danielle paused on the threshold to slay Jake with her eyes.

"You're too old for me, anyway," she snapped, then stalked through the office without so much as a word to Dorothy, who was watching openmouthed. At the entrance to the reception room, Danielle stopped dead, squared her shoulders, and made a U-turn. She marched over to the long counter built into the far wall that served as a home for assorted office equipment, picked up a covered cake plate that had somehow taken up residence there, and shot Jake, who hadn't moved, another killing look.

"And I'm taking my cake back," she added fiercely, and, cake plate in hand, marched back through the office and out of sight. Seconds later, the slam of the front door announced her departure. Jake winced reflexively as the force of it rattled the pictures on the walls.

"Damn," Pops said after a moment in which no one said anything. "I guess we can forget about that dinner."

"Looks that way." Jake tried not to sound as relieved as he felt.

"Do one of you two want to tell me what in tarnation just happened?" Dorothy asked.

"I think Jake just got dumped."

"Well." Dorothy ruffled up like an irritated hen as she hurried to take Jake's part. Her eyes met Jake's, and she shook her head. "If you ask me, you're better off. Any girl that would run around in her underwear like that, well, it's just not modest, and that's all I'm going to say."

"All the girls dress like that now," Pops objected. "I don't see any harm in it. Hell, it improves the scenery. Dotty, girl, you're just getting old."

"At least I've got the good sense to know it, instead of tricking myself out like a teen-ager," Dorothy, clearly affronted, shot back. "And as for ogling girls young enough to be your granddaughter—well, all I can say is, you ought to be ashamed."

Pops looked astounded. *"What?* Are you sayin' I ogled that girl? I never did. Well, no more'n I could help. I mean, when it's right there lookin' you in the face, what're you gonna do?"

Dorothy's mouth tightened at this, in Jake's opinion, truly foolhardy piece of truth-telling. Her cheeks flushed red. Her whole body seemed to swell.

"See?" she said. "See there? You are absolutely . . ."

"Wait." Slashing his hands through the air like a referee signaling a disallowed basket, Jake jumped in before the argument could deteriorate into a free-for-all. "Hold it right there, both of you. Danielle's my problem, not either of yours. Besides, we've got a business to run here, remember? Dorothy, I need that background check on Floyd Parker ASAP. I—"

"It's on your desk," she interrupted, still shooting Pops dirty looks. "Right there on top of the background checks for Donald Coomer and Maurice Johnson, which I got for you yesterday. If you check your inbox, you'll also find a copy of the convenience-store security tape from when Sarah got shot and all the security tape I could get from the jailhouse area around where Donald Coomer died, in case you want to look at it."

Jake sometimes had the disquieting suspicion that Dorothy could run the business without him or Pops or anyone else. This was one of those moments when the suspicion amounted to a near certainty.

"Good work," he said, trying not to sound like the wind had just been taken completely out of his sails. "Uh, get after that fingerprint report on the electrical cord Coomer used, would you?"

"It's there, too, in the manila folder with his name on it. Not that anything showed up." Dorothy reached beneath her desk and came up with her purse. "If you don't mind, I think I'm going to take an early lunch."

"Uh, no. Go ahead." Jake knew that being asked was just a courtesy anyway. When your elderly secretary has known you since you were seven years old, it's as much like you work for her as she works for you, he reflected wryly. Her cheeks still unnaturally red, Dorothy nodded and stood up.

Beating a figurative hasty retreat, Jake closed the sliding glass door and turned to look at his grandfather, who was staring through the glass at Dorothy's retreating figure as if he'd never seen her before.

"What'd I say?" he asked plaintively, shifting his gaze to Jake.

Jake could have clued him in, but trying to graft tact onto his grandfather was about as worthwhile as trying to shoo away the gator that was now, from all obvious signs, enjoying a midmorning nap on his walk.

"No clue," he said, dismissing the episode from his mind and getting on to business at last. "So, we have any luck yet on tracing that call that came into Sarah's house last night?"

Pops grimaced. "Charlie"—one of Pops's cronies, and an agency employee—"did a real nice job on that, but it still didn't do no good. The call originated from a cell phone registered to an Edisto Island lady, Mrs. Linda Ross, real nice. She didn't use the phone a lot, hadn't missed it until I called to ask about it, but doesn't remember having it after Monday night, when she thinks she left it in her car. My guess is she either lost it or it was stolen. Either way, it don't help us a bit figuring out who made that call."

Jake blew out his breath in a sigh and dropped into the chair Pops had vacated earlier. He'd known that the call wouldn't be traceable, of course, at least not to the person who'd made it. Life was never that easy.

"No chance that she or any of her family had anything to do with it?" he asked without any real hope.

Pops shook his head. "Don't think so. She's a soccer-mom type, he's a doctor, two young kids, fine, upstanding people."

Jake closed his eyes for a minute. Sitting out here in the enervating heat, with the air so thick and moist you could almost swim in it and the swampy smell of water and green things curling beneath his nostrils, he was suddenly reminded of just how tired he was. The last two nights, he had gotten practically no sleep at all, and, he realized, he was starting to feel it.

"Sarah upset?" Pops asked.

Jake forced his eyes open and his mind back on track with an effort. Pops was sitting now, too, across the table from him, hands folded across his waist, looking thoughtfully off into the distance.

"You can imagine."

"Yeah. Terrible thing." Pops shook his head regretfully.

Jake didn't really feel like talking about it, so he switched the conversation back to business. "So what happened with DVS?"

Pops glanced at him and shrugged. "They were ticked because Austin"—a twenty-two-year-old who was the agency's newest hire and was still pretty much in training mode—"was letting all the shoplifters he caught off with a warning."

DVS was a huge drugstore chain with locations throughout the South, and landing their chainwide security contract would be a nice addition to the business. But DVS was privately owned and picky about who they did business with, so they'd insisted on putting Hogan & Sons Investigations through a trial run that amounted to running the security in one store for a month. Which Austin had apparently screwed up.

"What'd he do that for?"

"Felt sorry for them, he said." Pops grinned suddenly. "You gotta love that kid. He's got heart."

"You fire him?" Jake knew the answer to that before he even asked the question. In the agency's good-cop/bad-cop dramas, he was invariably the only one who got the whole bad-cop concept.

"Hell no, he's saving up money for grad school." Pops put his feet up on the lower rail and leaned back in his chair. "Don't worry, though. I fixed the DVS thing for us."

"How?" Jake was almost afraid to ask.

"I told 'em that if they'd give us the contract, we'd do the first three months of chainwide surveillance for free."

"What?" Jake sat bolt upright in his chair, his eyes riveted on his grandfather's face. There was a reason Pops had needed a buyout so badly that he'd called Jake home seven years before. On his watch, the agency had been hemorrhaging money. And this was one of the reasons why. "Damn it, Pops, do you have any idea . . .?"

His cell phone started to ring. It was in his pocket under the marshmallows. Jake pulled the bag out, dropped it on the table, and managed to get his phone open before the caller could hang up.

"Hogan."

"Uh, Jake? This is Austin."

Jake's eyes cut to Pops. A feeling of foreboding tightened his stomach. "Yeah?"

"You know how I was supposed to be watching Miss Mason at the courthouse?" No, Jake really hadn't known that. Dave Menucchi, septuagenarian buddy of Pops and reliable, longtime agency employee, was supposed to be keeping an eye on Sarah for the day. Just for Jake's peace of mind. On the down-low, which meant that nobody up to and including Sarah was supposed to catch him at it. "Well, I, um, can't find her."

11

"You can't find her?" Jake cast a narrow-eyed glance at Pops, who had propped his elbows on the table and was leaning toward him, listening with obvious concern.

"I followed her up from the basement, and then she stopped and was talking to these two men in the hall. I didn't want to walk right past her because I figured she'd make me, you know? So I ducked into the men's room. When I came out, she was gone, but I thought that was cool because she was scheduled to be in Courtroom A right then. Only she wasn't. Some guy was handling her case. As far as I can tell, she's not anywhere in the courthouse." He broke off, and Jake could almost feel him sweating through the phone. "I'm real sorry, Jake. What do you want me to do?"

It was too soon for the little *frisson* of alarm that snaked down Jake's spine, and he knew it. There were a million places Sarah could legitimately be. The thing was, though, so much had happened to her lately that his nerves were on edge.

"Stay put until I get back to you. Let me see if I can track her down."

Jake disconnected, scowled at his grandfather, who'd clearly heard everything, and punched the button that automatically connected his cell phone to Sarah's. "Maybe I'm disremembering this, but I thought I told you to tell *Dave* to keep an eye on Sarah."

The connection was made. Sarah's phone rang in his ear.

"I had to switch him with Austin. DVS didn't want Austin back."

Jake groaned. Then he listened to Sarah's away message; said, "Hey, call me back" after the freaking tone; and was on his feet and heading for the door before he finished talking.

"I thought you said you didn't think Sarah was in any real danger." Pops was on his feet, too, looking as worried as Jake felt. "You want me to come with you?"

"No, you go on and do those witness interviews we have scheduled this afternoon for Helitzer." Then, because he didn't want his grandfather fretting when there was probably no need, he added, "I *don't* think she's in any real danger, but I just don't feel like taking a chance on being wrong. I'll call you when I find her."

As an afterthought, and just in case, he grabbed his Glock out of his desk on the way out the door.

That man better be at home," Crystal said. She was sitting in the front passenger seat of Sarah's car, sucking nervously on a mint that Sarah had offered her. One leg was curled up beside her, and she was massaging her bare foot as she spoke. The missing stiletto was lying on its side in the passenger footwell. "I got to be at work at five. Friday's a big night at Godfather's."

"You think he can fix it?" Sarah asked. They were talking about Crystal's boyfriend, and her car, which, Sarah had discovered when she had walked disconsolately out of the courthouse, had died in a handicapped spot right out front. Coming down the wide courthouse steps, she had spotted Crystal and a pair of strange men—obviously passersby who had been bedazzled by copious cleavage into helping—peering beneath the hood of an older, pale yellow Lincoln. Sarah had stopped to see what was wrong, and the upshot of the matter was that she was presently giving Crystal a ride home so that, Crystal hoped, she would be able to rouse her presumably sleeping boyfriend (wherever he was, whatever he was doing, he wasn't answering the phone, which had led Crystal to conclude that he must still be in bed at noon-ish) and get him to return with her and fix her car.

"He fixed it before," Crystal said, crunching on the last of the mint. The faint scent of peppermint filled the car. As she kneaded the ball of her foot, she wiggled her perfectly manicured toes. "I'm just worried they'll tow it before we can get back."

It was a legitimate worry. Crystal had a handicapped tag hanging from her rearview mirror, left over from a broken leg suffered some months ago, but it had expired long since. All it would take was a cop with enough interest—or vision—to read the dates scribbled on the tag, and the car was gone. Sarah, however, was betting against there being such a cop. At least, not until the car had been there long enough to provoke interest in and of itself.

"It's just a thought, but next time you come to court, you might want to park in the lot behind the building. It's free."

Crystal shook her head. "Too many cop cars back there. In case you haven't noticed, cops don't like me much right now."

"I've noticed," Sarah said, but stopped short of adding that she was experiencing much the same phenomenon herself. Crystal kicked off her other shoe, changed positions, and started to work on the other foot.

"It's cause I'm on my feet fourteen hours a day," Crystal explained as she caught Sarah's sidelong glance. "They hurt all the time."

Sarah didn't bother to suggest that Crystal might find relief in switching to lower-heeled shoes. She'd been around Crystal enough now to understand that she considered the four-inch slides a vital part of the package.

"That sucks," she said instead, and Crystal laughed and nodded.

At that moment they were about fifteen miles west of Beaufort, having driven out along I-21 past the sprawling bedroom communities, heading toward Burton. About a mile back, right as the strip malls had started to be replaced by feed stores and log-home showcases and establishments selling John Deere tractors, they had turned off the main route onto a narrow country road that wound first through tobacco fields and then entered a ragged stretch of low country woods. Scrub pine grew shoulder to shoulder with palmettos and twenty-foot-tall banana trees amidst tangles of groundsel bushes covered in tiny white blossoms. Ahead, the blacktop forked. The left fork wound on through the woods. The right fork led out of the trees and over train tracks nestled into a bed of white gravel that gleamed in the sun.

"Which way?" Sarah asked.

"Right."

Sarah obediently went right, braking as the car reached the tracks, which were marked only with a small warning sign. She looked both ways, then bumped cautiously over. Once they were—almost literally, Sarah felt—on the wrong side of the tracks, she saw the trailer park immediately. Occupying perhaps a hundred acres of flat farmland, mobile homes were lined up in neat rows, most with older cars or pickup trucks parked out front, a fair number with such amenities as wading pools or gas grills alongside. Heat shimmering from the collective roofs of the small, metal community formed a hazy veil rising toward the sky. The sign at the entrance read *Paradise Homes,* but Sarah didn't think many people, including Crystal, had ever found much paradise within its confines. Just as she herself, who had spent her teenage years in a trailer park called Sunshine Estates that could have been this one's twin, had never found a lot of what was implied in the word *sunshine* when she had lived there.

Sarah could picture the inside of that trailer still: The aluminum front door led directly into a living room that was maybe eight by twelve feet, with cheap faux pine paneling on the walls and a pair of big jalousie windows directly opposite each other, one in the front wall and one in the back, neither of which admitted much light. In the living room had been the TV, an orange tweed couch, a brown plush chair, and a small round table with four chairs where they ate. To the right of the living room was her mother's bedroom, just large enough for a queen-sized bed and a dresser, the top of which was always crowded with the perfume bottles her mother liked to collect. To the left was the tiny galley kitchen, the bathroom/laundry room combination, and, last but not least, Sarah's room. Its walls, too, had been dark with the laminated paneling, and it was big enough for only a twin bed. But Sarah had hung bright yellow curtains at the two windows, put a red-and-yellow sunburst quilt she'd bought at a yard sale on her bed, and built shelves to hold her beloved paperbacks that were the only books she could afford. Their cheerful covers lining the walls had made what could have been a dark little hole of a room warm and welcoming. She had lost herself for hours in those books, and they had introduced her to worlds far different from Sunshine Estates. Introduced her to possibilities, to lives she could have that didn't involve drinking and fighting and broken marriages and constant worry about whether there would be enough money to pay the light bill or the rent. Sarah had longed for a life like that with the intensity of a starving child longing for food.

With her father long out of the picture, she and her thrice-divorced mother had moved into the tin can, as her mother had disdainfully referred to their new home, when Sarah was twelve. Compared to the rickety but spacious farmhouse in rural Santee County where they'd lived for the past two years with her mother's third husband and his teenage son and daughter, the trailer was definitely cramped quarters. But at least the violent fights between her mother and stepfather were over. Sarah had considered that a definite plus. And the trailer park was on the outskirts of Columbia, the state capital, which had seemed like a big city at the time to country-raised Sarah. There was even a bus to take her to school, which was her refuge and where she excelled. Her mother continued to drink herself into a stupor on the average of once a week—screwdrivers were her drink of choice; Sarah still couldn't stand the smell of orange juice—but that had been one of life's constants and Sarah had learned to deal with it long since. She coped by putting her mother to bed when she passed out on the floor, mixing her the tomato-juice-and-vodka hangover remedy she preferred when she woke up moaning in distress, going to work (part-time at the drugstore near the high school, and then, as she got older, waitressing) and to school, and retreating into books whenever reality got too awful, as it frequently did. Even well into her thirties, as she had been when they had lived in Sunshine Estates, her beautician mother had been the ultimate party girl: Liquor and men were the highlights of her life. Her daughter made up her mind at a young age to avoid both as much as possible.

Then, during Sarah's junior year of high school, Candy, as her mother liked her only child to call her, met Jerry Lowe. Lowe was a sober man, a lay preacher, and a charismatic despot who worked sporadically as a roofer. Candy married him, moved him into the trailer, and was soon totally under his thumb. Candy's drinking improved, but in every other way, life in Sunshine Estates went from routinely but bearably unhappy to nightmarish.

Lowe had an eye for his pretty new step-daughter. Candy, when Sarah told her about the roving hands, the "accidental" brushes of his body against hers, and finally the attempted forced kiss that had been the last straw, sided with Lowe and accused Sarah of enticing her new husband.

Three months shy of high-school graduation, Sarah was on her own. She moved out of the trailer and into town. She rented a room from an elderly couple who had turned their big, rundown old house into a boarding house for University of South Carolina students. Working two jobs, she managed to support herself while finishing high school and even, with the aid of good grades and sympathetic teachers, was able to put together a financial-aid package that would allow her to attend the University of South Carolina in the fall. She still saw her mother occasionally, but their relationship was tainted by Candy's continued dogged belief in Lowe. Sarah, she insisted, should just tell the truth, apologize, and all would be forgiven. It hurt to realize that her own mother was deliberately choosing not to believe her, but that was the way it was. Even at eighteen, Sarah was enough of a pragmatist to suck it up and get on with her life as best she could.

Then, into the picture had walked Robby Mason. A big, buff redhead with an easy laugh and enough charm for three men, he was two years older but, thanks to a stint in the military right out of high school, a freshman like herself. For the first time in her life, Sarah fell head over heels. By Christmas, she was pregnant; by February, Robby had done the right thing and married her; and two days after her nineteenth birthday in August, Lexie was born.

And Sarah's life changed forever. When that little red-haired baby was placed in her arms for the first time, when she looked down at her and met the big, blue eyes that were so like her own, she made a vow: Lexie was going to have a better life than anything she or Robby had ever known. With that in mind, Sarah had rededicated herself to school, and every minute that wasn't about school or work was about Lexie. Dismayed by Sarah's sudden conversion from adoring girlfriend to fiercely determined young mother, Robby had started looking elsewhere for excitement and eventually, after telling Sarah she just wasn't fun anymore and that he wasn't ready to be a father, had taken off. Just like that. What had hurt the most, Sarah realized after the initial shock, was that Lexie would grow up just as she herself had, in a broken home. There was nothing Sarah could do to make Robby come back, and when she was being honest with herself, she faced the truth that except for Lexie's sake, she really didn't want him to. The spark behind them had died when she'd realized he wasn't prepared to sacrifice an iota of his fun for the benefit of his daughter, or his wife. Left to make it on her own, Sarah had done just that: She'd gotten through college, and then, in an accomplishment she'd been so proud of, that she had assured little Lexie would make their lives better than anything that either of them could imagine, she had been accepted into the University of South Carolina School of Law. After her first year, Sarah had already been pegged as one of her class's stars. Her grades had been first-rate, and her work ethic, as one of her professors had told her, was simply outstanding. Which was why Sarah had won the coveted *paid* internship in the Beaufort County District Attorney's office the summer after her first year of law school—and why she and Lexie had been living in Beaufort the summer that Lexie disappeared.

But Sarah couldn't, wouldn't, think about that. Not now. There was no point in unlocking the door to the torture chamber that was the memory of that time. She had to concentrate on keeping her car on the narrow gravel road that led around the perimeter of the trailer park. She had to concentrate on breathing steadily, in and out. She had to concentrate on the cool rush of the air-conditioning against her bare arms—in deference to the steamy heat, she had shed her jacket in favor of her short-sleeved white blouse—and the smell of peppermint, and the rhythmic movements of the woman beside her as she continued to massage her feet.

In other words, she had to concentrate on the present.

"Oh, look, there he is. That's Eddie," Crystal said, the excitement in her voice chasing away the last clinging cobwebs of the past as Sarah pulled up in front of the battered double-wide to which the other woman had pointed.

Clearly energized by the sight of her boyfriend, Crystal sat up straight and slid her feet into her shoes as Sarah looked toward a man in a wife-beater and black nylon athletic shorts, who stepped through the screen door as though drawn by the sound of the tires crunching over gravel. With the screen banging shut behind him, he stopped on the small stoop to plant his fists on his narrow hips and stare hard at the car. Hastily undoing her seat belt, clearly in a hurry to get out of the car, Crystal threw Sarah a smile that was almost shy.

"Hey, thanks for the ride."

Sarah nodded. Crystal's boyfriend was something of a surprise. The picture she'd conjured up in her head was of a greasedhaired *Sopranos* type, or maybe someone vaguely hip-hop. This guy was at least a decade younger than Crystal, for one thing, and there was no bling, nothing flashy at all about him. He didn't even look to be one of those beer-guzzling, good-ole-boy types that, by default, she might have been able to imagine Crystal with. This man was at most in his mid-twenties, with shoulder-length dirty blond hair and corpse-pale skin that looked like it had never seen the sun. He was about five ten and not particularly muscular, and there was a just-crawled-out-from-under-a-rock quality to him that creeped Sarah out a little. That, plus Crystal's way-too-eager-to-please manner now that she had spotted him, made her wonder about just what kind of relationship they had.

"Eddie doesn't look too happy," Sarah observed in a carefully neutral tone as Crystal reached for the door handle. "You sure you're going to be all right?"

"Yeah. He's probably just wondering who I got in the car with me. He don't like me to hang around with strangers too much." Crystal opened the door and slid out. "If you were a man, he'd be pissed. He gets real jealous if he thinks I'm with another man. Well, except for work, that is. 'Cause then he knows it's my job."

It was stupid of her, Sarah knew, but she had gotten to where she felt protective of Crystal. Probably it was the whole trailer-park thing: In some way, it was almost like she and Crystal were sisters under the skin. She *wanted* Crystal to succeed, to get her new life on track. The woman might have made a few wrong turns along the way, but she was doing her best to overcome the obstacles fate had strewn in her path and make a life for herself with the tools she had to work with, and that was all any of them could do.

"You've got my number," Sarah said. "Call me if Officer McIntyre or anyone else like that bothers you again. Or if anything else comes up."

"Yeah, I will."

Closing the door, Crystal hurried across the gravel toward Eddie, who was still scowling at the car. Putting the transmission into reverse, Sarah backed out of the narrow driveway. Having reached the first of the two concrete blocks that served as steps to the stoop, Crystal turned and waved at her. Eddie's eyes narrowed as he glared at Sarah through the windshield.

The malevolence in his gaze made her frown.

Maybe there's glare on the windshield and he can't see that I'm a woman, Sarah thought. Maybe he thinks he's got a rival. Or maybe he's just an asshole.

All giving-the-stranger-the-benefit-of-the-doubt impulses aside, she was going with the latter.

Even as she drove away, she kept glancing back through the rearview mirror to see how he would greet Crystal. From his expression, she expected something, an argument, maybe a grabbed arm or a blow. Nothing like that happened, although admittedly the clouds of pale dust the tires kicked up from the gravel partially obscured her view. But as far as she could tell, they merely exchanged a few apparently unheated words, and then they went inside the trailer.

And Sarah was left to remind herself that insofar as anything other than her victim status was concerned, Crystal was *not* her problem. One of the first things you learn as a prosecutor is that you cannot get personally involved with the people you represent. There are too many problems, too much need, and you can't carry the weight of it all and function. She knew that, but still it was sometimes hard to remember that in the final analysis, the cases she took on and the people associated with them were just part of her job and nothing more.

Crystal included.

It was, Sarah saw as she left the mobile-home park behind and turned east onto I-21, nearly one o'clock. Right about now she should have been getting ready to appear before Judge Prince to argue against the defense's motion to suppress evidence in an arson-for-profit case. Instead, Duncan was handling it, and for the first time that she could remember in years, she had time on her hands and nothing at all scheduled to fill it.

Once, a long time ago, she would have been excited at the idea of a whole afternoon with nothing to do. The thing was, though, time was her enemy now. Time brought with it the opportunity to brood, to dwell, to go over details in her mind that were best left to lie undisturbed. Even now, as traffic flowed around her, as a semi rattled past and a camper hauling a boat cut in front of her and a teenage boy with spiked orange hair bopped to some unheard beat every time she glanced in her rearview mirror, she had to fight to keep from replaying Lexie's phone call in her mind. No, *not* Lexie's. A phone call made by some other little girl who couldn't pronounce the word *scared.* Who, in fact, mispronounced it in exactly the same way Lexie had.

What were the chances of that?

Probably better than the chances that her daughter, who would be twelve now, was alive, calling her, and still sounding exactly the same as she had at age five.

Especially given the fact that, as part of the searching behavior she had learned was typical for parents who have lost a child, it was possible—not certain, by any means, but *possible*—that she had projected onto the voice on the phone exactly the intonation she had most longed to hear.

Oh, God, was that the explanation? Had she simply heard that mispronounced "scehwed" because she had wanted so much to believe that it was really Lexie calling her?

A lump formed in her throat at the thought.

Stop it, Sarah ordered herself, and wrenched her mind off the phone call with what felt like a physical effort, forcing herself to concentrate on something else altogether. The Helitzer case. Yes, that was good: all-consuming. If she was going to win it, she had to go into court with every single *t* crossed and *i* dotted. The forensic evidence was both helpful and not. For every expert they had found to swear that the position in which the body had been found, for example, and the depth and shape of the injuries to the skull made an accidental fall unlikely, the defense would have another expert prepared to testify to the opposite. Hairs found on the body were consistent with the husband's, but since he *was* her husband, the defense could make a perfectly reasonable case that the hairs had every right to be there. Besides, other hairs had been found on the body as well, some still unidentified. To further weaken any case that might be made from forensics alone, the scrapings taken from beneath Susan's fingernails held no trace of foreign human tissue, which indicated that she had not fought back against whomever or whatever had killed her. Sarah's pet theory was that Susan had never seen the blow coming, that her husband had simply come up behind her and attacked her without warning. Sarah's go-to motive (which meant that she was still casting around to see if she could come up with something stronger before she had to lay it out for a jury) was that the couple had quarreled over Mitchell's girlfriend (she had him behind the eight ball on that one; the girlfriend was even prepared to testify) and Susan had threatened to leave him. As she had prepared to make good on her threat, Mitchell had struck her down. To put the case away, to feel confident that a jury would see what she saw in the evidence, what she would really like to find was some sort of record of prior violence on the part of Mitchell Helitzer, preferably against his wife or some other woman. So far, she'd come up with nothing, but Jake and his firm had been and would continue doing exhaustive witness interviews with people who had known Mitchell from childhood onward to uncover anything they could, all the way up to the day she needed to present it in court, so maybe something would still turn up.

Barring the discovery of a figurative smoking gun, though, the case could go either way. To win justice for Susan Helitzer, she was going to need every ounce of skill she possessed. A few mistakes on the defense's part and a dollop of luck besides were probably more than she could hope for, but they would be welcome, too.

The bebopping kid roared by on the left,

distracting her. After he had passed, Sarah glanced reflexively in her rearview mirror again.

Her eyes widened.

A squad car was closing on her fast. Not as if it wanted her to pull over, but as if its driver was in a hurry to get somewhere. The thing that made her pulse rate quicken, though, was the identity of the driver: Brian McIntyre. With his partner on suspension until the grand jury chose to either indict or dismiss the rape case that she would bring before it the following week, he was alone in the car.

It just seemed way too suspicious that he was so far outside his usual haunts and coming from the direction of Crystal's residence besides. Had he been cruising around Paradise Homes?

Attempted intimidation of a witness was the phrase that sprang to mind, but of course she had no way to prove it. She didn't even have a camera with which to take a picture of him in case a way of proving what he might or might not be up to occurred to her later. The best she could do was call her office voicemail and leave a message for herself about what was happening. At least then there would be a record of McIntyre's presence this far out on I-21, with the date and time automatically affixed to it.

Sarah reached down to conduct a quick, one-handed fumble in the console between the seats before she remembered that she had left her phone in her blazer pocket. And her blazer, like her briefcase, was locked in the trunk of the car.

Okay, the whole make-a-contemporaneous-record thing clearly isn't going to happen.

Not that it really mattered. A picture taken through her car window wouldn't have proved that McIntyre was harassing Crystal. Neither would a voicemail message recording his presence behind her. He had as much right to be on I-21 as every other car on the road. As much right as she did herself.

Even if he'd been served with the TRO—which he hadn't yet, there was no way there had been enough time—he was not within the prescribed hundred yards of Crystal in any case. Her suspicions, coupled with his presence on I-21, were simply not enough to even accuse him of anything, much less haul him before Judge Wessell with the objective of having him thrown in jail.

There was, Sarah realized with a galling sense of helplessness as the squad car narrowed the gap between them, simply nothing she could do. Except glare at him through the rearview mirror, of course.

McIntyre was right behind her now, in full uniform, so close that she was able to see every detail of his body to mid-chest, where the dashboard blocked it from view. A tall, skinny man with brown hound-dog eyes and a black combover that merely brought attention to what it was trying to hide—namely, that he was going bald—McIntyre hadn't come within Sarah's orbit before Crystal had accused his partner of rape. Since then, she had learned a lot about him, and very little of what she had learned was reassuring. He and his partner, Gary Bertoli, were said to be as close as brothers. They generally worked the rougher areas around the bars and nightspots of downtown, and they were known on the streets as, in the words of one of her confidential informants, "arrogant pricks." Like Bertoli, McIntyre was married with children. Unlike Bertoli, who was laying low in the aftermath of being suspended, he apparently didn't have the good sense to stay away from the victim in the interim before formal charges were brought—or not.

A big silver Suburban barreled past on the left, and Sarah, acting on impulse more than anything, pulled into the passing lane and fell in behind it, then had to stomp the gas to keep up as the Suburban flew past the line of slower-moving vehicles on the right. The roar of speeding traffic filled her ears. Her Sentra shook slightly as it sought to keep up with the behemoth in front of it. Another glance in her rearview mirror caused Sarah to grit her teeth: Despite her instinctive attempt to get away from him, McIntyre was still behind her. Practically on her bumper, in fact. If for any reason she was forced to hit her brakes, he would run right into her.

She could see him clearly through the mirror. She was almost positive—not entirely, but almost—that he could see her, too. That he knew perfectly well who it was behind the wheel of the car he was tailgating. That he was, in fact, staying so close behind her on purpose.

The question was, what purpose?

Brian McIntyre had been one of the first cops on the scene when she had been shot. The thought flashed through her brain like a bolt of lightning.

Frantic questions followed in its wake: What if the third shooter theory was wrong? What if this Floyd Parker, whose pickup by the cops had been making her feel infinitely safer, had had nothing to do with her being shot at all?

What if McIntyre was on her tail for the purpose of taking another shot at her? Or making some other—could anyone say forced car accident?—attempt on her life?

Sarah's heart pounded. Her shoulders tensed. Her mouth went dry. The steering wheel vibrated against her palms as both hands clamped around it. A glance back in her rearview mirror confirmed what she already suspected: McIntyre knew exactly who was behind the wheel of the car in front of him.

For the briefest of milliseconds, his eyes met hers through the mirror. Still, it was enough. He knew it was her, all right. There was no way she was wrong about the recognition she saw in his face.

Sarah took a deep breath, gritted her

teeth, and switched her attention back to the road.

Sandwiched now between an eighteen-wheeler on her right and the narrow strip of grassy median that was all that separated her from a rush of oncoming traffic to her left, Sarah realized that she had nowhere to go. Whatever McIntyre had in mind, there was nothing she could do to thwart him for the moment. All she could do was drive. If she hit her brakes, if she tried to slow down, he might very well slam into her. If he slammed into her, his heavy Crown Victoria would force her much lighter car into the back of the oversized, truck-like Suburban in front of her, or to the right, into the rattling metal box of the semi's trailer, or to the left, for a head-on collision with oncoming traffic.

None of which offered much chance for her to emerge from her vehicle alive and unharmed.

Which might very well be the point.

The bottom line was: no prosecutor, no case. All it would take would be a little tap on her rear bumper, and Bertoli got his own customized get-out-of-jail-free card.

Sarah felt sweat popping out along her

hairline. The steel wall of the semi to her right blurred into silver nothingness. The median to her left became a thin green line. Keeping her eyes fixed on the boxlike rear of the Suburban in front of her, she concentrated on her driving as her speedometer crept up toward eighty. Way too fast for this stretch of road. Catastrophic in an accident. Nearly thirty miles over the speed limit.

Where, oh where, was one of those fabled rural speed traps when you needed it? Somebody cue up Boss Hogg.

Sarah cursed herself for not remembering that her cell phone was in her jacket before she put it in her trunk. Besides turning on her flashers, which she couldn't see accomplishing much under the circumstances, she had no way to summon help. She was as much on her own in the middle of this bright and busy highway as she would be if she were being pursued through a deserted forest in the dead of night.

Glancing compulsively in her rearview mirror, her gaze encountered McIntyre's again. His bumper was inches from hers, so close that the merest tap on her brakes would cause an almost instantaneous crash. She knew it, and he knew it, too.

As his gaze held hers for the fraction of a heartbeat that she permitted herself to look away from the road, she could tell from the way his eyes mocked her even as his thin lips stretched into a gloating smile.

He knew she was afraid, and was laughing at her.

The knowledge sent fury coursing through her veins. Her spine stiffened. Her chin came up. Whether she was about to die or not, she wasn't going cringing into that good night.

Thrusting her hand into the air where he would be sure to see it, Sarah gave him a one-fingered wave.

We who are about to die salute you, creep.

At least, she saw as she checked his reaction in the mirror, she had the satisfaction of knowing that she'd managed to wipe the smirk off his face.

Then the Suburban pulled on past the semi, and Sarah, following, glimpsed a little patch of daylight between the semi's cab and the car in front of it. That was all she needed. Grasping the wheel with both hands again, holding her breath, she whipped her car into it with maybe a foot to spare at both ends. The semi honked its horn in noisy protest. McIntyre zoomed past.

And flipped her the bird.

Every muscle in Sarah's body seemed to go limp as, keeping close on the Suburban's bumper, the squad car then sped on out of sight.

She was still feeling slightly shaky fifteen minutes later as she slowed for the red light at the intersection where the Quik-Pik reigned. It was once again open for business. Since it was a Friday afternoon in August, which meant that many people got off early from work and were gearing up for their various weekend pursuits despite a forecast that called for a repeat of last night's shower, traffic at the store was heavy. Shoppers hurried in and out of the doors. Cars gassed up at the pumps. More were parked in a row in front of the big windows, which had already been replaced, even to the point of having the usual advertising banners hung in them: a twelve-pack of Pepsi for $3.99; ice at fifty cents for ten pounds; Saturday night's Lotto. The coroner hadn't even released Mary's body yet, but already the tribute to her was gone from the big sign out front, which was back to trumpeting the price of gas in foot-high black letters.

And so the wheel turned and life went on, just like life always did.

Sarah wondered who was working the cash register. Had they known Mary? No way to guess. Were they afraid of dying at the hands of robbers? If they were, they were sublimating that fear to the necessity of earning a living.

The bottom line was, everybody had to eat.

Speaking of eating, she wasn't sure how much dog food there was in the house, or how much human food, either, for that matter, but she knew even as she had the thought that she would never be able to step foot in that Quik-Pik again as long as she lived.

She had just become an official Kroger shopper.

The light turned green, and Sarah drove on through the intersection, eager to put as much distance between herself and the Quik-Pik as possible. As she passed Wang's Oriental Palace, she glanced quickly down the alley where she had last seen the other survivor of that terrible night. Today the alley was empty, of course, except for the Dumpster and the sunflowers and ragweed and thistles blowing in the breeze.

Another four blocks and she would be home, for the first time in years, early on a Friday afternoon.

Checking the dashboard clock, Sarah realized that it wasn't even two o'clock yet. She still had hours and hours of time to fill. The Helitzer file was in her briefcase; she could go home and work on that, or the Lutz case, which was also in there, or make some phone calls, or . . .

Sarah realized suddenly that the only place she wanted to be less than the Quik-Pik was her own home.

Just thinking about walking in that front door made her heart feel as if it were being squeezed by a giant fist. Lexie's voice, or rather, the voice from that damned phone call, would be impossible to silence. Sarah knew that she needed to check the toys she had packed away, the toys that Jake had found scattered across her bedroom floor, just to see if there was anything amiss with them, anything that would shed some kind of light on why they had been out.

But she already knew that she wasn't ready to face going through those toys either. Not right now.

The pain was too close to the surface.

On impulse, she turned right at the next cross street. There would never be a better opportunity than right now to check out where Angela Barillas lived.

12

Beaufort Landing Apartments were public housing, which meant that the main criteria for moving in was that you had to be poor. Twenty identical brick boxes were set at angles on a flat, five-acre parcel of ground. One hundred twenty families overflowed those boxes, leaving laundry hanging on balconies and bicycles crowding hallways and Dumpsters piled high. Roughly half that number of beat-up-looking cars waited in the parking lot. Sparse strips of burned-up grass stretched between the buildings like the latticework on fancy apple pies. A few ratty bushes straggled tiredly here and there. There was not a single tree to be seen.

It was summer, so the kids weren't in school. Some were in day care, some were at camp somewhere, and some had other places to be besides this sweltering island in the middle of the mixed residential/commercial district, which was quite a few steps down the social ladder even from Sarah's own modest neighborhood. Still, there were enough children swarming over the metal playground equipment so that she had some hope of finding her quarry.

After parking her car, Sarah got out.

Immediately, the steamy heat embraced her like a too-friendly relative. Tall purple-gray thunderheads were piling up in the distance like mountains at the edge of a field of sky blue, and the air already seemed to be taking on additional moisture in anticipation of the coming rain. Sarah squinted against the glare coming off the parked cars, and her headache kicked it up a notch, reminding her that her pain medication was wearing off. Her knees felt wobbly, and as she paused for a minute to make sure they were with the program, the requisite fine sheen of sweat broke over her, making her clothes feel as if they were sticking to her skin. She'd forgotten she was wearing pantyhose and heels along with her skirt and blouse until the hothouse conditions reminded her. There was nothing to do about it, she acknowledged as she sucked it up and headed toward the play area, which was in the middle of the complex. She had no other clothes or shoes with her, and stripping off her pantyhose wouldn't be worth the effort.

Rattling window units and the *swoosh* of an occasional passing car formed a backdrop to the shrieking children. Sarah inhaled the scent of hot tar and fabric softener—somewhere nearby someone was obviously doing laundry—as she rounded the corner of the nearest building and then hesitated, surveying the scene. The strips of grass converged into a modest rectangle. What had seemed like dozens of children playing there sorted itself out into perhaps fifteen, most of them looking younger than ten. The children were a mix of genders and ethnic types, some scaling the metal polygon climbing apparatus, some dangling on creaky swings, some digging holes in a nearby patch of earth that from the holes already in it had obviously long been given over to that purpose. Two girls worked energetically at keeping a tired-looking see-saw in operation. A boy hurtled down a dented slide, screaming that the metal surface was too hot as he descended on his back. Like all the others, he was, of course, wearing shorts. He kicked his bare legs in the air all the way down, clearly trying to keep them off the hot slide.

As far as Sarah could tell, adults, like trees, were nonexistent. Perhaps they were supervising from inside, watching the play area out the windows.

Somewhat to her surprise, Sarah spotted Angela Barillas almost at once. She was sitting alone on one of several metal benches that had been placed around the play area, clearly for the use of the nowhere-in-evidence supervising adults.

Today the child was wearing a gray T-shirt that was a size or two too large with baggy purple shorts. She sat cross-legged, with her head bent so that her tangle of coffee-brown hair spilled forward, hiding her face. A book was open on her lap.

Little girls in general tugged at Sarah's

heart to the point where she tended to avoid them whenever possible. A little girl with a book—that hit so close to home that her throat tightened and she almost turned away.

Like herself as a child, Lexie had loved books. From the time she was old enough to understand, Sarah had read to her every single night before bed. Winnie-the-Pooh had been a particular favorite of them both. Sarah had teasingly called her daughter Tigger, telling her that it was because she was bouncy and full of fun, fun, fun. It also had more than a little to do with her coppery curls, but since, at age five, Lexie was already starting to bemoan the genetic tie that had made her a redhead, Sarah hadn't mentioned that.

She'd been using those beloved Winnie-the-Pooh books to try to teach Lexie to read right before she'd disappeared, and making good progress with it, too.

The memory made Sarah ache. But it did not make her leave.

Taking a deep breath, she sat down on the bench beside Angela, careful to keep some space between them. The girl looked up, her big, brown eyes widening in surprise and then—was it horror?—as she clearly recognized Sarah.

"Hi." Sarah braced for the possibility that the child might very well bolt. "Remember me? I'm Sarah."

"Are you a ghost?" Angela's voice was barely louder than a breath. Her eyes were now as round as hubcaps.

Sarah shook her head. "No. Of course not. Anyway, who ever heard of a ghost with a Band-Aid?" She touched it. "Or one that showed up at a playground in the middle of the day, for that matter."

Angela still regarded her suspiciously but, Sarah thought, with a touch less fear. "You got shot. I saw you. Just like Mary. She died."

"I didn't die, though. I just got this Band-Aid."

Sarah saw relief flicker across the child's face, and realized that Angela was prepared to take her at her word. But if she had thought that persuading the small skeptic that she wasn't a ghost might improve their relationship, she clearly had another think coming. Instead of looking scared, the little girl now scowled fiercely at her.

"So what do you want, then?" she asked. Her tone was as hostile as her expression.

"I just wanted to make sure you got home okay yesterday. Your sister—that was your sister you were carrying, right?—looked heavy."

"She weighs a *ton.*" Some of the child's hostility dissipated as Sarah hit on what was obviously something with which she wholeheartedly agreed. Angela cast a quick glance at the dirt-diggers, and Sarah, following her gaze, thought she recognized the smallest of the children grubbing away as her littlest sister. "I got to watch her, though. Mama says she's my 'sponsibility."

"What's her name?" Sarah asked, anxious to keep this relatively friendly exchange going.

"Sophia."

"How old is she?"

"Three." Angela shot another quick look at her sister, then scowled at Sarah again as she obviously remembered her grievance. "Why didn't you try to help Mary, the other night in the store?"

Sarah's smile faltered. Childlike, Angela had gone right to the heart of what was troubling her, and Sarah quite simply didn't know what to answer.

"I didn't know how to," she said after a moment spent deciding that absolute truth was her only option. "I was scared, and I couldn't think of anything to do to help."

Angela's frown eased a little. "I was scared, too." She glanced down at her book and sighed. "I really liked Mary. She was nice. Why did they have to kill her?"

Sarah shook her head. She had no answer for that. "It's hard when people we care about die."

Angela nodded in solemn agreement. "Sometimes she'd give us things from the store. The night the bad men came, I walked up there and she said I could get some baloney out of the case and take a loaf of bread. 'Cause there wasn't nothing at home to eat, and Sergio was hungry. You know how boys are."

There was a wealth of affectionate contempt in her tone as she said that last.

"Sergio's one of your brothers?"

"Yeah. He's five. Lizbeth is seven. I'm nine, and Rafael is ten. Usually Rafael takes care of Sergio, and I take care of Lizbeth and Sophia. Only Rafael couldn't go to the store that night, on account of he was sick. So I had to go."

"Your mom wasn't home?"

Angela shook her head. "She was at the restaurant, working. She works at Wang's until midnight most nights. Then during the day she's at the drugstore. She comes home in between and fixes supper. Or sometimes, if she doesn't have time, she gets us food at Wang's and sticks it outside in a garbage bag, so nobody won't know what it is. She says she'd get fired if they knew." Angela shrugged. "It's hard being a grown-up. You got to make lots of money for rent and food and stuff."

"I know."

A beat passed in which they both watched the playing children. A gusting breeze blew through, ruffling hair and flapping laundry. The brief stir in the humidity was welcome, and Sarah recognized it for what it was: a warning of rain to come. A glance at the gathering clouds on the horizon confirmed it. They were stacking up higher than ever, and starting to move inland.

"When I get a little older, I'm going get a

job and help my mama. So she won't have to work so hard."

The vow touched Sarah's heart. Clearly, Angela might lack material things, but she was loved. As far as Sarah was concerned, the word *neglectful* was no longer quite so easy to apply to Angela's mother.

"Your mom would be really proud to hear you say that."

"See, she don't have no one else to help her. It's just her and us kids now."

"So where's your dad?"

"Oh, he took off a long time ago. Sergio and Sophia's dad took off, too. Mama says good riddance to 'em, and she don't want no more men."

Bravo for Mama. Sarah was starting to like the woman, sight unseen.

"Hey, Angie. You seen Serge?" A young, thin boy ran up to the bench and stopped, planting his hands on his hips and bending almost double as he fought to catch his breath. It was hard to be certain, but he had the same coffee-colored hair, tan complexion, and slim build that Angie did, and looked vaguely familiar besides. Sarah was pretty certain that this must be the oldest

Barillas sibling. What had Angie said his name was? Rafael? And he was ten.

"Did you lose him again?" Angie looked more disgusted than alarmed. Turning down the corner of the page she was on, she closed the book. It was called *Inkheart,* Sarah saw at a glance, and realized with a pang that it must have been published fairly recently. She, the child who had read everything, had never read it. Lexie, who had loved books, too, would never get a chance to read it. Sarah was still dealing with the unfairness of that as Angie unfolded her coltish legs to get to her feet. "You know you got to watch him every minute. Mama'll skin you alive if he's lost."

"He's not *lost.*" With a last wheezing breath, Rafael straightened to his full height, which meant that the top of his head was at approximately the same level now as Sarah's. The thing was, though, she was sitting down. "We was having a race, is all, and he got away from me. For a little kid, he's pretty fast."

There were equal parts admiration and envy in his tone.

Angie's expression had turned censorious. "You know you're not supposed to be running anyway. You got asthma, remember?"

With the book clutched close to her thin chest, she scanned the play area as she spoke, clearly searching for the missing Sergio.

"Well, you're not supposed to be talking to strangers," Rafael retorted. He was looking at Sarah now as a suspicious frown formed on his face. "Hey, isn't this that lady who was chasing us the other day? The one you said was dead?"

"Hi, Rafael." Sarah thought about standing up but was afraid of scaring the children off. "I'm Sarah. And I am definitely not dead."

"You can kind of tell by the Band-Aid," Angie said to her brother in a helpful tone.

Sarah smiled at the boy. Rafael continued scrutinizing her as if he remained not entirely convinced that she was, indeed, among the living.

Note to self: Definitely need to invest in some blush.

"There he is!" Angie pointed toward the apartment building directly opposite. A swiftly closing door caught Sarah's eye.

Seconds later, a small, impish face pressed against the glass in the top of the door.

"Serge!" Rafael took off in hot pursuit. The small face disappeared from the window, and Sarah gathered that the chase was on.

"You're not supposed to run!" Angie yelled after her brother. If Rafael heard, he made no sign. Angie shook her head in a very adult gesture of disgust, then looked back at Sarah.

"You want anything else? 'Cause we got to go in now. It's getting close to Sophia's nap time."

What to say that wouldn't sound impossibly clumsy—or intrusive?

"Do you have food in the house? I could go get some groceries." Okay, so that was probably both clumsy and intrusive. The thought that Angie and her siblings might be hungry bothered her a lot.

Angie shook her head, already on the move toward her sister. "It's Friday. Mama'll go to the store."

Friday being payday, Sarah realized as she hurried to fall into step beside her.

"I'd like us to be friends, Angie. You know, the two of us went through a really bad experience together. Maybe we can make something good come out of it."

Angie cast her a sidelong glance. She was looking suspicious again. Clearly, her mother's warnings about strangers were percolating through her head. Smart kid— smart mother.

"Yeah, okay." Angie's tone held no sincerity at all. Sarah realized that the child was anxious to get rid of her now. Maybe she was afraid her mother would find out that she'd been talking to a stranger, and she'd get in trouble. Or maybe she just couldn't help associating Sarah with Mary's death. In any case, they reached the digging spot— not a sandbox, but a strip of grass where children had apparently, at some previous time, just started digging holes—and Angie stopped beside her sister, who was plunked down on the ground, gouging away at the just barely damp earth with a spoon.

"Come on, So. It's time to go in."

Sophia looked up, her dirt-caked spoon suspended in midair. She was a dirty-faced cherub with eyes the size and color of walnuts and tangled curls hanging mop-like to her shoulders. Her pink T-shirt was streaked with dirt, and the front right pocket of her blue terry-cloth shorts was ripped almost off so that it hung precariously by one corner. Her chubby little feet were bare and filthy.

They reminded Sarah of Lexie's feet. Lexie had loved to run around barefoot in the summer. Like the rest of her, her feet had been childishly plump, and they'd often been dirty. . . .

Sarah's heart give a great, painful throb.

This was why she avoided little girls. In the thousand different ways that they resembled Lexie, they each had the power to break her heart.

"No," Sophia said mutinously, and threw the spoon. It flew harmlessly past, but Angie, with the air of an exasperated mother, swooped down on her little sister and hauled her into her arms.

"No, no, no, no, no!" Sophia screamed, struggling. Angie juggled both the enraged toddler and her book with practiced ease. From somewhere she produced a pink pacifier, which she thrust into Sophia's open mouth. For a moment the issue hung in the balance, but then Sophia clamped her lips around the pacifier and peace once again reigned.

"Tell your mother we talked, okay? And that I'll phone her," Sarah called after the retreating Angie. Leaving a verbal message with a reluctant nine-year-old seemed inadequate, but at the moment she was feeling an almost overwhelming need to escape. The two little girls, the one with her book and the other with her plump cheeks and bare feet and toddler temper, were too vivid a reminder of what she had lost. "Bye, Angie. Bye, Sophia."

Neither one of them answered. Angie was already halfway to the building the boy had entered, Sophia propped on her hip. Sarah had the feeling that she was well on her way to being forgotten.

"Lizbeth! We got to go in!" Angie yelled over her shoulder, and the third sister, who Sarah had not realized was on the jungle gym, came running. She looked like a smaller version of Angie as she hurried to join her sisters.

Sarah watched them until they disappeared inside the building, then turned to leave. Another breezy gust swept through the complex, blowing sheets of newspaper out of a nearby Dumpster so that they sailed through the air like gulls. The day was darkening as the thick bank of rain clouds rolled in from the sea, and the gathering gloom almost exactly matched her mood. The last two days had left her feeling fragile, mentally even more than physically. Like drops of water wearing away rock, each reminder of Lexie was slowly but steadily eroding the defenses she had built up so painstakingly over the years. If she wasn't careful, if she didn't re-gird her defenses and carefully guard her bruised and bloodied heart from further trauma, the results could be bad. She would once again be left with nothing to protect her from the throbbing core of pain at the center of her being that had never gone away and, she was beginning to fear, never really would.

A squad car trolled down the most distant lane of the parking lot, and Sarah eyed it narrowly as she headed toward her car. It was, she realized, the first time in her life that the sight of a police car had provoked automatic wariness.

Welcome to how the other half lives, she told herself wryly, even as she took only a few seconds to dismiss the possibility that it could be McIntyre. She was as sure as it was possible to be that he hadn't followed her, and, anyway, it wasn't his car. No, this was a routine patrol, designed to make the residents of the complex feel safe and would-be wrongdoers feel nervous.

And never mind that she was feeling nervous, too.

The parking lot was filling up now as the people who had taken off from work a little early to get a head start on the weekend continued to come home. A heavy-set, fifty-ish woman in some kind of blue uniform huffed and puffed as she walked past Sarah, heading toward the buildings. A younger Latina woman got out of a green Taurus, then opened the back door to get a little boy out of his car seat. A tall black man paused beside his white Blazer on the far side of the lot, watching the cruiser with the kind of stillness that hinted of prior unpleasant experience with the police. No doubt sensing fear, the officer drove on over to talk to him.

Sarah was so busy watching their interaction that she had her door unlocked and her hand on the handle when she saw it.

A finger or something similar had scrawled a single word in the fine layer of dust on the driver's-side window of her car: *Eeyore.*

It hit her like a jolt of electricity to the chest.

She froze, staring. Her eyes widened. Her heart jackhammered. Her breathing suspended. Her stomach dropped clear down to the soles of her shoes. The world seemed to tilt on its axis.

Her keys dropped from her hand to hit the ground with a small, metallic clatter.

Eeyore was the code word that she and Lexie had chosen, the secret reassurance that was to be used if anyone other than Sarah ever tried to pick up Lexie. No one had known about it except the two of them.

Yet here it was. Written in dust on her car window.

Sarah didn't even realize that her knees had given way until they smacked against the hot asphalt beside the car.

13

In the end, as far as the police were concerned, a word scrawled in dust on a car window didn't amount to very much. Even *that* word. Even when Sarah reminded them about Lexie and told them what the word meant. It wasn't even that they were against her, angry at her, punishing her for pressing a rape case against two of their own. It was just that they weren't all that interested.

Were even, in fact, a little perturbed that while they were dealing with Sarah's collapse and subsequent near hysterical demands, the black guy in the Blazer took advantage of the commotion to drive away. Now there, their attitudes seemed to say, went some real crime.

If she hadn't used every bit of her clout as an Assistant DA, they would have done nothing at all. As it was, she managed to get a couple of detectives she knew on the scene, managed to get pictures taken of the window and have the left side of the car dusted for fingerprints and some of the gathered residents questioned.

Nobody knew anything.

"Even if they did, they wouldn't tell us," Detective Carl Sexton told her as the mobile crime unit was packing up in preparation for leaving the scene. His blue eyes were as baggy and hooded as a bloodhound's, but there was sympathy for her in their rheumy depths. He was gray-haired, maybe five eight or so and a little paunchy, one year away from retirement and the father of three grown daughters, which in Sarah's opinion made all the difference in his attitude this afternoon. She had worked with him on numerous cases, and knew him to be a stand-up guy. Better yet, he didn't seem to hold Crystal's case against her.

"Could've been a kid just playing around,

nothing to do with your daughter at all." His partner, Detective Janet Kelso, was a trim brunette in her forties. She rested an arm on the hood of the patrol car and leaned in to talk to Sarah, who was sitting in the cruiser's backseat with the door open, watching as the police did their work. "Or . . ."

Her eyes rested significantly on Sarah's hands, which were clenched in her lap. Sarah realized in the few seconds that her gaze locked with Kelso's that her physically subordinate position worked for the detectives in that she had to look up at them, which theoretically placed them in a position of power. She'd used the whole power position technique herself more than once while interviewing witnesses. But she was too physically and mentally drained at the moment to take back her authority by sliding out of the car and standing up.

"I already told you, I didn't write that word on my window," she said wearily. "Why would I?"

Kelso shrugged.

"It was just something that we needed to clear up." At least Sexton had the grace to sound apologetic.

"Whoever did this almost has to be the same person who made the phone call to my house last night. The one that sounded like it was from my daughter."

She'd had to go through the whole story again. The phone call that had been earth-shattering to her was, as far as the police department in general was concerned, a few sentences on a report that probably still had yet to be filed. It was one among hundreds of pieces of paper that would be generated over the weekend, and it would be lost among the crush of constantly accumulating paperwork. Unless she saw to it that it wasn't. Which she fully intended to do.

"We're going to follow up on that, too." Sexton's tone was soothing, while Kelso looked impatient.

"You ever consider that those pain meds you're taking might be making you hallucinate?" Despite her expression, Kelso's question wasn't unkind. With a significant glance at Sarah's Band-Aid and obvious knowledge of the wound she had recently suffered, Kelso had already inquired about any medications Sarah was on. Sarah had answered honestly. *Bad move,* she thought now. But then, the truth was the truth, wherever it led. At least Kelso was exploring the possibilities. "A doctor put my sister on codeine once, and she was seeing wolves in the bathroom."

"There's a record of the phone call," Sarah pointed out.

"But not what was said."

"No. Not what was said."

The crime unit van rolled past, on its way out of the lot, just as a fat drop of rain splattered on the pavement near Kelso's feet. Thunder rumbled overhead, the sound more of a warning growl than a roar.

"Uh-oh." Kelso glanced up.

"Wouldn't you know," Sexton said as more raindrops fell, striking his shoulder and Kelso's cheek and the pavement again with ominous *plops.* "I was supposed to play golf after work."

The two patrol officers whose cruiser Sarah was sitting in hurried back to their car.

"All done here," one of them said as Sexton glanced at them. They slid inside the cruiser, clearly eager to get in out of the rain that was beginning to fall in a slow but steady rhythm. The driver, a recent Police Academy graduate whose name Sarah couldn't remember, twisted around to look at her through the mesh barrier that separated the front seats from the back.

"Can we give you a lift somewhere, ma'am?"

That *ma'am* caught her attention. He was a beardless youth of, maybe, twenty-six or-seven. At most five years younger than she was, which begged the question: Just how old did she look, anyhow?

She felt ancient, used up, destroyed by grief. Clearly some of that showed.

"No. Thanks." Sarah took a deep breath and got out of the car. Drops of rain sprinkled down on her as if she were a hunk of meat being salted for the grill. The wet splashes felt good against her skin. The damp-earth smell of rain hung in the air, and she breathed it in deeply in an effort to reorient herself to the present. She was still in shock, she knew, still focused so much on Lexie and the past that the here and now was a little fuzzy. Sexton and Kelso had stepped back to give her room to get out, and as she stepped out of the way of the door, Sexton closed it behind her and waved the cruiser off.

It left with a *swoosh* of tires on pavement.

A glance around the parking lot told Sarah that the small crowd that had gathered was leaving, too, making haste to get inside before they got soaked. As far as they were concerned, the show in the parking lot was clearly ending, and, anyway, nobody wanted to stand around in the rain.

There was nothing left for Sarah to do but walk over to her car. It was a journey of perhaps thirty feet, but it felt impossibly far. The rain was falling faster now, wetting her hair and blouse, spilling down her cheeks like tears.

Tears from heaven. The phrase twisted like a knife in her gut.

Eeyore was almost unreadable by the time she stood next to the driver's-side door, looking down at it, smeared by the residue of the dark powder they'd used to take fingerprints from the glass and metal, and now, along with the powder, in the process of being washed away by rain. Sarah watched the fat drops sliding down the glass, obliterating the *E,* the *y,* the *o,* and felt her eyes burn with tears of her own.

No. She would not cry. Not again.

Fiercely, she blinked the tears back and

swallowed hard to ease the lump forming in her throat.

All she could do for Lexie now was be strong.

"You sure you don't want a lift, Sarah?" Sexton was beside her, and Kelso, too, Sarah saw as she glanced up at them. They were standing in the now steadily falling rain, watching her, getting wet on her behalf, and she felt vaguely bad about that. "One of us could drive your car home for you. It'd be no trouble."

"No, I'll be fine, thanks."

At least her voice was strong, stronger than she felt. Her hands were steady, too, as reached beneath the now almost unreadable *Eeyore* to grasp the handle and open the door. Unless she was ready to believe that her daughter was a spirit, a ghost, and was trying to reach out to her from the great beyond, then this, like the phone call, was the work of a person. A malicious, sick, twisted soul who wanted to wound her past bearing.

If she crumpled, if she gave way to grief, then they won. She would be damned before she would give them that satisfaction.

She got in, glad to be out of the rain but

not closing the door yet because Sexton and Kelso were still standing there, looking at her. Except for them, the entire parking lot area was now empty of people. Everyone had disappeared inside.

"I'll put a Priority One on those fingerprints." Sexton had to raise his voice to be heard over the quick patter of the rain. His hair was rapidly being plastered against his skull, his light gray suit jacket was turning splotchy from the shoulders down, and his face was slick and wet.

"You never know, something may turn up." Kelso said that in a way that told Sarah the detective held out little hope of it. Then she looked at Sexton. "You ready to go?"

"Yeah."

Kelso gave Sarah a tight little smile, then hurried off toward their car, ducking her head against the quickening shower.

"We'll do what we can, Sarah," Sexton said. "I know this is hard for you."

"I appreciate it."

Sexton nodded and turned away, too, walking quickly after Kelso. Sarah closed her door and put the key in the ignition. The interior of the car was surprisingly dark and smelled of her damp clothes. Starting the engine, she turned the headlights on low, backed out of the parking space, then put the transmission in drive and followed Sexton and Kelso out of the lot. Turning on the windshield wipers, she kept her eyes glued to the back of their unmarked car as the sound of the wipers' gentle swishing joined in with the soothing rush of the rain and the slight squelching of the tires to create a should-have-been soporific backdrop. Since she was in such a state that her surroundings were very nearly lost on her, the soothing sounds had no effect. Still, her periphery vision was impossible to turn off, and with the best will in the world she could not avoid seeing it: the last smudged traces of *Eeyore* weeping as they were washed away.

It was a little while before she realized that she was still blindly following the glowing red taillights of Sexton and Kelso's car. Instead of turning right out of the lot, which would have been the shortest route to her house, she had turned left. Shock must have paralyzed her thought processes for a while, she realized as she came back to full awareness with the sensation of someone just waking up. She was already at the edge of the historic district, heading into town. Though it was still several hours until nightfall, the rain had brought with it an early twilight. Lights were on in a few of the big white mansions, and the giant live oaks lining the streets swayed in the rising wind as they gathered their bedraggled cloaks of Spanish moss close. Headlights were coming at her, blurry because of the rain, as people exited toward the suburbs.

Even as Sarah took stock of her whereabouts, she realized that she must have subconsciously meant to go this way all along. She wasn't following Sexton and Kelso at all. Clarity came as suddenly as a thunder clap. She was heading for the one place she usually tended to avoid at all costs: Waterfront Park.

The place where Lexie had been lost.

The need to go there now was so strong it was almost a compulsion. She felt as if, somehow, Lexie might be there. Which was stupid, and with the rational part of her mind, at least, she knew it. Lexie *wasn't* at Waterfront Park, hadn't been there since about five thirty p.m. on that sunny July day seven years before, and would almost certainly never be there again. But it was the last place they had been together on this earth, and as such, in the wake of everything that had happened, it called to her irresistibly.

The phone call, the strewn toys, the scrawled *Eeyore*—all had their beginnings at Waterfront Park. They might be only sadistic pranks, or they might have a darker purpose, such as revenge or . . . well, that was what she needed to figure out.

The thing was, if she rejected the idea that what was happening was some kind of telepathic communication from her daughter, then she was left with one inescapable conclusion: Some living, breathing person who was physically nearby had done those things—and he or she almost certainly had to know or have known Lexie either near the time of her disappearance or afterward.

They'd only come up with *Eeyore* as a code word about three weeks before Lexie had disappeared.

Searching behavior might account for the phone call's mispronounced *scared*. Anyone, even Sweetie-pie at a stretch, might have scattered those toys. But *Eeyore*—whoever had written that code word on her window almost had to have gotten it from Lexie herself. Because Sarah had never mentioned it to anyone.

Had Lexie maybe told it to her kidnapper?

The thought was horrifying. It was also electrifying. Maybe the person who was doing these terrible things knew what had happened to her daughter. Maybe she, Sarah, could find him.

Maybe—*please, please God*—she could find Lexie.

No matter where Lexie was now, no matter what had happened to her, one conclusion Sarah had come to over the years was that knowing had to be better than not knowing. Not to know was to be condemned to a horrible half-life existence for the rest of her days.

It was a long shot. But after all these years, it was the only shot she had.

Somewhere Sexton and Kelso must have turned off, because their car was no longer ahead of her. It didn't matter. She could see the indigo waters of Beaufort Bay now. White caps undulated across the normally placid surface like flutters of fine lace. Tied-up shrimp boats bobbed at the tall posts of the public dock. More boats were coming in ahead of the building storm.

She turned onto Bay Street, and minutes later she was parking at the curb across from Waterfront Park. The rain had slackened to an intermittent drizzle, she realized as she got out. There was no need to feed the meter. It was ten minutes after six, and after six, unless there was a special event, parking at the meters was free.

There had been a special event at the park that day, special over and above the end-of-season T-ball picnic. The annual Beaufort County Water Festival had been in full swing when they had arrived about five p.m., and she and Lexie had had to park in the Municipal Lot and walk a couple of blocks amid cheerful throngs all going to the same place they were. A water ski stunt spectacular was in progress out on the bay, and the crowd had been watching and cheering the skiers as she and Lexie neared the park. When that was over, there would be a tortoise race, an outdoor concert, and, finally, the Queen of Carolina and the Sea Islands Beauty Pageant, which would wind up the evening's festivities.

Not even feeling the drizzle now, Sarah

walked across the rain-slick, nearly deserted street and through the tall, brick pil-
lars that marked the park's entrance. This
was the way she and Lexie had come. Then,
the day had been steamy-hot and sunny,
and the grassy acres lining the waterfront
were packed with people. Now it was raining and overcast. The sky was purple-
tinged gray with an occasional rumble of
thunder warning of worse to come. A
breeze blew in from the bay, ruffling the
fronds of the palmettos lining the walk and
filling the air with salty scents from the fishing boats gliding past on their way to their
moorings. If there were other people in the
park, she didn't see them.

The first rule of investigating a crime was
to follow the evidence, no matter where it
took you. Starting once again at the beginning, that was what she was going to do.

She was going to retrace her steps that
day and, as much as possible, Lexie's steps
that day, and try to see the whole thing
through fresh eyes. Who had been there
then who might have reason to lash out at
her now?

It was a new perspective, and it brought
with it the tiniest flicker of renewed hope. If

she could just make that connection, she might, just might, uncover the link that would lead her to Lexie at last.

She'd been just twenty-four, slim but curvaceous in a tomato-red T-shirt, short denim skirt, and flip-flops, tanned and pretty with bright blue eyes, black hair spilling over her shoulders, and a ready smile. Men looked at her when she passed, and, while she had no time to waste on them, she'd been secretly pleased at their attention. You'd think, given the horror that was to come, that there would have been some sense of foreboding in the air, that she would have had a premonition that the world as she knew it was about to shatter into a million little pieces, but no. She'd been happy that day, convinced that despite difficult beginnings she was now moving in the right direction. Lexie had turned Sarah's life around, and Sarah could remember the sense of wholeness she had felt as she'd held her daughter's hand while they crossed the street. Once they were safe on the other side, Lexie had pulled away, of course, conscious of her new conviction that only babies held their mom's hands. Side by side, they had walked through the park to the pavilion where the awards ceremony would take place. As one of the parent volunteers, Sarah was expected to help set up. Everyone was supposed to bring a dish, and they would watch a tape of highlights of the season as they ate. Then the awards would be handed out.

"Mommy, why couldn't we bring Sweetie-pie?" Lexie had asked, skipping along beside her. Lexie had known the answer, because they'd had this discussion several times during the course of the day. But her daughter liked to chatter, and she loved Sweetie-pie. From the moment Lexie had picked him out of a litter of cowering, half-grown pups the Humane Society had thoughtfully (Sarah was being sarcastic here; the last thing any busy single mother needed in her life was a puppy) put on display in front of the grocery store where no child could miss it, Lexie had been his champion.

How many times had Sarah thought that if she'd only agreed to bring Sweetie-pie to the park that day, everything would have turned out differently? A million, at least. Lexie would have had Sweetie-pie with her when she'd gone skipping off, and Sweetie-pie, even then, hadn't been a dog to be trifled with. In all likelihood, if they'd brought Sweetie-pie with them as Lexie had wanted, Lexie would be here now.

If only, if only, if only. The two most useless words in the English language.

"Because there are too many people," Sarah had replied. It was the same answer she'd given before, and she would probably give it again before the day was out. Her cheerful, outgoing little daughter was nothing if not persistent. Sarah's tone was admittedly a little short, because the topic, in her opinion, had been discussed to death. Also, it was punishingly hot, she was worried about getting everything she'd brought home with her from work done before Monday, and she was juggling a way-too-cumbersome load that included a plastic bag containing Lexie's swimming gear, another one with the thank-you gift they were presenting to the coach, and the requisite Tupperware bowl containing her contribution to the covered-dish supper—tossed salad. It was lame, she knew, but she just didn't have time to cook, and the deli-prepared items some of the other mothers brought were budget busters for her. Add to all that the fact that Lexie had a tendency to dart ahead, and the park was really crowded, which made keeping an eye on her more difficult than usual, and yes, she was starting to feel a little stressed.

It killed Sarah now to remember that the final moments she had spent with her daughter had been filled with such petty concerns.

"Hey, little girl, you wanna buy a balloon?" A clown stepped toward Lexie, his hands full of dozens of bright Mylar balloons. He'd been in full clown regalia, bushy black wig, painted face complete with red rubber nose, colorful suit. He looked at Sarah, who closed the gap between herself and her daughter protectively fast. "Just one dollar."

"No, thanks," Lexie said before Sarah could, because even at five she knew that money was tight and there wasn't a lot for extras such as balloons. Then she had skipped on, sunny as ever, down the path that Sarah was following right now.

The memory made Sarah ache. Lexie would have loved a balloon. But at the time, saving a dollar had seemed more important.

If she had it to do over, she would have bought her daughter all the balloons in the world.

But one thing she had learned so painfully was that there were no do-overs in life.

The clown was a vivid memory, and now she reexamined it for the umpteenth time. He had been one of the first people who had come to Sarah's mind when it had become clear that Lexie had gone missing. In the aftermath, the police, she herself, and later Jake and his firm had thoroughly checked him out: As far as they'd been able to determine, he'd had nothing to do with it. And unless he was using a different name, he wasn't in her life now.

So she let that memory go and went on.

"Lexie!" A moment later, Lexie had been greeted rapturously by her friend Ginny, who was also on the T-ball team, while their teammates Todd and Andrew had walked on past as if they'd never seen the girls before in their lives. It was a coed team, but five- and six-year-old boys and girls mixed about as well as oil and water. They'd almost reached the pavilion by that time, and other parents had been around: Ginny's, Todd's, Andrew's—as it turned out, every

child on the team had had at least one parent present, and most of them two. Sarah
talked to nearly all of them as they started
setting up the tables and the kids played
nearby.

The parents had been checked out. For
the moment, for that reason, Sarah was giving them a pass. What she was trying to do
as she stepped up into the pavilion now
was envision the crowds that had surrounded them that day.

About the size of a basketball court, the
pavilion was one of three spaced out across
the park, and the T-ball team had reserved it
with the Parks Department for their function. It had a green metal roof with metal
support posts holding it up. The floor was
poured concrete, metal picnic tables
marched up the center in two neat rows,
and it was open on all four sides. Now the
pavilion was dark and gloomy, and damp air
smelling of rain rolled in from the bay. The
only sounds were the natural ones of rain
drumming against the roof, rustling leaves,
and, further away, waves splashing against
the narrow strip of sandy beach. Then, the
place had been full of talking, laughing,
happy adults and children, it had been hot

as Hades, and the smell of all sorts of yummy food had filled the air. Beyond the pavilion, a crowd the police had later estimated to number in the thousands filled the park. The tide of people moving past those four open walls had been never-ending. Locals, but a lot of out-of-towners, too. Tourists who'd come especially for the festivities. Participants in the exhibitions and their families and entourages. Vendors. Anybody. Everybody.

From the beginning, it was this mix of people that had made singling out suspects so hard.

Closing her eyes, Sarah tried to remember, tried to envision the scene, tried to fix the crowd in her mind so that she might be able to pick up on someone that she had missed before.

The conclusion she came to was: impossible. All she saw in her mind's eye was a huge, amorphous blur of color and movement. No one stood out. No one had ever, ever stood out.

Her breathing had quickened, Sarah realized as she opened her eyes, and her stomach was starting to churn. Glancing around, she spotted the table where she had put her salad down among the cheese grits, the peach cobbler, the ham biscuits, the green-bean casserole. Then she'd been hungry, and the smells had made her stomach rumble. Now just remembering them almost made her sick.

She'd been standing beside the table talking to Ginny's mother when Lexie had tugged on her arm.

"Emma's brought cake."

Sarah almost shuddered as she remembered Lexie saying that. Emma's mom had decided to kill two birds with one stone and celebrate her daughter's birthday at the awards ceremony. She had put the birthday cake on the right front table and, as the children had gathered around in excitement, had started lighting candles. That was when Lexie had begged to be allowed to go get cake.

And Sarah, God help her, had said *yes.*

It was about ten minutes later that Sarah had first missed her. Having filled plates with food for Lexie and herself, Sarah had gone to fetch Lexie from the crowd around the birthday girl so that they could sit down and eat together.

Lexie wasn't there.

Emma's mom remembered giving her a slice of cake.

Emma remembered her saying *I'll be six soon, too.*

Todd saw her at the edge of the pavilion with her plate almost empty, throwing the crumbs of cake that remained to a pair of eager seagulls.

After that, nothing. No one recalled seeing her again.

Disbelief, panic, stone-cold terror: Sarah remembered the progression of emotions she had experienced as it became increasingly clear that Lexie was nowhere to be found and a hard knot formed in her chest. The park had been packed with people that day. They were everywhere, walking the paths, sprawled on blankets in the grass, crowding the waterfront. With so many people, how was it possible that no one had seen Lexie walking away, being lured or dragged away, or, however it had happened, disappearing?

But no one—at least no one who would admit it—had.

Sarah had looked by herself at first, hurrying around the pavilion, calling Lexie's name. Then the other parents had joined in, then park security, then the police. Nightmarishly, the festival had continued around them. Shouts egging on the participants in the tortoise race had echoed in Sarah's ears even as she had run down the paths screaming her daughter's name.

By nightfall, Sarah had faced the horrible truth: Lexie was gone.

But even then she hadn't realized the enormity of it. She hadn't realized that *gone* meant *gone for good.* She hadn't realized that seven years later, she would still be searching for her daughter, and that all the efforts to find her—the boats dredging the bay, the barrage of publicity, the combined efforts of the police and the FBI and herself and Jake—would come up empty.

It was as if Lexie had simply vanished off the face of the earth—until the phone call last night, and then *Eeyore* today.

As rain hit her in the face, Sarah realized that she was no longer in the pavilion but walking down the narrow concrete path that led to the bay. This was the path she had searched first, frantically pushing past a knot of beer-swilling college boys and a laughing twentysomething couple and a mom with a toddler boy in a red umbrella stroller. Even as she retraced her footsteps, as the palmettos swayed and rustled on either side of her and the darkness-sensitive lights came on in the park one by one and the rain picked up until it was drenching her, the memories were flooding back. Vivid memories into which she delved with the intensity of an archeologist finding a still-sealed Pharaoh's tomb.

A man in a red-and-white-striped apron with a cart, selling hot dogs and soft pretzels: In her mind's eye, she searched his features, drew a blank. Another man, homeless from the look of him, bent over a metal trash can as if checking out its contents: nothing familiar about him. A video camera whirring, causing her to glance around to discover that she, along with the gaggle of uniformed cheerleaders behind her, was being recorded for posterity. She could see only the lower half of camera guy's face because video cameras then had required that you look through the viewfinder, but nothing about the bushy black mustache above a rather small, pursed mouth rang a bell.

Still, something hovered tantalizingly at

the edges of her consciousness, just out of reach.

What was it? Sarah tried to zero in on it, but the harder she tried, the more elusive the memories became.

By this time she was at the post-and-chain fence that restricted access to the beach to a few approved approaches. She only realized that she had reached it because she had to stop walking as she encountered the barrier. Rain washed over her, cool and tasting faintly salty on her lips. The soft murmur of it filled her ears. Her hair was wet, her clothes were wet, and she started to shiver a little as the breeze from the bay hit her full-on. She blinked to keep the water out of her eyes and folded her arms over her chest in a reflexive effort to conserve body heat as she stared out over the bay. A line of distant lights marked the opposite shore. The water itself was so dark that it looked nearly black, and the sky was only a little lighter. The whitecaps were taller now, and in the distance, she saw lightning flicker. The storm that had threatened for hours was approaching fast.

"Lexie," Sarah whispered into the dark and the rain, her voice a pale reflection of the agony that twisted inside her. "Lexie, where are you?"

Then, without warning, her peripheral vision picked up the dark outline of a man moving up fast behind her. Almost simultaneously, a hand closed around her arm. Startled out of her reverie, Sarah jumped and screamed, fighting to get away.

14

"What the sweet hell do you think you're doing?"

Despite the anger in it, the familiar voice had the effect of completely deflating Sarah's burgeoning fear. She stopped struggling and glared up at the shadowed face of the man looming beside her.

"Jesus, you scared the life out of me." She pressed a hand to her chest. Beneath it, she could feel the thudding of her heart. Taking a deep breath, she tried to calm her jangled nerves.

"I scared the life out of *you?* Do you know

how long I've been looking for you? You ever hear of answering your cell phone?"

Jake still gripped her arm. Sarah hadn't realized how cold she was until she felt the warmth of his hand against her chilled skin. There was just enough light from a distant streetlamp to allow her to see that his face was pale and his jaw was set. His eyes were narrowed against the rain driving in from the bay, which she realized was falling hard now. They both had to raise their voices to be heard over it.

"It's in the trunk of my car," Sarah remembered guiltily. Lightning flashed, closer at hand than before. A drumroll of thunder followed. Her eyes remained fixed on him, widening at the import of what she had to tell him. The words bubbled up from her throat in their eagerness to get out. "Jake, you won't believe what happened. Somebody wrote *Eeyore*—Lexie's and my code word—on my car window."

"I heard." Jake's tone was grim. His hand tightened around her arm. "You can tell me all about it when we're back at your house. If you don't have enough sense to come in out of the rain, I do."

"But Jake . . ."

"Come on."

Turning his back on the rain-laden gusts blowing in from the bay, he started walking quickly back the way she had come, propelling her along beside him. Sarah didn't resist. She was more glad to see him than she could say. If she had been thinking, if she had had room in her mind for anything other than Lexie, she would have fished her phone out of the trunk and called him as soon as she'd found that word on her window. But the police had been right there, and she'd been in such a state of shock that anything beyond making sure that word on the window was documented and investigated had been beyond her. The thing was, though, nobody could help her think this through like Jake. Unfortunately, the pace he was setting was killer, as if he was in a really big hurry to get out of the park, and it was definitely not conducive to any kind of serious conversation. In fact, it soon became too much for her altogether. Her legs were shaky, she found as she hurried beside him, and her knees felt rubbery and weak. Add to that the fact that the walkway was slick and she was trying to keep up with a striding man while wearing high heels, and something had to give. She pulled her arm free of his grip, and he paused and glanced back at her as she lagged behind.

"What?" he said.

"Could you slow down?"

"Sorry."

He waited for her, then moderated his pace, matching it to hers. After a moment or so, she tucked her hand in his arm and walked close beside him again, so that her shoulder butted into his arm and her side brushed his. He was wearing a dress shirt with the sleeves rolled up to the elbows, without a tie, and dark slacks. The shirt was wet, and she could feel the warm hardness of the muscle beneath through the sodden cloth. The rain had soaked her clothes, too, and for the first time she realized that she was shivering a little.

"Did you come out here *looking* for me?" she asked.

"No, I just happened to be in the neighborhood. . . ." He shot her a sardonic look. "Of course I came out here looking for you. I've been chasing around after you since not too long after you left the courthouse. Just to satisfy my curiosity, what part of *somebody might be out here who wants to kill you* are you having trouble understanding?"

"They picked Floyd Parker up. Morrison told me."

"Yeah, well, did he also tell you that it turns out that Floyd Parker has a rock-solid alibi? If he's the one who shot you, just about the entire choir of Mount Zion Baptist Church is going to hell, because they're all swearing he was there, picking up his mother from choir practice, when the robbery went down."

Sarah suddenly felt a little queasy. "Oh."

"Yeah, *oh.*"

They were passing the pavilion now. Rain was falling steadily, smelling of the bay, forming a silvery veil between them and their surroundings. The palmettos looked like tall, bristly sentinels on either side of the path, and the lights dotting the park glowed ghostly white. Beyond them, the rest of the park was dark and indistinct. Out of the corner of her eye, Sarah caught a glimpse of movement. Glancing around, she realized that she hadn't been alone in the park after all. The shadowy silhouette of a man perched on one of the tables in the pavilion swigged from some kind of container. Clearly he had sought and found a place out of the rain. He seemed to be looking their way, although it was impossible to be sure. To the left of the structure, another figure holding a newspaper over his head hurried across the grass toward the beach, head bent and shoulders hunched, as he tried to avoid getting wet. It was impossible to determine anything about him other than that he was a man. Up ahead, just beyond the entrance to the park, Sarah saw a dark-colored SUV cruising slowly down the street. Its headlights cut silvery swathes through the gloom, capturing the sheer force of the downpour in their beams.

If someone who wanted to kill her really was out there, she realized she'd just provided them with a hell of an opportunity. She also realized that she felt perfectly safe now—because she was with Jake. Which was kind of stupid when she thought about it. He was many things, but not bulletproof.

"So how'd you find me?" she asked after a moment. They were walking through the park gates now, and her Sentra was to the right up ahead. Jake's Acura was parked behind it.

"Morrison called me. After the police called him. Apparently, the word he got was that one of his Assistant DAs was having some kind of public nervous breakdown."

Indignation stopped Sarah dead in her tracks. Windblown rain swirled around her, glistening in the halogen glow of the street lamps, but she barely noticed.

"I was not. I was visiting Angie Barillas— she's a sweet little girl, Jake, and I think she's realized now that I only want to help her and her family—and when I got back to my car someone had written *Eeyore* in the dust on my window."

Jake came back to her, curled a hand around her elbow, and started her walking again.

"So I heard from Carl Sexton after I managed to track him down. He said that you were pretty freaked out about it."

"The thing is, nobody knew that *Eeyore* was our code word except Lexie and me." Urgency sharpened Sarah's voice. At Jake's silent prompting, she moved rapidly at his side as they crossed the street. Their footsteps slapped in tandem against the wet pavement. He seemed more tense than usual and kept casting quick, wary glances to the right and left. Sarah realized that he was looking for someone who might be following her, maybe waiting to take shot at her, and experienced an inward shudder. Now that she knew that the person who had shot her was still at large, she felt a little nervous, she realized. She also realized that she would have been feeling a lot more nervous if she hadn't been more concerned at the moment with the ramifications of the word that had been written on her car window.

"What makes you so sure?" Jake asked.

She looked up at him earnestly as they reached the Sentra. "I never told anyone about it. Don't you see, whoever wrote that almost had to have gotten it from Lexie. I think she might have told it to whoever took her."

They stopped beside the driver's side of her car. She had her back to the door, blinking up at him in an effort to see through the rain, while he frowned down at her. Rain washed over them, drumming on the roof of her car, splattering on the sidewalk. What light there was shone on her face. His was in shadow.

"So your theory is that he wrote it on your car window this afternoon?" There was no mistaking the grim edge to his voice. His eyes looked black in the uncertain light. His brows nearly met above them.

Sarah nodded. "I think so. Yes."

"If that's the case—and you notice I only say 'if,' because, thank God, there are other explanations—then you realize that the sick bastard who took your daughter must be following you, that he's trying to either frighten or harm you, and that means you may very well be in danger from him too, always assuming that he's not the same guy who took a shot at you at the Quik-Pik? You ever think that under the circumstances, coming out to a deserted park alone might not be a good idea?"

He was practically yelling by the time he finished, and he didn't give her a chance to answer. Instead, he took her keys from her hand, punched the button to unlock the doors, and marched her around to the passenger's side. The rain was falling in sheets now, but it didn't really matter. They were both so wet, they couldn't get much wetter.

"What . . .?"

He didn't give her a chance to say anything else. "Get in. I'm driving you home."

She did, and as she slid inside, she was immediately conscious of how good it felt to get out of the rain. He shut the door on her, and she shook her head a little to get the worst of the rain off and then ran her hands through her hair, pushing the soaked strands back from her face. The Band-Aid, loosened by the downpour, came off in her fingers. Sarah glanced at it in surprise. It was wet and limp, a dead Band-Aid, and she wadded it up and pushed it into the small trash bag she kept in the passenger footwell. Then she flipped the mirrored visor down to inspect the damage. To her surprise, her hair almost covered the wound, which was far less noticeable anyway without the giant Band-Aid. When Jake opened the door and dropped into the driver's seat a moment later, dripping all over her faux leather upholstery even more than she was herself, she flipped the visor closed again, forgot all about the state of her head, and frowned at him.

"What other explanation?" she demanded instantly. It was shadowy and dark inside the small car, and the smell of rain and damp clothing filled the air. He was close, taking up more than his fair share of space, as he always did. It felt as if they were cocooned inside the small car, with the blanketing rain insulating them from the world outside.

He shot her an impatient look. His face was shiny wet, and raindrops glistened on his hair. "For starters, maybe Lexie told somebody *before* she went missing. I haven't had a whole hell of a lot of experience with five-year-old girls, but from what I have seen, they're not that great at keeping secrets. Maybe whomever she told *before* she went missing has a problem with you now. Or maybe whomever she told repeated it to someone else, or told the police, which means it's written down somewhere in all the mountains of paperwork the case has generated. Hell, anyone could have found out about it by now."

The logic of that was obvious now that it was pointed out to her. Sarah took a deep, steadying breath as the tiny flicker of hope that had sprung to life inside her was all but snuffed out, then opened her mouth to dispute what she recognized was, indeed, a likelier scenario than the one she had been imagining. But whatever she had been going to say was lost as he pulled a pistol out of his waistband and, leaning past her, stowed in it her glove compartment.

"Why do you have that?"

In the beginning, when they'd first met, he had carried a gun a good portion of the time. Gradually, as the heat and Beaufort's relative lack of crime and his own distance from his law enforcement years mellowed him out, he had started carrying it less and less often until, in the last couple of years, he rarely carried a gun at all.

"Oh, I don't know, maybe I just felt like heading out in the rain and bagging a couple of gulls."

Okay, his sarcasm wasn't appreciated. Her eyes narrowed at him as he started the car, then, with a single glance at her, turned on the heat. Of course, the air that came blasting out of the vents was cold at first, and she shivered as it hit her. Even with the rain, the outside temperature was still probably in the upper seventies, but she was freezing, she realized as she crossed her arms over her chest. Her teeth would have chattered if she'd let them.

"You know, there's no need to be sarcastic."

"Why not? Maybe I feel sarcastic." Pulling out into the street, he did a U-turn and headed back the way she had come. The headlights were on, and they illuminated the park gates and a long expanse of green as they swept past.

"Look, I'm sorry if you were worried about me."

Jake laughed. It was not a sound of amusement. Sarah's lips compressed. The thing was, though, she was really glad to see him, glad he'd come in search of her. Her preoccupation with finding out what had happened to Lexie had admittedly made her blind to any danger she herself might be facing. Under the circumstances, it was good to know that he had her back. If he was inclined to be a little cranky about the whole thing, well, she would just bear with him until the crankiness wore off. Then maybe he could help her figure this thing out.

"What about your car?" Her tone was carefully neutral.

"I'll pick it up later." Braking at the inter-section, he pulled out onto I-21. There were a few other cars on the street, most of them heading the same way they were: out of town.

"So, I hear Morrison gave you the afternoon off."

"Told me to take the afternoon off. There's a difference. He said Judge Schwartzman thought I was looking wobbly."

"Smart judge." There was still a definite edge to Jake's voice. He was as wet as she was. His black hair glistened as the headlights from an oncoming car swept the Sentra's interior. His collar was wilted and his shirt clung to his wide chest and broad shoulders. His jaw had a hard set to it that told her he was committed to nursing his grievance for at least a little while longer. He glanced at her. "You ever think of taking Morrison's advice and just going on home and recuperating from a strenuous couple of days? Like any sensible human being would do?"

Sarah would have stiffened if she'd had the energy. Since she didn't, she used her words. "You know what, I could do without the attitude. Maybe we should go back and get your car and I should just drive myself home. Alone."

Again with the unamused laugh.

"Not happening, honey, and you know it. And, just to clue you in, I'm not crazy about your attitude, either."

They were in the historic district now. More lights were on in the great white houses, and the live oaks on either side of the road were so wet that they seemed to be weeping. Jake swerved around a passengerless horse-drawn carriage that seemed to be hurrying somewhere, probably to a barn or some place that afforded protection from the downpour. Sarah could just barely hear the clop of the horse's hooves over the rush of the rain.

"So where'd you go after you left the courthouse?" he asked.

"Crystal's car broke down. I gave her a ride home."

"Crystal?"

"Crystal Stumbo. I helped her take out a TRO against Brian McIntyre this morning." Jake's mouth tightened, and Sarah interpreted that to mean that he disapproved, just as she'd known he would. Luckily, his approval was not required. "She lives out almost to Burton, in a trailer park. Coincidentally—or not—McIntyre was out that way, too, in his squad car. He followed me back into town."

Something in her voice prompted him to shoot her a sharp look.

"So what happened?"

"He rode my bumper for a while. Way too close, in fast-moving, heavy traffic. He did it deliberately, too, I could tell, like he was trying to frighten me. Or threaten me. Then I managed to get out of his way, and he went on past. In retrospect, it turned out to be no big deal."

"Oh, yeah?"

"Pretty much."

"This wouldn't be the same McIntyre you were worried might be the guy who shot you, would it? Oh, wait, since he's the only McIntyre in the department, it must be. I can see where having him follow right on your bumper might be no big deal."

Sarah ignored the sarcasm this time. "Well, at least he didn't take a shot at me. He just flipped me the bird." She paused, remembering. "Oh, and—it's probably coincidence, but you never know—there was a squad car with a couple of uniforms in it already in the parking lot when I found the writing on my window."

"Sounds like the fan club was out in force today."

Sarah glanced sideways at him. There was no doubt about it: Jake was in a snit. He was driving too fast for the conditions, with a kind of controlled savagery, so that the Sentra sliced through the rain, its tires sluicing through the runoff on the road. He was frowning, his eyes narrowed and his mouth in a firm line.

Since she didn't feel like having the fight he was clearly spoiling for, she didn't reply. They reached the intersection with the Quik-Pik, which was apparently still doing brisk business despite its recent history and the rain. The cars at the pumps and the glowing interior served as a graphic reminder that life goes on.

Jake turned onto Davis, and the Quik-Pik was thankfully behind them.

He broke the silence. "You know, just for the record, this whole death-wish thing you've got going on is starting to get to me."

This time Sarah did stiffen. Her eyes slewed around to him. "What?"

He shot her a grim look. "You think I don't know what's going on inside your head?

You can't deal with the fact that your daughter's gone and you've still got your life to live. So you're doing your damned stubborn best not to live it."

Sarah's mouth dropped open. She glared at him. "You're nuts. I don't know what you're talking about."

"Oh, yeah? Well, let's start with the obvious. On Wednesday, you get shot in the head. A police guard is posted outside your room to keep whoever did it from trying it again. On Thursday, I'm so wor-ried about your well-being that I drive you home from the hospital and stay the night with you, just in case someone might actually be thinking about knocking you off. On Friday, after a hell of a night, you sneak out of bed at the crack of dawn and go haring off without any protection whatsoever. I track you down to the courthouse, where, you're right, you're probably safe enough. So I heave a big sigh of relief, you do what you can to improve the situation by pissing off as many people as possible, and then you disappear without a word to anyone. You do everything in your power to give anybody who might want to kill you a sporting chance at it, until I finally manage to track you down again. Alone in a deserted park. If that's not a manifestation of a death wish, then you tell me, what is it?"

Sarah spluttered. She'd never actually thought of it like that. "An . . . an unfortunate series of events."

Jake snorted and whipped the Sentra into her driveway. With no lights on and the rain pouring down on it, her house looked dark and depressing, and maybe even a little sinister. The thought of Sweetie-pie waiting inside was heartening, but Sarah was glad to have Jake with her all the same. Even if he was starting to really annoy her.

"So, let's look at the rest of your life." He put the car in park, cut the ignition and killed the lights, then turned to look at her. "How's your social life? You got a boyfriend? You date?"

Sarah gave him a killer glare without bothering to reply.

He continued relentlessly: "Okay, scrap that. What was the last movie you saw?"

"*Scary Movie,*" she answered instantly, then could have bitten her tongue off. She remembered the occasion perfectly: She had watched the DVD with him, in his living room, while he'd scarfed down mountains of popcorn and candy and soda and she'd sipped a Diet Coke.

"And that would have been—what? Sometime last summer? As in a year ago?"

She knew she should have bitten her tongue off.

"So? I've been busy."

"Uh-huh. Remember how we used to go fishing sometimes, early Sunday mornings? How come you stopped coming with me?"

"It's called sleep."

"Bullshit. You were having a good time, and you couldn't take that, so you quit coming. No good time for Sarah."

"That's a load of crap."

"Is it? So tell me, you got any hobbies? Special interests? TV shows you're really into?"

"I watch the news." *When she had time,* she added, but not out loud.

"Yeah." He managed to pack a wealth of scorn into that one word. "Read any good books lately?"

Damn it, he knew her too well. This wasn't fair. Reading had once been her escape, books her favorite things in the world. She hadn't opened one for pleasure since Lexie had disappeared.

The most aggravating part was that he didn't even have to read her answer in her face to know what it was.

"Okay, scrap that, too," he said when she didn't reply. "You don't date, you don't go to movies, you don't have a hobby, you don't watch TV, you don't read. Mind telling me just exactly what you do do for fun?"

"I have fun." She sounded defensive, even to her own ears. "I work out. I play with Sweetie-pie. I . . ."

"Come off it, Sarah, you're talking to me here, remember? I know you. I didn't ask you how you fill your time when you're not actually working. I asked you what you do for fun."

So maybe he had her there. She had no social life, and he knew it. Also, she didn't really do much that constituted fun. And he knew that, too.

"I have a demanding job. . . ."

"Fun. I'm asking you about fun."

Okay, enough was enough. He was starting to make her mad.

"Well, golly gee, maybe I should join a bowling league," she shot back. "Or maybe

I should do what you do and make a hobby out of picking up baby blondes."

With that, she got out of the car and stalked toward her front door. In the car, she'd started to warm up and, with the heater blowing on her, dry off a little. But as soon as she stepped outside, the rain hit her full force, and she was soaked again in an instant.

Damn it.

"Maybe you should at that." Jake was right behind her, practically yelling in her ear. "That would at least be better than the way you're living now."

"There is nothing wrong with the way I'm living now." Sarah made it to her small front porch, opened the screen—and remembered that he had her keys. Even as she slanted a fulminating look back over her shoulder at him, he was already reaching around her to insert the key in the lock. She turned the knob, and then, as the door opened, practically fell into the sanctuary of her front hallway. Jake followed her, and as she turned on the light he shut the front door behind them. Sweetie-pie greeted her with his customary woof, and she patted his head as she glared at Jake, who, not incidentally, was dripping all over her hard-wood floor.

"Isn't there?"

"No."

Throwing the word at him over her shoulder, she headed for the bathroom to get some towels while he stopped in the place where the entry hall met the hall that led to the bedrooms to yell after her.

"The hell there isn't."

Sarah came back and tossed two big beige towels at him as she silently deplored the mess they were making on the floor. Then, rubbing her hair dry, she walked past him into the kitchen to let Sweetie-pie out, flipping on the light as she went. As the dog stopped on the covered back porch, looking warily out at the downpour, she shut the door on him and turned back. Jake was standing in the middle of the kitchen with a towel draped around his shoulders while he eased off his soaked shoes. A puddle had already formed around him, Sarah saw as she eyed him up and down. She kicked off her own shoes, glad the floor in the kitchen was tile.

"I'm going to take a shower," she said, refusing to continue the fight, and headed back toward the bathroom again to do just that.

"You think I'm not being serious?" He was right behind her as she reached the hall. He caught her arm, stopping her in full flight. "You need evidence? Take a look at this place."

Sarah turned and glared at him, yanking her arm free in the process. He was barely an arm's length away, so close that she had to look up to meet his eyes. The hall was narrow, and as she took a step back, her shoulder brushed the smooth, white wall, leaving a damp mark in its wake.

"Look, if you have a problem with my house, you're welcome—more than wel-come, in fact—to go home to yours."

Ignoring that, he gestured toward the living room and kitchen, small sections of both of which they could see from the hall.

"You notice anything when you look around? I do. No pictures on the walls. No curtains. No rugs on the damned floors." His voice was rising. "The furniture's cheap. It's ugly. It's uncomfortable."

"Are you criticizing my decorating?" Sarah demanded, outraged.

Jake snorted. "Decorating? Don't give me that. You didn't decorate. You went out and you deliberately bought the bare minimum of stuff you needed to furnish this place. You deliberately bought cheap, and you deliberately bought ugly. Everything's brown, tan"—he paused, pulled the towel hanging around his neck off, and shook it at here—"hell, even the damned towels are tan."

"So I like earth tones," Sarah said through her teeth. "Sue me."

"The hell you do." Jake's eyes swept over her. "Look at your clothes. You dress like a woman twice your age. You never wear anything colorful or pretty or, God forbid, sexy. Everything you wear is black or gray or . . ."

"They're called neutrals," Sarah interrupted, seething. "They're business-appropriate. What, are you an expert on women's clothing now?"

"No," Jake said. "But when I first met you, you were wearing a bright red T-shirt and a short denim skirt that showed off your legs. I can still remember because you looked good in them. Your apartment—remember what your apartment looked like? The one you and Lexie lived in? I do."

"Stop," Sarah said. "Just stop right now."

"It was yellow. The walls. A soft, pale yellow that made you feel welcome as soon as you walked in the door. The couch was old, but you'd thrown a red quilt over it and it was bright and comfortable. There were curtains. Rugs. Pictures on the walls. Books on the shelves. Photographs in frames. Flowers on the table. A damned plant in your kitchen window."

"The flowers were plastic. The plant was dying." Sarah felt as if her heart was constricting. It was all she could do to breathe. The images he conjured up made her ache as she tried to force them out of her head.

"Maybe they were, but that's not the point. The point is that the place you lived in then was a home, not a damned mausoleum. The clothes you wore were pretty, sexy. Since then, it's like you're deliberately trying to deny yourself anything that could possibly bring you pleasure. You don't even eat, for God's sake."

"So what if I don't?" Sarah cried, stung almost past bearing. "Why don't you damned well just mind your own business? What's it to you?"

"This," Jake said in a goaded tone. Then he pushed her back against the wall, slid a hand along the side of her neck, and covered her mouth with his.

15

The shock of it held her perfectly still for a moment. Her hands flattened against his chest as if she would push him off her, but she didn't push. His lips were cool when they first touched hers, but as he slanted his mouth across hers, they almost instantly warmed up. He kissed her hungrily, ardently, his mouth moving on hers, his tongue sliding between her parted lips—she must have gasped with surprise when she'd first realized what he was doing, because she couldn't account for their opening in any other way. Her head reeled as he licked urgently into her mouth. He tasted of rain and the outdoors, and she could feel the rough beginnings of stubble on his cheeks and jaw rubbing against her smooth skin. He was leaning against her, pinning her in place with his weight so that she was trapped between him and the cool plaster wall at her back. She was suddenly supremely conscious of how big he was, how solidly muscular, how strong. Heat radiated from him, penetrating his wet clothes and her wet clothes so that she could feel the imprint of his body everywhere they touched. With a sense of disbelief so strong that it verged on unreality, she realized that he was hard with wanting her.

Then his hand moved, sliding down her body to flatten urgently over the slight curve of her breast.

She could feel the heat of that hand, the strength of it, steaming into her skin through the thin layers of her clothing.

Her hands curled into fists around the cool, wet cotton of his shirt as her breast seemed to swell into his palm.

Still, she did not push him off.

His mouth lifted away from hers, just barely, just enough so that she could breathe, could try to wrap her mind around what was happening, could process the sensations that were shooting along her nerve endings. Her eyes were on a level with his broad shoulders, she realized, and as she looked up past the strong column of his neck at the hard, dark, impossibly familiar face looming over hers, she saw that his eyes were open, too. For the span of perhaps a heartbeat they stared at each other as the very air around them seemed to sizzle with electricity. His eyes were black and heavy-lidded and hot with desire, gleaming with a raw, masculine intensity that she had never seen in them before. Hers—who knows what he could read in hers? Surprise, maybe disbelief, a sense that the world as she knew it had just spun hopelessly out of control.

This was not supposed to happen. This couldn't be happening. This was Jake, her good buddy, her best pal.

Not her lover.

"Kiss me back, Sarah." His voice was low, thick, a little unsteady, sounding like nothing she had ever heard come out of Jake's mouth before. He touched her mouth with his; stroked his tongue tantalizingly along her lower lip; brushed a soft, searing kiss against the corner of her mouth; then lifted his head so that perhaps an inch at most separated his mouth from hers.

She stared up at him, unblinking, mesmerized by the war that sheer physical sensation was waging against emotion and memory and the habit of years.

"Damn it, kiss me back." The warmth of his breath feathered across her damp lips. His mouth touched hers, softly, barely there.

She quivered, sucking in air as the hand covering her breast moved. His head lifted, and his eyes locked with hers again as he slid his thumb, very deliberately, back and forth over the layers of thin white nylon and flimsy bra covering her nipple. Her body responded instantly, her nipple hardening to urgent attention as a shaft of heat shot clear down to her toes.

Her eyes widened in astonishment.

Something flared in his eyes, a blast of heat, of passion, as if to acknowledge the physical response she couldn't control. Then he kissed her again.

This time his mouth made her dizzy. His kiss was greedy, devouring. Closing her eyes, she clung to his shirt as if to a lifeline.

She let him kiss her, not resisting but not responding either, as her long-deprived body battled with her fiercely rejecting mind. It had been so long since she'd had any kind of sexual contact, felt any kind of sexual response, that the feel of his mouth on hers, his hand on her breast, his hard body pressing her into the wall, was a revelation. Her body burned, and the sheer unexpected pleasure of it absolutely blew her away.

His mouth left hers, slid down to her throat. Sarah went weak-kneed as the hot, moist pressure of his lips nuzzled the sensitive chord at the side of her throat, pressed lingering kisses into the delicate hollow where her neck joined her shoulder. A tiny tremor shook her, and he must have felt it because he murmured something incomprehensible against her skin. Then his hand was somehow underneath her blouse, her bra, warm and sure as it moved sensuously over her still-damp skin. She knew his hand well: It was broad-palmed, long-fingered, eminently capable. And now it was cupping and caressing her bare breast.

Her breathing suspended. Her heart pounded. Her bones seemed to melt. The pleasant throbbing that had begun inside her intensified in an instant into an urgent, burning quake.

Yes, oh, yes, she thought with feverish intensity, even as her muscles seemed to dissolve and soaring passion rendered her light-headed.

He must have sensed her response, because his hand tightened on her breast. Her skin was silky smooth and cool from the dampness of her clothes. His was hot and faintly rough. Her breast was small, tender, malleable. His hand was big enough to cover it completely, hard enough to be unmistakably masculine, insistent with desire but gentle for all that. She could feel her nipple, pebble-hard, jutting into his palm. The pleasure was so intense that it was almost an ache, and she wanted more. Needed more.

Needed *him.*

He lifted his head, touched his lips to hers. Once, twice. Gently. Ravishingly.

"Kiss me back, Sarah," he whispered against her mouth.

I want to. Oh, God, I want to.

The response sprang fully formed into her mind, but she didn't say it. She wanted to do what he asked, wanted to wrap her arms around his neck and press her body to his and surrender to the fire that was raging between them more than she had ever imagined she could want such a thing—so much that her knees trembled and her head whirled and her body burned.

I can't. . . .

Thoughts of loss, of grief, of love and loyalty and never letting go swirled through her brain, coalescing into those two words, and just as quickly as they did, her body began to shut down.

"No." Her rejection was swift and forceful. Turning her head aside, she roughly shoved him away.

Somewhere, so far removed from the two of them that the sound could have been coming from a distant planet, the phone began to ring.

For a moment, the briefest of moments, she barely registered the sound as her eyes remained locked with his. She was breathing in quick little pants, getting herself under control, deliberately freezing him out. He was close, so close that she could have lifted a hand and laid it flat on his chest, standing with his arms hanging loosely at his sides, hands flexing, breathing heavily.

His eyes were hot, a dark flush rode high on his cheekbones, and an unmistakable sexual urgency seemed to radiate from him, supercharging the air around them.

Ring.

The phone. This time it forced its way into her consciousness. It was the first time she had heard the phone in her house ring since Lexie's—*no, not Lexie's*—since the traumatic call that had jerked her from sleep.

Galvanized (*What if it's Lexie—the same person—calling back?*), Sarah pushed past him and raced for the kitchen.

"Don't touch it," Jake called after her. There was a roughness to his voice, an undernote of anger that spoke to what had just happened between them. "Let the machine pick it up."

Not snatching up that receiver was the hardest thing in the world. Sarah stood there, breathing hard, her hand hovering above the plain black phone sitting on her kitchen counter, staring at the phone as if she could see through it.

Lexie—what if it's Lexie on the line?

And never mind that she knew, *knew,* that the little girl's voice that had upset her so much could not possibly have belonged to

Lexie. Her heart—poor, foolish thing—still refused to be convinced.

After two more rings, the answering machine kicked in. Heart thudding, Sarah listened to her own voice telling the caller to please leave a message.

"This is Dr. True's office. We're just calling to remind you that Sweetie-pie is due for his shots."

There was more, but Sarah didn't hear it. Her hand dropped as if it had turned to lead, and she turned away from the phone, sick at heart. She had hoped it was Lexie—or, rather, the voice that sounded like Lexie— again, she realized. It was idiotic to want something that she knew wasn't real, that had caused her so much pain, but no matter how phony it was, that agonizing phone call had felt like the first true link she had had to her daughter in seven years.

Jake was standing in the kitchen doorway watching her, grim-faced. Even soaked to the skin and shoeless as he was, he looked formidable, and she realized that she would have felt even more lost than she already did if he had not been there.

Their eyes met. The memory of that searing kiss hung in the air between them.

"Jake . . ." Her tone was tentative as she fumbled to come up with the words that would put things right between them. She *felt* tentative, uncertain of her ground, uncertain of him. What she wanted was her best friend back. The problem was, this stony-faced man with the hard mouth and smoldering eyes wasn't him.

"Forget it," he said before she could come up with anything remotely like the words she needed. "Kissing you was a mistake, all right? I shouldn't have done it. Chalk it up to very little sleep and a couple of long, stressful days."

"But . . ." Her instinct was to talk it out, to smooth things over, to do what she could to take their relationship back to where it had been before.

"I said forget it." He turned away, then glanced back over his shoulder at her. "Take a shower, get dressed, throw some clothes and whatever else you need in a bag. We're spending the weekend at my place."

"Your place?" She frowned as she followed him from the kitchen. He was using the towel he had shaken at her to wipe the water off her hardwood floors. This was clearly not the moment to remind him that she possessed a mop for that purpose, so she didn't. "Why? I have—"

"Because I'm tired," he interrupted. "I need sleep. So do you. And there's no way in hell either of us is going to be able to get any rest at all here, with you jumping like a scalded cat every time the phone rings and all kinds of reminders of Lexie and what's been going on with that around every-where."

She knew what he meant: the phone in her bedroom that, whenever she glanced at it, she still thought of as a link to her daughter. The toys in the closet that she still hadn't gone through. A hundred and one other things. He was right—of course he was right—but still, it pained her to think of just walking away from this house where Lexie suddenly seemed almost alive again. Somewhere deep in her mind, it was as if years spent learning to live with the painful reality of what had happened had been erased, and her daughter's disappearance was once again fresh and raw.

He straightened, balling the damp towel in his hands. Sarah was standing in the kitchen doorway now. Lights were on in the kitchen and the front hall, but where he stood, in almost the exact same spot where he had kissed her, was shadowed. Too shadowed to allow her to decipher his expression.

"You know," she said uncertainly, because everything between them was suddenly different now and she felt a little awkward with him for the first time in years, *"you* could go get a good night's sleep at your house and I could stay here. I've got Sweetie-pie. I'll be perfectly safe. And . . . and"—she had just remembered, and was surprised to find that the memory displeased her—"anyway, you've got a date to eat pork chops."

She tried a smile. He didn't smile back. For a moment he held her gaze, his eyes dark and unreadable in the shadowy hall, and then he turned and walked away. Into the bathroom. When he reemerged a moment or so later, his hands were empty.

He had put the towel in the hamper, Sarah realized.

"She dumped me. Danielle. This morning." His tone was as expressionless as his face.

Sarah's eyes widened. He *had* had a stressful day. No wonder he'd been cranky from the moment she'd set eyes on him. It hadn't been all about her at all. Which made her both feel better and, at the same time, idiotically, worse.

"Oh, dear. I'm sorry," she offered, feeling as if she was on firmer ground. After all, wasn't being there for each other one of the cornerstones of their relationship? "Are you okay?"

His mouth tightened as if in irritation. His eyes narrowed at her. "Go take a shower, Sarah, would you please?"

"Really. Go on home and go to bed. You don't have to worry about me."

"Right. Like I'm going to leave you. Would you quit being a total pain in my ass and just go take a goddamned shower?"

His mood hadn't improved noticeably by the time they reached his place. It was nearly nine o'clock—still raining, although not quite as hard as before—and night was falling fast. The other cars on the road—and, since this was Friday night and people were out and about, going to dinner, movies, and the mall, there were quite a few of them—all had their headlights on. In the backseat, Sweetie-pie stood in the middle, swaying with the curves in the road, smelling of damp dog while taking a vital interest in the food on Sarah's lap. In the front seat, Jake drove in silence while Sarah, whose few attempts at conversation since emerging from the shower had been shot down with monosyllabic replies, cast him the occasional sidelong glance. The radio played a little too loudly. Since Jake, who almost never listened to the radio while driving, had turned it on, Sarah took the pulsing music as a clear indication that he didn't want to talk to her.

All-righty, then.

"Grab the food, hang on to the dog, and I'll get everything else," Jake said as they pulled into the lot beside his building. "Everything else" consisted of Sarah's small overnight case; her briefcase, which had been retrieved from the trunk along with her cell phone, which was now in the pocket of the rain jacket she wore over a T-shirt and jeans; and a plastic grocery bag containing a bag of Kibbles 'n Bits and Sweetie-pie's dishes. The food referred to their supper, which had come from a quick side trip through McDonald's drive-through. Mindful of Jake's assertion that she didn't eat, Sarah had made it a point to ostentatiously nibble one fry after another ever since the bags had landed on her lap, where they rode for the duration to protect the contents from Sweetie-pie. Plus, she had ordered a hamburger with everything on it and small fries in addition to her usual side salad.

She did eat, so there.

To further underscore the point of how mistaken Jake was about her, the T-shirt she was wearing was bubble-gum pink, with a large crown and the words *Queen of Torts* in red across the front. Okay, so maybe it had been last year's joke Christmas gift from the office party, and maybe she had never worn it before, and maybe she'd had to search every nook and cranny of her dresser to come up with it. Still, it was emphatically *not* a neutral.

Hah.

Since Sweetie-pie was no fan of rain, they made it inside without him having to sniff at every rock and blade of grass, as he usually did when visiting unfamiliar places. Once inside, of course, he had to shake off the loathsome water, drawing a grimace from

Jake as droplets were flung all around the reception area.

"Sorry." Sarah had to grin. Jake's love-hate relationship with Sweetie-pie was a continual source of amusement to her, no matter what else was going on in her life. Except for a flinty-eyed glance, Jake ignored that, and Sarah found herself looking at his broad back as he led the way through the darkened offices on the bottom two floors to his apartment on the third. Like the building and the business, the apartment had originally belonged to his grandfather, who'd lived in it for a while after his wife had died. Pops had moved into a nearby retirement community upon selling the business to Jake and ostensibly retiring, and the apartment had been rented out. Then, when Jake lost his house when his wife had been awarded it in their divorce—she had subsequently sold it and moved to Chicago—Jake had moved into the apartment. Jake had stayed on in the apartment, mostly, Sarah suspected, out of sheer inertia, because his business was certainly successful enough to allow him to live somewhere else if he chose. The apartment was comfortable, he'd said when Sarah had asked him about it, and plenty big enough for him. She suspected that, manlike, he simply didn't want to go to the trouble of moving when there was no pressing need.

"You're being a total jackass about this, you know," Sarah said after about fifteen more minutes of near silence, during which they'd entered Jake's apartment, put the food on the table, and eaten while staring at the talking heads on *Headline News,* which he'd turned on and which, Sarah knew, was serving the same function as the car radio. Or, at least, he'd eaten, scarfing down a Big Mac and fries like he was starving and slurping up a large Coke. She, on the other hand, was still faintly queasy from all the grease she'd forced down in the car to prove a point that he probably hadn't gotten anyway, so she had taken a single bite of her burger and was picking at her salad. She couldn't even look at the fries anymore.

He dragged his gaze from the TV long enough to glance at her. "Oh, yeah?"

Now there you go, that was progress. His reply actually consisted of two syllables.

"I don't know why you're so bent out of shape. Since I'm not a mind reader, you're going to have to tell me. Are you upset about Danielle? Or mad at me because you kissed me and I didn't melt like butter in your arms?"

His brows twitched together. "I'm tired, okay?"

He transferred his attention back to the TV, where they were talking stock prices. She'd known Jake a long time, and on the strength of that, she was willing to bet the rent that he wasn't finding what was being said on-screen all that riveting. But he focused intently on it nonetheless.

"Bullshit. You're mad. It's about the kiss, isn't it? Not Danielle."

He glanced at her again. This time his expression said quite clearly that if she'd been a mosquito, he would have gladly swatted her.

"You're right about one thing: You're definitely not a mind reader." There he went with the sarcasm again. As far as Sarah was concerned, as tones of voice went, that one was growing kind of old.

Her lips pursed, but she persevered. "You caught me by surprise, okay? The last thing I was expecting was for you to kiss me. We've known each other for seven years, and you've never kissed me before."

His expression lightened fractionally as a touch of humor glinted in his eyes. "What can I say? First time for everything."

"Just so you know, I wasn't *rejecting* you." That was the point she wanted to make clear. Watching his face, she saw the grimness around his eyes and mouth return and continued hurriedly, "It's just—I *care* about you. And you care about me. As friends. And that's very, very special, and I don't want to lose it."

Jake snorted. "What are we, five years old? That sounds like it came straight out of kindergarten. It was a kiss, all right? One damned kiss in seven years, so would you quit making it into such a big deal?"

"I will if you will."

"Honey, one kiss might loom large in your life, but in mine . . ." He shrugged, his voice trailing off, but his meaning was clear: Over the last seven years, for him, there'd been lots of kisses. *Hundreds,* Sarah thought, hazily calculating. No, probably thousands. She did a quick mental review of his girlfriends, and found to her annoyance that she wasn't enjoying herself one bit.

"Well, that makes it all better," she said tartly.

"You wouldn't be jealous, now, would you?"

She responded with outrage. "No!"

"Just asking."

He gave another of those maddening shrugs, snagged a couple of her fries—he'd eaten all of his—polished them off, and finished his Coke, his attention once more on the TV. Watching him, Sarah simmered, then sighed inwardly. No matter what he said, he was still mad, she could tell. And he was a lot more affected by what had happened between them than he was willing to let on.

She tried again. "Look, it's me, you know? Not you. It's not that you didn't turn me on, if that's the part that's bothering you. It's just . . . I just don't feel comfortable having a . . . a sexual relationship with anyone. Even you."

This attempt at total honesty did not go over quite as planned. It did not reestablish the bond of trust and openness between them as she had hoped. It got Jake's attention, though. His eyes fixed on her, narrowing. His jaw tightened.

"I'm aware, okay? Remember that whole not-letting-yourself-have-any-pleasure conversation we had? I'd say this is a prime example. And by the way, just for the record, one measly damned kiss does not a sexual relationship make."

Sarah ignored that last in favor of glaring at him. "Just because I didn't pull off my clothes and hop into bed with you at the first touch of your lips on mine doesn't mean I won't let myself experience pleasure. I experience plenty of pleasure." Then, realizing how that sounded, she quickly added, "In other ways."

Jake's mouth thinned. "You keep telling yourself that, and sooner or later you might even start believing it's true." He stood up. "Okay, end of discussion. I'm going to go take a shower."

Sarah was still simmering as he walked away. He kept no extra clothes at her house, and her clothes were way too small to even begin to fit his big frame, which meant he was still wearing the clothes he'd gotten soaked in earlier. They had basically dried on him by this time. They were probably still a little clammy. He was probably a little uncomfortable. That was probably why he was experiencing this sudden, acute urge to grab a shower.

The moon was probably made of green cheese, too.

He was just making sure he got in the last word.

"Face facts: You're wrong," she called after him.

He glanced back over his shoulder at her.

"Nice shirt," he said. "Did you pull that out of mothballs just for me?"

Then he laughed and disappeared into his bedroom, leaving her glaring after him.

Along with a private bathroom and closet space, Jake's bedroom took up the whole south side of the apartment. The living room, dining area, and kitchen were in the center, and then another smaller bedroom, a bathroom, and a tiny office completed the space. The same decorator who had done the downstairs offices had overseen the updating of the apartment, so it was a nice, masculine mixture of grays and blacks, with deep red accents. And yes, there were rugs and pictures and curtains in the appropriate places, which, yes again, her house did lack.

The thing was, though, Jake had used a decorator, which, when you came right down to the whole accessorizing thing, was cheating. And she, Sarah, had been busy. Really, really busy. Just because she hadn't made use of her inner Martha Stewart did not mean that she was—how had Jake put it?—deliberately denying herself anything that could bring her pleasure.

Did it?

Unbidden, that sizzling kiss and the way it had made her feel did an instant replay in her mind. Her first response had been shock, her second, heat. Hunger. Wanting. But even as her body had experienced a fierce sexual charge, her mind had rejected any idea of satisfying it.

So what did that say?

Probably nothing that she wanted to examine too closely.

Unless, maybe, she was prepared to admit that Jake just might be right.

Glumly, Sarah disposed of what was left of her burger and fries by feeding them to Sweetie-pie, who was nearly as indiscriminate as Jake in his choice of food. Then she took a couple more bites of salad, gave up on the whole eating-to-prove-a-point concept since Jake was no longer around to be impressed, and threw the rest away.

It wasn't that she didn't eat, she thought

defensively. It was just that she'd made a mistake with the fries. And it wasn't necessarily that she wouldn't allow herself to enjoy sex. It was more that she wasn't sure she wanted sex in her life again, especially not now, with everything else that was going on. And then there was the fact that Jake was her best friend and that their relationship was too important to her to mess up. Besides, Jake's kiss had been unexpected, to say the least. As she had told him, he'd caught her by surprise. Maybe, with some warning, her response would have been different. Anyway, to borrow a page from Jake's excuse book, she'd had a stressful day.

Moving to the couch—it was a nice one, long and deep, upholstered in a charcoal-gray suedelike material with deep red pillows at each end—she curled up, remote control in hand, and stared at the TV. It was typical Jake: plasma, big, affixed to the wall, state-of-the-art.

Not that she was, at the moment, taking in a single image or hearing a single word playing on it.

Forget Jake's grouchiness, and the kiss, and the whole detour on which it had taken their friendship. The thing she needed to focus on right now was that someone had written *Eeyore* on her car window. The question was, who? Could Jake be right? Could her and Lexie's secret word be part of the record somewhere?Jake had copies of most everything pertaining to Lexie's disappearance—the police files, the FBI files, the results of his own investigation, photos, video- and audio tapes, everything except the actual forensic evidence, of which there was precious little—on the premises. She personally had poured over them so many times that she knew whole sections by heart, but maybe she'd missed something. He kept his current records, including Lexie's, one floor below where she was sitting, in what had once been a bedroom and was now given over to hundreds of files.

Could she possibly have overlooked the part where someone had told an investigator about their secret code word?

The only way to be sure was to check. Sarah was on her feet, remote forgotten on the couch, heading downstairs for the files even before the decision to do so had finished forming in her brain. With Sweetie-pie click-clacking behind her, she went down-stairs and retrieved as much as she could carry, which amounted to a backbreaking armload of manila folders stuffed to burst-ing with paper. There was four times as much still to come, plus the boxes of pho-tos and tapes, but she figured she could go through it in a few hours if she just worked methodically. She had just plunked the lot in her arms down on the cleared dining table and begun sorting them into piles, ready to start going through each and every file again page by page, when Jake emerged from his bedroom.

He stopped halfway to the table to frown at her. "What're you doing?"

"Getting ready to go through the files on Lexie's disappearance to see if it's in here anywhere that *Eeyore* was our code word."

"You know, I can put some people on that tomorrow and get it done a lot quicker than you can do it yourself."

Sarah stopped sorting and looked at him. Barefoot, he padded toward her, comfort-able in an old gray Gamecocks T-shirt and jeans. His hair was ruffled and looked like it was still slightly damp from his shower, a five o'clock shadow darkened his cheeks and chin, and there were faint, tired shadows beneath his eyes. The well-washed T-shirt hugged his broad shoulders and wide chest, and his jeans emphasized the long, powerful muscles of his thighs. It had been a long time since Sarah had thought of him as anything but Jake, her best friend, but now it was as if she were seeing him properly for the first time, and she realized that he was a very attractive man.

Hot, even.

That she should even think such a thought bothered her. Then, putting blame where blame was due, she concluded, *It's all the fault of that damned kiss.*

It had changed everything. Where before they had been as comfortable with each other as family, now a new element had entered into their relationship. A slight uneasiness, a sense of unfamiliarity, a barely perceptible tension hung in the air.

She didn't have time for this.

"They might miss something." She resumed sorting, then sat down and opened a file. Immediately, a copy of the "missing" flier she and hundreds of volunteers had passed out in the first days and weeks after

Lexie's disappearance looked up at her. Her daughter's picture was front and center.

Sarah couldn't help it. She winced and closed her eyes.

"Damn it, Sarah." Jake must have realized, because he came over to stand beside her.

Get a grip, Sarah told herself fiercely, and opened her eyes again just as he flipped the flier over so that Lexie was no longer looking up at her. Instead, Sarah found herself staring at Xeroxed photos of the park, six to a page, and tried to let the breath she'd caught out softly, so that he wouldn't hear. There was the pavilion, the sidewalks, the grassy areas, the beach. As the pictures had been taken several days after Lexie had gone missing, though, they held little of interest to her, and Sarah flipped through them quickly.

"You know this is not about Lexie, don't you?" His voice was grim. He was still standing beside her, but she didn't look up at him. She didn't want to see the compassion for her that she knew would be there in his eyes. "Something bad is happening here, for sure, but it's not about Lexie, per se. Her disappearance is just the weapon somebody is using to get under your skin."

"Who?" Blindly, Sarah flipped another page. She still didn't look up at him. As much as she didn't want to see the pity in his eyes, she didn't want him to see the pain in hers, either. "And why?"

"I don't know. But I do know that it's not some ghostly manifestation of your daughter trying to get in touch with you—oh, yeah, I know you; I know that thought's occurred. What we're dealing with here is a living, breathing person who has it in for you. Who may have shot you and may still be looking for an opportunity to kill you. Who definitely is capitalizing on the tragedy in your past for their own ends. Either somebody who hates you or somebody with something to gain. One of your current cases, maybe, like Stumbo or Herlitzer or whatever the hell else you're working on. Or somebody you've pissed off pretty badly in the past." He paused, and the faintest note of humor entered his voice. "Hell, now that I think about it, the number could be legion."

That caused her to look up, and to even give him a wry little smile. "Gee, thanks."

The look in his eyes turned almost rueful.

He loomed above her, tall and solid and looking capable of taking on all comers, one hand gripping the back of her chair.

"Give it a rest for tonight, Sarah. You won't miss anything if you leave it until tomorrow." His voice had gone soft, almost coaxing.

For a moment, she was tempted. Just put it out of her head, relax with him, watch TV—they hadn't done that in a long time.

But she couldn't. She absolutely could not.

No matter how much she might agree with his assessment of what was going on, no matter how much logic might tell her that at its core this truly wasn't about Lexie, her heart was convinced that it was. And that made every second she wasn't hunting for the truth a second wasted.

"See, the thing is, no one knew about *Eeyore*," she said. "I'm almost positive. If I find it in here, then I know you're right and I can let it go. If I don't . . ."

Her voice trailed off, and her gaze slid back down to the papers in front of her: a typed summary of a witness interview with someone who'd been in the park when Lexie had disappeared. It was stapled on top of an actual transcript of the interview. To be thorough, to be sure, Sarah realized that she was going to have to read every word. Suppressing a sigh, she flipped the summary back and began.

Without another word, Jake moved, sitting down at the table opposite her. He picked up the next file in the stack and started going through it.

He would do whatever she needed, just as he always had. It was good to realize that no matter what else was going on between them, Jake still had her back.

Two hours later, they were still at it. The worst part was, although they discussed a lot of possibilities, batting things back and forth, arguing them through, they had come up with absolutely nothing new.

"Okay, enough." Jake had just finished the file he was going through, and he reached across the table to close the one she was working on.

Sarah would have protested, but she was so bleary-eyed that she still saw the paper she had been looking at even thought the file was now closed, which told her that it was, indeed, time to quit. What they were doing was useless if they weren't thorough.

Sadly, she realized with a glance around the table, they weren't much more than halfway through the pile she had carried upstairs. Thinking of all the material that remained downstairs, her shoulders slumped.

This was going to take forever, and not only was there was no guarantee of success, there was actually only the slimmest chance of it.

"Bed," Jake said firmly, standing up.

Of their own accord, Sarah's eyes flew to his face. Given what now lay between them, the word, with all its connotations, was loaded. She must be tired to react so strongly, Sarah thought, surprised at herself, and tried to dismiss the jumbled images—his mouth on hers, his hand on her breast, the hardness of his body, that first instinctive response of hers—that whirled through her head in its wake. But he must have read something of what was going through her mind in her eyes—damn the man, he knew her too well—because his eyes darkened and his lips firmed.

"It's almost midnight," he continued. "I'm beat."

Sarah was standing up, not all that surprised to find that she was lightheaded and a little unsteady on her feet, when he thrust his hands into the front pockets of his jeans, rocked back on his heels, and added, "So, you sleeping with me?"

16

For a moment Sarah simply looked at him across the table, a little wide-eyed she was sure, as she remembered that last night she had, indeed, slept in his arms.

A lot had changed since then.

Then he grinned at her, the kind of slow-dawning, faintly lopsided, charming grin that he hadn't given her in a long time.

"I take that look on your face for a 'no,'" he said, and she realized that he had been teasing her.

She smiled, too, relieved. If he was getting his sense of humor back, things were looking up. At least he didn't seem to be mad at her any longer.

Sweetie-pie, who'd been sleeping beside her feet, stood up, too, stretched, and looked up at her inquiringly.

"You want to go out?" she asked him. Then, to Jake, as Sweetie-pie replied with an affirmative brightening of his eyes, "I need to take him out."

"I'll do it."

Sarah was already heading for Sweetie-pie's leash, which she'd left on the coffee table in front of the couch. Sweetie-pie, who knew the way things worked, was right beside her.

"You?" She looked around at Jake skeptically as she scooped the leash from the table and clipped it to Sweetie-pie's collar.

"You see any other suicidal idiot around?" Sarah laughed.

"You'd do that for me?" She batted her eyelashes at him.

"There's not much I wouldn't do for you." His voice was wry, and he grimaced as he took the leash from her. He looked down at Sweetie-pie, who was on his feet, pressing his big body close against Sarah's legs. Sweetie-pie looked up at him, and his doggy lip curled. It wasn't quite a sneer, but it came close. "But I have to admit, this is stretching it."

"I'll come with you."

Jake shook his head. "You stay here. Just in case there's somebody out there who wants to take another shot at you."

Sarah's stomach tightened. "You think there is?"

"I don't know. For somebody to find you over at that housing project, they almost had to be following you. Is it the same person who shot you? Hard to tell, but it's not the kind of thing I'd want to be wrong about." He started moving toward the door, then paused as he reached the end of the leash and Sweetie-pie stayed firmly planted. "Of course, if whoever this is is really interested in killing you, you practically gave him a printed invitation to the party when you went walking all on your lonesome in the park. Your still being alive strikes me as a good sign, but then again, unlike some people, even cold-blooded killers sometimes draw the line at running around in a pouring rainstorm."

She gave him a withering look. "Shut up, Jake."

He smiled mockingly at her, then glanced down at the immovable object at the other end of the leash. "Come *on,* Sweetie-pie."

With a glance up at Sarah, Sweetie-pie began to move with obvious reluctance, and Jake headed for the door again.

Sarah, meanwhile, had a hideous thought.

"Do you think he followed me *here*?" At the idea that whoever was behind this might be outside right now, that he might be shadowing her everywhere she went, her heart kicked up a notch. The realization that it hadn't occurred to her earlier that she might very well have been followed made her feel slightly stupid.

"I hope so," Jake said grimly, one hand on the knob as he glanced back over his shoulder at her. "I've got a couple of people outside, watching the house. If he did, we've got him." He opened the door, looked down at the dog, who was looking back at Sarah longingly, then met Sarah's gaze. "You're down with the whole stay-inside-until-I-get-back thing, right?"

Sarah nodded wordlessly. Sweetie-pie must have sensed her sudden tension, because the curl in his lip became more pronounced—pronounced enough to reveal a threatening glimmer of teeth.

"Good," Jake said, then glanced down. His tone changed, rising about half an octave to the fakest-sounding near falsetto that Sarah had ever heard this side of Jack Nicholson in *The Shining.* "Good dog, Sweetie-pie. Let's go potty."

Even under the circumstances, Sarah smiled.

Sweetie-pie looked up at him with clear loathing, then allowed himself to be escorted from the room.

They were gone only about fifteen minutes. Having waited on tenterhooks, Sarah sprang up off the couch as they entered. Clearly it was still raining; Jake's shoulders and upper body were dry—she assumed he'd picked up an umbrella or some such protection on the way out—but raindrops splotched his jeans from mid-thigh down. Sweetie-pie's coat glistened, and he smelled damp, but he didn't shake. Sarah assumed he'd done that downstairs. Probably in Jake's reception room again.

"Anything?" Sarah asked as he handed her Sweetie-pie's leash. She unclipped it from his collar and patted his big head. He heaved a sigh and padded off toward the kitchen area, where she had put his food and water dishes.

Jake shook his head. "No. Listen, just so you know, you've got nothing to worry about. There'll be people out there watching the house all night. Plus, the burglar alarm's on. And you'll have Cujo in your room. You can sleep like a baby." The merest hint of a smile curved his lips. "Even without me."

He was teasing her again, but she was too glad of this further proof that their relationship was back on track to ruffle up at him.

"You're the best, Jake."

"Careful, you'll be getting me all hot and bothered here." His voice was dry. He walked over to the couch, picked up the remote, and turned off the TV. Then he glanced over his shoulder at her. "Go on to bed, Sarah."

She did. The double bed in Jake's guestroom was comfortable, as was the room itself. Her oft-laundered sleep shirt—it was pale blue, mid-thigh-length, and decorated with a picture of a sleeping kitten—was soft and familiar. Sweetie-pie was under the bed, and she could hear him breathing, which was comforting. The rain pattering against the windows was soothing. The burglar alarm and the fact that Jake had people watching the house were reassuring. But what really made her feel safe enough to surrender to sleep was the knowledge that Jake was nearby. All she had to do was call out his name, and he would come running, she knew. One yell, one too-loud thud, one out-of-the-way sound, and he would be at her side in an instant.

And so, secure in that knowledge, she resorted to her usual mantra and fell asleep. Dreams came, as they always did. Sarah didn't usually remember most of them, but sometimes she awoke feeling comforted and thought that perhaps Lexie had visited her in her dreams. Other times, she awoke weeping and guessed that she had relived her daughter's disappearance. Tonight, though, she awoke with a scream.

For a long moment after she'd been jolted from sleep by her own frightened cry, she lay unmoving, flat on her back, her fists clenched around the covers, which she clasped to her chest, staring sightlessly up at the ceiling. Her heart pounded. Her breathing came fast. What had awakened her? She didn't know. She knew only that whatever it was had brought her screaming from sleep. Jake would arrive any second, she knew, and she listened for his hasty footsteps even as her breathing steadied and her frantic heartbeat slowed. The room stayed dark, quiet. Nothing moved. No one—read, Jake—came. Under the bed, Sweetie-pie continued to sleep, the sound of his breathing rhythmic and undisturbed. As the last mists of sleep cleared, Sarah understood that she'd had a nightmare. A nightmare disturbing enough to make her cry out in her sleep. It was hazy now, but she could vaguely remember that a one-eyed creature had been chasing her, and when she turned it had been right in her face, whirring away . . .

A video camera. A *man* with a video camera. In the park. Filming her up close and personal not long after Lexie had disappeared, while she'd been almost out of her mind with terror yet still not totally without hope for her daughter's safe recovery, and a bevy of scarlet-and-white-clad cheerleaders had performed their routines behind her.

In the aftermath of Lexie's disappearance, the police had taken, or been given, dozens of hours of videotape shot in the park that day. An appeal had gone out for every scrap of footage that had been shot at the festival, and the public had responded in spades. Sarah knew, because she had watched every minute of every one, looking fruitlessly for any clue that might lead to Lexie. There had been nothing useful.

The thing was, though, there had also been no footage of herself in close-up, staring wild-eyed into a camera while a bunch of cheerleaders cavorted behind her.

The tape should have been there. The fact that it wasn't was significant. Maybe. Or maybe not.

Maybe it was there but she had missed it, or even watched it and forgotten about it. After all, it had been years since she had looked at those tapes. And she hadn't been looking for herself in front of a background of cheerleaders at the time. Until she'd walked through the park the previous evening with her memory on overdrive, she'd forgotten all about that man with the camera.

But thinking about it now, in the aftermath of her only hazily remembered dream, it seemed that he had been inordinately interested in *her.* And clearly her subconscious had been disturbed enough by the memory to process it again in the form of a dream. A dream that had frightened her into screaming herself awake.

The pertinent question was, had that man really been taping *her,* in particular, rather than, say, the cheerleaders? And if so, why? The answer that percolated up from her subconscious made her sick: Having done something with Lexie, could he then possibly have been recording Lexie's mother's reaction to her disappearance?

Probably not. Surely not. Her imagination was almost certainly getting the best of her here, as it had many, many times since Lexie had vanished. Still, what she remembered of the cameraman stayed fixed in her mind: middle-aged, average height, a burly build, a small, pursed mouth beneath a bushy, black mustache. And that was all. The only other detail about him that she could recall was the damned camera that had blocked the rest of his face.

But it was more than she had ever had before. If this guy had truly had something to do with Lexie's disappearance—and she knew it was a stretch, a big stretch, but she was ready, willing, and able to grasp at the flimsiest of straws at this point—then it was a starting point. A few details, a thumbnail sketch of somebody to look for—they'd never had even that much before. And as little as it was, it might make all the difference.

Even as she started to get all excited, Sarah warned herself not to.

The first thing to do was to review the tapes to make sure she hadn't just overlooked the footage containing those jumping cheerleaders.

She slid out of bed and padded softly into the living room. The digital clock on the TV read three sixteen a.m. She'd been asleep a little more than three hours, but she felt totally energized.

Purpose, like hope, did that to a person.

The tapes were downstairs. No way was she going to be able to sleep again until she had watched them. Fortunately, unlike the files, there was no need to go through all of them. Each was labeled with the name of the person who'd done the filming—throw out all the women—the time the recording had begun—throw out anything after five

forty-five p.m.—and the approximate locations included in the footage.

Moving quietly so as not to wake Jake—
so much for her assumption that one unto-
ward noise would bring him rushing to her
rescue, she thought wryly—she went downstairs and sorted through the videotapes.
When she was finished, she was left with
eight that were possibilities. Then she
turned out the light and carried them upstairs. Once inside the apartment, she quietly put the stack on the coffee table, then
stood still for a moment to catch her breath.
Over the myriad night sounds of the apartment, she could hear two sets of competing
snores, Jake's and Sweetie-pie's. Pondering her own personal twist on one of life's
great questions—if a person screamed in an
apartment and no one heard her, had she
really made a sound?—she walked over to
Jake's bedroom door, which was open, presumably so that he could hear her if she
needed him, which clearly hadn't worked
out as he'd hoped. She listened to him
snoring for a moment longer, then softly
closed his door so that she wouldn't wake
him. Then she returned to the living area,
turned on the lamp beside the couch,

picked up the shortest tape—they ranged from seven minutes to an hour—and made a hideous discovery.

His big, fancy, state-of-the-art TV played only DVDs.

For a moment, the discovery floored her. She thought longingly of her own crappy old TV, with its hopelessly out-of-date VCR. The tapes would play fine on that. The possibility of simply packing up the tapes and Sweetie-pie and heading home occurred to her, only to be almost instantly dismissed. Jake's warning that someone who wanted to kill her might be out there had sunk in this time, and without the impetus of extreme emotional duress, she wasn't quite that stupid. Then she remembered the small, white TV that Dorothy kept in the break room on the second floor, where she retreated most days to eat her lunch and watch her favorite daytime soap. It had a VCR built into it. Scooping up the tapes, Sarah hurried back downstairs.

The break room was right next to the file room. It was small, maybe eight feet by ten feet, and, since it was Dorothy's retreat, it had mostly escaped the ministrations of the decorator. One wall was devoted exclusively to kitchen-style cabinets and a counter where the TV waited. It also held a small refrigerator, a microwave, and a sink. The walls were painted a soft blue, and a blue floral couch with a shell-framed mirror above it took up the wall opposite the cabinets. Against the far wall stood a card table with four chairs, where Dorothy, and anyone else who wanted to join her, often ate. Blue-checked café curtains covered the small window.

Sarah flipped on the overhead light, slid the first tape into the VCR, turned the volume down as low as possible so as not to risk disturbing Jake (not that, disillusioned as she now was, she really considered there was much likelihood of that), and settled into the couch to watch.

The footage was of two little boys kicking around a beach ball. There was a glimpse of the pavilion in the background, but, since it was filmed at the children's eye level—the cameraman must have been crouching or kneeling—not much besides the children was captured. Even the background figures were cut off at the waist.

The second tape was of a dog chasing a Frisbee near the sidewalk that led from the pavilion to the beach. Background figures were visible in this one, though just from watching it, none seemed to be of particular interest. Sarah vowed to freeze-frame it and go over each individual in the crowd later, on the off-chance that the man who had filmed her in front of the cheerleaders might be visible.

The third tape was taken inside the pavilion by a relative of Andrew, the same Andrew who was on Lexie's T-ball team. It basically featured Andrew, Andrew, and more Andrew, and Sarah remembered it well. She'd watched it a dozen times in the first few months after Lexie's disappearance, because there was a glimpse of her daughter in it. Just a glimpse, a flash of coppery ponytails tied up with blue ribbons skipping through the background. Quick as a sneeze, and she was gone.

Sarah popped that one out as soon as she realized what it was. But still, she wasn't quick enough to prevent a squeezing pain from gripping her heart.

She quickly replaced it with another tape, feeding it into the VCR's slot and sinking back into the couch as the image of a young woman eating a hot dog and waving at the camera appeared on the TV. The . . .

"Christ, Sarah, it's four in the morning."

Jake appeared in the doorway so suddenly that Sarah jumped. Her bare feet, which had been tucked beneath her, hit the floor. His hair was mussed, his eyes were bloodshot, and he was wearing only his jeans. His broad, heavily muscled shoulders nearly filled the doorway, and his wide chest sported a neat triangle of curling black hair. It had been a while since she'd noticed what he looked like without his shirt, and she was interested to observe that despite his hideous diet, he looked pretty good. Fit, even. Not cut, no six-pack abs, but reasonably trim around the midsection.

Okay, now that the genie was out of the bottle, there was clearly no putting it back: The precise word that sprang into her mind as her eyes ran over him was *sexy.* She couldn't believe that until tonight she had never really thought of him in that light before. He'd always been just Jake to her: a strong arm to lean on, a keen mind to bend itself to her needs as necessary, a pal to hang out with, somebody she knew, without any doubt whatsoever, she could count on to be there for her.

For years now he'd been the closest thing to family she had left, and it hit her with the force of a cream pie to the face that before tonight, she had never even really looked at him objectively.

Because if she had, how in the world could she possibly have missed the fact that he was sexy?

He was right, she thought, suddenly appalled: Since Lexie had disappeared, her grief had all but rendered her deaf and dumb and blind to the world around her. In every way that mattered, she had cut herself off from life.

She must have been staring at him all glassy-eyed as she experienced this profound psychological breakthrough, because with a single glance at what she was watching, he moved between her and the TV, folded his arms over his chest, and glared at her.

"This is sick, you know that?"

"What? I'm watching . . ."

He cut her off. "I know what you're watching. You think I haven't watched the tapes from that day often enough myself to recognize them when I see them?" He blew out his breath in a sigh, and some of the edge left his voice. "So, you want to tell me why you're watching them *now*?"

Glancing past him at the section of TV screen that was still visible, she saw that the young woman, having finished her hot dog, was blowing kisses at the camera.

"I remembered something," Sarah said as Jake turned off the TV, punching the button with rather more savagery than the action called for. Dealing with the he-was-right stuff would have to wait: First she needed to fill him in on what she was almost convinced was a real breakthrough in the case. "Right after Lexie disappeared, when I was running around looking for her, there was a man with a video camera filming me. A bunch of cheerleaders were performing behind me, but he was focusing the camera on *me,* I'm almost sure. I wanted to see if that tape had been turned in, because if it hasn't been . . ."

Just talking about it, Sarah got excited all over again.

"Did I mention that it's four o'clock in the damned morning?" Jake interrupted, growling. "You didn't go to bed until mid-night."

"I'm not tired." Sarah dismissed that impatiently. "Jake, listen, I—"

"Well, I'm tired. You ever think about that? I'm so damned tired, I'm practically seeing double here."

"So go back to bed. I just want to watch—"

"You should be tired. You should be falling down exhausted. You keep this up and you're going to kill yourself for real."

"I'm not that fragile. I—"

His eyes narrowed and his jaw tensed as she spoke. He broke in ruthlessly.

"The hell you're not. Have you taken a good look in the mirror lately?" He reached down, caught her hand, and hauled her to her feet. Turning her around, placing both hands on her shoulders, he brought her face-to-face with her reflection in the mirror above the couch. He loomed big and dark behind her, and Sarah thought that it was probably the marked contrast with his size and swarthiness that made her own reflection appear so slight and pale. Her hair was ruffled, angling back away from her face so that her wound was barely visible, but she was sure that it was its ink-blackness that made her skin look so paper-white. As for the bluish shadows under her eyes—well, admittedly, she hadn't slept for a while. And the prominence of her cheekbones? Eating hadn't been a big priority, either. In fact, now that she thought about it, she hadn't had breakfast. Or lunch.

He had a point. She did look kind of fragile. Not that she meant to agree with him: It would give him too much ammunition.

Her chin went up. "So?"

Their eyes met through the mirror. His hands tightened. They looked tan and very masculine against the soft powder blue of her sleep shirt. Their size emphasized the narrowness of her shoulders. He was so close behind her that she could feel the solid strength of him just brushing her back. She was suddenly supremely aware of the fact that he wasn't wearing a shirt. She began feeling way too warm and thought—hoped—the cause must be the heat of his body radiating into hers.

Any other explanation added up to a complication that at the moment she just didn't need. She pulled away from his hold and turned to face him. For good measure, and because she was suddenly way too conscious that she was naked beneath her sleep shirt and that just a few hours before, he'd had his hands on her breasts, she crossed her arms in front of her and matched him frown for frown.

His eyes held hers. "You're running on nothing but fumes here, and if you keep on like this, you're going to collapse. Then what good will you be to Lexie or anyone else, hmm?"

Sarah hadn't thought of that.

Her frown faded. She licked her lips.

"It's just . . . I feel like I'm closer to finding out what happened to Lexie than I have been in a long time. In my dream I saw this guy with a camera, and I remembered that he had actually been there in the park. I can remember some things about him, so that if I'm right we can actually get a little bit of a physical description together. That's why I needed to look at the tapes. If the one he shot isn't here, then . . ."

"It still won't be here tomorrow. Come on, Sarah. Maybe you don't need sleep, but I do, and I sure as hell can't get any with you down here doing this."

Sarah was still resisting the pangs of guilt she knew he was intentionally inflicting on her when he made an impatient sound. Then he reached out, caught one of her hands, and started walking, pulling her after him into the hall, flicking off the light as he passed the switch.

"The tapes . . ." Sarah protested, looking back.

"Trust me. They're not going anywhere."

Only a faint glow from his apartment, the door of which he'd left ajar, provided any illumination at all, leaving the hall shrouded in shadow. The narrow stairs that led from the second to the third floor were dark at the bottom, light at the top.

He stopped at the bottom, pulled her up beside him like a fisherman hauling in his catch, then dropped her hand and gestured to her to precede him up the stairs.

Despite her efforts not to succumb, the guilt had taken root. Without a word, Sarah climbed, although she knew she was too wired to sleep. The thing was, though, Jake wasn't. Much as she would rather be watching the tapes right now, she would go back to bed and lie there staring at the ceiling for Jake. At least until she was sure he was asleep again.

"I'm sorry I woke you up," she said, meaning it, when they were back in his apartment. He had just locked the door and was turning to scowl at her some more. She yawned hugely, for effect, and moved to the lamp beside the couch, which she'd left on. "You're right, I *am* tired. I'll see you in the morning, okay?"

"Wait a minute. Say that again." His scowl lightened fractionally as he padded barefoot toward her.

"I'm tired?" She was fumbling beneath the shade for the little knob that turned off the lamp.

"No. I'm talking about the part where you said 'You're right.' I don't think I've ever heard you say that before."

"Oh."

He was close now, and she looked up at him, taking in the narrowed brown eyes under the stubby fringe of black lashes; the stubble darkening his chin; the hint of grimness that still hovered around his mouth; the sturdy column of his neck; the broad, bare shoulders; the wide, hair-roughened chest tapering out above strong hips and powerful legs in well-worn jeans, with a single comprehensive glance. He was as familiar to her as her own reflection, and yet, suddenly, she got the feeling that maybe she didn't really know him that well at all.

The thought was exciting.

Sarah registered that little jolt of sexual awareness with a slight sense of shock. Maybe, now that she'd recognized how closed off her emotions had been, she was starting to get them back.

Once again, this disturbance in the force, as it were, could be laid right at the door of that damned kiss.

This is not a good time to get your groove back, she told herself, but that didn't keep her heart from suddenly beating a little faster as he stopped in front of her. As insurance, even as her fingers found and gripped the tiny knob, she released it again and straightened, letting her hand drop to her side. Plunging them into darkness was probably not something she needed to do. Not until she got a handle on how this whole psychological reawakening thing was going to work out for her.

"Well?" Jake folded his arms, clearly waiting. Sarah noticed as if it were something new that his arms were deeply tanned and brawny with muscle, and instantly switched her gaze to his face.

"Fine: You're right." She realized that she had practically snapped the words at him in her agitation, sighed, and gave up the fight with herself. The thing about Jake and her was, they'd always been honest with each other. Playing it any other way just wasn't fair to either of them. "I would say, about a lot of things, actually, except I'm afraid that giving you that kind of credit would go to straight to your head."

He looked cautious. "What kind of things are we talking about here?"

"You know. Everything you said to me when we had that argument earlier. I think the theme was, I don't have any fun."

"You don't," he said, as if the reminder was all that was needed to get him fired up again. "You work all the time, you don't sleep—right now being a case in point—you—"

She interrupted, narrowing her eyes at him. "Okay, I got the message already." Then she added, "Can I ask you something?"

"Why do I have the feeling that this is going to be a loaded question?"

She ignored that. "Why did you kiss me? And don't give me that stuff about you having a stressful day, either. The truth."

His jaw hardened. Wariness flickered in his eyes. "Honey, you can't handle the truth."

He said it lightly, as a joke, but if he thought that he was going to get away with leaving it at that, he was sadly mistaken: He wasn't putting her off that easily.

"I want to know why you kissed me, Jake." She searched his eyes. "I deserve to know."

A beat passed. His mouth twisted in a half-smile. Then he did something surprising: He took her hands, lifted them to his mouth, and kissed them, one at a time. Sarah's eyes widened as she watched his lips press into her smooth, pale skin. It was the kind of romantic gesture she never would have believed Jake capable of, and it dazzled her. Her pulse quickened. Her breathing went all uneven. She felt the heat of those kisses clear down to her toes.

Then she lifted her eyes to meet his again.

They were dark and hot above their clasped hands.

"See, the thing is," he said, "maybe I'm tired of us being best friends."

17

"This wouldn't be because I'm a major pain in the ass, would it?" Sarah managed, struggling to keep it light even as her heart started tap-dancing in her chest.

"There's that." He was looking surprisingly grim for a man who had just kissed her hands, she decided. "You know you're killing me here, right?"

"Think you could be a little more specific?" Forget tap-dancing. Her heart was doing calisthenics. "Killing you how, exactly? Are we talking no sleep, or too much aggravation, or—"

"All those," he said, interrupting. There was a husky undertone to his voice. "Plus— and this is the main one—I'm crazy about you."

The calisthenics turned into higher-level gymnastics. Their hands were still linked, although their arms had dropped to their sides now. His eyes had gone so dark that they were almost black. His mouth was wry.

Sarah suddenly felt breathless. She didn't know who the person was who was listening to him say these things, but it didn't seem like it could possibly be her. It felt too good. It had been, she realized, a long, long time since something had felt this good.

Best to proceed cautiously, like a grandma strapping on roller skates for the first time in decades. "So what are you saying?"

"You need me to draw you a diagram here?" He grimaced, and his hands tightened on hers. "Okay, fine. I want some changes in our relationship. I want to take you out to dinner. I want to take you to the movies, out on my boat, on vacation with me. Hell, since we're being so honest, let me spell it out—I want to take you to bed.

That's what I want. But you—see, you're the problem. You can't even kiss me back."

Her pulse was going crazy now, and suddenly there was an electric tension in the air.

"We could work on that," she said, holding his gaze.

Something flared in his eyes. Something hot, and dark, and dangerous, and Sarah felt her heart skip a beat in response. Her mouth went dry. Her breathing came too fast.

"Oh, yeah?"

"Yeah."

Then, keeping his grip on her hands, their bodies not touching at all but still generating a swift, fierce heat between them, he leaned toward her and kissed her. It was a gentle kiss, barely there, no more pressure than the brush of butterfly wings across her lips.

The heat exploded into a full-blown conflagration. His touch seared her skin. Her bones melted.

Sarah realized that her eyes were still open, because they were looking into his. And what she saw for her there in his eyes made her breath catch and her heart pound like a kettledrum. They were heavy-lidded, dark with desire, aflame with wanting her. But there was something else, too. There, beyond the flames, behind the sexiness, they were vulnerable.

The idea that Jake, always so big and tough and capable, always with the answer to every question she or anyone else had ever thought to ask, always in command of himself, always steady and strong, was vulnerable because of her, broke the last lingering bond that had been holding her inside her prison of grief for so long.

She closed her eyes. She took a step forward so that she was right up against him, her breasts pressing against his bare chest with only the thin layer of her sleep shirt between them, her legs brushing the long muscles of his. Her nipples tightened instantly as the heat and hardness of his body penetrated. Her stomach clenched. Something deep inside her body quickened and began to throb.

And she kissed him back.

For an instant, no more, he went very still as her lips moved against his, as she licked into his mouth, as if he was taking in this new development. Then he muttered something undecipherable against her lips and wrapped his arms around her, pulling her so close that her swelling breasts were flattened against him so that she was lifted off her feet onto her tiptoes, so that their bodies were practically melded into one, and kissed her like he was starved for the taste of her mouth.

I love the way you kiss. The thought surfaced through the steam. Had she said it aloud? She didn't know. She was so shaken, so turned on, so *amazed* that she could feel like this that she couldn't be sure.

But whether or not she had, he was still kissing her, hot, deep kisses that made her body quake and burn, made her go all light-headed and weak-kneed. His lips were firm and warm, and his tongue was hot and demanding, and he knew what to do with both, which she registered with a flicker of combined excitement and displeasure. His arms were hard around her, his hands splayed across her back, and Sarah could feel the rapid thudding of his heart against her breasts. Or maybe it was her own heart that she could feel beating so hard. She was so bedazzled, she couldn't be sure.

This is Jake, she thought fuzzily as she wrapped her arms around his neck and kissed him back with all the pent-up passion of years, exploring his mouth as he was exploring hers, a little clumsily maybe, but so hungrily, so needily, that she was burning up with the thrill of it. Because it was Jake she was kissing, this explosion of passion she was experiencing was even more unbelievable. Whoever would have thought that Jake, her good buddy, her old pal, her best friend Jake, could make her feel like this?

His mouth left hers then to trail kisses down the side of her neck. Sarah took a deep, shaken breath and with the influx of oxygen got a little bit of cognitive function going again. This was taking a turn she hadn't foreseen, getting hotter faster than she had imagined it possibly could. . . .

"You realize," she murmured into his ear as he pressed his mouth to the tender spot where her neck and shoulder joined, "that we may be messing up a really great friendship here."

He stilled and drew in a breath, then lifted his head to look down at her. His arms loosened fractionally, allowing her to come down off her toes. His eyes were dark with passion. His face was flushed with it. He was faintly breathless, his chest rising and falling faster than usual against her breasts. His skin was damp with sweat, too, she discovered as, impulsively, instinctively, she slid her hands out along the warm, firm-muscled breadth of his bare shoulders.

God, his shoulders were wide. And muscular. How could she possibly not have noticed how wide and muscular they were before?

"You know, that's a chance I'm prepared to take." His voice was rougher, lower, thicker than she had ever heard it before. He was looking at her carefully despite the hungry blaze in his eyes, and Sarah realized that he was gauging her reaction to what was happening between them.

The thing about Jake was, he could always be counted on to do what he could to take care of her.

The knowledge that she could pull back any time, could step away from him and he wouldn't do a thing to try to prevent her, wouldn't hold it against her, would in fact do his best to make walking away easy for her, eased the last little niggle of the panic that had been fighting to claw its way back into her consciousness. This was Jake, and because it was Jake she was going to go with it.

"Yeah, me too," she said, watching his face while she ran her hands back over his shoulders with deliberate sensuousness and clasped them behind his neck again.

His eyes went obsidian on her.

So she rose up on her tiptoes again and kissed him.

He inhaled sharply against her mouth. His arms tightened around her. For a moment he went motionless, letting her kiss him, letting her press her lips to his and lick into his mouth and snuggle up against him. Then he shifted his grip, bending her so that her head was pillowed against his shoulder, so that she was just off-balance enough to have to cling to him, and took control of the kiss with an expertise that made her head whirl. She could feel the rising tension in him, the urgency, the need. The muscles in his shoulders and neck were tight beneath her hands. She stroked his warm neck, his back, then threaded her fingers through the crisp hairs at his nape and arched up so that her breasts pressed harder against his chest. One of his hands slid down her back to cup her bottom, molding her against him.

She felt the evidence of his desire between them, and made a tiny sound deep in her throat.

"Christ, Sarah." He raised his head, and she opened her eyes in time to watch as he shook it as if to clear it. Then he moved again, sliding an arm beneath her knees, lifting her clear up off her feet and into his arms.

He started walking with her, his arms strong and hard around her. His eyes were as shiny black as jet now, and dark color suffused his face. He was breathing fast, and it was clear that he wanted her. Badly.

Well, the thing was, she wanted him, too.

"Jake," she said, more out of wonder that this was Jake, and her, and they were actually doing this than for any other reason. Her arms were looped around his neck, and he carried her as if she weighed nothing at all—toward his bedroom, she realized with a quick glance around, and suddenly it was all she could do to breathe.

"Sarah." Despite the hard wanting in his face, his mouth curved into the slightest of smiles for her. "So, you getting cold feet yet?"

They were at the open door to his bedroom, which, in contrast to the living area that was suffused with a soft, incandescent glow, was dark and shadowy. He had to turn sideways to get her over the threshold, and it was then, with this slightly awkward maneuver, this sobering passage from light into darkness, that she registered the enormity of what she was doing, the impossibility of it, the dangers and pitfalls and potential heartbreak that littered the landscape that lay ahead. Panic raised its head again, raking its icy claws through her consciousness, whispering to her to stop now while she still could.

If she slept with Jake, their relationship—to say nothing of her life—would be forever changed.

"Oh, what the hell," she said aloud, as much to squash the panic as to answer him. "Let's do this."

"Good attitude," he said, and laughed.

Then his eyes blazed at her and he kissed her again, hard and sure, as they cleared the doorway and the shadows swallowed them up. Seconds later he laid her on his bed and came down beside her, and that one tiny moment of doubt was lost in a rush of heat.

Sarah registered the softness of the mattress, and the tumbled state of the bed, and the warm scent of Jake on the pillows, even as he kicked the covers to the floor and slid his hands up under her sleep shirt.

His kiss was slow, sensual, and drugging. His palms stroked upward over her thighs and hips and rib cage and breasts, trailing fire in their wake, making her body quake and tighten and arch against his hands like a kitten being stroked. He kissed her and petted her until she trembled and clung— and until he had her sleep shirt bunched under her armpits.

"How about we take this off?" he whispered and kissed her ear, his tongue delving inside the delicate swirl as his teeth nibbled at her lobe. Temporarily unable to talk, Sarah sucked in air but had no objection and demonstrated this by lifting her arms over her head and raising herself up a little so that he could pull the garment off.

Then she was naked.

Nothing in her life had ever been quite as mind-blowing as the idea that she was naked in bed with Jake.

Pure heat shot through her as she felt the cool caress of the air-conditioning against her bare skin, and the smoothness of the sheet against her back, and the weight of his gaze sliding over her. The bedroom was dark, but not so dark that they couldn't see each other. Jake's eyes were everywhere, touching on the creamy globes of her small breasts with their nipples looking all dark and pointy in that uncertain light, moving over the delicate curve of her waist and hips, taking in the black-velvet delta between her thighs, sliding down the slender length of her legs.

"You're beautiful," he said, and she said "thank you" because it just kind of seemed like the thing to do, and closed her eyes.

He rolled on top of her, his weight pressing her down into the mattress, and it was only as she felt his hips rock into her and his leg slide between hers that she realized that he was still wearing his jeans.

The idea that she was naked and he wasn't made her dizzy. She quivered a little at the sheer excitement of it. Then his lips found hers again and she twined her arms around his neck and kissed him back with hungry abandon. She brushed her lips across his face, kissed his jaw, his throat, reveling in the salty taste of him and the prickliness of the stubble on his cheeks and chin. His wide chest was faintly damp and rough with hair and absolutely, indisputably masculine, and she loved the way it felt against her breasts. His broad back was warm, too, and also damp, all sleek skin covering long, thick muscles that flexed beneath her stroking hands. He moved against her, heavy and hot and hard with wanting, and his hands found her breasts and her body, prodded by that long, muscular leg, began to quake and burn.

When his mouth left hers to nuzzle her throat, she dug her nails into his shoulders and squeezed his tantalizing leg between both of hers and opened her eyes and gasped for air.

"God, you're good at this," she managed to say in a reasonably normal voice as his thigh rocked into her and his mouth trailed fire along her collarbone before crawling up the gentle slope of her right breast, which his hand cradled in readiness.

At that, he lifted his head to look at her. His eyes gleamed hotly at her through the darkness. She could just see the quick answering curve of his mouth.

"Honey, you have no idea," he said, and

she was just registering that his voice was thick and low but held a thread of humor, too, when his mouth found her nipple and his hand slid down over her stomach to delve between her legs.

Sarah's heart lurched. Her stomach clenched. Her legs tried to close instinctively, but his thigh was between them and there was nothing she could do. Then his hand found her, and there was nothing she wanted to do. She lay there panting, eyes closed, quivering with shock and growing, unbelievable delight as his fingers sought out her most secret places and taught her their secrets, too, and his mouth teased her breasts with wet-hot fire.

How could I have lived without this? That was the thought that ricocheted through her dazed brain.

When he moved again, his mouth leaving her breasts to kiss its way down her stomach, her eyes opened. She was trembling, weak with longing, her body pulsing with need. Her heart was pounding so hard and she was breathing so erratically now that any kind of intelligent conversation was beyond her. She murmured an incoherent protest, clutching at his shoulders, but he either didn't understand or wasn't in any mood to comply. Her hands gripped the sheet, her fingers digging into the mattress as he moved beyond their reach, stroking her legs apart, kissing her in between them.

Her body clenched. Taken by surprise at the dark, hot thrill of it, Sarah arched up against that tantalizing mouth and cried out.

His mouth was scalding hot. His lips and tongue were knowledgeable and sure. He licked into her, gentling her with his hands, sliding them beneath her to grip her bottom and hold her still for him. Her body burned and clutched and melted as he taught her how truly pleasurable surrendering to the needs of her own hungering body could be. He had her moving for him, moaning for him, absolutely mindless with wanting him.

Then he left her.

Breathing hard, trembling, legs and body shifting restlessly, Sarah opened her eyes and found the tall, broad shape of him standing beside the bed.

"Jake?" Her voice was unsteady as she strained to see through the shadows. She was weak with longing, wanting him so much, needing him. . . . The faint metallic sound of a zipper being lowered told her that he was taking off his pants.

"One minute."

She got just a glimpse of him naked— *Jake naked*—and her eyes widened a little as she registered that he was big all over— *hung* was the word she thought—and swollen with desire for her. Then she heard the sound of a drawer opening, and watched what he was doing, and realized that he was, as always, doing what he could to take care of her.

And never mind that it rankled a little that he had condoms right there in his nightstand, ready to whip out at a moment's notice. That was a thought for another time, when she wasn't quite so turned on.

"I've been thinking about this for months," he said as he came back down onto the bed with her. There was a huskiness to his voice that made her throat go dry.

"Months?" she murmured, distracted, as his leg slid between hers again. Only now it was bare just like the rest of him, warm and firm with muscle and abrasive with hair, and it was joined by its fellow. Her legs, soft and pliant now, parted to accommodate him, and her heart started thudding and she felt hot all over again from just thinking about what they were getting ready to do.

"Maybe years. Feels like forever." He pressed down on top of her, and she was so ready, so hungry for him that her arms went around him and her legs went around him and she arched up against him *right that second* because she just couldn't wait any longer. Then he kissed her, a hard, hungry, urgent kiss that made her dizzier than she already was, and pushed inside her, huge and hot and filling her to bursting.

It felt so good—so incredibly, impossibly good—that she couldn't believe it. She clutched at him, crying out. He did it again, slow and deep, deliberately making her feel every bit of the exquisite sensation of it.

"Jake," she moaned, and his name was so familiar on her lips that it shocked her. *This is Jake inside me,* she thought with disbelief, and suddenly that was thrilling, too. Her nails dug into his back and her hips arched up off the mattress and she kissed him with a fierce abandon that was like nothing she had ever felt before.

Then he was taking her, hard and fast,

kissing her mindless, hands everywhere, moving with her, rocking her into the mattress, driving her wild, making her cry out over and over again.

"Sarah," he groaned through clenched teeth at the end, *"oh God, Sarah,"* as he came into her with a series of fierce, deep thrusts that made her shudder and shake and come. Without warning, the world exploded against her closed lids like thousands of brilliantly hued fireballs, and her body convulsed around him and she remembered again just at that last fiery instant that it was Jake she was doing this with, Jake who was naked with her and on her and in her, and that made it even better, nirvana times ten thousand.

"Sarah," he groaned again, fiercely, as he felt the cataclysm that shook her. Then he drove deep inside her one last time and finally, shuddering, found his own release.

She was still floating, still lost in dark, blissful space somewhere, when he kissed her mouth and rolled off her, rolled off the bed, and disappeared. By the time she had wrapped her mind around that, had gotten her heavy lids to open and had registered that the bed was indeed empty and was, in fact, cooling rapidly without him in it beside her, he was back, tossing the covers which he'd kicked off earlier over her so that at least the air-conditioning wasn't freezing her out any longer.

"Miss me?" he asked, sliding back in beside her and pulling the covers up around them both.

"Mmm," she murmured as he pressed a quick kiss to her mouth, muffling what would have been an honest *yes,* and curved against him even as his arm around her pulled her close. He smelled so good and felt so good, so familiar and safe and yet so different, so sexy, that her eyes closed and for a moment all she could do was luxuriate in the sheer bliss of it. They settled in with him on his back and her head on his shoulder, her arm draped casually across his chest, her leg curved on top of his thighs. Sarah experienced an odd sense of déjà vu and realized that she had lain with him like this before, the only other time they had slept together, but this time was different because they were naked and they had done it and that made everything between them strange, everything between them new.

As in, no more best friends.

"Now what?" Her eyes popped open on the thought. Panic threatened to raise its ugly head. Her hand froze in the middle of absentmindedly stroking his chest, and she tilted her head back so that she could see his face. His dear, familiar face that was suddenly almost a stranger's, too.

He slanted a look down at her. "I don't know. I was thinking, maybe—you on top."

"What?" For a moment, Sarah was so surprised that she blinked at him. Then she saw his mouth curve—the kind of curve she'd watched it make thousands of times before without realizing that his patented slow half-smile was sexy—and figured out that he was teasing her. Again.

Okay, that was normal.

"I'm not joking."

"Me neither." As if to prove it, he gripped her waist and lifted her and shifted sideways and there she was, lying on top of him, sprawled out on his chest with her legs tangled with his.

The evidence that he really might not be

joking lay right there between them. It was distracting, to say the least.

"What I meant was, where do we go from here?"

His hands found her bottom, stroked it, and settled there, big and warm as they splayed over her cheeks, holding her against him. Her heart beat faster, and suddenly she was breathless again.

"I know what you meant." He sighed. "Sarah, honey, could we table the discussion until tomorrow? I'm tired."

His hands slid down to her thighs, parted them, positioning them on either side of him so that she could feel him, hard and hot and ready now, rigid against her. His fingers brushed suggestively between her legs, and her body, newly sensitized, quickened and started to burn.

It was obvious what he had in mind. The funny thing was, she was all of a sudden inclined that way, too.

"I thought you were tired," she murmured as he sat up and started nuzzling her breasts. She was straddling his lap, her hands on his shoulders holding on, and she moved against him and kissed his bristly cheek even as she murmured the words in his ear.

"Not that tired."

He reached sideways, and she could hear the drawer opening and feel him groping inside it.

She stiffened.

Okay, getting mad was stupid. It was infantile. She was a grown woman, she knew all about his girlfriends, and he was protecting her, after all.

"Jake."

"Hmm?"

"Just for the record—no more blondes."

He stopped what he was doing to peer at her through the shadows. She could see the dark, hot gleam of his eyes, feel the weight of his gaze, but had no idea in the world what he was thinking.

"They were just to keep me from getting bored while I waited."

"Waited for what?"

"You," he said, and kissed her. Then he pushed inside her, and what they were doing felt so amazing that she forgot everything but that. By the time they were finished she was exhausted, drained, absolutely worn out but spendidly so, and she subsided on top of him with a replete sigh.

Minutes later, she was asleep.

It was after nine a.m.—way late for him—when Jake finally stirred. One bleary-eyed glance at the clock confirmed it: He'd had something less than three hours of sleep. Gray light filtered in through the curtains, which, since the material was designed to block the sun, meant that it was bright as hell outside. Luckily, it was Saturday, so his schedule was flexible. In fact—and here he slanted a glance at Sarah, who, since they were curled up together like spoons, her back to his front, was turned away from him, still sound asleep—he was surprised he was awake at all. For days now he'd had practically no sleep, and by all rights he should be completely dead to the world. But for whatever reason, he wasn't. He felt surprisingly good, surprisingly awake, surprisingly energetic. In fact, he felt kind of like a kid on Christmas morning, bursting with good cheer, filled to overflowing with peace on earth and joy to the world and all that sappy stuff. He felt, in a word, *happy,* like a man who had gotten everything he had ever wanted, and he realized that that could be summed up in a single word, too: Sarah.

He'd been waiting for her all these years, marking time, hanging around, and he hadn't even realized it until last night, when she'd ordered him to knock it off with the blondes. The answer he'd given her then was true, and until the words had come out of his mouth, he'd been blind to it.

Now he knew.

Which might or might not be a good thing.

A little sheepishly, he recognized the state of being in which he found himself. It even had a name: crazy in love. The question was, did she feel the same?

She'd made love to him like she meant it. But, as he knew from experience, that didn't have to mean a thing.

Sarah had issues, serious issues, which they were going to have to work through. But if she gave him a chance, he was willing to do whatever it took to help her put the past behind her. Behind them both. Because whatever happened to her now happened to him, too.

Hell, even if he hadn't seen it before, from the very first day they met, hadn't it always been that way?

He cast another glance at her—he was lying on his back now, and she was turned away from him, her head pillowed on his biceps, her knees drawn up toward her chest—and let his eyes linger on the slender shape of her. The quilt was tucked beneath her arm and curved around her body so that she was modestly covered in front, but since he had rolled over to check the clock, the covers gaped away from her in back, and he could see every delectable inch. His eyes traced the sleek curves of her shoulder and waist and hip, and the length of her legs, and lingered on the gorgeous heart-shaped contours of her ass, while his heartbeat kicked up a notch and erotic images from the night before replayed themselves like his own private porn film in his head.

Just remembering the taste of her, the warm, silky texture of her skin, how she had squirmed beneath him, her breathless little cries as he had reminded her what pleasure was all about, made him horny all over again.

Now the faint scent of the floral shampoo

she used wafted past his nostrils. The heat of her body reached out to him like caressing hands. The feel of her warm cheek snuggled against his arm, and the whisper of her breath on his skin, sent tingles of anticipation shooting out along his nerve endings.

Of course, it was also possible that those tingles signified that his arm had gone to sleep beneath the weight of her head.

The thing was, she was naked, and in his bed, and he knew he could make her want him again in about a minute.

But the other thing was, she was Sarah, and she had to be beyond tired, and she really, really needed sleep.

And the bottom line was, he wanted Sarah to have whatever she needed.

He had already made up his mind to leave her be and let her sleep when a strange scraping sound on the other side of the bedroom door that he had closed last night before falling asleep made him stiffen and cast a wary glance that way.

It took him just a few seconds to figure out what it was: Sweetie-pie, of course. A lively memory of the animal's previous intrusion into a room where he lay sleeping was what had prompted him to get up and shut the door in the first place. Now the damned dog probably had to go out. Its scratching was also probably what had awakened him to begin with.

What he didn't want was to have it wake Sarah. Muttering a curse under his breath, moving as carefully as he could, Jake eased his arm out from under her head, rolled off the bed, tucked the covers back in around her, grabbed his clothes from the floor, and hotfooted it toward the door.

The dog scratched at it again just as he got his hand on the knob. He cast one more glance back at Sarah, who hadn't moved.

You're mine, he thought with sudden fierce conviction, and then edged his way out the door, literally in the teeth of the man-eating mongrel—which was also, he supposed, part of the whole *you're mine* deal.

Which just goes to prove that there really was a fly for every ointment.

Could anybody say "hello, stepdog?"

And if that wasn't enough to turn him off Sarah, then he was so far gone that there was no help for him anywhere.

Instead of using the outside entrance to his apartment—there was one, a staircase that climbed the back of the building, which he used only on the rare occasions when whatever he was doing required privacy— he and Sweetie-pie went back down through the house, retracing their route from the previous night. A glance told him that the burglar alarm was off, so he wasn't too surprised to find Dorothy at her desk, even though she officially had weekends off. She had her back to him as she pecked away madly at the Mac's keyboard, and was giving off hostility in waves.

That being the case, he also wasn't surprised to find Pops standing at the sliding glass door, looking out. Outside, the day matched Jake's mood: sunny and bright. It was probably already getting really hot out there, too.

". . . not my fault," Pops was saying plaintively as Jake came within earshot.

"Morning," Jake called in passing. He didn't know what Sweetie-pie's holding capacity was, but he didn't want to find out. Also, he didn't want to get in the middle of whatever drama was going on between his grandpa and his secretary. He had plenty of drama of his own going on right now without any help from them, thank you very much.

"Hey, Hoss." Pops turned away from the door a little too quickly, which got Jake's attention. Something about the movement just looked guilty. "Sarah spend the night?"

It wasn't a loaded question. His and Sarah's long-standing friendship was too well known for her overnight presence in his apartment to occasion any but the most casual interest from either Pops or Dorothy. But still, under the circumstances, it made Jake feel just the tiniest bit self-conscious.

He really was going to have to look into moving sometime soon.

"Yeah," he said, and would have passed on through if Pops's guilty movement hadn't prompted him to look just a little harder through the patio door, which, he discovered, was about eighteen inches ajar.

Like Pops had been on his way out.

Only to be stopped by the presence of an enormous gator on the deck.

Jake spotted the huge reptile with disbelief just as Sweetie-pie erupted into a frenzy of barking and charged, yanking the leash out of Jake's unprepared hand.

"Shit!" Jake yelled. Then, "Shut the door!" as he leaped in hot pursuit.

But it was already too late.

Sweetie-pie exploded through the opening with suicidal fury, roaring like the monster he was, about two seconds away, according to Jake's appalled calculations, from becoming stepdog lunch.

18

An instant spent visualizing Sarah's reaction should her pet go the way of the poodle was all it took. Jake channeled his inner damn fool and raced to the rescue.

"Sweetie-pie! *No!*"

Fortunately, the gator was a little slow on the uptake. The huge, hysterical hound practically vibrating with noisy aggression just a foot or so from the end of its snout appeared to take it by surprise. It blinked, its bulbous golden eyes seeming to require a second to refocus. Its attention, Jake saw as he barreled through the door he shoved wide, had been very much occupied with the marshmallows strewn across the weathered wood planks. A tattered, nearly empty plastic bag lay at the edge of the table. Jake experienced a momentary flashback to the bag of marshmallows he'd pulled from his pocket the previous day and had an explanation for the gator's presence on his deck.

The thing was so big that only the first seven or so feet of its bumpy, mud-colored body was on the deck; the last three feet of its tail still trailed down the steps.

One good chomp of those jaws and Sweetie-pie was toast. And the gator—not unreasonably, since the moronic mutt was darting in and out, snapping at its nose—was starting to look a tad ticked off. Cold with fear, Jake planted a foot in the middle of those marshmallows, snatched up the end of the leash despite the fact that doing so put his hand way too close to a truly impressive set of snaggly yellow gator teeth, and yanked backward with all his might.

Just as the gator lunged.

Sweetie-pie yelped and levitated, bouncing upward like he had springs on his feet. Leash in hand, yanking the dog toward him

like a fish on a line, Jake careened backward, stumbling over the threshold, past
Pops and Dorothy, who were both watching in wide-eyed, openmouthed astonishment.

Unfortunately, he saw to his horror as he
regained his balance and the leash
smacked him in the face, Sweetie-pie was
no longer attached to the other end of it.
The dog's collar was there, still fastened,
dangling in a limp loop that had just made
smarting contact with his right cheekbone,
but Sweetie-pie was no longer wearing the
collar.

Clearly it hadn't been on tight enough,
because it had pulled right off over his head.

Even as Jake had that moment of terrible realization, Sweetie-pie hit the deck on
all fours again and the gator went after him.

"Sweetie-pie! *Here!* Here, boy!" Jake
yelled, scrambling for the door, but if the
dog heard, he clearly didn't have the whole
run-for-your-life thing down, because he
kept up the attack.

The deck wasn't that big. The dog had
nowhere to go. He bounced around like a
kangaroo on speed, letting loose with an
explosion of barks and snarls and snaps at

his opponent that was loud and ferocious enough to scare a flock of gulls out of the live oaks in the backyard and drown out the motor of a passing runabout. The gator heaved itself after him, knocking over a chair, rattling the glass on the table as he surged beneath it. Clearly it was only a matter of moments until Sweetie-pie was sushi.

Sarah would be sick with grief.

"Shit," Jake groaned, and did the only thing he could think of: He launched himself at Sweetie-pie like the defensive back he had once been. Two bounds and he was back on the field, feeling about as smart as if he had just leapt between King Kong and Godzilla. Grabbing Sweetie-pie around the torso—

"Jesus, Jake! *Move!"* Pops shrieked.

"Get! *Get!"* That was Dorothy, flailing away at the gator with a broom she'd obviously had the presence of mind to snatch out of the utility cabinet.

Jake hurtled the dog, and himself, over the railing.

They crashed the six feet or so to the ground. The grass was thick and the ground beneath was softened from the previous day's rain. Still, Jake hit hard enough to knock the wind out of himself. For a moment he lay unmoving, feeling like he was spread-eagled over a boulder, until the boulder shuddered and he realized that he'd smacked down right on top of Sweetie-pie.

Give him the boulder any day.

"Get! Get! Get!" *Whack! Whack! Whack!* From the deck, Dorothy clearly was still working the broom.

"Hoss! You okay down there?" Pops called.

Lacking the breath to reply, Jake sensed movement to his left, turned his head and found himself eyeball to eyeball with Sweetie-pie. For a moment they stared at each other, dark brown eyes locked with dark brown eyes, apparently equally stunned. Then Sweetie-pie sucked in air, and his lip began to curl.

And not in a good way.

"Good dog, Sweetie-pie," Jake wheezed, praying he wasn't about to lose a nose. In the background, he could see the redoubtable Dorothy coming down the deck stairs, sensible shoes, housedress (today's was mint-green), old-lady bun and all, smacking the ground in front of her with the broom at every step. Ahead of her rushed the gator, hightailing it down the walk toward the water.

Clearly, it knew when it had met its match.

Sweetie-pie must have sensed that his enemy was escaping, because his head turned in that direction. Then he heaved himself out from under Jake, shook himself, and tottered off in hot pursuit of his retreating opponent. His gait was crooked, his barks more falsetto than ferocious, but he had won the day. The gator slithered into the water and disappeared with a splash. Sweetie-pie held the bank, loudly triumphant.

"You're welcome," Jake muttered in the general direction of the noise.

"That was *awesome,* man." Austin appeared within his field of vision, leaning over Jake from behind so that his long, blond hair fell over his face. He was a tall, thin, reasonably good-looking kid in baggy khaki shorts and a Day-Glo orange polo shirt. Since he was one of two guys currently on watch outside the house in case the person harassing Sarah made life easy on all of them and showed up, his presence wasn't

surprising. Except for the shirt, which probably violated the whole don't-let-the-bad-
guy-spot-you spirit of the assignment, and
the fact that he'd been posted in a parked
car in front of the house.

"You okay?" The other person leaning
over him was Dave Menucchi, who'd been
assigned to cover the back of the house
from the vantage point of Jake's boat.
Fifteen years younger than Pops, he was,
unlike Pops in his jeans and navy Herman's
Crab Shack T-shirt, dressed in respectable
geezer gear: tan polyester sansabelt slacks
and a plaid, short-sleeved button-up shirt.
He had a round, nearly unwrinkled face, full
head of iron-gray hair, and a Santa Claus
belly. At Christmastime, he occasionally
played you-know-who for the local Macy's.

"Yeah," Jake managed, although breathing still took work. Pops was hurrying
toward him. Dorothy, broom in hand, was,
too. Several passers-by—probably Big
Jim's patients—a conclusion Jake reached
because one was wearing a green napkin
clipped around her neck and another was
carrying a magazine—had gathered in the
near corner of the parking lot to watch,
peering toward the center of the action—

that would be him—with nervous interest. No sissy, he got up. Or, rather, started to get up. Last time he'd played defensive back, he'd been a kid. Now that he was thirty-nine, getting up after a hit like that took a little work. He rolled onto his hands and knees, got his feet beneath him, and thus worked his way upright, doing his best not to wince as he made the final mistake of straightening his spine.

A glance down at himself told him that the parts of him that weren't sporting grass stains were streaked with mud.

Down by the water, Sweetie-pie quit barking and expressed his blatant disrespect for the vanquished gator by hiking his leg over a rock.

Pops and Dorothy reached him at the same time. Dorothy looked grim. Pops was grinning from ear to ear.

"Hoss, we need to talk." Pops's eyes twinkled at him. Now that his only grandson had escaped with all his limbs intact, he was finding the Jake and Gator show hilarious. "That was plumb crazy, what you did. Molly'd been a little bit faster, we'd be calling you peg-leg about now."

"Damn right we need to talk," Jake

growled. "No more feeding the damn gators."

Pops's control deserted him at that, and he let out a snort of laugher, then held up a conciliatory hand at the look on Jake's face. "Okay. Jeez. Who knew? Anyway, you're the one who left the marshmallows out on the deck."

"How can you laugh? He could've been badly hurt." Dorothy glared at Pops. "Because of you and your foolishness."

"Me? You gotta blame something, blame that dog of Sarah's. What's it's name, Koochie-koo? The funny thing is, Jake hates that dog." Pops started laughing again.

Jake observed sourly that only Dorothy had the grace to look concerned for his well-being. Austin and Dave were also snickering, but—since they weren't kin to him and could, theoretically at least, be fired—they were being a little more subtle about it.

He also observed that he was still holding on to Sweetie-pie's leash. And that Sweetie-pie himself was now trotting off along the bank, probably hoping to find the gator and go on to round two.

"Damn it to hell and back anyway," Jake said in disgust, his hand clenching the leash. But there was no help for it: The dog had to be fetched. With a single blistering look around that encompassed three of his four employees, he made tracks across the grass after Sweetie-pie, trying his best not to limp.

"Here, Sweetie-pie."

Then, because Sweetie-pie kept on going and Sarah loved the damned dog and he knew from personal experience that the messed-up mutt responded best to feminine tones, he jettisoned any hope of retaining his self-respect and called "Here, Sweetie-pie" again—only this time using his best soprano.

And he tried not to let the bursts of laughter that erupted behind him damage his self-esteem beyond repair.

By the time he caught up to Sweetie-pie, talked his way in close enough to slip the collar over the dog's head, and then managed to drag him back to the house, a good hour had passed. There was, he was relieved to see as he approached the deck, no gator in sight. The backyard was empty except for a crow picking at the grass. Sweetie-pie wanted to hang around and eagerly sniff the deck—obviously, his enemy's scent lingered—but Jake was in no mood to humor him and so they went inside. Pops was kicked back in Dorothy's chair, his back to the computer, which he couldn't work anyway, his hands steepled over his belt buckle, a meditative look on his face.

"What?" Jake asked after a single glance at his face.

"They went out to brunch."

"Who?"

"Dorothy and that . . . that . . . Dave."

"So?" Sweetie-pie was tugging at the leash, wanting to get back upstairs to Sarah. For once, Jake thought, he and the dog were of a single mind.

"They didn't invite me."

"So?" This time impatience tinged Jake's tone.

"I think he likes her. I think it's like a date."

"So?" Jake said for the third time.

"So . . . so . . ." Pops's voice trailed off. He was frowning, clearly less than happy. "So nothing, I guess."

Jake's eyes narrowed on his grandfather.

"You don't want her to go to brunch with Dave, then you ask her to brunch yourself."

"Me?" Pops looked stunned. "Ask out Dorothy?"

"Why not?"

"Well . . . well . . . she's too old for me, for one thing."

Jake rolled his eyes. "Pops, she's at least ten years younger than you. You're eighty-six years old, remember? *God* is not too old for you."

Pops's mouth compressed. "What, are you a comedian now?"

Jake was getting tired of the whole conversation. He was dirty, he had a big dog on a short leash, and Sarah was waiting in his bed upstairs. If he was lucky, he might have time before she awoke to take a shower and slip in beside her.

"I'm serious," he said. "You and Dorothy have been pussyfooting around each other for years. Maybe she's getting tired of it. Maybe she's ready to look in another direction—like at Dave."

Pops grimaced. "She's been mad at me ever since I bought my motorcycle. She told me to grow up." He sounded mildly indignant.

"Maybe you should offer to take her for a ride on it."

"Dorothy?" Pops sounded horrified at the thought.

Jake shrugged. "Why not? The worst she can do is say no." Putting the subject out of his mind, he gave in to Sweetie-pie's urging and his own inclination and started moving toward the stairs. Then he paused and turned back to look at Pops. "Look, you know that word that was written on Sarah's car window yesterday? *Eeyore*?"

Jake had filled Pops in on what was happening the day before, while he'd been on his way to the park in search of Sarah.

"Yeah?"

"It was a code word she and Lexie had. She thinks no one knew it except the two of them. I want you to get some people going over the records we have to see if there was any mention of it anywhere. Any suggestion of anything like that, tell them to flag it and let me know."

"They in Current Files?"

"Yeah, except for some Sarah took upstairs last night. I'll bring them down later. Get Austin in here, he can start on the ones that are still in the file room. Tell him to be real thorough. There's almost no chance he's doing any good outside anyway. And call everybody else in, too. Today they're all on the clock."

"Will do."

"And when Dorothy gets back, tell her to check with me, would you? I want some background checks run on some people." Like Brian McIntyre and all the cops involved in the Stumbo case, for example, and Mitchell Helitzer and his close associates, and anyone else he or Sarah might be able to come up with who might have something to gain if Sarah were dead, or unable to function as a prosecutor for the time being. "I'll get her a list of names. And when I do, you might start checking those same names to see where all those people were yesterday afternoon. Anybody on that list without a solid alibi for the approximate time that word was written on Sarah's car, I want them flagged, too."

"Okay." Pops turned in his chair, then looked back over his shoulder at Jake. "Uh, Hoss, you do remember that we got all that loss data for Beta Corp. to analyze by Monday? Which is why Dorothy and I were in here this morning to begin with. And Charlie's out right now wrapping up the last of the witness interviews for the Kane trial, which the prosecutor's office also needs by Monday. We do all this other stuff, we're gonna be stretched pretty thin."

Jake blew out a sigh, trying not to think about what he was going to be paying out this month in terms of overtime. "Yeah, I know. Hopefully, we can get it all done. The work pertaining to Sarah, though—it takes priority. I got a bad feeling here."

"You know, talk about two people pussy-footing around each other—"

His grandfather's meaning was unmistakable. For years now, he'd been telling Jake he ought to give Sarah a whirl, and Jake had been brushing him off. So maybe the old coot was right sometimes.

Not that Jake meant to tell him so. At least, not until he and Sarah had a little more time to get used to this new wrinkle in their relationship themselves.

"Hey, my business," Jake interrupted before the digression went any further, and with a click of his tongue at Sweetie-pie, who had flopped at his feet and now rose reluctantly, recommenced heading for the stairs.

"Yeah, yeah." Pops, having heard the whole keep-your-nose-out-of-my-love-life routine since Jake was approximately fifteen, waved this familiar warning away. "You're gonna do what you want anyway, no matter what I say."

Jake ignored that.

"I'll shower and change and be back," Jake said, mentally kissing all thoughts of climbing back into bed with Sarah good-bye. He had too damned much to do this morning. Well, unless it was a quickie. The thought made his blood heat.

"Tell Sarah I said hi," Pops said, and picked up the phone. He punched in numbers as Jake, with Sweetie-pie trailing behind, went upstairs.

Stepping quietly through the door to his apartment a few minutes later, Jake saw that the curtains were pulled back so that the sun poured in, and inhaled the smell of fresh coffee. Clearly Sarah was up. *I'm home,* was the thought that went through his mind as he unclipped Sweetie-pie's leash, and it hit him that these were not the typical words that normally went through his head when he stepped over his own threshold. Now that he thought about it, in fact, this was the first time his apartment had really felt like home to him, rather than just a place where he was staying for a while. As he straightened he realized that never before, not when he was married and not in all the years since, had he felt this sense of being in exactly the right place in the world for him. As the dog padded away toward the kitchen, he examined the implications almost ruefully. It was because Sarah was there, of course. He didn't usually have women stay over, and when he did, he was always anxious to get them out as fast as possible the next morning. He wasn't, as he had discovered about himself long ago, an afterglow kind of guy.

Except now he was. With Sarah, he could definitely do afterglow. Maybe even afterglow forever.

Assuming Sarah was in the kitchen, Jake trailed after Sweetie-pie, his heart beating way too fast for a thirty-nine-year-old man who had long since given up counting the notches on his bedposts.

The shiny-bright Christmas-morning feeling was back.

Just before he reached the kitchen door, Sarah walked out of his bedroom. He stopped where he was—she hadn't seen him yet—and let his eyes move over her. She was freshly showered and dressed in a black T-shirt that hugged the small, high curves of her breasts and white jeans that emphasized her narrow hips and the slender length of her legs. A shaft of sunlight touched the short ruffle of her hair, and it gleamed like a blackbird's wing as it angled around the delicate bones of her face. There were faint shadows beneath her eyes—it was still relatively early, just past ten thirty, which meant that even if she was just out of bed she still hadn't gotten enough sleep—and her mouth looked exceptionally full and lush, like it was slightly swollen from his kisses.

The thought made his body tighten.

She was beautiful and elegant and sexy as hell—and his.

A keeper.

I'm not throwing this one back, he thought just as she seemed to sense his presence beside the kitchen door and swung those big blue eyes toward him.

"Hey," he said softly as she spotted him, and smiled at her.

"Hey," she said back. Her answering smile was more a perfunctory stretching of her lips than anything, and it quickly died away. It was a casual, no-big-deal kind of greeting, and under the circumstances it felt just plain wrong. She kept walking, giving him a really nice view of her particularly fine ass as she passed.

Okay, so she wasn't going to run across the room and fling herself into his arms. He could deal.

"I went through the rest of the tapes while you were gone," she said to him over her shoulder, still much more remote than anything he'd been expecting. "The one I was looking for isn't in there. I'm going to have Sue Turner"—Turner did composite drawings for the police department—"make a sketch of the guy who was doing the filming."

Jake folded his arms over his chest. "Are you now?"

She nodded. "It probably won't lead to anything. Basically, all I remember is a kind of sturdily built guy with a mustache, and the camera."

"It could still turn into something," Jake said, and she nodded again.

"That's what I'm hoping."

The dining table with its piles of manila folders was in front of him. With the curtains open, the wall of windows let bright golden sunlight spill over it and the living area to his left. Sarah kept on walking, keeping the dining table between them. She paused near the table to pick up something from near the floor—the table blocked his vision, so he couldn't tell exactly what—and then picked up the pace again. He had thought maybe the couch was her goal, but then he realized that she was headed toward the door.

With her overnight case in her hand.

"Where are you going?" he asked. Her attitude left him feeling a little angry, a little deflated, and, yes, if truth be told, a little hurt.

She glanced at him again, a cool, sideways glance that had no trace of romance in it. Jake figured that he might not always be the sharpest knife in the drawer, but even he was starting to get the picture here: crazy in love did not appear to describe Sarah's state of mind.

"Out." Her eyes slid over him as she reached the door. She paused, one hand closing on the knob.

"Out?" Jake repeated, his eyebrows lifting. He hadn't been expecting a big hearts-and-flowers routine—well, maybe he had, which underscored the problem with expectations—but this chilly distancing act was starting to get to him. Big time.

Even Sarah seemed to feel that her comment called for further explanation. She nodded.

"Duncan called. Pat Letts's office notified our office yesterday that they're going to be asking for a postponement on Helitzer on Monday. They're also filing a motion to suppress statements he made to police without an attorney present. We're going to meet for lunch and talk about how to respond, and discuss strategy for the trial. Oh, and he said that the coroner's office released Mary's body late yesterday. The funeral is scheduled for tomorrow afternoon."

"You're kidding me here, right?"

"No, of course I'm not kidding." She gave

him another of those cool glances. "It's at four, at Our Lady of the Sorrows Church on Hudson Street." She frowned a little as her gaze moved over him again. "What happened to you, anyway? You're all muddy."

"I fell down outside." He wasn't in the mood to go into it further. Far be it from him to use for leverage the fact that he'd saved her dog from being a gator munchie.

"Oh." With no further apparent interest in hearing more, she turned the knob and started to open the door.

"Wait a minute. Hold it right there." Jake moved then, closing the space between them in a few quick strides, while she watched him coming toward her with a shuttered expression that he'd never seen on her face before—at least, not for him. He pushed the door closed again—she let her hand fall away from the knob—and gripped her wrist. Her skin felt cool and sleek, her bones frail beneath his encircling hand. He could feel her pulse galloping beneath his fingers. He was close now, maybe a foot away, so close that she had to look up at him to meet his eyes. So close that he could smell the sweetness of her shampoo.

"You're not seriously planning to go out to lunch with Duncan, are you?"

Her brows rose. "Do you have some kind of problem with that?"

Jake took a deep breath.

"Wow." He studied her face. That remote look in her eyes was, he discovered, starting to bother him a whole hell of a lot. "Yeah, actually, I do. In fact, I have several problems with it. Let me just start with the most pressing: Remember yesterday, how we were talking about there maybe being somebody out there who wants to kill you?"

Sarah's lips tightened. "I'm meeting Duncan at the Macaroni Grill. I don't think anybody's likely to shoot me there."

Probably not, but he still didn't like it. And, yes, maybe a couple of those reasons were personal. Although he'd let that damned gator eat him before he'd ever admit to the first twinge of jealousy of Ken Duncan.

"You ever thought that it might be Duncan who's behind this?"

Surprise followed by skepticism flared in Sarah's eyes. "No, I never did."

"Then maybe you should, because he could be, because he's got something to gain. He'd probably get the Helitzer trial, for one, if something happened to you. That's pretty high-profile, wouldn't you say? Hell, he might even get your job."

"Now you're being ridiculous."

"Am I? I've been thinking about it. Nothing in life is random, and that includes everything that's happened to you these last few days. It's almost got to be all connected, it's too coincidental otherwise. And the corollary to that is, whoever is doing this has something to gain by it. Okay, it's probably not Duncan, but it could be. It could be a lot of people, some of whom we probably haven't even thought of yet. Until we figure it out, you need to stay out of harm's way."

"What do you want me to do, put myself on virtual house arrest?"

"It's better than being dead."

Her eyes narrowed at him. "So what are you suggesting? That I hide in your apartment until whoever shot me is identified, if he ever is? That you go with me everywhere I go? That's not going to work for either of us. I have a job, and things I have to do. So do you. I appreciate everything you've done for me, I appreciate you taking care of me like you have, but I'm taking my life back. I'm going to lunch with Duncan, for starters, and then I'll be back to pick up Sweetie-pie, if you'll let him stay here until then, and go through your files on Lexie. Then I'm going home, and tonight I'm going sleep there all by myself, just like I've been doing for years. Tomorrow I'm going to Mary's funeral, and Monday I'm going to work. If anything comes up I can't deal with on my own, I'll let you know."

Good-bye was there in her voice, polite but unmistakable, uttered in the kind of coolly dismissive tone that he would never in a million years have expected Sarah to employ with him. He didn't like it. In fact, he didn't like it a whole hell of a lot.

A silent beat passed in which they held each other's eyes.

Then Jake said softly, "Now who's being a jackass about something?"

Sarah stiffened. "I don't know what you're talking about."

She pulled her wrist away from him, and he let her go. He knew her well enough to know that she was lying through her teeth. She knew exactly what he was talking about. But he was suddenly ready, willing, and able to spell it out for her anyway.

"I'm talking about last night. About you and me. In bed together. Naked. Making love." He almost enjoyed watching the color rise in her cheeks.

Her eyes flashed at him. "You don't get it, do you? That's one reason I can't stay here anymore. It was a mistake, okay? A huge mistake. I should never have let it happen. I told you we were ruining our friendship, and we did."

He'd known it was coming, had expected it since, basically, she'd started talking, but hearing her put it into words like that made him wild.

He laughed, but even to his own ears it was an ugly sound.

"Oh, yeah, I get it. I get it just fine. It's like the fishing. You liked it too much. It felt good, didn't it?" He was practically talking through clenched teeth now. "No feeling good for Sarah, isn't that right?"

Her mouth twisted. Her eyes blazed at him.

"Go to hell." She pushed past him, pulling open the door, then took two quick steps across the landing and ran down the stairs.

It was all Jake could do to keep himself from chasing after her. It was also all he could do to keep himself from cursing a blue streak or kicking the door or in general giving vent to the burning mix of emotions that churned inside him as she whisked out of sight and he listened to her feet clattering away down the stairs.

Just minutes later, he heard the distant slam of the front door and felt like he'd been punched in the gut.

Forget Christmas morning, he told himself grimly. *Pal, you've just been Scrooged.*

Then he headed downstairs, slowly and calmly, and gave Pops, who greeted him with raised eyebrows and a lurking grin, the kind of look that made him swallow whatever joshing comment he'd been about to make. And he sent Charlie, who'd just walked in, after Sarah with instructions to keep an eye on her on the down-low and let him know if anything came up. And finally, he went back upstairs, showered and changed, then went off in search of Brian McIntyre, for whom he had a personal, direct, and in-your-face message: *Come within a mile of Sarah again, and I'll make sure you regret it every day for the rest of your life.*

* * *

Hundreds of mourners turned out for Mary's funeral. The small church was packed with family, friends, neighbors, and acquaintances as well as the merely curious, drawn by the publicity and the sensational nature of the death. The pews were filled to overflowing. People stood in the aisles and lined up in rows at the back of the church. It was a Catholic service, full of incense and candles and prayers and hymns. Sarah, seated with strangers in a crowded pew near the back, barely heard a single word of it. She kept seeing, over and over again, the beseeching look in Mary's eyes as their gazes had locked a few minutes before the other woman had died. And then, the explosion of blood and gore . . .

There's nothing I could have done, Sarah told herself, but it didn't help. It didn't make the lump in her throat or the sick feeling in the pit of her stomach go away.

When the service was over, when the flower-topped casket had been carried out, when the weeping daughters and grandchildren had passed down the aisle to pile into the limousine that would follow the hearse to the cemetery, Sarah rose and filed out too. In the crowded nave, she paused to exchange a few desultory comments with some of the mourners she knew, a couple of the cops who were working the case, a lawyer from the Victims of Crimes office, a woman from her own neighborhood. Just as she was about to pass through the wide arched doors to the steamy heat of the porch and sun-crisped grass and parking lot beyond, a hand touched her arm.

"Mrs. Mason?" The voice had a slight Hispanic accent. Sarah looked around to see a small, plump, fortyish woman with a tanned complexion and liquid dark eyes behind her. She wore a short-sleeved black dress and had her long, black hair piled in a bun on the top of her head. Her round face was wet with tears and she held a chubby little girl Sarah thought she recognized in her arms.

"Yes?" The little girl, and the other children crowding close to her, made it easy to guess the woman's identity.

"I am Rosa Barillas," she said, confirming what Sarah already was sure of. "I want to thank you for saving my Angie's life."

"You're welcome." What Sarah really wanted to say was *I had to because, you see, once I had a daughter, too.* But she didn't. Instead she smiled at Rosa, and then smiled at her children—the two boys, Rafael and Sergio, the middle daughter, Lizbeth, and Angie—too. The inexorable forward motion of the crowd behind them propelled them all through the doors, onto the porch, and then down the steps to the lawn. A TV camera crew was set up out front, Sarah saw, and realized that the murdered woman's service would make the evening news. Incongruously, sunlight drenched the scene, reflecting off the roofs of cars and the camera lens and odd bits and pieces of jewelry worn by the mourners. It bounced off the female reporter's blonde hair, and, glancing that way, Sarah recognized Hayley Winston. People parted like the Red Sea around her and her crew, streaming toward the parking lot, which was filled to overflowing with cars, some of which were already in motion as they pulled into line behind the hearse.

"Angie has something she wants to give you," Rosa said, opening her purse as they paused in an awkward little clump not far from the camera crew. She fumbled inside it for a moment, then came up with a tissue-wrapped bundle about the size of a pack of cards, which she passed to Angie.

"Go on," Rosa murmured to her daughter, and Angie stepped out from behind her mother and held the package out to Sarah almost shyly.

"Thank you," Angie said, and Sarah recognized a mother's determined coaching behind the words. She also saw that Angie's face, like Rosa's, was streaked with drying tears.

"Thank *you*." Sarah accepted the package, which was light as air, and crouched down in front of Angie to open it. Pulling the tape carefully away from the tissue paper, she peeled the paper back to behold an exquisite little angel, hand-crocheted from silvery-white yarn.

"Because you were her angel that night," Rosa said.

"It's beautiful." Sarah balanced the delicate little thing on the palm of her hand. She smiled at Angie. "I'll treasure it."

"That's it. That's the money shot." The barely audible murmur made Sarah look sharply around. It came from the Channel 5 cameraman, who, along with Hayley Winston, was standing behind her, his camera perched on his shoulder. He was obviously zeroing in on the angel on Sarah's hand.

Sarah blinked at them in outraged astonishment.

"Will you miss your friend Mary?" Hayley Winston thrust the microphone in her hand toward Angie before Sarah could react.

"I wish she never had to die. I wish I could see her again," the little girl whispered and burst into tears. Then she took off running. With an apologetic look for Sarah, Rosa and the other children rushed after her.

Sarah surged to her feet, staring indignantly at Hayley Winston. But the woman and her crew were already moving away from her. The camera was once again pointed at the reporter, who was speaking into it.

"And so we have a touching finale to the funeral of Mary Jo White: an angel presented by little Angela Barillas to the woman who saved her life, Beaufort County Assistant District Attorney Sarah Mason."

If there was more, Sarah suddenly didn't want to hear it. Carefully closing her fingers around the angel, she turned her back on the TV crew and hurried after the Barillas family, who were piling into an ancient mini-van when she caught up with them.

"Mrs. Barillas," Sarah said, and Rosa, who was just climbing into the driver's seat while the sliding door closed on her brood in the back, turned to look at her questioningly even as she reached for handle to close the open door.

"I'd like to stay in touch." Sarah offered one of her business cards, and the other woman took it. "If you—or the children—ever need anything, call me."

Rosa looked down at the card and nodded. "Thank you."

"Mama, we're dying back here," one of the children—Sarah thought it was Sergio—yelled, and the rest loudly chimed in. Rafael, in the front passenger seat, waved his hand in front of his face and mimed panting.

"I must go," Rosa said, and Sarah nodded and stepped back. The van door closed and the engine started, which meant that the air-conditioner presumably did, too.

Sarah turned and walked away toward the far side of the parking lot, where her

Sentra waited in the broiling sun. Unlocking the door, she got in, wincing a little as the backs of her legs, which, in deference to the heat, were bare beneath her sleeveless black dress, made contact with the sizzling vinyl seat, and set the small angel safely down on the passenger seat. Turning on the car, recoiling from the hot blast of air that shot from the air-conditioning vents, she quickly rolled down her windows to let the worst of the heat escape.

Then she backed out, swung around, and drove toward the back of the line that was already moving out on its way to the grave site.

She was still waiting to pull into line when her cell phone rang. Sarah scooped it out of the console between the seats and squinted at the display. The sun made the incoming number hard to read. . . .

It was, she saw with some surprise, her number. Her home number. Somebody— who, she couldn't imagine—was calling her cell phone from her house.

Flipping open the phone, she pushed the button and answered. "Hello?"

"I want to come home, Mommy," Lexie

whimpered. "I want you to sing me our lull-aby. Please, Mommy. Please."

And then the plaintive notes of *When You Wish Upon a Star* tinkled through the phone.

19

"Jake! Jake! Something's up!" Austin's frantic voice had sounded through Jake's cell phone and echoed in his ears as he drove toward Sarah's house with a grim disregard for both speed limits and the usual rules of the road. Austin had shadowed Sarah to the funeral, hanging back, keeping watch, and was actually one row over in the parking lot when her Sentra had peeled out of there like, according to Austin, a bat out of hell. To Austin's credit, he had managed to stay with her, keeping her in sight without, he was pretty sure, her ever spotting him. Not that Sarah's spotting ability seemed to be particularly good at the moment. Jake himself had been at the funeral, standing in the back, and he was willing to bet dollars to doughnuts she'd never known it. Austin had stayed in his car in the parking lot, observing Sarah's vehicle and the main entrance of the church, which was fortunate because Jake had hung back in the vestry to give Sarah time to get clear. Now, as Jake pulled into her driveway, Austin waved at him from the driver's seat of the green Rav4 parked a little way up the street. Getting out of the car, Jake waved back in acknowledgment as he strode up the walk, took the two steps to the porch in a single bound, and started to fit his key into the lock.

Which, as it turned out, wasn't necessary. The door not only wasn't locked, it wasn't even shut. It swung inward as he touched it.

Not good.

He pulled his Glock from the small of his back and walked through the door.

"Sarah?" Heart racing, gun hand pointed at the floor but ready to jerk into position at an instant's notice, he moved quickly through the entry hall. Sweetie-pie emerged stiff-legged from the direction of the bedrooms to greet him with a snarl. Figuring that Sweetie-pie was coming from wherever Sarah was, Jake went by him with nothing more than a muttered "good dog" and didn't get his leg torn off, which Jake counted as a sign of true progress in their relationship. Sarah's bedroom door was open, and even before he reached it he could hear the eerie tinkling music-box tune that had so creeped him out when he had heard it before.

When you wish upon a star . . .

"Sarah?" His muscles were tense and ready for action and his adrenaline was pumping. He wasn't sure what he was going to find, and at first, when he saw her kneeling on her bedroom floor in her black funeral dress with her head bowed over that damned white unicorn and the rest of Lexie's toys scattered around her, he was relieved. At least she didn't appear to have suffered any physical harm.

Then he realized that she was shaking. Holding on to that damned toy for all she was worth and shaking like a leaf. The sight acted like a vice closing around his heart.

"Christ, Sarah," he said, and shoved his

pistol back into his waistband as he went toward her.

Sarah looked up at him and realized that there was no one else on earth whom she would rather see in that moment of extremis. Since walking out of his apartment, she hadn't seen him, hadn't heard from him, and had accepted the pain of their broken relationship as just one more heartache in a life that had been filled with them. Pain was something she was familiar with, something she had learned to live with, to cope with, and she had told herself that in time she would adjust to this newest one, too. But now, now that her heart had been ripped from its moorings again, she needed him, she realized. Needed him and wanted him with her. Far too badly to do anything but be glad he was there.

"She called me," Sarah said over the unicorn's tinkling tune as he crouched down beside her. "On my cell phone. From here, in this house. She said, 'I want to come home, Mommy. I want you to sing me our lullaby.' And then I heard this." She touched the unicorn. After all these years, its plush side still felt velvety soft beneath her fingers. "Lexie loved this song. We sang it every night."

Her voice cracked on that last part.

"Sarah . . ." Jake reached out and took the unicorn from her, and Sarah let him. He very carefully set it upright on the floor, and the music stopped. She looked at it sitting there and felt cold all over. Lexie had gotten it for Christmas, the last Christmas before she had disappeared. Every night thereafter, she had taken it into bed with her, and they would sing along with it, and then Sarah would set the unicorn on the nightstand beside Lexie's bed to watch over her during the night.

Her heart ached, remembering.

Jake was talking again, and it took a real effort to tune in. "You know somebody is doing this to try to get to you. Short of killing you—and they may have tried that, too, when you were shot—this is the best way to throw you off the rails. Somebody knows that, and they're using it. That's all this is. It isn't Lexie, Sarah."

His words hit her like small stones of reason. It was all Sarah could do not to flinch. He was right, she knew he was right, but . . .

"How could they know about our lullaby?" Her throat felt raw and painful from the sobs she refused to give in to. Her eyes seemed to burn from her unshed tears. "It's like *Eeyore.* How could anyone know that?"

On Saturday afternoon, after her meeting with Duncan, she'd come back to Jake's office. Jake wasn't there, but Pops and Dorothy and Austin were, going through the files on Lexie's disappearance, searching for any mention of Eeyore. She'd joined in, and they'd combed all the records without finding even a hint of what they were looking for. But, as Pops had pointed out to her, sounding so much like Jake that she had felt her heart clutch, it was possible that there were other records, other files, at some of the agencies that had been involved in the search for Lexie. The FBI, for example, would have their own set, as would the Beaufort PD, and the Center for Missing Children—any of those might contain a few documents that were missing from Jake's set. And any of those documents might contain the reference to Eeyore. Just because they hadn't found it, Pops said, didn't mean the information still wasn't out there somewhere.

But Sarah didn't think it was.

"I don't know, honey." Jake's voice was rough with compassion for her. "Somebody knows about it, though, and we're going to find out who. I promise. We're pulling out all the stops."

"It was Lexie's voice," she said, because she couldn't hold it in any longer. "I know it's impossible, but . . . it was Lexie's voice. Her sweet little five-year-old voice. I'd swear to it."

Her voice broke, and her control did, too. She reached out for him blindly, and his arms came around her, pulling her close, holding her tight. Being in his arms again felt so familiar, so safe and right and comforting that she thought *Jake* just once with a fierce, piercing sense of home-coming and then wrapped her arms around his neck and pressed her face into his shoulder and clung like she would never let go again.

She didn't cry. She refused to cry. Jake was right, she knew, someone was doing this to her deliberately, and to succumb to tears, to the ocean of grief and despair and heartbreak that these despicable acts had tapped, would be to let him win.

But try as she might, she couldn't stop herself from trembling from head to toe. She couldn't stop her heart from pounding or her stomach from knotting. She couldn't stop her breathing from going all raspy and ragged.

"Sarah," he said. And, "It's okay." Things like that. Things she didn't even really hear, except for the comforting sound of them. Things that were unremarkable, unmemorable, except for the deep, familiar timbre of the voice that said them.

"I need to call the police," she said after a little while, not really surprised to find that her voice sounded nothing like her usual one.

"I'll do it. From my cell phone. If somebody called you from this house, then they had to have touched either the phone in the kitchen or the one in the bedroom. There might be fingerprints."

Sarah felt a quick glimmer of hope—fingerprints might lead to an ID—and nodded. Jake stood up and pulled her up with him. For a moment longer, she leaned against him, drawing strength from him, absorbing his warmth through her skin, deliberately willing the last of the trembling to stop. When it did, she gritted her teeth and straightened her shoulders and stepped away from him, out of his arms, and walked into the living room where she made it to the big leather chair before her knees gave out on her. Jake followed her as far as the front hall, then stopped where she could see him as he talked into his cell phone. He was, she saw, wearing a dark suit and tie, and a white shirt, and she wondered briefly where he had been.

A pair of uniforms showed up, followed shortly thereafter by Sexton and Kelso, who Sarah insisted be called for continuity's sake. They were professional, they did their jobs, and if any of them felt any animosity toward her about the Stumbo case, at least it didn't show. By the time they left again, it was well past eight o'clock. Sarah was back in the chair with Sweetie-pie at her feet, not having wanted to watch as Lexie's toys were dusted for fingerprints along with both phones and the doors, as well as assorted interior surfaces that the officers felt an intruder might have touched. They took Sarah's statement, talked to Jake, determined that he had the only other key to her house so far as Sarah knew, canvassed the neighborhood to see if anyone had seen anything, which no one had, and shook their heads over the whole thing. Nobody said it, but Sarah could tell from their expressions: Nothing was taken, there was no sign of a break-in, and she, her house, and belongings were physically fine. This was going into the files as a low-priority crime.

When they were gone, Jake, who'd seen them out, walked back into the living room and stood, looking down at her with his hands resting loosely on his hips.

"You're coming home with me," he said as she looked up at him inquiringly. "I'm not leaving you here. If someone got in, got past the dog, and made a call from your telephone, they can get in again. You're not safe here."

Sarah met his eyes mutely. Then she nodded, and when he reached for her hand, she let him pull her to her feet. He was right, she could see that he was right, and, anyway, staying in the house last night alone except for Sweetie-pie had been a nightmare. Lexie's shade had been everywhere, and the thought that someone might be lurking out there in the dark, waiting for her to fall asleep before sneaking inside, had never been far from her mind. Sleeping in either bed had proved impossible, so finally she had carried a pillow and blanket to the couch, where she had eventually dozed off while watching TV. It wasn't something she cared to do again. Especially not now, after this.

Now she no longer felt even marginally safe in her own house.

"Those prints they lifted—when will they know whose they are?"

"It takes a while," Jake said, which she knew. "I'll talk to some people, see what I can do to hurry things along."

Sarah met his gaze. She could read what he was thinking as clearly as if he had said the words aloud. "Whoever is doing this isn't dumb enough to have left prints."

"Probably not, but you never know."

She knew, and so, from his expression, did he.

"You don't think . . . it couldn't be Lexie, could it? Somehow? Making these calls?" Sarah couldn't help it. The idea had sunk talons into her heart and wouldn't let go.

Jake's eyes darkened. "I don't see how."

"No." Sarah did her best to let the impossible hope go. She took a deep breath.

"I have to get some things," she said, remembering that the next day was Monday and no matter what else was going on in her life, she still had to go to work.

Jake waited while she gathered what she needed, and then he carried her things out to his car. She trailed behind him with Sweetie-pie, then hesitated when he opened the back door of the Acura for the dog to jump in.

"I need my car," she said. "For in the morning."

Jake studied her face. "You up to driving?"

Sarah nodded.

"Okay, I'll follow you."

It didn't take long to get to his building, but by the time Sarah pulled into the parking lot, the sun was starting to sink below the western horizon in a blaze of pinks and purples and oranges. The sky over the inlet behind the house was already deepening to indigo, and a chorus of bullfrogs was in full swing not far away. The mosquitoes were out in force, and lightning bugs were blinking on and off like Christmas lights. The steamy brilliance of the day was yielding to the pleasant heat of a sultry summer's night. Sarah picked up the little crocheted angel from where it still rested in the passenger seat, tucked it carefully into the small, black purse she had retrieved from the top shelf of her closet to replace the one the police were still holding for evidence, and got out of the car. She opened the back door for Sweetie-pie, then stood listening to the whirr of insects and various splashes from the direction of the water as Jake's Acura pulled in beside her.

"I ordered pizza," he said as he joined her, and Sarah made a face at him. He grinned unrepentantly at her, typical junk-food-scarfing Jake, and suddenly Sarah felt as though their relationship was almost back to normal again.

"The part that's really bothering me is the damned dog," Jake said as he followed her and Sweetie-pie up the stairs. "How'd they get past him? Is there somebody he likes, a vet or something, maybe? A groomer? A pizza delivery boy? Anybody?"

Sarah didn't have to think about that for very long.

"No." She and Sweetie-pie had reached

the third-floor landing by that time, and she spoke over her shoulder. "Not as far as I know. At least, not well enough to let them in the house."

"He should be chewing this guy up."

From the thoughtful tone of it, Sarah realized that Jake was talking to himself, and she didn't reply as she walked into his apartment. He followed her, pulling something out from beneath his coat as he walked, and Sarah's eyes widened as she realized that he'd been carrying a gun. *For me,* she thought as he tucked it away in a drawer in the table beside the couch, and the fact that Jake was carrying a gun again underlined the danger he thought she might be in.

In her desperation to follow this new trail that seemed to be leading her toward Lexie, she'd almost forgotten about that.

"Where have you been, anyway?" Sarah asked a few minutes later. She had dropped onto the couch as he closed the curtains, and was watching now as he stood beside the dining table shrugging out of his suit jacket and pulling off his tie. Sweetie-pie was napping beside the coffee table. Sarah was still shaken, still weak and sick inside, but she couldn't help the little flicker of sexual awareness that she felt as her eyes slid over him. It caught her by surprise, made her faintly uncomfortable. He was still Jake, her best friend Jake, but now there was something new between them, a kind of intangible vibration that she could sense in the air, and she was looking at him in a way she had never really looked at him before. She couldn't help noticing the breadth of his shoulders in the white shirt, or how powerfully he was built. The hard handsomeness of his features would never have registered on her even forty-eight hours previously. Nor would she have felt the least bit of awkwardness at the prospect of spending the night in his apartment.

But now she did.

If Jake was experiencing any of the same uneasiness, he gave no sign of it. Draping both garments over the back of one of the dining chairs, he sent her a wry look.

"Funeral."

That was unexpected enough that Sarah blinked.

"Funeral?" Her eyes widened as the only

possible answer occurred to her. "Mary's funeral?"

Jake nodded. He unbuttoned his cuffs, then started rolling his sleeves up past his elbows. Again, that flicker of awareness caught her by surprise: His forearms looked tan and strong, and his hands were big and long-fingered and unmistakably masculine.

Okay, those were details that she would just as soon have remained oblivious to. There was no room in her life for a boyfriend, a lover. But Jake—there was room for Jake. She needed Jake. As she had learned over the past twenty-four hours, he mattered to her. A whole hell of a lot. Her life had felt empty and bleak when she had thought he was no longer going to be a part of it. What she wanted to do now was simply wipe the whole sex thing out of their relationship, just erase that one night from both their memories, and have them go back to what they had been for so long, each other's closest friend.

"I didn't see you," she said, determinedly pushing anything other than their friendship out of her mind.

"I was there."

Then Sarah thought of something. She had been so upset before that it was only just now occurring to her that Jake had shown up at her house with uncannily accurate timing.

"How did you know that . . . that something had happened?" That she had needed him was what she meant, but she didn't say it, because it said way more about the complicated nature of their relationship than she felt ready to get into at the moment.

Jake looked faintly guilty, and then Sarah knew.

"You were following me," she said accusingly. There was a definite edge of indignation to her voice. Not too much, because she had been so very thankful to see him. But still . . .

"Actually, right at that moment, Austin was. He called me."

Then Sarah saw the whole thing. She narrowed her eyes at him. When she thought of the miserable night she had spent, of how on edge and nervous and ready to jump at the slightest sound she had been, she felt like kicking herself. She should have realized. If she'd been thinking halfway straight, she would have realized. How long had she known Jake, after all?

He wasn't the man to just give up and go away.

"So who staked out my house last night?" Her tone was dry.

Jake had the shifty look of a man contemplating a lie. Sarah's eyes caught his, and he sighed.

"I was in the back. Thank God for your privacy fence, or one of your neighbors surely would have spotted me and called the cops. Dave was out front."

Before she could say anything, the doorbell rang, and Jake went downstairs to answer it.

Saved by the pizza, Sarah thought, but since it really felt kind of good to know that Jake been watching her back despite the fact that they had been on the outs at the time, she let the subject drop.

By the time the pizza was almost gone— well, since she had no appetite whatsoever, by the time his pizza was almost gone—she was big-eyed with exhaustion. Her elbows were on the table, her chin was in her hands, and it was all she could do to stay upright in her chair. But she already knew that if she tried to go to bed, she wouldn't be able to sleep.

Shadowy monsters that she couldn't quite see haunted her dreams.

"I'm going to take the dog out," Jake said and stood up. "You go on to bed."

Sarah blinked at him. He was gathering up the remains of their meal, and as he picked up the box containing her pizza, he cast her virtually untouched pie a grim glance.

"You need to eat more," he said.

"I know." She took a deep breath as he called Sweetie-pie and the dog looked up, then creakily got to his feet. The thing was, this was Jake, and she pretty much knew the way he worked. He hadn't forgotten about their sexual encounter any more than she had. It lay there between them, unacknowledged but impossible to completely dismiss. The only way to put the issue behind them was to address it directly, Sarah realized. Take the bull by the horns, as it were. Shine a light on the elephant in the middle of the room.

"Jake."

"Yeah?" He put the box on the ground for Sweetie-pie, who started gobbling the contents down with the eagerness of a dog whose normal diet didn't include a lot of pizza, and straightened to look at her inquiringly when she didn't continue.

Okay, just spit it out. It was ridiculous to feel bashful with *Jake.*

"Thanks for not letting wh—" With the best will in the world she stuttered slightly over what to call it, settling for the wimpiest euphemism in the world. "What happened ruin our friendship."

"What happened?" he repeated blankly, his eyebrows lifting at her in apparent incomprehension.

The thing was, though, she wasn't falling for that. He knew perfectly well what she was talking about, and she knew it.

"Yes," she said, eyes narrowing at him.

"Are you by any chance talking about us getting it on the other night?"

So much for delicacy.

"You know I am."

"Oh," he said. "Well, I just wanted to make sure." Then, when that earned him a full-blown glare that should by rights have had him cringing in shame, his eyes twinkled at her. "You're welcome."

For a moment, Sarah simply looked at him.

"Jackass," she said, but without any particular heat. He grinned at her, a little mockingly, and suddenly it was all right, things were back to normal between them again, and she felt some of the tension that had been knotting her stomach start to fade. Jake was right, he had to be right, what was happening to her here was harassment in its most vicious form but nothing more, and she would survive it as she had survived everything else.

That which doesn't kill me makes me stronger: words to live by.

"Go to bed, Sarah," Jake said again then, and took Sweetie-pie for his walk.

She did go to bed, worn-out from the emotions and events of the last few days, and if she had bad dreams, at least they didn't wake her, and in the morning she didn't remember them.

Maybe it had something to do with the little crocheted angel that Angie Barillas had given her, which she had put on her bedside table before she went to sleep. It had seemed to glow for a few seconds after she'd turned off her light, and she had still been looking at it when she'd fallen asleep.

Maybe it had stood guard over her dreams through the night.

20

"It's been seven years since Lexie disappeared. Why did this start happening now? Something had to trigger it," Jake said to Pops.

It was shortly after seven thirty the next morning. Jake, with Sweetie-pie in tow, was just coming in from what was starting to feel like his regular gig of dog-walking when Pops had roared up on his motorcycle. Jake had practically shuddered at the sight of it: After walking out of his building on Saturday morning with the day's agenda firmly set in his mind, he had been reminded by the absence of his car from the parking lot that he had no wheels. Pops had given him a lift on that thing to pick up his car, a hair-raising ride that Jake had vowed never to repeat on pain of death (probably his). Pops was now walking in with him, and Jake had just finished filling him in on the call from "Lexie" that Sarah had received the day before.

"She got that promotion," Pops observed. Today's T-shirt was from the recent Stones tour, the one with the big red kissy lips and wagging tongue. Add jeans, boots, and Pops's shiny dome, and he was once again a happening dude.

"That was three months ago." Jake carefully closed the front door behind them. After Sweetie-pie's close encounter with Molly, he was careful to walk the dog only along the sidewalk that ran in front of the building. "I've asked Sarah, but she can't think of anything specific that could have set somebody off."

The problem with discussing this with Sarah was, he and she were coming at this from two separate angles: He was looking at it from the perspective of searching for a person who would want to harm Sarah, and she was looking to learn who could have kidnapped Lexie. These lines of inquiry did not necessarily intersect. In Jake's mind, it was quite possible that whoever was tormenting Sarah had had nothing whatsoever to do with Lexie's disappearance, and was simply using it as the most obvious means to drive her around the bend. To Sarah, all roads led to Lexie. It was as simple as that.

"No run-ins with anybody or anything like that?"

Jake shook his head. "Nothing that stood out in her mind, anyway."

They were in the big downstairs office now. Pops dropped into Dorothy's chair, and Jake, with Sweetie-pie at his side, went to double-check the sliding glass door to make sure it was securely shut. It was, and the deck was free of gators, and the early morning sun rising over the intercoastal waterway was as round and yellow as an egg yolk as it climbed the bright blue sky. It was already hot, and was due to get hotter still, and the humidity was thickening like cooking gravy. Everything was status quo, a typical August morning, except that somewhere out there, someone hated Sarah enough to inflict the cruelest possible torture on her. Maybe even hated her enough to kill her.

Jake was going to track that someone down if it took him the rest of his life.

"Maybe you're looking at it ass-backwards," Pops said thoughtfully, rocking back in the chair. "Maybe it's not something that already happened that's got this guy het up but something that's getting ready to happen. Something that whoever this is doesn't want Sarah to be a part of, or reach, or do."

"I thought of that." Jake turned away from the view outside the window to meet his grandfather's gaze. "And I've been looking into it. The problem is, she's got a lot of stuff going on right now. The Helitzer trial is the big thing. Then there's that rape case against those two cops. And she's prose-cuting a couple of bank robbers, and a big-time drug dealer she wouldn't cut a deal with, and a teacher accused of having sex with an underage boy, and . . . well, the list just goes on and on. Plus, there's that Women Against Rape class she helps out at, so there's a whole 'nother group of peo-ple to look at. And the people she works with, who knows, maybe one of them wants her out of the way for some reason. Hell, maybe she's ticked off a neighbor. There are so many possibilities, it's like looking for one particular blade of grass on a golf course."

"Whoever this guy is, he knows that the way to hurt her is through her kid," Pops said. "That should narrow the list down some. It's been seven years. A lot of these people wouldn't know she even had a kid."

Jake shook his head. "I don't think that makes a difference. There was so much publicity about that. And it's easy to find out. You can Google her and it comes up."

"Google," Pops said with the scorn of someone to whom the Internet was a continuing mystery. "What the hell is that? You tell me, what kind of world is this when you can just type in a name and—"

The sound of footsteps coming lightly down the stairs caused him to break off and glance in that direction. Jake looked that way, too. Sweetie-pie, who'd been flopped on his belly staring longingly out the window, lifted his head and looked around, then came to his feet. Moments later, Sarah, in a loose-fitting charcoal-gray skirt suit, silky white blouse, and chunky-heeled pumps (the absolute unsexiness of which caused Jake to officially rest his case about her clothes), hurried into view, clearly on her way out the door.

Despite the fact that she'd slept soundly last night—he knew because he'd checked on her several times—she still looked pale and tired and—the word he wanted was probably *haunted.* And yet she was still so beautiful that his heart stuttered a little just because he was looking at her.

Fool, he told himself. Because that's what he'd always privately thought about men who hankered after women who didn't want them. He'd seen plenty of them in the course of his work as a private investigator, men in the throes of divorce who were still in love with their wives, other men who couldn't believe that the cutie they were canoodling with was just after their money or was canoodling with somebody else on the side, all sorts of lovesick idiots making themselves crazy over that one woman they thought they just had to have. What he'd wanted to say to each and every one was: *There are plenty of fish in the sea. Get over it and move on.*

Now his lack of sympathy and fellow feeling were coming back to bite him in the ass.

There might be lots of fish in the sea, but this was the only one he wanted.

Mine, he thought as she paused in the doorway to shoot him a quick smile. *And I don't mean as best friends, either.*

But that was all she was offering.

"Hey," she said to him. "Thanks for taking Sweetie-pie out."

"Not a problem." Jake glanced down at the dog, who was standing beside him looking hopefully at Sarah. The thing about her taking the dog out was that somebody might be waiting out there to shoot her. The probability lessened as the days without someone trying it again passed, but it was still a risk that he wasn't prepared to take, which meant that he and Sweetie-pie were clearly destined to become bosom buddies. "I think we're bonded now. He didn't even snarl at me once."

"See, I told you he loved you." She smiled at Pops. "Hello, Pops," she said as she walked into the room and patted Sweetie-pie on the head.

"Mornin', Sarah. Where you headin' out to so early?"

"Work," she said, transferring her gaze back to Jake. It was clear from her attitude that she was determined not to let this thing beat her down, and he admired her more than ever for that. "Did you guys ever finish up the witness interviews for *Helitzer*?"

"Yeah. Nothing interesting. Charlie'll be dropping them off this morning."

"Great. How about you? Will I see you sometime today?"

"Probably." *Oh, yeah. Wild horses couldn't keep me away,* he thought, but he didn't say it. Instead, he frowned at her. "You're not going anywhere besides your office and the courthouse, right? No driving strippers home or anything like that?"

"I swear," Sarah said, because they'd already had a talk about the best way for her to stay safe until this was over. Of course, Jake thought, he meant to have somebody tailing her throughout the day regardless, even though he'd sorta, kinda promised her he wouldn't. "Listen, I've got to go. See you later."

She was already on the move.

"Later."

"Bye, Pops."

"Bye, Sarah."

She was almost through the door that led into the reception room when she glanced back over her shoulder at Jake.

"By the way, who's following me today? Just so I know who to look out for?"

Okay, so she knew the way things worked with him. Jake had to grin. "It's Charlie this morning. Since he has to go over to the DA's office anyway."

"Tell him I'm probably going to stop for coffee," she said. "You're out."

Then she was gone, her footsteps muffled by carpet, the front door closing behind her with a dull click.

Jake only realized that he was still grinning like a fool when he encountered his grandfather's knowing gaze.

"What?" he said, losing the grin.

"Nothing." Pops shrugged. "At least, nothing new. Hell, Hoss, I knew it was love when you took on that gator for her."

"I did not—" Jake began, only to be interrupted by the arrival of Dorothy. His secretary, summery in pale yellow, bustled in, gave him a nod, bestowed a disapproving look on Sweetie-pie, and ostentatiously ignored Pops, who quickly vacated her chair.

"I saw Sarah," she said, tucking her purse

under her desk and smoothing her skirt beneath her as she sat down in the chair Pops had abandoned. "That poor child looks worn-out. She needs a vacation. Does she know Charlie is following her? Because I thought I saw her wave at him."

"She knows," Jake said.

"Seems like Hoss here ain't so good at keeping things on the down-low." Pops moved to stand beside Jake.

Jake started to reply, but Dorothy got in first.

"Speaking of keeping things on the down-low," she said, her eyes fixing on Pops, her expression turning testy, "maybe you want to tell me just when we got a company policy against employees seeing each other socially? Because I've been here something like forty years, and when Dave told me that you told him about that policy, well, all I can say is that was the first I'd ever heard of it."

Pops looked uncomfortable. His eyes slid sideways to his grandson. Jake recognized the look in them from a lifetime's worth of experience: It was *Help, I need you to save my bacon.* "Jake—"

"I'm out of this," Jake said, holding up a hand. "This is—"

Your business, he was going to say, but he got cut off by the ringing of his cell phone. Fishing it out of his pocket, he checked the display, frowned, and moved away to answer.

"Hi, um, it's Doris Linker." Jake still hadn't placed the name when the caller further identified herself. "Uh, Maurice Johnson's sister. You know how you said you'd pay us a thousand dollars if we called you as soon as Maurice woke up? Well, he's awake."

"How is it, Ms. Letts, that you have had nearly a year to prepare for this trial, and Ms. Mason has had—what? Three, four months? And yet she is ready to go to trial and you are not?"

Sarah tried not to look pleased as Judge Schwartzman turned the full force of his judicial disapproval on Pat Letts, who was swinging for the fences today in a candy-red suit that was eye-catching enough to make Sarah almost envious. It was not, however, having the effect on Judge Schwartzman that Letts had obviously hoped for. Or maybe it was, but the pair of reporters busily scribbling away in the back were acting as an antidote. Whatever, things were certainly not going opposing counsel's way.

Letts looked taken aback, but she recovered with admirable sang-froid. "The complexity of the case is such, Your Honor, that . . ."

"I don't want to hear it, Ms. Letts. You think I haven't been on the bench long enough to recognize a delaying tactic when one is argued before me?" Judge Schwartzman frowned at Letts. Then, as Sarah was carefully not smiling and Letts was just as carefully not acting chagrined, Judge Schwartzman leaned toward them, his blue eyes stern over his bifocals. "And I will remind you both that voir dire starts next Wednesday. I expect no more delays. Motion denied."

He banged the gavel down, then stood up and left the dais, shaking out his black judicial robes as he went. The United States flag and the State of South Carolina flag behind the dais fluttered in the wake of his passing. The bailiff moved toward the court reporter, who was leaning back in her chair, and a murmur passed over the courtroom signifying the start of the lunch break. Sarah let out a silent sigh of relief. She wasn't at the top of her game today, and she knew it; she was having trouble concentrating because of yesterday's phone call from Lexie, or whoever it was who had sounded so much like Lexie, continually gnawing around the edges of her consciousness. But she wasn't letting it get to her—well, at least not any more than she could help. She was up here doing her job, going to bat for the crime victims she was paid to represent, keeping on keeping on. She might be holding together with difficulty, but she was holding together, and that was the important thing.

"Old turd," Letts muttered under her breath as she and Sarah each turned away to get their things from counsel table, and Sarah glanced at her in surprise. But if she thought that such an unprofessional aside might mark the start of a thaw in her relations with opposing counsel, she was wrong. Letts gathered up her things and stalked out of the courtroom without so much as another glance at Sarah. An assistant, a younger woman Sarah didn't know, hurried after her. Today there was no sign of Mitchell Helitzer, for which Sarah was thankful.

"That was surprisingly easy," Duncan said under his breath as he fell into step beside Sarah. Since he would be acting as her co-counsel once the trial started, his presence today wasn't in any way out of order. Still, since the DA's office was drowning under an ocean of work, it was department policy that a single prosecutor handle minor matters like today's hearing. Therefore, having Duncan show up two minutes before the hearing started had been a surprise.

"So what are you doing here?" she asked. He was walking up the aisle beside her as the courtroom emptied around them. The reporters who'd been sitting in the back were gone.

"Morrison told me to come." Duncan shrugged. "Ask him, not me."

Sarah meant to. Just as soon as she got back to the office. Every other Monday afternoon at three was a mandatory staff meeting. This was one of those Mondays, so Morrison would be in.

They pushed through the double doors together.

Letts was leaning against the dark-paneled wall near the stairs, talking on her cell phone. Despite the shuffling human tide between them, her to-die-for suit stood out like a ruby in a pile of gravel, making her impossible to miss. Sarah guessed that she was reporting the results of the hearing to someone, probably either an associate at her firm or Mitchell Helitzer himself.

"You want to grab some lunch?" Duncan asked as they went down the stairs together.

Sarah glanced up at him. He was smiling at her, his blue eyes crinkling at the corners, handsome in a little-boyish way that she knew a lot of women would find appealing. She liked him, they worked well together, and the lunch they'd shared on Saturday had been both friendly and productive. But still, there was something in his manner toward her that told her that maybe Jake was right: Maybe his interest in her went beyond the professional. She didn't want to encourage that.

Like she'd told him before, she didn't date.

"Thanks, but I'm working through," she said, which was true. He nodded, and as they reached the first floor he headed on toward the metal detectors, and with a wave Sarah turned toward the ladies' room. She had just finished drying her hands and was opening the door to leave again as Letts walked through it.

They almost jostled shoulders, and Letts stopped to glare at her.

"Just so you know, my client is innocent," Letts said. "And I'm really going to enjoy proving it in court."

"See, the thing is, we have a different take on this." Sarah gave her a brittle little smile. "I think your client is guilty as hell, and I'm really going to enjoy nailing his ass to the wall."

With that, she pushed on out into the hall.

"I love it when you talk dirty like that," Jake's voice said in her ear, and Sarah whirled to find him smiling wryly at her. Clearly he had overheard at least her part of her exchange with Letts. "So, who you busy pissing off now?"

Sarah told him. "What are you doing here?" she concluded.

"I'll tell you over lunch. You free?"

For Jake? "Sure," she said, "but I've only got about forty-five minutes."

"Plenty of time." Jake took her arm and steered her toward the metal detectors. He was wearing a tan summer-weight sport jacket with navy slacks, a white shirt, and a navy tie, and just looking at him made some of the tension that had built up in her neck and shoulders relax. "So, you want McDonald's or Arby's or what?"

Sarah groaned.

They ended up at Marco's deli across the street, where Sarah had chicken noodle soup and Jake had a meatball hoagie with extra cheese and fries. Hold the health benefits.

"They were following you," Jake said when they were seated with their food at a little table in the corner. Marco's was popular with the regular courthouse crowd, the judges and clerks and lawyers and officers of the court, and the place was crowded. Sarah had already waved at several people she knew, as had Jake. "Maurice Johnson and Donald Coomer. They drove to your house, saw you come out, and followed you to the Quik-Pik. That's when they got the idea to rob it: When they saw you go inside. Seems Johnson's brother's girlfriend used to work there, and she said they always took in a lot of money."

"What?" Sarah stopped eating, her spoon suspended halfway to her mouth as she stared at him. "Who told you that?"

Jake looked smug. "Maurice Johnson. He's conscious and talking. At least, he was when I left the hospital."

Sarah goggled at him, spilled some soup, and quickly put the spoon back in her bowl. That was so much information to take in, she didn't know where to start first.

"How did you know he was conscious?"

"I told his family that if he woke up to where he could talk and make sense, and I was the first person to talk to him, I'd pay them a thousand dollars. They called this morning."

"Is that even legal?" Sarah was still gaping at him even as she mopped up her spill with some paper napkins she'd pulled from the holder on the table. "I *know* it's not ethical."

"Hey, I'm an investigator, not a lawyer. The same rules don't apply." His appetite clearly unaffected by the bombshell he had dropped on her, he took a big bite out of his hoagie, chewed, and swallowed. "My guiding principle is: Whatever it takes to get the job done."

"What job?" Sarah was still turning over the implications of what he'd said in her mind.

"Keeping you safe. Finding out who shot you and why. Finding out who's making these phone calls. And figuring out how it's all related. And I'm starting to think it is."

"You think the shooting's related to the phone calls?" She'd completely forgotten about her soup, and he frowned meaningfully at the still-steaming white crookery bowl in front of her.

"Eat," he said, and when she picked up her spoon again he continued. "Johnson said it was Coomer's idea to go to your house. Of course, he could be lying to protect his ass, but he says he doesn't know why. He said they got there just as you were getting in your car, and they followed you to the Quik-Pik. They sat outside for a minute, watching through the glass windows, and that's when Coomer got the idea to rob the place."

"But why were they following me in the first place?" Sarah tried not to shiver as it all ran through her mind again in a kaleidoscope of lightning-fast vignettes—Skeleton Boy cornering her near the cold cases, Duke threatening and then shooting Mary, Angie's screaming eruption from beneath the table, their frantic flight from the store, the impact of the bullet smacking into her head.

"Johnson said he doesn't know. He said he was just with Coomer, along for the ride."

Having swallowed another mouthful of soup that practically stuck in her throat, Sarah put down her spoon again.

"So what do you think happened?"

Jake's eyes met hers over the hoagie in his hands. They were dark, hard, unsmiling—the eyes of the FBI agent he had once been.

"I think somebody either hired or coerced them—maybe just Coomer, maybe both of them—to scare you, rattle you. Maybe to hurt you, maybe even to kill you, I don't know yet. Whatever, things got messed up when you went to the Quik-Pik unexpectedly, so they decided to wing it, which is always a mistake for stupid guys, and during the course of winging it, the situation went to hell on a slide."

"Skeleton Boy said Duke's name," Sarah remembered.

"What?"

"Johnson called Coomer 'Duke,' his street name, right before Duke shot Mary."

"Yeah." Jake resumed eating his hoagie. "You see what I mean."

"You mean Mary was killed because of me?" Sarah suddenly felt sick.

Jake met her gaze. "Mary was killed because of being in the wrong place at the wrong time and having the misfortune to run into two stupid, violent thugs."

Who were in the store because of me. Sarah recognized the truth of that, and sent a little prayer heavenward, begging for forgiveness from Mary.

Her gaze met Jake's. "So who do you think shot me?"

"That," said Jake, his eyes once again hard as agate, "is the million-dollar question. I don't know yet, but I sure as hell mean to find out."

Neither one of them said anything for a moment. Noticing Jake's eyes narrowing critically on her bowl, Sarah picked up her spoon again. She didn't eat, no way could she possibly eat now, but she stirred the soup with her spoon in hopes of creating a diversion.

"And how does this relate to the calls?" she asked.

"I'm still working through the possibilities, so this is probably not one hundred percent right, you understand, but I think that when the whole have-the-two-vicious-punks-rob-beat-rape-kill-whatever-you scenario didn't play out like somebody hoped, the somebody being the person who hired Coomer, this person decided to get creative. Creative meaning having a little girl who sounds like your missing daughter call you and say pathetic things."

Lexie. Just remembering that voice over the phone made Sarah lightheaded. Had it really been another little girl who only sounded like her?

"But why?" Sarah was so shaken, she put down the spoon.

Jake shook his head. "I'm still working on that. Likewise the who. And if you don't want to dry up and blow away before we get this figured out, you need to eat."

Sarah picked up the spoon again. With his watchful eyes on her, she took a sip of broth. For a moment neither of them said anything more as he finished his meal and she kept up the pretext of eating soup.

"Why would he tell you all that?" Sarah asked eventually, as the iron hand that had seized her heart loosened its grip a little. "Johnson, I mean."

Having downed the last of his fries, Jake wiped his hands on a napkin. "I told him that if he talked, I'd cut him a deal: no murder one charge, no death penalty hanging over his head, no more than ten years in the hoosegow."

Sarah's eyes widened. "You don't have the authority to make a deal like that."

Jake shrugged and grinned. "So I lied."

Sarah was still searching for the words with which to answer that when movement nearby caught her eye. She glanced up absentmindedly, only to find Duncan signaling for his check from a table nearby, where he'd been eating with another man. For a moment their gazes met, and Sarah, remembering that she'd told him she meant to work through lunch, felt faintly guilty. He nodded acknowledgment at her, and she waggled her fingers at him.

"What?" Jake asked, as he took in her gesture and her face.

"Duncan's over there. He asked me to lunch, and I told him I had to work through."

"So you got a better offer." Clearly indifferent to Duncan's possible disgruntlement, Jake signaled for the check. The waitress brought it right over while Duncan continued to do his best to attract the same waitress's attention without any luck. Sarah might even have been impressed if she hadn't known the waitress, who was one of Dorothy's granddaughters, and, like her grandmother, doted on Jake.

"What time you think you'll be home?" Jake asked as they were going out the door together.

"Seven-ish," Sarah answered automatically, because it was Monday and she usually got home about that time to let Sweetie-pie out before heading out to her gym. Then she registered that *home* now meant Jake's place, where he would presumably be waiting for her. Her heart gave an odd little hiccup at the thought. *Home,* the way Jake said it, had a nice ring to it.

"I'll be there." He walked her across the street and saw her safely inside the courthouse, where he left her. The last thing he said to her was, "By the way, just so you know, Dave's on for the afternoon."

Later that day, after the staff meeting, Sarah cornered Morrison in his office. It was nearly six thirty, because the meeting had run long, as staff meetings always tended to do, and Morrison was on his feet behind his desk, methodically engaged in packing up his briefcase, when she tapped on his open door and then walked in. As DA, he had the pick of the offices in the nondescript seventies-era high-rise not far from the courthouse that they all worked in, but that wasn't saying much. Like hers and everybody else's, his office was basically a cubicle with a metal desk, metal bookshelves filled to overflowing with books and papers lining the walls, a rolling chair behind the desk, and a couple of standard office chairs pulled up in front of it. The only thing that made his office more desirable than any of the others was that it was located in a corner of the building, which gave him a magnificent view of Beaufort Bay to the east and the historic district to the north.

The double helping of windows also meant that the office was air-conditioning-challenged, a problem that Morrison was constantly trying to have fixed.

"Yeah?" Having finished loading his briefcase, Morrison snapped it shut and looked at her inquiringly.

"Why did you send Duncan over to the postponement hearing on *Helitzer?*" Sarah asked without preamble.

A shadow crossed Morrison's face. "Because I thought you might need backup."

"I've never needed backup before. I certainly don't need it for a run-of-the-mill hearing."

Morrison seemed to hesitate. Then he gestured toward the visitors' chairs in front of his desk.

"Sit down, why don't you, Sarah?"

Uh-oh. This can't be good. Morrison never asks any of his staff to sit down.

Sarah gave him a level look and pointedly did not sit down. "Whatever it is, you can tell me while I'm on my feet. I promise not to faint on you."

Morrison's lips thinned. His hazel eyes seemed to take her measure through the rimless glasses that magnified them slightly, momentarily giving him the look of some big-eyed predatory insect, like a praying mantis.

"I heard about that latest harassing phone call you had Sunday night. I wasn't sure you'd be up to much after that."

"I'm always up to doing my job."

"And you do a good one, Sarah. I give you that." He turned squarely to face her, and Sarah braced for the *but* that she could feel coming her way. "I'm getting calls from people. They tell me you seem wiped out, shaky on your feet, not your usual self. I can see some of that for myself just looking at you now. Hell, no wonder, you've had a rough few days. I understand that. And believe me, I sympathize. But we've got some big trials coming up, a lot going on, and Duncan's capable. I want you to bring him up to speed, just in case . . ."

His voice trailed off. Sarah was already bristling with indignation.

"Just in case what? I go off the deep end? I crack up?"

Morrison didn't laugh. He didn't even smile.

"In case you need to take some time off," he said evenly. "This is a high-pressure job, and you have a lot going on in your personal life right now. I have to think about the well-being of the office."

"Are you telling me my job is on the line here because I got shot and some nutcase is harassing me?" Sarah was angry, but she was also slightly stunned. If she were to lose her job . . . She went icy inside as she realized that without it, she would be lost. Without work to fill the minutes, the hours, her *life*—what would she do?

Morrison held up a placating hand. "All I'm saying is I want Duncan thoroughly briefed."

"In case he needs to take over for me. If that's not saying my job is on the line, I don't know what it is saying."

A beat passed in which their eyes held, hers stormy to mask her fear, his faintly apologetic and at the same time unyielding.

Morrison sighed. "What I meant was, in case you should want to do something like take a leave of absence. Or—"

They were interrupted by a quick rap at the door, which was still standing open. Sarah looked around to see Lynnie, her twenty-six-year-old, slender, attractive, Chinese-American administrative assistant, looking apologetically at her.

"I'm sorry to interrupt," Lynnie said in her soft voice. "But there's an emergency call for you, Sarah."

"Can we finish discussing this later?" Sarah only made it a question to observe the employee-boss protocol. What she was really saying, and she knew Morrison knew it, was, We *will* finish discussing this later.

"Sure." Morrison sighed, and Sarah, with another simmering look for him, went off to answer her phone.

"Mrs. Mason?" Sarah recognized the Hispanic-accented voice on the other end of the line even before Rosa Barillas identified herself. "I am so sorry to call you at work, but I don't know what else to do. Angie is missing. Please, can you help me?"

21

"My baby. My baby. Please, Holy Mother, look after her, bring her back to me. Oh, she is just little. My baby." Rosa Barillas's broken murmurs were like barbed wire wrapping themselves around Sarah's heart. By ten p.m., a crowd, including Sarah, had gathered in the Barillas's small, threadbare apartment. Rosa was on the couch, wrapped in a blanket, a cup of coffee and a pastry untouched on the table at her elbow. Periodically, she would slip off the couch and drop to her knees on the floor, clasping her hands and offering up frantic prayers for her daughter's safety.

The atmosphere was heavy with grief, thick with terror. People talked in hushed tones, as if they were at a funeral already. The two older children, Rafael and Lizbeth, huddled big-eyed in a corner under the care of someone Sarah thought might be an aunt. Sophia and Sergio had fallen asleep not long before and had been carried from the apartment to spend the night elsewhere. A constantly changing tide of people swirled through the apartment—police, visitors, reporters, all stopping to say a few words to the distraught mother. Sarah, for one, knew the clock was ticking. As she had learned in the dreadful aftermath of Lexie's disappearance, after the first forty-eight hours, the chance of recovering a missing child alive drops to practically zero.

It was like lightning striking twice. It wasn't supposed to happen. But it had.

Angie had apparently vanished off the face of the earth.

The last anyone had seen of her had been around three p.m. She had been outside her apartment building, watching Sophia dig in the dirt, waiting for a load of laundry to finish so that she could put it in the dryer. A number of children, including Rafael, Sergio, and Lizbeth, had been running around, playing hide and seek. There had been a lot of screaming, a lot of laughter, innumerable sounds that might have masked a cry or scream. But no one—at least, no one who was admitting to it—had seen or heard anything unusual. When Rafael had first noticed that Angie was not on the bench reading, as she liked to do while the rest of them played, he had assumed that she was in the laundry room. But she never came back.

At first just Rafael had searched for her, sort of casually, then growing more and more worried. Then all the Barillas children, with Rafael carrying Sophia, had looked all over the apartment complex, searching everywhere they knew. Rafael had even run up to the Quik-Pik and Wang's Oriental Palace to see if Angie, for some unknown reason, could have walked up there without telling anyone where she was going. Finally, their friends had joined in the search, too, and the parents who were home, and some other adults. By the time it was agreed that Angie was not in anyone else's apartment, not in any of the nooks and crannies where the children liked to hide, not sunning herself on the roof where the young, unmarried women liked to lounge, it was after five o'clock and Rosa had come home.

Rosa was mistrustful of the police. She was always afraid that they would come and try to take her children from her, that they would send her back to Guatemala, where she was from, that they would arrest her, deport her, do something bad to her or her children. But when she saw that Angie was not there, when she heard Rafael and the other children's story, when the neighbors told her how they had looked and looked for Angie without finding her, then she had called the police. And after that she had called Sarah, the lady lawyer, the Assistant District Attorney that in her mind was a person of immense stature, of power. Sarah knew this because Rosa told her so, clinging to her hand as she begged her for help.

Sarah gave what little help she could, calling Jake, calling the detectives whom she knew, but she was sick with fear that nothing any of them could do was going to do any good.

It was like déjà vu all over again. The police came, looking again in every place where everyone had already searched, asking questions, taking statements, going door to door. Jake put in a call to his friends at the FBI, and they came and went to work. Jake himself threw the full resources of Hogan & Sons Investigations into the effort. Neighbors and friends joined with strangers to form search parties that scoured nearby streets and fields, and walked the banks of the creek behind the complex. Just before sundown, the media arrived in force, Hayley Winston and her rivals, setting up camp in the parking lot. Except for the identity of the players, it was all, *all,* just like before.

When Lexie had disappeared.

Just like it had been then, the consensus was stranger abduction.

The possibility that Angie's disappearance was linked in some way to Lexie's, or at least to the phone calls Sarah had been receiving, preyed on Sarah's mind. And Angie had been on TV with her, not once but twice. Could there be a connection? All anyone would tell her was that the possibility was being checked out.

Sarah felt like she was caught up in a nightmare. It was all she could do not to just start screaming, to start shrieking and pulling her hair out and then running, running away as fast as she could, but she didn't. She didn't do any of the things she felt like doing. She alone knew what the pain felt like, the desperation and disbelief, the sense of unreality, the terror, the whispered bargains with God.

She alone knew that holding on to hope did not mean that hope would be answered. She alone knew the true horror that Rosa was enduring.

And so she stayed beside the other woman, stayed through the onslaught of relatives and friends and neighbors, through the questions from law enforcement and the media, and Rosa clung to her, because they both recognized that they were now members of a terrible sisterhood, and she knew, as Sarah did, that Sarah was the only one who truly understood.

Twelve hours passed. Morning came. Sarah called in to work, taking a vacation day, and if it confirmed Morrison's fear that her personal life was getting in the way of her job, well, for the moment there was just nothing else she could do. She had to stay. Angie's picture was on TV, in the papers. Eighteen hours. Food was set out, but no one ate. Twenty-four hours. One full day. The searchers were working in shifts now, as were the police. The FBI had come and gone and come and gone. The media issued an update with the evening news: nine-year-old Angela Barillas, still missing. Everyone was exhausted. People went home, came back. Rosa fell asleep on the couch.

It was night again by then, eight, nine, ten p.m. The golden hours were ticking inexorably past. Angie was somewhere. Maybe even still alive.

Or maybe not.

Hope was running out with the slow inevitability of sand dropping through an hourglass. Sarah prayed that Rosa had not yet fully realized that.

"Sarah." Jake stopped beside her, bent down, and put a hand on her shoulder, shaking her gently to full awareness. Only then did Sarah realize that she had been dozing, sitting on the floor near Rosa because all the furniture was occupied, with her legs curled beneath her and her head pillowed on her arm draped atop an end table. "Come on. We're going home."

She blinked at him stupidly for a moment, not quite fully awake, not quite understanding. He was bleary-eyed and sporting a lot of black stubble, his white shirt, which was rolled up past his elbows, wrinkled and faintly grubby, his navy slacks bearing dust stains around the cuffs. The apartment was still bustling as people came and went, but the sounds were muffled as everyone clearly tried to be respectful of Rosa's uneasy sleep.

"I can't. . . ." Sarah began, glancing at Rosa, who was huddled beneath a blue blanket that someone had draped over her so that just the top of her head was visible.

"Yes, you can," Jake interrupted ruthlessly. His voice was low out of deference to Rosa, but it held a steely note that she had heard in it just a time or two before. "And you are, if I have to carry you out of here. For God's sake, Sarah, you're not doing anyone any good right now. And you're killing yourself."

He was right, and Sarah knew it. She was so tired she was dizzy with it, so empty that she was way beyond feeling hungry, so heartsick and devastated that her heart felt like a huge, gaping wound.

And none of it made any difference. She and the rest of them could stand vigil for eternity, and it wouldn't matter. All the pain in the world wouldn't change a thing.

As she had learned with Lexie, that was the bitter truth.

"Yes, all right," she said, her weariness plain in her voice, and let him pull her to her feet. On the way out the door, she gently touched the shoulder of one of the relatives, a sister of Rosa's maybe, who was knitting away in a hard kitchen chair that had been pulled into duty in the living room. "Tell Rosa I'll be back in the morning."

The woman nodded wordlessly, and Sarah let Jake take her away.

Once they were back in the apartment, Sarah dropped bonelessly onto the couch. Sweetie-pie came click-clacking over from somewhere and stopped in front of her to look at her gravely.

"Pops already took him out," Jake said as the dog laid his head in her lap, offering wordless comfort as if he sensed, in the way that dogs sometimes do, that something was terribly wrong. Jake disappeared into the kitchen, but Sweetie-pie, instead of following him as he generally did because the kitchen was the source of treats, stayed with her. As Sarah stroked his big head, it occurred to her that the dog had also been through this before. When Lexie had gone missing, Sweetie-pie had suffered, too.

"Good dog," Sarah whispered, and took comfort from the silent weight of his head on her thigh, and the sleek warmth of his coat beneath her hand.

"Okay, one house special coming up." Jake came out of the kitchen carrying something. "Go lie down, Sweetie-pie."

As the dog complied, Sarah looked up, her eyes widening as Jake set his burden down on the coffee table in front of her. On a white dinner plate rested a yellow bowl. In the bowl was—chicken noodle soup.

"You made me soup?" There was a hint of incredulity in her voice.

"You like soup. I made soup. So eat." He stood beside the couch, hands resting loosely on his hips, looking down at her.

Jake rarely cooked. Making breakfast—and that was very much an occasional thing—was about as good as his culinary talent got. The fact that he had made soup for her . . .

"Thank you." She drew the words out and even dredged up a glimmer of a smile for him. He was taking care of her, just like he was always taking care of her, and the knowledge that he was there, that he cared, that he had her back, comforted her, too.

"It's canned, but it's better than nothing." He still stood over her, and she knew what he was waiting for, and knew, too, that she needed the nourishment. What had she eaten today? Not much. A few nibbles here and there.

"What about you?"

"Honey, believe me, I ate."

She spooned up some soup. It was hot, which was good, but it tasted salty on her tongue and felt almost slimy as it slid down her throat.

She kept on with it, grimly, because she knew she needed to eat and because he was watching her. After about a dozen mouthfuls, she gave up and reached for the TV remote as a diversion.

CSI. Sports. A *Seinfeld* rerun.

". . . just like Alexandra Mason seven

years ago, nine-year-old Angela Barillas . . ."

Oh, God, the news. Just like the soup, TV was something for which she suddenly had no appetite. She hastily clicked it off.

"Do you think whoever is behind the calls I've been getting took her?" she asked flatly. That was the fear that she couldn't shake off.

"I don't know. It's a possibility the cops are taking seriously."

"They're not going to find her, are they?" She was so tired she almost felt like she was floating now, her head resting against the back of the couch, her hands lying limply at her sides.

"We don't know that." *Oh, yes, they did,* Sarah thought, but she didn't say it. They both knew he was only saying that to keep any smidgen of hope that she might be harboring alive for as long as he could. "Listen, finish your soup and let's go to bed."

Sarah shook her head. "I can't finish it. I'm not hungry."

His lips tightened, but he didn't say anything.

Sarah carried the plates into the kitchen, then took a quick shower—she felt so grimy, she couldn't bear the thought of going to sleep without one—pulled on her sleep shirt, and fell into bed. Sweetie-pie was already snoring away beneath it.

When she turned out the light, the little crocheted angel seemed to glow.

Lexie, Sarah thought as her gaze fixed on it and anguish overwhelmed her. Then, *Angie.*

She prayed that God had them both in his keeping while tears streamed down her face.

Exhausted as she was, sleep wouldn't come. Every time she closed her eyes, hideous images scrolled through her mind. After a while she couldn't take it anymore, and she got up and walked soundlessly into the living room. The apartment was dark except for a few stray silver moonbeams that filtered in around the edges of the imperfectly closed curtains. Jake was asleep. His bedroom door was closed, but no line of light showed beneath it and she thought, if she listened hard, she could hear him snoring. Huddling in a corner of the couch, her knees drawn up to her chin and her arms wrapped around them, she wept, silently, but as though her heart was broken.

Which it was.

She didn't even hear him until he materialized beside the couch. She jumped a little when she sensed him there, and looked up. Backlit by moonbeams, he was little more than a large, dark shape, a denser shadow in a room full of them.

"Christ, Sarah, what the hell are you doing up?" He sounded grouchy—angry, even. "What part of 'you need sleep' don't you understand?"

The thing was, he didn't know that, until the instant she had become aware of him beside her, she had been crying. She didn't want him to know, desperately didn't want him to know. To cry was to appear weak, vulnerable, helpless, all those things that she wasn't and never would be. And if he knew she was crying, he would hurt for her.

She didn't want that, either.

She drew a deep, hopefully unheard, breath and let it out again. Mopping up the tears would be to give herself away, so she didn't do it.

"I just got up to get a drink of water," she said in as normal a voice as she could muster, and got to her feet.

What she didn't expect was that the

moonbeams that backlit him would fall full on her face.

"Right." His voice was grim. His hands reached for her, closed around her arms, pulled her toward him.

"It's okay to cry, Sarah," he continued in a different, softer voice. "Just like it's okay to eat and sleep and go out and play in the sun and make love and . . ."

"I can't," she said, even as she made contact with his firm, warm body and discovered that he was wearing nothing but his boxers, even as her arms went around his neck and his arms wrapped around her waist. Tears were once again welling into her eyes, but she furiously blinked them back, looking up at him, meeting his gaze through the shadows, knowing that he could see her expression even though she couldn't see his. "What good does it do to cry, when it doesn't bring Lexie back, or change a thing?" Her voice started to shake, and despite her words, the tears overflowed to spill down her cheeks. "And how can I sleep, when every time I close my eyes I see Lexie in my dreams? How can I eat, when I don't know if Lexie has food?

How can I enjoy the sun, when she's forever lost in the dark?"

"Sarah . . ." Her pain was reflected in his voice. His arms tightened around her and his hands slid up her back, pulling her close. She dropped her head, shying away from the moonlight, resting her forehead against his broad shoulder, wetting his skin with the last of her tears as he hugged her to him.

"How can I make love to you when it makes me feel like I'm letting her go?" she whispered brokenly against his skin as the familiar warmth of him, and feel of him, and smell of him enfolded her as surely as his arms. "I *can't*."

"You're not alone in this, you know." His arms were tight around her. She could feel his lips brushing her hair as he spoke and his hands smoothing her back through the thin cotton of her nightshirt, and the whole solid length of him against her, and she held on to him for dear life. For all the anguish that she was feeling, for all the emotion that surged between them, his tone was perfectly reasonable, calm and almost detached. "I'm in it with you, too. To see you so thin and pale and wired, to watch you frantically trying to fill every hour of every day with work or something like it, to know that you're going to deliberately deny yourself anything that you discover you particularly like, or that's fun, or that gives you pleasure—it kills me. It rips my heart out, Sarah."

The pain in his voice got through to her. She lifted her head then, to look at him. His eyes, black and glinting in the moonlight, met hers.

"I love you," he said. "More than anything in my life. And I think you love me, too."

She went still, perfectly still, while his words seeped through her skin, were picked up by her bloodstream and finally absorbed into her bruised and battered heart. Despite the shadows that cloaked them both, she could see the crow-blackness of his hair; his hard, high cheek-bones; his square, stubbled jaw. For years she had leaned on his broad shoulder, been steadied by his solid strength. He had been the one constant, immutable presence in her life, the person she had trusted most, the person she had known she could utterly rely on.

Her best friend, Jake.

And now, maybe for a long time now, although she had been too blind to see it, he was maybe something more.

"I think you're right," she said, and heard the faint note of surprise in her own voice. "I think I might."

He smiled then, the briefest curve of a smile that crinkled his skin and narrowed his eyes.

"Way to be sure," he said, and kissed her.

She kissed him back, and his arms locked around her as if he never meant to let her go. Sarah suddenly felt weak, as if all her muscles had dissolved into jelly, and her heart started to pound and her blood heated. His lips were hard and greedy but tender, too, and she met his hunger with an urgency of her own, with the yearning need of a soul that had been left wandering in the cold too long and had finally found its own source of light and warmth.

When his mouth left hers at last to slide across her cheek to her ear, she pressed tiny kisses into his neck. Then he picked her up in his arms and carried her into his bedroom and made love to her with a fierceness that blotted out everything except him, except them, that drove out all the pain and grief and fear and replaced it with heat, with desire, with pleasure.

And afterward, as abruptly as a breath snuffing a candle, they both fell fathoms deep asleep.

The distant ringing of a phone pulled Sarah from the depths. For a moment she lay blinking in the dark, curled against Jake, basking in the comfort, in the warmth, in the feel of his strong arms around her, in the sound of his snores above her head. Then she realized what she was hearing, and alarm shot through her veins: her cell phone, which she'd left on the night table in the other bedroom.

It was—a glance at the clock told her— three fourteen a.m.

The only news that it was possible to get at that hour was bad.

Wide awake now, Sarah slid out of bed and hotfooted it toward the source of the ringing.

Which, of course, cut off the moment she reached the threshold. A distinctive little tinkle told her a message was being left.

About Angie? Oh, God, was there news about Angie?

Or was it Lexie—the person who sounded like Lexie—again?

Her heart pounded as she picked up her phone and turned on the light. Flipping it open, she punched a button and saw that the last incoming call had been from an unfamiliar number.

Sarah held her breath as she waited for the message to play.

"Hi, it's Crystal." The other woman was talking fast, practically whispering. "Listen, I found out something about that missing little girl. I sent you an e-mail. Just click on the link and—" Crystal's voice broke off. "Shit, I got to go."

The last words were infused with fear.

By the time the message ended, Sarah's pulse was racing. She stood for a moment, staring down at the phone, trying to decided what to do. It was early Wednesday morning. From what Sarah knew of Crystal's schedule, she had probably just left work. Given the fear in her voice, calling her back might not be the best idea.

The thing to do first was check her e-mail.

Her laptop was in her briefcase in the trunk of her car, which was parked in the lot outside the Barillases' apartment. For a moment, Sarah was stymied. Then she remembered the computer in Jake's office. She could log on from there.

She went downstairs, turned on the light, sat in Dorothy's rolling chair, and turned on the computer. Its screen glowed at her, the desktop filled with unfamiliar Mac icons—she was a PC person herself. Locating the Internet link, she logged on under "guest," and managed to access her e-mail. Among a host of other messages were two sent back-to-back from Crystal. One was tagged *look at this,* the other *here.*

Sarah chose *look at this,* opened it, and found herself looking at a picture of a guy getting into old, blue Camaro. There was nothing about the guy or the car that meant anything to her, and she saw that there were eleven more pictures. She flipped to the next one—a red pickup truck with another unknown guy. The next one was a white Blazer with the driver practically invisible behind the wheel. The fourth one was a cop car with Brian McIntyre in it—and it was then that Sarah realized what she was looking at: pictures Crystal had taken with her digital camera of vehicles parked outside her house. If this showed what it appeared to show, then they had McIntyre dead to rights. He was in front of Crystal's home in violation of the TRO.

Which had what, exactly, to do with Angie, who Sarah presumed was the missing little girl Crystal was referring to? Sarah was busy trying to make the connection as she closed out of that e-mail and opened Crystal's other message.

It read: *I found this on Eddie's computer just now. I think he's been screwing around on me so I was checking up on him. I don't know what to do so—here. His password is "wormman."*

Crystal didn't sign it, but she did include a blue-lettered link to something called Paul's Playhouse.

Sarah clicked on it and was taken to what looked like a site that sold children's playground equipment. Small pictures of kids swinging on a swingset, sliding down a slide, splashing in an above-ground pool, and climbing into a treehouse surrounded the words, *Welcome to Paul's Playhouse.*

Beneath them, a small box requested a password.

She typed in *wormman.*

And seconds later found herself looking at Angie.

22

Angie was in a cage. The narrow, silver metal bars ran both vertically and horizontally, to form a grid. She lay curled up in a little ball in the corner, her eyes closed, her long, black hair spilling around her like a curtain. Something wide and grayish-colored—duct tape, Sarah thought—bound her wrists behind her and her ankles together. Another strip covered her mouth. Her orange T-shirt and denim shorts matched the description of what she had been wearing when she had disappeared. The camera was outside the cage, looking down at her from an angle. It was hard to be certain, but Sarah thought she was alive.

Her heart gave a great leap.

"Jake! Jake!" Sarah went flying up the stairs, ran breathless through the dark apartment, flipped on the light in his bedroom, and pounced on Jake as he lay snoring away. "Jake! Wake up!"

She was shaking his shoulder violently when he flopped over onto his back and opened his eyes to peer groggily up at her.

"You're killing me here," he groaned. "What now?"

"Get up! Get up! You've got to come downstairs with me! It's Angie!"

His eyes opened all the way and seemed to have to work to focus.

"What's Angie?"

"Would you get up?" Sarah tugged on his hand. Jake weighed a ton, there was no way she was moving him if he didn't want to move, and he was being about as energetic as a slug. "Angie's on the computer. Crystal sent me an e-mail link, and Angie came up."

"What?" He sat up, the covers falling down around his waist, and ran his hands over his hair. "Are you sure?"

"Yes, *yes*! Hurry, would you please?"

As she spoke, Jake swung his legs over the side of the bed and stood up, affording her a nice view of a very sexy body, which she would have enjoyed a whole lot more if she hadn't been practically going crazy with impatience.

"So you want to run that by me one more time?" He picked up his boxers from the floor, where they were crumpled beside her sleep shirt—she was wearing her white terry robe, which she had snatched from the spare bedroom before going downstairs—and pulled them on.

"Crystal—Crystal Stumbo"—Jake nodded to indicate he knew who she was talking about, and followed her as she hurried out of the room—"sent me an e-mail link to a site on the computer called Paul's Playhouse." She was talking to him over her shoulder as she rushed back down the stairs with him behind her. "I went there and entered her creepy boyfriend's password, and there was Angie. A picture of Angie. She's in a cage, and she's bound with what looks like duct tape, but I think she's alive."

They had reached the office by this time. Jake narrowed his eyes against the brightness of the overhead light, but Sarah made straight for the computer. The screen was black, blank. Panic assailed her. What if it was gone, what if the link had been lost, what if something had happened?

She grabbed the mouse, moved it, and the screen lit up.

Angie was still there.

Thank God.

Jake sucked in his breath. "Jesus H. Christ. It is her." He leaned closer, his hands closing on the back of Dorothy's chair as he studied the image. "My God, where is she?"

Sarah was already at the phone. Her pulse raced. Her breathing came fast and shallow, like she had been running. "Who should I call? The police, the FBI, who?"

"All of them." He still seemed to be taking it in. He glanced around at her. "Wait, give me the phone. It'll come better from me."

Sarah wasn't going to argue with that. It was, she knew, perfectly true. By this time, she had the feeling that she had pretty much been labeled the flake of the Western world by police and FBI alike.

"Hurry," she breathed.

"Oh, yeah."

Within ten minutes, Jake's office was swarming with law-enforcement types. Sexton and Kelso were there, along with a quartet of uniforms and Special Agent Gary Freeman, a tall, lanky thirtysomething redhead, and Special Agent Tom Delaney, a stocky, fortyish blond of medium height who was a friend of Jake's. Since it was still basically the middle of the night, everyone except the uniformed cops was wearing the most thrown-together of outfits. All, without exception, were grainy-eyed. Other than Kelso, who was sitting in a chair, pecking away at a laptop on the counter across the room, they were gathered in a tight semicircle around Dorothy's Mac. Agent Freeman, apparently the resident computer expert, was sitting in Dorothy's chair, working the mouse. Jake, dressed now in jeans, T-shirt, and sneakers, had his head together with Delaney, studying a color printout of the picture of Angie in the cage, trying to determine if there were any clues that might give a hint as to where she was and glancing up occasionally to see what was happening on the screen. Sarah, also wearing jeans, T-shirt, and sneakers, having told at least half a dozen times now the story of how Crystal had called her, gave Kelso the name of Crystal's boyfriend, which she was running through the computer for priors, and was practically leaning over the back of the chair as Agent Freeman tried to ascertain exactly what they were dealing with.

"It's a still picture, taken from a live feed, probably not more than a few hours old," he reported. "It's a super-encrypted site, almost impossible to log on to without the direct link that was provided, accessible only to select individuals who each seem to have been issued with an individual password, which I am presuming means that anyone's access can be cut off at any time without compromising the rest of the site." He paused for a moment, clicking the mouse, moving the cursor around the site. "There seem to be some hidden links here. . . ."

"Sarah, you want to come here for a minute?" Kelso called, and Sarah went over to stand behind her. "This him?"

Sarah glanced at the screen.

The guy was a whiter shade of pale, with dirty-blond hair worn in a mullet, a cut over his left eye, and a sulky scowl.

"Yeah, that's him."

It was a pair of mug shots, full face and profile. Prisoner number 823479T, Edward Mark Tanner, height: five ten, weight: 165, date of birth: March 3, 1978. Hair: blond; eyes: blue; identifying marks: scar on right hand, phoenix tattoo on right upper arm. Charge: DUI. The picture had been taken in September two years previously.

Phoenix tattoo on right upper arm.

Sarah looked more closely at the profile shot. Tanner was visible to mid-chest, and he was wearing a wife-beater. She could see most of the tattoo.

It was basically a big bird with its wings spread and its beak facing forward, and it looked familiar.

Her heart skipped a beat.

"Duke had one of those," she said. "I'm almost positive it was the same."

Kelso looked up. "Who the hell's Duke?"

"Donald Coomer. One of the guys who took part in the convenience store robbery where I was shot. The one who died in jail."

"Yo, gentlemen," Kelso called over her shoulder to the room in general. "We got something interesting here. Anybody know of a gang or some kind of organization with a phoenix tattoo as an identifying mark?"

Everybody except Freeman came to cluster around her and stare at Eddie Tanner's picture on the screen.

"I'm drawing a blank here." Sexton shook his head, and since nobody else said anything, that seemed to be the consensus.

"It's the same," Sarah said again, for the benefit of the newcomers. Her pulse was racing, and she was so cold suddenly that she wrapped her arms around herself. "I'm almost sure. One of the guys who robbed the convenience store had a tattoo just like this one." She glanced up at Jake, who was now standing beside her. "Duke," she added for clarification.

"Which means that there's a real good chance that all these things are connected." Jake echoed what she had been thinking.

Did they take Angie because of me? Please, no.

Her throat constricted.

"Yee-haw," Agent Freeman exclaimed. "I'm in."

Everybody rushed back across the room to gather around him. From her spot behind Freeman's left shoulder, Sarah watched with pounding heart as lines of writing popped up on a blue screen.

"There was a link to a chat room. . . ." Freeman said as he scanned what was materializing across the monitor in front of him.

He tensed, and Sarah read what had just appeared on the screen:

Big Dog: *Hello, Wormman. What are you doing here so late?*

"Fuck," Freeman muttered, which Sarah took to be a bad sign. Then he said, "Guys, we got a problem," and everyone in the room except Kelso, who was still working the laptop, drew in a collective breath.

At the same time he typed in:

Just checking things out.

"That sounds wrong, doesn't it?" he said on a note of panic to the room in general. "Why the fuck didn't I stay out of here? I should've known I couldn't just lurk. Fuck, fuck, *fuck.*"

The next line on the screen read:

SimonSays: *You know the auction closes at five a.m.*

"They're taking bids on her," Freeman said. "I thought so. The good news is, she's still alive then, for sure."

"Who are they? Any way to identify them?" Jake asked.

Freeman, his fingers still poised over the

keys, shook his head. "Not from here. They could be anybody. Anywhere. The Internet makes for a small world."

"Get out of there," Delaney said urgently. "We don't want to spook 'em."

"Easier said than done," Freeman snorted, and typed in:

I'm aware.
Big Dog: *You got a bid, Wormman?*

Freeman said, "Anybody want to chime in with suggestions, I'm all ears." Then, when no one said anything, he muttered, "Fuck, I'll pretend it's eBay."

And typed in:

I'll maybe jump in later. A little closer to the zero hour. Logging out for now.

Then he clicked the mouse again, and the chat room was gone. Everybody let out a collective breath as Angie's picture once again filled the screen.

Only this time it was a different picture, another still, a terrible moment frozen in time.

In it, Angie was awake and had struggled to her knees. She looked terrified. Her thickly lashed brown eyes were huge and spilling over with tears as they looked into the camera. The tape had been removed from her mouth. A red, chafed-looking rectangle around her lips showed where it had been. Her lips were parted, as if she were saying something.

Pain, sharp as a knife, stabbed through Sarah. The association was too close, too intimate. Besides her terror for Angie, she felt a rush of anguished connection with Lexie. Had her daughter been thrown in a cage, bound and terrified, too?

"Oh my God," she whispered, as all the blood seemed to rush from her head. She gripped the chair back hard and closed her eyes to combat the dizziness that swept her.

"You okay?" Jake was beside her, his arm circling her shoulders, and for a moment, as her head spun and her knees went weak, she leaned gratefully against him. A beat passed, and then she nodded to indicate that she was all right and concentrated on breathing. For now, for one more terrible now, she had to stay strong.

For Angie, this time.

"Fuck, we're losing it, we're losing it," Freeman cried.

Sarah opened her eyes just in time to see Angie's picture vanish from the screen. The Paul's Playhouse site with its now-grotesque pictures of happy children appeared instead. Then it convulsed and disappeared, too.

They were left staring blankly at an empty blue screen.

Sarah felt a sense of loss so intense that it was as if her insides were being ripped out.

"They made us," Freeman said. "Holy shit, I think they made us."

Fear closed Sarah's throat and sent a shudder coursing through her. Angie had been right there, right in front of them, and now she was gone. They'd lost her. Jake's arm tightened around her. Freeman rocked back in his chair. Delaney cursed. The sense of urgency in the room was suddenly as palpable as the hum of the air-conditioning, but the bottom line was that nobody seemed to know what to do.

"We got to make a move," Sexton said, looking around. "I say we pick this guy Tanner up right now."

"And the woman," Jake said. "Crystal Stumbo. They can tell us about the website, if nothing else. At this point, it's the only link to that little girl we have."

"You got an address on Tanner?" Delaney turned to Kelso, who was on her feet now, lifting a sheet of paper as it came out of the printer.

"Right here." She flapped the paper at him.

"I think he's staying with Crystal. In her trailer," Sarah said. She felt cold all over, her heart was beating way too fast, and her stomach churned to the point where she was nauseated, but she could deal with it. She *would* deal with it. Time was running out.

Kelso read from the paper. "This says forty-five West Homewood Drive, twenty-four C. It's an apartment." She looked up. "Hell, the address is two years old."

"We got an address on Crystal Stumbo?" Delaney asked. Freeman was on his feet now, and the tension in the room had hit fever pitch. People were moving restlessly, shuffling their feet, cracking knuckles, anxious to get going. But everybody was keeping it reined in, keeping their emotions in check. Clearly, nobody wanted to go off half-cocked.

Everybody knew: They were the only hope Angie had.

"I'll get one." Kelso turned back toward the laptop.

"I don't think you'll find it. She's only lived there for something like two months," Sarah said, her voice amazingly steady considering how destroyed she felt inside. "It's the Paradise Homes trailer park out toward Burton. I have the exact address in my files at the office, but I've been out there. I know where it is."

"You can show us?" Delaney asked.

Sarah nodded.

"Okay," he said, looking around. "Let's get this show on the road. We need to be quick. If they made us, like Freeman thinks, then they're covering their tracks *now*. But we also need to be real careful, and real quiet. The goal is to get these two people in custody and question them without letting any of their associates know what's gone down. That little girl's life may depend on it."

It was a little after four a.m. by the time the lights on Jake's car picked up the luminous white gravel that marked the railroad crossing just outside Paradise Homes. In the passenger seat beside him, Sarah leaned forward as they bumped over the tracks and then told him where to turn in. Directly behind them, in Delaney's silver Infiniti, rode Agents Delaney and Freeman. Behind them, in an unmarked police car, were Sexton and Kelso. Three squad cars brought up the rear, cruising along quietly, without lights flashing or sirens blaring. At this hour there was very little traffic on I-21 heading out toward Burton, and the cavalcade rushing through the night attracted no undue attention. The plan was for Sarah to point out the precise trailer, and then she and Jake were to pull on past and let the law-enforcement types handle things. Once the targets were secured, she would ride back with Crystal, on the theory that Crystal trusted her and would likely be more forthcoming with someone she knew.

"There." Sarah pointed to Crystal's home. Just looking at it made her mouth go dry. Would this work? Could Crystal and her repellent boyfriend actually lead them to Angie in time?

Please, God, please . . .

Parked in front of the trailer were Crystal's yellow Lincoln and a small blue pickup truck. As Jake rolled down the window and stuck his arm out, gesturing toward the trailer for the benefit of Delaney and Freeman, Sarah added in as calm a tone as she could muster, "That's Crystal's car. Looks like she's home. And her boyfriend, too."

"Let's hope."

Jake pulled on past as agreed, and his lights swept over the next trailer in line. This one was a little bigger, a double wide in two-tone tan and white. Its parking area held two vehicles, too, a green two-door Toyota and a gold GMC Jimmy, as well as a prefab wooden shed, a metal picnic table, and a trio of black plastic garbage cans complete with lids. There was no room for so much as the addition of a bicycle, so a third vehicle, a white Blazer, had been parked in the grass just behind the trailer. Sarah registered all the clutter absently as Jake sought a close place to park. He ended up making a U-turn, then pulling off the road onto the grassy verge. Once stopped, he quickly cut his lights in hopes of not rousting anyone from sleep who didn't need to be rousted. The yellow glow of a porch light beside the main door of the trailer they were parked behind held a pair of fluttering moths in thrall. Besides that, a few other dim porch lights shining at irregular intervals along the row of trailers, and the slashing white glare of headlights from the arriving cars, all was now dark and still within Sarah's field of vision. Not even a dog barked.

"You don't think Angie's in there, do you?" Sarah whispered through dry lips, then felt foolish for thinking that anyone could overhear. As long as they were inside the car, unless one of them started shouting, she and Jake were good.

He shook his head. "It looked like the wall behind the cage was corrugated metal. A warehouse, maybe. Not a trailer."

Sarah's breathing quickened as she watched the other cars cut their lights one by one and then pull up in front of the target residence. Once they did that, the first three were out of her sight: She couldn't see the front of Crystal's trailer. The last two, both squad cars, had their rear bumpers sticking out into the narrow road even after they stopped, because there wasn't enough parking to accommodate them. Sarah heard, faintly, the sound of car doors opening and closing, and her heart skipped a beat.

"It's going down," Jake said. She nodded, sitting there tense as a coiled spring, going quietly nuts inside. It was made worse because in order to protect her from any potential gunfire if the boyfriend resisted, they were parked so far outside the center of operations that she couldn't even see what was happening.

The thing about that particular style of trailer was, it didn't have a rear exit. Both doors opened onto the front. Going out a window was always an option, but as Sarah knew from experience, it was tough to do. No quick escape was happening that way.

On pins and needles now, Sarah leaned forward, watching for some sign that Crystal was out and she was needed. Her pulse drummed in her ears. Her stomach curled into a pretzel. Every sense she possessed was attuned to what was happening at the front of Crystal's trailer.

But as far as she could tell, nothing was.

"I can't stand this." Sarah glanced at Jake. The distant porch light illuminated the interior of the car just enough to allow her to see that he was looking tense, too. "I'm moving up to where I can at least see what's going on."

Being kept away from the action must have been at least as frustrating for Jake as it was for her—if it hadn't been for her, she knew him well enough to know he would have been right up there in the thick of things—because he didn't argue. He simply got out of the car when she did, then met up with her near the trunk.

"We're going to stay back out of the way," he said, low-voiced, as he curled a hand around her arm to ensure that she was going to do as he said. "Let the people who are getting paid for it do their jobs."

Sarah nodded agreement. She already felt better just because she was moving.

The night air was warm and still and smelled faintly of charcoal, as though someone had had a grill going earlier. Overhead, the sky was a deep midnight blue with a pale crescent moon and a few dim stars. Their feet crunched over the gravel roadway, the sound surprisingly loud over the muted murmurs of the night. An owl hooted somewhere off in the fringe of trees to the left.

It occurred to Sarah then that she should have been hearing something more germane to their purpose by now—like the sounds of someone being arrested, maybe, or a fight, or even a prolonged knocking if Crystal so far hadn't made it to the door. But she heard nothing beyond the sounds of the night as she and Jake circled around the corner of Crystal's trailer.

Something's gone wrong, Sarah thought when she got her first look at it, and her stomach cramped. *Maybe Crystal wasn't home after all. Maybe no one was. Maybe . . .*

The trailer's metal door was open, with the screen door standing wide. Inside, the lights were on in the main living area, and even as Sarah watched, more lights came on in the bedrooms at either end. Delaney, Freeman, Sexton, Kelso, and all six uniforms were nowhere to be seen, which meant that they almost had to be inside.

Which meant that there were a lot of people in that trailer, and they were all suspiciously quiet.

"Something's up," Jake said, and Sarah nodded. She suspected that he would have tried to leave her where they were and gone up to check things out for himself, except that he didn't like the idea of leaving her alone in the dark. Which was just as well, because she had absolutely no intention of being left.

"They've found something," she whispered, because it was the only explanation that made sense. He nodded and didn't even try to dissuade her as she skirted the police cars, making a semicircle that should have least afforded them a view of what was going on just inside the door. Instead, he moved with her, drawing the gun she hadn't even realized he was carrying as they came up behind Delaney's car.

"If there's any shooting, you hit the ground, you understand?" His voice was fierce. He let go of her arm, then reached into the pocket of his jeans and pulled out his keys, which he pushed into her hand. "If it looks bad, take the car and get the hell out of here."

"I will." She thrust his keys into her pocket, and then they were up beside Delaney's front bumper, and from there they could see inside the trailer's door.

Freeman was right there. She could see him clearly. He was standing with his back to the door, his red hair making him impossible to mistake. To his left, partly obscured by Freeman's body, stood Delaney. In the background, she could just see the top of Sexton's head.

They were all looking down at something that seemed to be on the floor at their feet.

Sarah's heart began to pound. She had a bad feeling, a terrible feeling. . . .

Without a word to Jake, she started to walk toward the open door. By the time she got there, she was practically running. He was right behind her, keeping pace but not trying to stop her. It was clear from the body language of the group inside the door that there was no danger. But it was equally clear that they were shocked and upset. . . .

Sarah saw the blood first, just as soon as she reached the top of the stoop: a bright scarlet pool with a surface sheen that made it gleam in the light. Then she saw the thick, curling strands of red hair lying in the blood, soaking it up so that it looked almost black in places. Finally, she saw the face with its skin gone gray from blood loss and the now garish-looking makeup standing out like a clown's, and she knew.

"Crystal's dead," she said to Jake behind her, because there was absolutely no doubt that she was. Crystal lay sprawled on her back on the pale blue wall-to-wall carpet, still wearing the black sequined halter and miniskirt that was her work uniform, her arms outspread, her legs in their fishnet stockings horribly splayed. She'd taken off her shoes. The sexy stilettos were there in front of the couch, one on its side as though she had just kicked them off. Had she come in, kicked off her shoes, checked the computer, placed the call to Sarah, and been killed? That's what it looked like.

Sarah's breath caught. Her stomach dropped.

She stepped on through the door, because there wasn't room on the stoop for both her and Jake, and then he was in the trailer, too, standing beside her in the small, inexpensively furnished living room that was so like the one she remembered from her childhood that it almost gave her the willies. Everyone glanced up at them as they entered. No one said anything. No one had to. It was obvious that this was a terrible tragedy, not just for Crystal but for Angie, too.

The tenuous thread that they had hoped would lead them to the little girl had just been cut.

"Shit." Jake sounded tired. "How long ago?"

"Not long," Sexton said. "She's still warm. At a guess, I'd say fifteen minutes max."

"They're covering their tracks," Delaney said. "We got to find that kid."

"I called Bob Parrent in Homicide," Sexton said. "They're on their way."

"No computer, but there's a space on a desk back here where it looks like one was," someone called from the back bedroom.

A glimpse of one of the uniforms moving from the bathroom to the back bedroom told Sarah where the others were. They were clearly searching the trailer.

"Okay," Sexton called back. Then, "Whoever killed her probably took it."

"What about Tanner?" Jake asked, moving on into the room and looking around.

"Not here," Sexton said. "I already put out an APB. We'll get him."

But will it be soon enough for Angie? Sarah didn't have to ask the question to know the answer: probably not. She folded her arms over her chest and tried to block the horrific picture of the little girl as they had last seen her out of her mind.

"Can we track some of the other people

in that chat room? Big Dog or SimonSays?" Sarah asked. She was sick to her stomach, light-headed with horror, and every nerve she possessed was raw with shock. But as a prosecutor, she was no stranger to crime scenes, and she tried to tap into that professional distance, to keep herself responding objectively so that she could function.

"Eventually," Freeman said. "But it might take some time."

Which we don't have. Sarah thought it, but didn't say it.

"You find her cell phone?" Jake asked, and she thought it was Sexton who said "not yet," but she couldn't be sure. With the best will in the world, she couldn't keep the personal out of it. Crystal's throat had been slit, Sarah saw, even though she was trying not to look, trying not to take in too many details, so that she could stay strong. A terrible gaping wound yawned like a huge smile across her neck from ear to ear. Blood as red as rubies still rolled thickly out. It covered her upper body like a coat of red paint, and was splattered across her right arm and the nearby chair and the wall. . . .

The horrible raw-meat smell of it was impossible to ignore any longer. Sarah closed her eyes, fighting to push it away, but she couldn't. She inhaled it, shuddered at the sweetish taste of it in her mouth, and thought of Mary.

Of the way her head had exploded.

Gorge rose in her throat.

She made it out the door just as the Homicide unit was coming up the steps. With a brief nod for Ian Kingsley and Carl Brown, whom she knew, she slid past them and walked quickly down to the end of the trailer. There, with one arm pressed against the cool metal for support, she bent almost double and vomited until there was nothing left inside her to come up.

She couldn't go back inside just yet, she thought as she straightened. She was too sick, too weak, too dizzy. Her forehead was beaded with cold sweat, and her legs felt as wobbly as Jell-O. If she had to look at Crystal again right now, she would probably pass out. What she needed to do, for just a few minutes, was find a cool, quiet place to sit down and regroup.

Jake's keys were in her pocket. She would sit in the Acura, turn on the air-conditioning, and close her eyes. In a few minutes, when she was better, she would go back.

Keeping one hand against the trailer for support for as long as she could, Sarah headed toward Jake's car, cutting diagonally across the gravel parking area next door, picking her way between the shed and the picnic table. There were so many cop cars arriving now, so many law-enforcement types of various descriptions running in and out, that she was surprised that half the trailer park wasn't awake. But apart from this little pocket of hyperactivity, the night remained quiet and still.

She was walking past the white Blazer parked behind the neighbor's trailer when the lights came on in the bedroom nearest the vehicle. If it hadn't been for that, for the quick illumination of the Blazer's interior that it provided, she never would have seen it.

The copy of *Inkheart* on the Blazer's back-seat.

Sarah stopped in her tracks, her eyes widening as that registered. She instantly forgot all about feeling ill.

Angie had been reading *Inkheart*. And now that Sarah thought about it, she remembered a white Blazer being in the parking lot when *Eeyore* was written on her car window. And among the digital pictures Crystal had sent her had been one of a white Blazer.

This white Blazer?

She could almost hear Jake saying it: *There's no such thing as coincidence.*

Her heart practically leaped out of her chest.

Whirling, she started to run back to Crystal's trailer, only to be yanked backward by a hard arm grabbing her around the neck in a choke hold. She screamed, but only a strangled croak emerged as the arm tightened brutally. Grabbing the crushing arm, digging her nails into bare male flesh, kicking her heel back into his kneecap, she fought for all she was worth—and was hit in the side by something that felt like the kick from a mule.

And just like that, everything went black.

23

"That's Tanner's truck out there. We called the plates in," Sexton said. He addressed this to Delaney, who was standing near the corpse's feet, talking on his cell phone, and who nodded by way of acknowledgment.

"So he's on foot?" Kelso asked.

Sexton shrugged. "Hard to say."

Jake wasn't paying much attention. The trailer was so crowded that it was getting hard to move now as the Homicide squad took over and the ad hoc Save Angie team prepared to take off.

Next step, arrived at by consensus: simultaneously search for Eddie Tanner and try to get the Internet service provider to give up an ID for whoever had set up Paul's Playhouse.

The clock was ticking. They all knew that. Crystal Stumbo's murder was gruesome evidence that time was running out even faster than before.

But Jake's main problem at the moment was that he couldn't find Sarah.

"Anybody seen Sarah Mason?" he asked the occupants of the living room in general. He'd already walked through the trailer once without spotting her, and his gut was starting to tense. Where the hell could she be?

One of the Homicide guys looked up from where he was wrapping rubber bands around the plastic bags that he had already put over the victim's hands.

"A woman was outside, puking her guts out at the end of the trailer, when I came in," he volunteered. "Short, dark hair, blue jeans."

Sarah. Christ, she'd gone outside? Nodding his thanks, Jake went out the door, which was still standing wide. The night was as dark as before, but there was a whole sea of vehicles parked around the trailer now, and law-enforcement types were swarming around like bees. From his vantage point on the stoop, he looked quickly around. No sign of her.

"Sarah?" he called.

No answer.

Then he went down the steps, sticking close to the trailer until he got to the end that the homicide detective would have had to pass to come in. Sure enough, there in the grass not far from where he stood was a puddle of vomit.

There was no other sign of Sarah.

Jake's pulse kicked up a couple of notches.

"Sarah?" he called again, louder, his eyes searching the darkness for her. He'd given her his keys, he remembered. Maybe she was waiting in the car.

Walking so fast now that he was almost running, he went to check. She wasn't there. Jake felt the hair rise on the back of his neck as he did a panicky 360, scanning the nearby trailers, the dark outline of trees to his left, the road and the vehicles jammed bumper to bumper around the crime scene.

"Sarah?" He yelled her name this time, not caring if he woke the whole world.

No response. Which he'd known there wouldn't be. Even as he ran back toward the trailer, he realized that the weird little warning vibe of danger that had been both a bane and a blessing to him for so long was shivering through his gut again.

Motion. Vibration. Something smooth yet resilient beneath her. Pain in her head and her arms and her side, and a curious floating lethargy, like nothing she had ever felt before.

Those were the things Sarah woke up to.

"So how long you think she'll be out for?" Those words, uttered in an unfamiliar male voice, were coming from somewhere close, somewhere in front of her.

"Got no idea," another unfamiliar male voice replied. "When I zapped that big ole dog of hers, though, he was out for a while."

Instinct warned Sarah to remain still, to let them think she was still unconscious, but she cracked her eyes open a little. For a moment she couldn't see anything, and cold fear shivered along her nerve endings.

Where was she? Then the sounds and motion touched a chord in her memory, and she realized that the reason she couldn't see was because it was night and she was in a car. In the backseat. Lying on her left side on the rear bench seat of an SUV, to be precise, with her hands tied behind her by something that felt rubbery and thick, maybe an extension cord, and her ankles bound, too, even more tightly, though by what she couldn't tell. The voices were coming from the front, where two men sat in bucket seats.

Digesting what she had heard, Sarah deduced that one of them had hit her with a stun gun. That would explain the pain in her side and her head, and the tingly weakness of her limbs. So the one in the passenger seat had zapped Sweetie-pie, had he? Then he must have been in her house. Had he pulled Lexie's toys out of the closet? Sarah's heart lurched at the thought. Dear God, had he maybe even been responsible for that phone call? But no way in hell could he have sounded like a little girl . . .

Opening her eyes a bit more, she strained to see something of the men that might help her identify them. There was no way to be sure, of course, but just from instinct, she guessed that one of them was Eddie Tanner.

Who had, in all probability, just murdered Crystal.

It was only then that Sarah fully realized that she was in terrible danger. She didn't know where these guys were taking her, but it wasn't on a picnic.

Her heart started to thud in slow, thick strokes. Suddenly she felt like she needed more air, but she had to be careful not to alter the rhythm of her breathing.

"D'you talk to him yet?" The guy in the passenger seat, the one she thought might be Tanner, sounded a little nervous. Wetting her lips, Sarah glanced carefully up through the seats again, and realized that by tilting her head just a little she could see small sections of both men's faces through the rearview mirror. The passenger's pasty white complexion made it all but certain: It was Tanner. The driver was a black man. Sarah guessed that he was probably the guy she had seen in the parking lot of Angie's apartment building. One of them must have written *Eeyore* on her window.

How did you know about that? That's what she wanted to scream at them. Were they the ones who had kidnapped Lexie, and Angie as well? Sarah felt nauseated again at the thought, and thanked God she didn't have anything left inside her to lose. But Tanner, at least, seemed too young to have abducted Lexie. Seven years ago, he would have been what? Twenty years old? As a prosecutor, though, she'd learned that twenty wasn't too young to be a monster.

"Yeah," the driver said. "I told him we had no choice but to grab her. She recognized my car. Or maybe it was that damned book you left in the backseat. Something."

"Is he pissed?"

"A little. He said he's getting tired of us always having to mop up your messes."

"*My* messes? *You* were the one who sent that damned stupid Duke to kill her and make it look like a burglary gone wrong, only he fucked it up. I tried to mop that mess up, remember?"

"You did a real good job of it, too." The driver's tone was faintly sneering. "She's still alive back there, fuckhead, in case you hadn't noticed. Next time you shoot somebody, make sure you kill them."

"She fucking tripped just as I fired."

"Yeah."

"Shit, is he still pissed about that?" Tanner sounded really nervous now. Sarah didn't know who "he" was, but whoever they were talking about was scary enough so that there was an edge of real fear in his voice. Did they maybe work for whoever had kidnapped Lexie? Or Angie? That made more sense. Then it occurred to her: *They probably know where Angie is. . . .*

There was the briefest of pauses. The SUV jolted over something, and Sarah instinctively tensed as she bounced. Her bent knees slid a little further over the edge of the seat. If they hit another bump, she was going down. Her hands and feet felt prickly and weird, and she realized they were asleep. She tried moving her fingers, wiggling her toes. Now that she was a little more awake and together, she became aware of the smooth midnight silk of the sky flying past beyond the windows, the jagged black outline of evergreens, and, closer at hand, the faint blue glow of the instrument panel. She could smell something, too— besides vinyl and stale car air—but she couldn't quite place what it was.

"He didn't appreciate the publicity, is all.

He had to change his game plan, and that's never good."

"That wasn't my fault." Tanner was really starting to sound agitated. Sarah recognized the emotion with a certain degree of fellow feeling: Her own pulse was rocketing through the roof. She was close to finding Angie, maybe close to finding out what had happened to Lexie, and even if she did, it wasn't going to do anybody any good. These losers would stop, sooner or later, and then she was guessing that she would be killed. The thought brought a fresh thrill of terror with it. Oh, God, she didn't want to die. . . .

A lightning picture of Jake appeared in her mind's eye, and for an instant she felt a flicker of hope. He would be going crazy by now, looking for her, pulling out all the stops. They were already searching for Tanner, and sooner or later they were bound to find him. The question was, would it be in time?

Tanner was still talking. "Look, I made those phone calls you told me to. You think it was easy, getting that kid's voice to come off those old tapes just right? But I did it. Hell, I did everything you asked. Who took out Duke, right there in the damned jail? Who grabbed that little girl out of the laundry room? I did, that's who. All you ever did was stay out there in the damned car and keep watch. And it wasn't my fault, about Crystal finding that link and sending it to her lady lawyer friend. The old man used my laptop. What was I supposed to do about that? I never even knew that link was on there."

She was able to move her hands a little, Sarah discovered. The cord that was binding them had some give. Whose voice had he gotten off some old tapes? *Could it have been Lexie's?* Lexie's real, precious little voice, as she had always thought? *And, who was the old man?* Even as she listened with pounding heart and sinking stomach, even as she tried to make sense out of what Tanner was saying, Sarah was moving her hands, twisting her wrists, trying to get some wiggle room.

She might be about to die, but if so, she wasn't going gently into that good night.

"No, I don't suppose you did." The driver's tone was faintly sarcastic.

"Anyway, I made up for it. I killed her, didn't I? Cut the nosy bitch's throat."

"You sure did. You ever think it might've been smarter to take her off somewhere and do it? Just askin'."

"You wanted me to kill her someplace special, you shoulda said. You just said kill her."

The car was slowing down, pulling over to the side of the road, and as Sarah realized that, she tensed.

Oh God, it's happening now. The car was bumping to a stop, and when it stopped, she was going to be killed. Sarah's lungs constricted so that it was suddenly difficult to breathe. Her fists clenched and with all the force she could discreetly apply she strained against the cord binding her.

"Why are you stopping here?" Tanner sounded surprised.

"Because there's a creek beside the road that would be the perfect place to dispose of a body."

"Oh." That answer seemed to satisfy Tanner, while Sarah was instantly drenched in cold sweat. Her heart pounded. Her pulse raced. Her mind darted around like a small creature in a trap. Her hands twisted, her fingers plucking at the cord. There was more give, but she wasn't going to have time. . . .

The car stopped.

Terror rose like bile in Sarah's throat. Her hands writhed desperately as she tried to work free. Her fingers encountered a knot and she explored it, pulled at it . . .

"Get out and see how far the creek is from the road," the driver said, shifting the transmission into park.

"Yeah, okay." Tanner opened the door, and the interior light came on. As he slid out, Sarah went still as a log, feigning unconsciousness as she desperately tried to come up with a plan. . . . Like what, kick whoever tried to pull her from the backseat in the balls with her bound feet, then hop away like the Energizer Bunny? Unfortunately, her self-defense training had consisted of a single Women Against Rape class. No kung fu stuff was going to happen here.

"It's right here." Tanner was standing outside the car now, and he ducked his head to look back in at the driver. "We can just pull her out and shoot her and push her in."

It was all Sarah could do not to pant with terror.

Lie still, she cautioned herself, peeking up at Tanner through her lashes. *Don't move.* Her only chance—*who are you kidding? You have no chance*—lay in the element of surprise.

"Good."

"Hey." Tanner was looking at the driver in alarm. "What're you doing?"

"Mopping up the mess," the driver said.

Sarah was still watching Tanner when a bullet exploded through his chest. He was wearing one of his wife-beaters, and the front of it suddenly seemed to bloom with scarlet gore. She squeaked and jumped— she couldn't help it—but the explosion of the gun at such close range hopefully masked the sound. Tanner gave a cry, wind-milled, and toppled backward. A crashing sound followed by a splash told her that he had probably fallen into the creek.

Instead of her? Or along with her?

The driver calmly got out of the car. As Sarah lay there, stunned, trembling, working hard not to hyperventilate, she remembered the *along with her* part and made her fingers move, made them work at that knot. She heard another shot from outside the car, and went all light-headed. Then the passenger door slammed, and a moment later the driver got back in the car and closed his own door.

Sarah recognized the acrid smell she was breathing in now. It was gunpowder.

"I know you're awake," the driver said, looking at her through the rearview mirror. "I heard you."

And before she could react to that, he turned around in the seat and zapped her with a stun gun.

When Sarah awoke again, the car still wasn't moving. Or, it had moved and stopped again. She couldn't be sure. She couldn't be sure how long she had been out, or where they were, or what had happened in the interim. She only knew that, first, she felt like she'd been run over by a freight train; second, it was even darker than it had been before; and, third, she could, very faintly, hear a man talking.

The good news was, her heart was pounding so hard that she had to be alive.

The bad news was, if something didn't change fast, she probably didn't have long to stay that way.

Okay. No time to lie here trying to collect her scrambled wits, or figure things out, or do anything except try to make hay while the sun didn't shine. She was sure—relatively sure—that she was alone in the vehicle. The reason it was so dark was because the engine had been turned off, which meant that the instrument panel was off along with the headlights.

When he'd hit her with the stun gun, she'd been on the verge of getting the knot loose. Her fingers attacked it again, desperately, and all of a sudden she could feel it loosening more, feel it coming free. She pulled again, and then she had it, it was undone, and with a quick twist of her hands the cord dropped away from her wrist.

Bringing her arms forward, giving her numb hands a quick shake to try to restore some blood flow, she pushed herself up just enough to peek out the window in the direction of the voice, and spotted her captor standing about six feet away from the driver's door, his back to her as he talked to a shadowy somebody in a pickup truck parked alongside. The impression she got was that they were waiting for someone.

Who? Sarah had a feeling that she didn't want to find out.

It took no more than a split second for

Sarah to register that the vehicles were in a large clearing ringed by trees, and that there was a building on the right, long and low, with enough lights turned on inside so that the small windows were dimly illuminated, spilling their glow into the night. Then she was grappling with the bungee cord that had been knotted around her ankles, not so much untying it as stretching it and pulling it off.

Suddenly, she was free. Another peek out the window told her that her captor was in the same position as before. The thing to do, she calculated quickly, was slip out the rear door on the passenger side and run like a rabbit with a tiger after it into the night.

The interior light. Her heart almost stopped when, with her hand on the door handle, she realized that she had forgotten it. The flash of light would draw instant attention to her escape.

Breathing like she had been running for miles, pulse pounding, Sarah used the curved end of the bungee cord to pry off the cover, then unscrewed the damned little lightbulb with shaking hands.

With another cautious glance toward her

still-talking captor, she then eased open the rear door and slipped out.

The night is darkest in the hours before the dawn.

Sarah remembered that quote from somewhere, and it was true. The night was now nearly as dark as the inside of a cave. It was still warm, but a slight breeze had arisen. The moon was a pale ghost of itself dropping down toward the ruffle of treetops that marked the western horizon. The few visible stars seemed to have almost burned themselves out. The faint smell of diesel fuel hung in the air, and she wondered if the building might be some sort of garage. Whatever, skirting around the back of it and then melting away into the trees beyond seemed like the best plan.

She was shaky, weak-kneed, and a little dizzy, she discovered as she slunk toward the trees, keeping close to the metal wall and taking care to stay below the windows and to make as little noise as possible. A glance inside the building told her that it was a boat storage facility, which, since it was August and prime boating season, meant that it held a lot of empty trailers but only a couple of boats. No one appeared to be inside it, which Sarah counted as a good thing. Any second now she expected to hear a shout that meant her escape had been discovered. The thought made her jittery, quick to jump at every movement or sound. As soon as she was in the trees, she would run like her life depended on it, which it did. But for now, she needed to be very quick but also very quiet. . . .

What made her look in the last window, she didn't know. Was it accident? Instinct, maybe? Whatever, she glanced inside, and found herself looking into a small storage room that had been cordoned off by unpainted plywood walls from the rest of the building's interior. It was empty, except for a large cage of the type one might use to confine a big dog.

In the cage was Angie.

Sarah's breathing stopped. Her heart thumped like it was trying to beat its way out of her chest. She froze, staring through the dingy glass, hardly able to believe what she was seeing.

The child was curled up in a ball on the floor of the cage, her eyes closed, her long, black hair spilling over the rest of her face so that Sarah couldn't see her expression.

She looked thin and pale and so helpless that Sarah's heart broke in two.

She couldn't leave her. No matter if it cost her her own life, she couldn't leave her.

Taking a deep breath, Sarah retraced her steps. About ten feet back, she had passed a door.

Her heart was in her throat as she tried the knob. It was unlocked. As she cautiously opened the door, light poured out in a brazen advertisement of her presence.

Just as she had seen through the window, there was no one about inside the building. Sarah stepped through the door, closing it quietly behind her to keep the spill of light from giving her presence away, then slipped toward the storage room on the right. Being caught in the light made her feel hideously exposed. Pulse racing, mouth dry, sure that she would be discovered at any second, she ran as quietly as she could to the storage room and tried the door.

It was locked.

Heart pounding like a jackhammer now, knees weak with fear, Sarah looked desperately around and spotted a set of keys on a table against the wall. Snatching them up, wincing at their jingle, she ran back to the door and found one that looked like it might fit the lock.

It did.

Opening the door, she stepped inside and closed the door behind her again. The room was maybe eight by ten feet, three plywood walls with the metal wall of the building as the fourth, and it was stiflingly hot, even so late at night. The smell of human waste was strong, and as she rushed toward the cage, Sarah saw that there was an open bucket in the far corner of it. Clearly, Angie had been using it as a toilet.

"Angie! Angie!" If the child was awake and conscious she gave no sign of it. She just stayed curled in her little ball, and Sarah didn't like to think what she must have endured to make her so unresponsive. Sarah dropped to her knees in front of the cage.

"*Angie. It's Sarah.*"

Angie moved then. She opened her eyes and lifted her head, shaking her hair back from her face.

"Sarah?" Her voice was tiny, the merest breath, and Sarah's heart broke for her all over again even as discovered that the cage door was fitted with a padlock. Picking it up to examine it, she heard a whirr behind her and jumped like she'd been shot. Glancing around, she discovered the camera mounted on the wall opposite the cage. It must be motion-sensitive, she realized, and now it was filming.

Sarah imagined the pictures that were now beaming over the Internet, and her blood ran cold.

Their small window of time was slamming shut.

Don't panic, she told herself, even as panic mushroomed inside her.

The padlock took a key. And there was a small silver key on the ring that looked as if it might fit. Again, the jingle as she shifted them made her wince.

"Are you here to take me home?" Angie's whisper sounded rusty, as if she'd been crying. She struggled to her knees.

"Yes. *Shh,* be quiet. We can't let anybody hear us." Sarah's fingers trembled so much that she could barely fit the key in the lock. She was on pins and needles, glancing behind her, glancing at the window, glancing at the camera, her every sense attuned to any sound or movement beyond that room. Even the silence struck her as ominous. Any second now . . .

The key turned in the lock, and she pulled the padlock open. Seconds later she swung the cage door wide and Angie literally fell out into her arms.

The child was still bound hand and foot with duct tape.

"I want my mama," Angie whimpered as Sarah's arms closed around her.

"I know." Sarah scooped her up against her chest, stood up with some difficulty, and rushed toward the door. Freeing her from the duct tape would take too long. They couldn't have much time left. Minutes, seconds . . .

"Are they still here? The bad men?" Angie was looking fearfully around. Sarah could feel her trembling.

"Yes. That's why we have to be so quiet," Sarah whispered, juggling child and doorknob and yet somehow managing to get the door open and both of them through it. Angie wasn't really heavy, maybe sixty pounds at most, but carrying her was awkward and Sarah's own muscles had been weakened by the stun gun. "I'll get you to your mama as quick as I can, I promise. Just be very, very quiet now. . . ."

Angie's eyes were wide and frightened as Sarah closed the door again in the hope that it might slow down the discovery that the child was missing, then ran heavily across the open space toward the door that led outside. Sarah herself was way beyond terror now. Her heart was pounding so hard that she could barely hear anything over the drumming of her own blood in her ears. Her pulse raced. She could scarcely breathe. She cast a single petrified glance around the still-empty warehouse, then got that last door open, too, and slid out into the night.

The door was still closing behind them when she heard a shout from the front of the building.

"She's gone!"

Terror gave wings to her feet, strength to her limbs. Legs pumping like pistons, she clutched Angie close and fled toward the trees as all hell broke loose at the front of the building. Car doors slammed. More shouts rang out: It sounded like four or five different voices. Lights came on all around the building—big, white halogen lights that for a moment caught them in their glare.

Then Sarah practically dove into the sheltering darkness of the trees.

She ran as far as she could, as fast as she could, which wasn't actually very far or fast at all. Flashlights bobbed through the darkness behind them; shouts rang out. The sounds of pursuit gave wings to her feet. Her legs got tangled in the undergrowth. Branches slapped her in the face. She tried to shield Angie as best she could, tried to comfort her, but the child was sobbing, trembling, terrified. Finally, Sarah had to stop, had to put Angie down, had to catch her breath. She collapsed, panting, on the dew-damp ground, with both of them scooting for concealment under the inky shadow of a spirea bush. Its sweet fragrance made a stark contrast to the terror-filled night.

"I'm so scared," Angie whispered as Sarah bent her head and put her teeth to the duct tape that bound the child's wrists. Sarah was trembling herself, with effort and fear. Adrenaline pumped through her veins like speed, and she was so winded, it actually hurt to draw breath.

"I know. It's going to be okay." Sarah managed to make a tiny rip in the tape, and then another, and another. Angie made a sharp little sound as Sarah finally pulled the tape away from her skin.

"That hurt." Angie brought her arms

around in front of her, shaking her hands, rubbing her arms. "My hands are asleep."

"They'll be better in a minute."

"I want to go home."

"You're going home as soon as we can get you there." Sarah gnawed away at the tape around Angie's ankles.

"Are they going to find us?"

"No. We're just going to be really, really quiet."

The tape tore at last. Sarah ripped at it, and finally Angie was free. Sarah helped her rub her legs, and then Angie curled up on the thick padding of fallen leaves, huddling close again at Sarah's side as they rested for a moment. Sarah wrapped her arms around her, holding her close, providing what comfort she could. The branches of the spirea hung down around them, providing a sense of security that Sarah knew was false. There were sounds around them, too, tree frogs piping and insects whirring and a sudden rustling that Sarah thought must have been made by a small animal skittering through the leaves, but nothing more sinister. She could see an occasional flicker of light through the swaying branches, which she thought must be a searcher's flashlight. Maybe they could just hide here until help came.

If help came.

Jake, where are you? Sarah thought despairingly. He was looking for her, she knew. Looking frantically, desperately, leaving no stone unturned. But Tanner was dead now. He wasn't going to be picked up and questioned. The chances of rescue coming anytime soon were looking increasingly remote.

They were going to have to save themselves.

Dawn would break soon. In the daylight, they would be easy to spot. The only plan she could come up with was to put as much distance as possible between them and their pursuers.

She looked down at the small head resting so trustingly against her, and felt her heart turn over. She hadn't been able to save Lexie, but maybe she could save this child.

She tightened her arm around the little girl.

"Sweetie, we've got to move. We're going to walk and walk and walk until we get somewhere safe."

Angie nodded.

Sarah had just let go of her when she heard a footfall, and saw the dark shape of a man's shoe and pant leg just beyond the spill of the bush. Her heart lurched. Her breathing suspended. She grabbed Angie's arm to alert her, to warn her to silence, but there was no need. The child was rigid with fear. Her eyes were riveted on the same thing Sarah had seen.

Then a flashlight shone down through the spirea's branches, catching Sarah full in the face.

"Gotcha." It was a man's voice, triumphant. The branches were swept aside, and Sarah found herself looking straight up into the mouth of a gun—and Mitchell Helitzer's gloating face.

Beside her, Angie screamed.

24

"Run, Angie." Those were the words that sprang to Sarah's lips, but it was too late: Somebody reached beneath the bush and grabbed the screaming child, pulling her out even as she fought and tried to hold on to Sarah.

"Help me, Sarah! Help me!"

Sarah tried, but Angie was torn from her grasp. The Blazer's driver had the little girl, Sarah saw, wrapping both arms around her waist and carrying her fighting and screaming away.

"No," Sarah cried, scrambling after her on

all fours, trying to catch her, to save her. Helitzer was right on top of her, grabbing her arm, holding her back despite her struggles. When she tried to get to her feet, he kicked her viciously in the side. The force of it lifted her off the ground, then dropped her back down onto it again as the pain made her cry out and see stars and almost pass out.

For a moment, Sarah could do nothing but lie on her stomach, trying to breathe, dizzy with pain. When Helitzer squatted down beside her, roughly pushing her onto her side and pointing his gun at her face, Angie's anguished screams were already dying away.

"Hello, bitch," Helitzer said, and Sarah knew it all right then, understood the motive behind everything, and hated him. But she was winded and hurting and her mind was working frantically, trying to come up with a plan, some way she could get through this and survive and save Angie, too, and so she did not reply.

The flashlight was on the ground nearby, its beam casting twisting shadows across the tiny clearing. It also provided enough illumination so that she could see his face, his expressions, as he leaned over her. A piece of torn duct tape stuck partly out from

under the spirea bush. With the one coolly
objective part of her mind remaining to her,
Sarah wondered if that was what the
searchers had seen that had given her and
Angie away.

Angie. The thought of the child's fate was
like a raw, aching wound in her chest.

"You're going to die." Helitzer moved the
gun until it was just inches from the tip of
her nose. He was watching her closely, enjoying the moment, enjoying her fear. "I'm
going to blow your face off."

Jake would grieve forever. Sarah felt a
great welling of sorrow at the thought. She
of all people knew how terrible grief
could be.

She realized that she was fighting to survive for Jake, too.

"Killing me is not going to help you beat
the rap for killing your wife," Sarah said,
wheezing a little from the pain in her ribs.
"They'll just assign another prosecutor.
That's how the justice system works."

"I *own* the fucking justice system. Except
for you, and I'm getting ready to take care of
that little problem right now." He touched
the tip of her nose with his gun almost play-
fully. "You still think you're going to . . ."

Sarah heard something, a faint shuffling in the leaves nearby, and her senses went on red alert. Helitzer must have heard it, too, because he broke off, his gaze shifting in the direction of the sound.

"There you are," a familiar voice said, the tone incongruously cheerful. "I've been looking for you."

Sarah's breath caught and her eyes widened as a portly figure stepped into view: *Judge Schwartzman?* was her first incredulous thought. Her second was, *Oh, thank God, the cavalry's here.* But Helitzer didn't look scared, merely impatient. He didn't jump up and run away or throw down his weapon and surrender. He merely frowned.

"What are you doing here?"

Judge Schwartzman came closer. Sarah saw to her horror that he, too, was carrying a gun. She didn't know what that meant, but her instincts were shouting *nothing good.*

"Please help me," she said to him, just in case her instincts were wrong. He stopped right beside Helitzer and looked down at her. Sarah met his gaze beseechingly and knew then that something was indeed very

wrong. *I own the fucking justice system.* Helitzer's words echoed through her mind. But
still, she had to try. "He's going to kill me.
And there's a little girl . . ."

"Shut up." Helitzer slanted a vicious
glance down at her. The mouth of the gun
had shifted, she saw, not much but enough
so that it was no longer pointing right at her
face, and Sarah had wild thoughts of seizing
it and rolling away, or simply jumping up and
running. *Wonder Woman . . .* unfortunately,
there was no one like that here.

Judge Schwartzman ignored her plea in
favor of replying to Helitzer. "The auction
ended at five. There's a buyer. Since kid-
napping little Angie was your idea—and I
have to admit, it worked better than anything else to take this lady here out of her
game—I presume you want a cut?"

"I don't give a shit about a cut."

"Fine, then. You won't object if I go ahead
and have them put the girl in my van? I'll
drive her as far as Memphis, and somebody
will meet us and take her on from there."

"Pervert," Helitzer's voice was heavy with
contempt.

"I know," Judge Schwartzman said sadly,
and shot Helitzer through the head.

Sarah saw the black, dime-sized hole appear above Helitzer's temple, saw his eyes widen and his lips part as if in surprise, and then watched him topple over sideways, with utter stupefaction. She didn't scream, it happened too fast, and there was no firecracker-loud explosion, just the dull thunk of impact and the smell of gunpowder. That, the tiny, still-objective part of her brain told her, meant that his weapon had a silencer.

It was all very quick and very quiet.

One second Helitzer was getting ready to kill her, and the next he was dead.

"Thus end all tyrants," Schwartzman muttered, lowering the gun.

"Oh, thank God." Sarah scrambled to her feet as disbelief was replaced with a spurt of pure euphoria. Judge Schwartzman was one of the good guys, she'd known he had to be, and her instincts could go hang. She looked down at the corpse, which was sprawled clumsily on its side, then back up at him.

"Thank you," she said with heartfelt gratitude, but even as the words left her mouth she saw that his gun was now aimed at her.

Right at her chest, from three feet away. There was no way he could miss.

She sucked in air. Her eyes flew to his face. "Judge?"

"I'm sorry about this, Sarah." He shook his head regretfully. "I really am. But this is the only way I can get my life back. I kill him, I kill you, and I kill the two numskulls guarding little Angie in her cage, and it's over. I walk away with no one the wiser. Like I said, I get my life back."

"What are you talking about?" Her pulse thundered in her ears. Her mouth was suddenly dry. Her eyes fixed on his face, and it didn't make her feel any better, or any less afraid, to realize that his expression was truly regretful.

"Look, I never wanted to hurt you. It was all him, that bastard. He killed his wife, you know. Beat her to death. He admitted it to me, came to my house, and flat-out admitted it, then told me I was going to make sure the case never came to trial or he was going to see to it that everybody found out about Paul's Playhouse. And he was going to have you killed. That night you were shot? He sent one of his thugs to kill you. He was furious when they screwed up and it resulted in all that publicity. He was afraid that if he tried again so soon it would seem suspicious, that the investigation might go deep enough to lead back to him, and that's the only reason you're still alive right now. That's when he came up with the idea of having me use those tapes of your daughter to upset you, to drive you off the case." He shook his head sadly. "See, Duncan's in his pocket, just like me. Just like Carver was. He is—was—blackmailing all of us. Carver had a stroke over it. But you—there was nothing to blackmail you with. Only your daughter."

Sarah suddenly couldn't breathe. She momentarily forgot about the gun in his hand, about everything else he was saying. "Tapes—of Lexie? You have tapes of Lexie?"

He nodded. "She was such a pretty, spunky little girl, Sarah. And I didn't know you then. I never would have taken her if I'd known you." Sarah's heart clutched as she stared at him with disbelief. Suddenly, she realized where she had seen his mouth before. It was small, and pursed in repose, and it was the mouth she had seen below the video camera that terrible day in the park.

As she realized it, she went all light-headed. The expression on her face must have been a terrible thing to behold, because his voice suddenly turned almost pleading. "You've seen how Paul's Playhouse works. One of us will choose a child, keep her until we're tired of her, then sell her to whoever wants her. There are several children available right now, as a matter of fact. And we always tape everything, from the time of capture. There's big money in the tapes, you know. They can be sold separately." He paused to cast a glance of loathing at Helitzer's body. "You know how he's supposed to be this big importer/exporter? What he really sells is—was—porn. All kinds of porn, worldwide. Which is how he found Paul's Playhouse. And me."

He was sounding sad again, but Sarah didn't care if he was filled to the brim with remorse. He was a monster, and if there was any justice in the universe, a lightning bolt would flash from the heavens about now and strike him dead.

"You taped me that day in the park," Sarah said through stiff lips. For the moment, the plan was to keep him talking, to buy time while she came up with a better plan. If he killed her, he would escape unpunished, and Angie would be lost forever just like Lexie had been. And there were more children at risk. If there was any possible way, she was going to try to get them help as well.

He nodded again. "I like to tape the moms, too. That's my own special touch, and I must say I'm rather well known for it in certain circles. I have one special van with a cage in back of it, and I always use that one. I knock the girl out with chloroform, lock her in the cage, then come back and tape the relatives running around all frantic as they look for the child. Especially the mom. Sometimes I show a tape of the mom to the child, and it helps establish control. Plus, to some people it adds a little something to the package."

Monster didn't even begin to describe this man. There wasn't a word bad enough. Sarah thought about Lexie, about her sweet little daughter at this degenerate's mercy, and felt the gorge rise in her throat. Anger, fierce and pulsing, began to rush through her veins, forcing out her fear, strengthening her. This man was the one she had sought for so long. This man had taken Lexie.

"What did you do with her?" Sarah had to know. More than anything in life, she needed to find her daughter. Not just for her own sense of closure, but for Lexie's sake. Lexie deserved to be near people who loved her. "Where is she?"

"I wish I could tell you." There was that regretful tone again. If Sarah had had a weapon, she would have slain him right then. "I only kept her for about a week. I don't kill them, you know. I never kill them. I just—play."

Play. That was the word that did it. Sarah had never experienced homicidal fury before, but she did then. She went for him, screaming and charging at him like a wounded animal, knocking him off balance so that he went stumbling back under the onslaught. He tried to fend her off, but she'd caught him by surprise.

"*Ah!*" he yelled as he tripped on something and went down. Then she was on top, slugging him, her fists smashing into his fat face, his throat, any part of him she could reach.

For the first time in her life, she knew what it was to want to kill.

But the bottom line was that she was

small and he was big, and he rolled with her and trapped her beneath him and put his gun to her head.

"Bitch," he said, as the cool, hard steel pushed against her temple. They were both panting with exertion, but his right eye was swollen and bloody scratches marked his face and he was getting a fat lip. He was going to kill her now, she knew, she could see it in his eyes, no more remorse from him, but she was fiercely glad that she had at least marked him before she died.

Take that for Lexie, she thought, and spat full in his ugly face.

His face contorted with anger and his gun hand moved. Sarah closed her eyes.

"Police! Don't move!" The shout, from somewhere near at hand, caused her eyes to pop open again. Sarah heard the rush of footsteps, the crashing of foliage, and more shouts of warning, but for a moment, one timeless moment as the mouth of the gun nuzzled her temple and eternity stared her in the face, her eyes locked with Schwartzman's.

Then his hand jerked and he pulled the trigger.

* * *

Jake reached them just that instant too late. He had reminded himself of Superman, moving faster than a speeding bullet as he'd followed the sounds of Sarah's screams, his heart pounding like a trip-hammer and his blood racing through his veins as he'd gone crashing through the woods with half the Beaufort PD and a good percentage of the FBI in tow.

He had seen them as he'd raced through the trees, caught blood-chilling glimpses of the man on top of her, of the gun to her head, but he hadn't been close enough, hadn't been able to take a shot for fear of hitting her, too, so all that was left to him to do was scream "Police, don't move," just like the officers behind him.

Then the gun went off, and blood and bits of bone and brain matter flew everywhere. His heart stopped. He almost pissed his pants. He let loose with a primeval cry of anguish and leaped for them, grabbing the bastard by the shoulder, rolling him off her— and then discovered that the guy's face was blown away.

He'd shot himself in the head. Not Sarah.

Jake's knees gave out. He sank down on the thick cushion of loam just as she sat up. She was covered with blood and gore and leaves and God knew what else, and nothing had ever looked so beautiful to him in his life.

"Thank God," he said, like it was a prayer. Then she sucked in air and wrapped her arms around his neck. He wrapped his arms around her, too, and held her like he would never let go again.

A little later that morning, Sarah witnessed Angie's reunion with her mother. They were both at the hospital, where the police had insisted on taking them. Sarah had checked out fine, but Angie they wanted to keep. Sarah had just stepped inside Angie's room when Rosa came barreling through the door.

"My baby! Where's my baby?" Rosa cried, even as Angie, clean and clad now in a green hospital gown, sat up in bed.

"Mama!" She held out her arms, and Rosa flew into them, and they both burst into noisy sobs. Sarah cried a little, too, as did most of the relatives who had followed Rosa into the room.

Then she left the room to give them the privacy they deserved.

Jake was right outside. He hadn't been more than a couple of steps away from her since he'd rolled Judge Schwartzman off her three hours earlier. She had already told him everything, including what she'd learned of Lexie's fate. In turn, he had told her what had happened after she'd gone missing, and how they'd finally found the boat warehouse because of Tanner, who had not died, but had managed to dial 911 on his cell phone despite being critically injured.

"So you doing okay?" he asked as they headed down the hallway toward the elevator together. Now that Sarah had been released, they were going home, to his apartment, by mutual agreement. It was, Sarah reflected wryly, one more day of work that she was going to have to miss. Under the circumstances, though, she hoped Morrison would prove tolerant.

They reached the elevator bank, and Jake punched the down button.

"Yes." She knew that he was referring to

her reaction to what she now knew of Lexie's fate. "What I've learned over the years is, knowing's better than not knowing. The thing is, though, I've hoped and prayed for so long. Now that I know, I feel sort of . . . empty inside. Like there's nothing left for me in life."

"Hey," he said as the elevator arrived with a *ping* and the doors slid open. "What about me?"

She looked up at him then, a little surprised.

"Well, of course there's you," she said as they stepped into the elevator together. Then she realized that that sounded like she was taking him for granted, which she did, and which, in her opinion, was a good thing. But just to clarify, she added, "I love you."

He smiled at her, that slight curve of his mouth that now had the power to make her blood heat and her heart sing, and said, "I love you, too."

Then, as the elevator doors slid closed, he kissed her.

And neither one of them remembered to push the lobby button for a very long time.

* * *

It was late the following afternoon, and Jake had just pulled into his parking lot in time to witness something he'd never thought he'd live to see—to wit, Pops taking Dorothy for a ride on his motorcycle—when he got the call he'd been both expecting and dreading.

"I thought you ought to be the one to break it to her," Morrison said. "They found Lexie."

25

Sarah stood in the living room of her house, so on edge that she could hardly stand still as she looked out the window, waiting for the arrival of the police car that would bring Lexie home to her.

She'd gotten her miracle after all. Her daughter was alive. After tracing the Paul's Playhouse ring through records left in Judge Schwartzman's house, they'd found her in a remote farmhouse in Utah, where a man was keeping her as one of his many wives.

It seemed impossible, unreal. Seven

years. Would she even recognize her own daughter?

"You okay?" Jake asked. He was right behind her, waiting with her, and he knew how excited she was, how jittery and afraid.

Would Lexie remember her?

A squad car pulled up out front, stopped, and two cops got out. Sarah's heart started to race. Her blood pounded in her ears. She suddenly felt short of breath.

One of the cops—Sarah couldn't have described him for the life of her—opened the rear passenger door, and a slender, red-haired girl wearing a long denim skirt and a simple white blouse got out.

"Oh my God, there she is." Sarah turned to Jake, who put an arm around her and squeezed. She dared another peek out the window. "She's so tall."

They were walking up the lawn, the girl and the cops, and suddenly Sarah couldn't stand to look. She'd known that the daughter who was being returned to her wasn't going to be the same as the daughter who had been taken, not in looks and probably not in a lot of other ways as well, but still, the girl she'd pictured had been the plump, smiling five-year-old.

But they were almost at the door now, and Sarah hurried forward to open it.

Sweetie-pie hurtled from the bedroom, giving voice to a volley of ferocious barks before she could even say hello, or get a proper, close-up look at her daughter.

The officers froze. Sarah, who had just pushed the screen door open, cast Sweetie-pie an impatient look, with *Shut up, Sweetie-pie* trembling on the tip of her tongue.

But her daughter brushed past her, walking right inside the house, ignoring Jake, who was standing in the entrance to the living room, staring at the dog. The dog stopped barking to stare at her, too.

"Sweetie-pie?" her daughter said. Sarah watched with bated breath as Sweetie-pie walked slowly, cautiously toward her, seeming to sniff the air.

Then her daughter dropped to her knees and opened her arms, and the dog rushed into them, wagging his tail.

For an instant, no longer, Sarah watched. Then she dropped to her knees beside dog and girl, and said, "Lexie?"

Her daughter turned her head to look at

her, and Sarah found herself gazing into Lexie's indigo-blue eyes.

And the hard, cold knot that had lived inside her heart for seven years seemed to melt.

"Mommy?" Lexie was staring at her, too, as if she was trying to merge this older face with the one she remembered. "I never forgot you. I used to dream about you. I thought you were an angel."

"Lexie," Sarah said again, this time with heartfelt conviction. Tears pouring from her eyes, she wrapped her arms around her daughter, and Lexie hugged her back, and Sweetie-pie wagged his tail, and Jake smiled at her.

And Sarah thought, *My cup runneth over.*